PRAISE FOR
JULIA FENTON'S
BLACK TIE ONLY

The dazzling nationwide bestseller! A royal celebration for the rich and famous overflows with champagne, secrets, and explosive scandal . . .

"Wow! What a wonderful read. Fast-paced with lots of glitz, glamour, and sex . . . You can't put it down."
—MICHELLE GREEN

"Slick . . . entertaining."   —*Publishers Weekly*

"An engrossing tale that will take you behind the scenes of the most glamorous gala of the decade."
—EILEEN GOUDGE

"This is one party you won't want to miss."
—RUTH RYAN LANGAN

"Glitz, glamour, sex . . . an instant summer hit!"
—*Library Journal*

"High-powered glitter, sex and adventure. Julia Fenton has created one of those rare novels you can't put down. She's outdone Collins, Krantz, and Robbins."
—PAMELA BELLWOOD

DEAR READER,

At the end of this book you'll find a special sneak preview of a dazzling new novel by Nora Roberts, the *New York Times* bestselling author of *Carnal Innocence* and *Genuine Lies*. It's called *Honest Illusions*—and it's honestly her best.

We hope you agree.
The Publishers.

Jove titles by Julia Fenton

BLACK TIE ONLY
BLUE ORCHIDS

BLUE ORCHIDS

Julia Fenton

JOVE BOOKS, NEW YORK

BLUE ORCHIDS

A Jove Book / published by arrangement with
the author

PRINTING HISTORY
Jove edition / July 1992

ISBN: 0-515-10875-8

Jove Books are published by The Berkley Publishing Group,
200 Madison Avenue, New York, New York 10016.
The name ''JOVE'' and the ''J'' logo
are trademarks belonging to Jove Publications, Inc.

PRINTED IN THE UNITED STATES OF AMERICA

10 9 8 7 6 5 4 3 2 1

For my Rick, in deepest love and affection,
the light of my life,
and for Michael and Andy, always so dear

and

to the family, ever so important for support and love in these tumultuous times: Ed, Dolly, Manny, patriarch Ben, matriarch Stella, and all the other Fentons, Saffirs, and Smiths, wherever they are, and then . . .

there's Mary . . . in a special category all by herself.
God love you all!

Also, I always have to let Cynthia and Robert, the two "squirts," know that everything I write is inspired by my love for and pride in them.

Also, a special thank-you to some dear, wonderful friends, Sheila Clifford, Stephanie Mary deFratis, Gail Etter, Phyllis Factor, Bonnie Sue Harris, Cassandra Lippman, Sheila McCarthy, Alexandra Rellinger, Marilyn Turner, and Karen Warner, for putting up with all my various moods and nonsense for the past several years.

Acknowledgments

First, I would like to thank Leslie Gelbman of the Putnam/Berkley Publishing Group, our wonderful editor who believed not only in me but also in this project from start to finish.

A big thank-you to the following individuals and companies who have kindly provided valuable services to Valentina, Orchid, and the rest of the *Blue Orchids* family during the preparation of this manuscript.

Transportation:

Ginny Borowsky, Manager, Special Services, American Airlines, Chicago; Catherine E. Schaffer, Manager, National Accounts, U.S.A., British Airways, New York; Mel Farr Agencies—Ford, Lincoln-Mercury, Toyota; Frank Audette of AudetteCadillac; Avis Car Rental; and Janet Randolph, Book-Couzens Travel Service.

Medical:

Arthur B. Eisenbrey, MD; Richard J. Feldman, MD; Meryl M. Fenton, M.D.; Kenneth Gitlin, MD; H. John "Tony" Jacob, MD; William Meyers, MD, and his wife, Irene; Hershel Sandberg, MD; Rahul Sangal, MD, and his wife, JoAnne; Marshall Shapiro, MD; and Howard Topcik, DDS.

Judges:

The Honorable Avern Cohn, Barry Grant, Lawrence Glazer, Roman S. Gribbs, and Fred Harris, who all gave their specialized assistance.

Hotels:

The Mayflower, New York, NY, Michael Fenn, general manager; Helmsley Windsor, New York, NY, Isel Garcia, sales coordinator; Bel Air, Bel Air, CA, Ulrich Krauer, general manager pro-tem; Beverly Hills, Beverly Hills, CA, Karman

Beriker, general manager; Holiday Inn, Golden Mile, Hong
Kong, Hari Harilela; Hyatt on Sunset, Hollywood, CA, Robert
Simeone, general manager.

Restaurants:

Beau Jack's, W. Bloomfield, MI, Gary Cochran; Chasen's,
Los Angeles, CA, Ralph Woodworth; Dan Tana's, Los An-
geles, CA, Dan Tana; Bistro Gardens, Los Angeles, CA;
Jimmy's, Los Angeles, CA; Le Dôme, Los Angeles, CA;
Norm's Diner, Farmington Hills, MI, Randy Burgess; Polo
Lounge, Beverly Hills Hotel, Beverly Hills, CA; Rib Joint,
Los Angeles, CA; Spago's, Los Angeles, CA; Tatou, New
York, NY; Arriva's, Warren, MI, Sammy Loccricio; and also
Chef Vincenzo Bassonetti of Cafe Vincenzo, Garden City, MI.

In addition, I would also like to thank the following, in
alphabetical order: Joan and Lloyd Adelson; the Mel Ball
Orchestra; Robert Beneditti and Cliff Raven, Sunset Strip
Tattoo; the Beznos brothers, Harold, Jerry and Norman;
David Boor, Merrill Lynch; Mary Kathryn Boyer; Keith and
Svetlana Braun; Nancy Coffey; Joe and Carolyn Collins;
Norman and William Dabish of Powerhouse Gym; the
Christopher Dingell family; U.S. Congressman John
Dingell, Jr., and his wife, Debby; John F. and Marian
Dodge; Joe and Vera Dresner; Milt and Linda Dresner;
Margaret Duda; Bill and Sheila Ellman; Howard and
Rebecca Emmer; the Mel Farr family; Oscar and Didi
Feldman; Constance Fenton; Margie Fenton; the Peter Fink
family; Richard M. Fitz; U.S. Congressman William Ford;
David Gac; Larry and Theresa Gaynor, Nailco, Inc., Livo-
nia, MI; Ralph and Erica Gerson; John and Marion Ginopo-
lis; Peter Ginopolis; Larry and Loretta Globerson; John
Gould, graduate student, Slavic Languages, University of
Michigan; the Gray Brothers, Duane, Loren, and Max; Erica
Haber, University of Michigan Department of Slavic Languages; the Meg Harris family; Jean and Will Haughey; the
John Hertel family; Bruce Himrod, U.S. Air Force Reserve;
the Michael Horowitz family; the Alan Hurvitz family;
Mary Jacobs, Harmony House; the Stuart W. Kallman
family; the George Killeen family; the Joseph Kopicki
family, Joe and Jennifer Kopicki; Steve and Marie Kopicki;

Helen Kovach, Russian Department, Oakland University, Rochester, MI; U.S. Senator Carl Levin and Helen Galen of his staff; Mira Linder; Mickey and Joyce Lolich; Fred and Marlene Manfra; Burt Meisel; Ethel Mellen, the Flower Company; Mickey Meltzer; Bobbee Meyer of Miami Beach, FL; Tillie Milgrom; Mike and Peggy Miller; Steve and Julie Mott; Joe Muer, Jr., Muer's Oyster House; Warren D. Munsey, production/recording engineer, and Dale Tallant, production engineer, Ron Rose Productions, Southfield, MI; Robert Nederlander, Nederlander Theatrical Organization, and Kathleen Raitt, assistant to James Nederlander, Nederlander Theatrical Organization.

Also Ronald M. and Linda Parz; Shari Raby; Lois Pincus; Mel Ravitz; Dave and Lois Robinson; the Mel Rosenhaus family; Dolly Rotenberg and Charlotte Silverstone, the Party Planners, Birmingham, MI; Tom and Diane Schoerith; Richard and Sheila Sloan; Howard Perry Rothberg; Eric Rubin and Michelle Bova, Eastern European Desk, U.S. Department of State; David, Tim, Pete and Terry from the Franklin Racquet and Health Club, along with good friends Shelton Adler, Paul Brownlee, Skip Davis, Francine Greenfield, Mike Kanka, Irwin Lieberman and John O'Brien; Robert Levin; the Louis Rudolph family; Richard Saffir; Charlie Sanders; Douglas and Sydell Schubot; Sr. Mary Patricia, St. Vincent–Sarah Fisher Home for Children, Farmington Hills, MI; Tom and Diane Schoenith; Irv and Mary Katie Seligman; Mark and Lois Shaevsky; Joe and Edna Slavik; Vi Slowly, Fisher Theater, Detroit, MI; Edward Slotkin; Frank and Marty Stella; Ted and Anne Swift; Anthony Tewes, Tewes Financial Services; Sam Tootalian; Steve Wilen; Larry and Kimberley Wilkinson; Mark Yoffe, PhD, Russian literature, University of Michigan, and Albert Zuckerman, Writer's House, New York, NY.

And last, but not least, sincere thanks to Robert L. Fenton, entertainment lawyer and producer of *Best Friends,* an NBC-TV Movie of the Week, and Julia Grice, *New York Times* best-selling author of *Lovefire, Tender Prey, Jagged Light,* and others. Without my "dream team" there would have been no *Blue Orchids.*

The characters in this book are all fictional—that is, they come out of my imagination. If they bear any resemblance to specific individuals, this is a matter of coincidence. It was not my intention. I have created fictional events that use the names of certain celebrities or very prominent people and I put them in places they were not, saying words they did not. The actions and motivations of the characters named after real people are entirely fictitious and should not be considered real or factual. Simply put, there is no connection between the characters in the novel and the people whose names I have used. If I have caused embarrassment to anyone in any manner, I wish, here and now, to apologize—openly and most sincerely. Without the stars of our world, we would all be much poorer.

Julia Fenton
June 1991

BLUE ORCHIDS

DR. ZHIVAGO
A COMEBACK FOR VALENTINA?
by Joe Donovan

UPI–New York. Will _Dr. Zhivago_, the most eagerly awaited musical in 20 years, be a triumphant comeback for Valentina? Will the $7 million gamble bring Broadway to its feet next Thursday evening at the new Lederer Theater on 52nd Street?

The musical is based on the 1965 movie classic, _Dr. Zhivago,_ and was staged by producer Keith Leonard as a comeback vehicle for Valentina, who retired after her near-fatal accident in 1988 at Continental Studios in Los Angeles.

With the book written by Orchid Lederer, who also plays a supporting role, lyrics by Avram Kahn and score by Jerry Steinhaus, the show has been plagued with problems including, backstage sources say, serious disagreements among certain members of the cast.

''Nonsense,'' denies Leonard, 38-year-old Broadway maverick with five Tonys already on his shelf. ''All shows have a few problems—I consider that a positive. Valentina is incandescent in this role. This is the apex of her career, as first-nighters will see tomorrow night!''

Also appearing will be _Dirty Dancing_'s Patrick Swayze, and Winona Ryder, in their first Broadway roles . . .

Chapter

One

THE TANG OF Fendi bath oil rose sensuously into the air. One graceful white arm reached upward, as Valentina Lederer smoothed soapsuds down her elegant forearm, continuing the soapy sweep to the curves that had recently adorned the front cover of *Sports Illustrated*'s swimsuit issue.

From her bath, she could look across Central Park, the jeweled necklace of skyscrapers blurred with rain, as more lights twinkled on in the growing darkness.

Rain. She glanced toward sterling silver clock hands. *4:45!*

Damn . . . Valentina sprang out of the tub, scented water running off her. Grabbing one of the thick towels, she pummeled her skin vigorously, then raced through to her dressing room.

The enormous room held garments arranged by function. Evening wear, a welter of chiffon, silk, organza, and lamé. Suits, casuals, jeans. Built-in drawers for silk lingerie, and a wall for shoes, purses, and accessories. A three-way mirror on the door reflected Valentina's body, the long, beautifully shaped dancer's legs, the rounded breasts that had never seen silicone, the shaped fluff of black pubic silk.

Valentina hurried, slipping into the first pair of panties she found, a skimpy thong. Then stockings, with lace tops. Sexy. She felt wired, and the warm bath hadn't done anything for her opening-night jitters. This was her night.

1

She'd hit rock bottom but was on the way up, and after tonight, she prayed, the media would never have the opportunity to pan her again.

"I won't bother with makeup," she decided, grabbing a Bob Mackie white leather jumpsuit, which slid on like butter, hugging her hips. "Cher with curves," *People* said about her. She smiled, liking the comparison. She loved clothes, loved being sultry and flashy . . .

And now . . . her hair! Hastily Valentina released the pins, allowing the black curls to fall below her shoulders. The curls, still damp, were tight and springy.

No time now to comb them. They'd do that at the theater . . .

She rushed through the apartment, scooping up her purse, pausing long enough to hurry into the nursery, where the nanny was rocking her year-old daughter, Krista, to sleep. The baby had Valentina's jet-black hair, the same green eyes, and her impossibly clear, fresh skin.

"I'm leaving, Mrs. Davies. Wish me luck," she said, bending down to kiss Krista. She breathed in the sweet fragrance of the imported baby shampoo.

"Baby, I love you," she whispered. "I love you so much."

The little girl puckered her face sleepily.

"Best of luck, Miss Lederer," said the nanny. "The *very* best."

"Thank you, Mrs. Davies."

She tore herself away from the baby, and hurried down toward the large coat closet. Opening it she pulled a sleek white sable off the hanger and flung it over her shoulders. At the door, she paused before an old photograph that hung on a wall. Taken in the fifties, it showed a graceful ballet dancer with hair of sleek ebony, and dark, sad eyes.

"Mama," Valentina whispered, lingering for a second, reaching out to touch the glass. "I will do it. I will, for both you and Keith. I promise you!"

Emerging from the elevator, Valentina crossed the lobby at a run, the extravagant white coat flying behind her.

Sammy, the doorman, had spotted her and was already signaling Newt Hoffman, her driver.

Rain was still pelting down as Sammy, sheltering her under his huge umbrella, helped her into the white limo.

"Don't worry, Miss Lederer." Newt smiled in the rearview mirror as they sat in traffic between Sixty-fifth and Sixty-sixth streets. After five years, he knew her moods. "As soon as we get to Central Park South, I'll cut over. We'll be there in time, no problem."

"Thanks, Newton. Damn it . . . I'm all nerves. But once I'm at the theater, I'll be okay."

"More than okay, Miss Lederer!"

Her performance, yes. Over months of rehearsals and during the tryout in Boston, she'd honed it to perfection. But she couldn't shake a sense of foreboding, a feeling that something beyond everyone's control was going to happen.

Please. Valentina whispered a silent prayer. *Let all the strange happenings I'm so worried about be only my imagination . . . let them only be coincidences. Everything has to be wonderful.*

"Lord," she sighed, feeling the old twinge in her back. It was right in front of her, in black and white, but she couldn't make sense of it.

Pietro Mazzini, the director . . . bruise marks around his throat carefully concealed with an ascot.

Bettina, their obsessive choreographer, suddenly disappearing three weeks ago.

And Jinna Jones, an ordinary chorus dancer, first dropped from the show, then reinstated. Why?

Leaning back, Valentina concentrated on taking deep breaths. In, out, calm and slow, relaxing. Between here and the theater, she would create her own little island of peace. She would relax herself. Keith needed the hit as badly as she did, and she wanted it so desperately for him. Her fiancé had poured everything he had into this production, and if it failed, he could go bankrupt—straight down the tubes. He'd let his work slide to care for his dying wife. Valentina wanted Keith to have a long, solid Broadway run. The best gift she could give him.

"Here we go, Miss Lederer," Newt said reassuringly as the big car eased forward. "We're moving now."

"Thank you," Valentina murmured.

A raspberry silk teddy barely concealing her shapely buttocks, burnished auburn hair streaming around her shoulders, Orchid Lederer rushed from living room to bedroom, then to the walk-in closet of her Park Avenue penthouse, glancing anxiously around the perfumed spill of lingerie, clothes, newspapers, and marked-up versions of her revised screenplay. The place reeked of her perfume, Escada, and held a tingling aura of musky sexuality.

Screw it—the brooch for Valentina. Where the hell had she put it? It was an *apology,* for God's sake. It spoke of a lifetime of love, hate, regret. She was tired, so tired, of the seven-year rift between them, the dead, empty spot at the center of her being that could only be filled by Valentina's love.

Releasing a frustrated sigh, Orchid walked into the large, mirrored bathroom, and spotted the jewelry box from Van Cleef and Arpels lying on a small table.

She lifted the cover and pulled out the specially designed brooch.

Two exquisite orchids entwined their stems together, the iridescent blue-violet petals shimmering in the light, diamonds placed to resemble dewdrops.

Blue Orchids. She and Valentina had rocketed to stardom ten years earlier, then split up, their quarrel as public as the Supremes' had been. "*Please* make Valentina love you. Because if she loves you, she loves me too. I mean it," she whispered, staring at the pin. Her barely audible plea was drowned out as the telephone shrilled. Orchid snatched it up.

"Miss Lederer? This is your service, with your second reminder call. You should be leaving for the theater."

"Yes, yes, yes," she cried, adding a hasty "Thanks," before slamming the phone into its cradle. She dashed back into the walk-in closet and wriggled into a pair of tight jeans. Then, after slithering into a black silk T-shirt that showed off her small breasts, she tossed on a hip-hugging black leather jacket and pulled on black snakeskin cowboy boots. As a last gesture she grabbed the jewelry box and stuffed it into the jacket pocket.

Five minutes later, as Orchid sighed and settled back, her cab pulling away from the curb, her stomach was clenched in a hard knot.

Valentina hadn't called!

Rain sprayed against the stage door of the Lederer Theater, pelting the gathering crowd held back by uniformed security teams.

Keith Leonard, the thirty-eight-year-old producer of *Dr. Zhivago,* stepped out of his cab, frowning, his strides long as he started toward the theater door. He was tall, his eyes as blue as the Rio Grande, and his rugged face showed the effects of the intense pressure he had been under for weeks.

Vans from Channel 7 Eyewitness News and WNBC-TV were double-parked in a loading area. Already a small drenched crowd had gathered, one girl holding a wet placard that said, *Valentina, We Love You!*

All a good sign for a hit, he thought. The last three years of a depressed economy had taxed his resources, and now he needed a real blockbuster—and his skittish backers were depending on it. But this one was for Valentina. Without it, she might go into a tailspin again.

A tall, bulky man in a trench coat hurried out of the crowd. "Joe Donovan, *LA Times.* Just a few questions. I know this is a busy night."

"Sorry. Excuse me—"

The man persisted. "Mr. Leonard, what are your feelings about Valentina's comeback?"

"I've already given several interviews and so has Valentina. I think we've covered the waterfront. She's terrific, a wonderful singer and actress who worked like hell and deserves a hit. Something we hope tonight's performance is going to bring us."

"I know, but how about something more personal . . .

your immediate feelings about tonight? After all, she's your fiancée.''

"No interview until after the show," Keith snapped.

Keith nodded to the security man, Bill Kopicki, and started through the door, only to be blocked by a young man in a dark suit, wearing an earpiece.

"Sorry, sir, you're not allowed in this part of the theater.''

"What the hell do you mean, I'm not allowed? I'm the producer.''

"Do you have a pass?''

"The pass? No, dammit, I left it at home. I'm the *producer*. You're not regular security. Where's Billy?'' he added, looking around for the young guard he had seen only moments before.

"This is Department of State business.''

"Department of *State*? What the hell does that mean?''

"Sorry, sir. Do you have someone who can identify you?''

"What the—Goddammit, yes! Billy!'' Keith was in a rage when he finally found the security guard, who identified him. Something *was* wrong.

Once inside, the frenetic backstage world closed around Keith, a world he'd been part of since his first Tony-winning musical, *San Antonio!*, in 1975. Awards for shows he'd produced crowded several shelves in his study at home—eleven Tonys, along with several Obies, New York Drama Critics awards, and two Oscars—all the most coveted prizes, many won before he was thirty.

Dark-haired Winona Ryder, of *Great Balls of Fire* and *Heathers* fame, hurried past swathed in a shiny black rain slicker, mumbling her first lines under her breath.

The assistant director came scurrying out of Makeup. "Mr. Leonard, Valentina's not here yet. Orchid's late too. This fucking rain . . .''

"Well, curtain time doesn't wait for rain, Sue. Have Makeup and Wardrobe stand by.''

He kept on walking down the corridor to his small office,

and closed the door. Switching on the lights, he allowed his eyes to rest on a photograph of Valentina from *People* magazine's "50 Most Beautiful People" issue. "Lovingly for Keith, who knows all he has done," was the scrawled inscription.

The tabloids had hounded her for months, after the near-fatal fall she'd taken three years ago at Continental studios, her back operations, her subsequent addiction to drugs, and her messy divorce from LA doctor Paul Jensen.

As he took in the slanted emerald eyes feathered with long lashes, her high cheekbones that lent an air of fragile mystery to her perfect features, Keith felt his eyes moisten. God, he adored her! She was warm, giving, the most sexually uninhibited woman he'd ever known. He could have a better time with her barefoot and in jeans on the beach than he would on a night out at "21" with any other woman. Her courage touched him, her vulnerability drew him into her, and he loved the fact that, despite all her professionalism, she needed him.

His lips set in a grim line, he took a key out of his pocket and unlocked the bottom desk drawer, reached in and pulled out a snub-nosed .38 special, then shoved it into a pocket and shrugged on the jacket again, its fabric hiding the pistol from casual view. Just a little insurance.

Then he glanced at a folded newspaper on his desk, where a picture of United States Senator Charles Willingham occupied the upper right quadrant. The feisty old southerner was a one-man drug crusade. A man with powerful enemies. He loathed the Medellín drug cartel and they reciprocated the feeling. Keith suspected that whatever was going down tonight, it centered around Willingham.

At the Sign of the Dove, the low murmuring of diners and discreet waiters created a world where nothing as mundane as a rainstorm might intrude.

Senator Charles Willingham, six feet tall and 230 pounds of southern politician, pushed away his plate, which had contained duck à l'orange on a bed of browned rice with mushrooms and garnished with white asparagus. His usual hearty appetite had failed him tonight. He had things on his mind—a lot to do in the next hour and a half.

"I've really *got* to hurry," said his perky thirty-two-year-old fiancée, Jinna, taking a last sip of tea. "I have to warm up. I'm still shaky on that second-act reprise. Oh, Jesus. I just hope I don't freeze 'like I did in Boston. I want this so badly, Charlie baby. I *need* this show!"

Willingham looked across the table, feeling a spasm of guilt. Jinna had lived and breathed Broadway for the past four years and he knew that maybe he was being selfish for hoping that she'd be a dancer only for a year or two longer, as she'd promised him when they got engaged. He worried sometimes that success would make her forget that promise. Dammit, he wanted babies, at least three of them. He was sixty now, and could still shoot off the old rocket, but how long would it last? A young woman like Jinna might not even understand how he felt time slipping by so fast.

A dynasty with himself as progenitor. First, his appointment as secretary of state, which the President had virtually promised him. He'd be the first southern secretary of state since Cordell Hull, in the Roosevelt administration. Then, children. Maybe someday a son of his in the White House. All very possible. He could be another Joe Kennedy.

Jinna was glancing at her watch. "I should go," she repeated. She added, "Now, you *will* be there, won't you? Charlie, you promised me. I don't want this to be like Boston. You know how important it is to me."

"I'll go now with you, darlin', if you're still worried," he said, snapping his fingers for the waiter. "You know I always keep promises."

"No!" Jinna was already on her feet. "Babe-ums, they won't let you past security, it's crazy backstage, and there's nowhere you could wait. I told the driver to circle the block. He'll be right outside. No sense you getting wet, too, in all that rain." Jinna reached for his hand. "Oh, Charlie . . . sweetie pie . . . I do love you so much. Wish me luck, will you? Tell me to break a leg."

"Break a leg? Why, honey, I'd never—"

"Charlie, Charlie, what will I do with you? 'Break a leg' means 'good luck' in theater talk."

"All right, then," he drawled. "Break a leg, honey . . . but don't break both of them because then how can we ever make love?"

Her laughter was swift and nervous, and then she was gone, threading her way through the tables. The best thing that had ever happened to him.

After Jinna's departure, the smile faded from the senator's craggy face. He moodily picked up his coffee cup, his face reflecting in the dark brew. Then the reflection broke apart, disintegrating, as he brought the cup to his lips.

The effect was unsettling. Damn . . . was it all getting to him? He hadn't told Jinna about the State Department's warnings, his "alternative" plans for tonight's performance. Even his staff didn't know about the switch, except for Tommy Lee, his chief bodyguard. The drug cartel had targeted him for a hit because he was asking the Senate for economic sanctions against Colombia.

Assassination? Not him, not after all these years. A loony had tried it in 1968. It hadn't kept him down even two weeks. He was as tough and stubborn a bastard as ever walked the hallowed halls of the Senate, and he took crap from no one.

He would fool the bastards good!

The room, in a hotel bordering Times Square, was small and anonymous. Steam filled the room, drifting out of the bathroom where the shower had been running for the past twenty minutes.

Naked, a muscular thirty-one-year-old South American stepped out of the shower, toweling off a body sheened with water droplets. Black hair, olive-black eyes, dusky skin.

Araña breathed deeply.

Araña had "proven loyalty" at twelve, killing a rich drunk in a Buenos Aires barrio, and now killing gave a pleasure as intense as cocaine—and as habit forming.

The South American strode to the double bed and began rummaging in the large suitcase, well stocked with makeup, wigs, and other articles purchased from theatrical supply houses. For tonight's role a mouth prosthesis would be needed, along with special plastic that, used properly, would simulate the dewlaps and wrinkles of aging. Araña had become an amazing mimic and an expert with disguise, like a changeable shadow able to blend into any crowd, "becoming" anyone, male or female.

Both the CIA and Mossad, even the KGB, had used the South American on more than one occasion. A rebellious labor leader in an Eastern bloc country. Colombian federal judges—eight or ten of them. A French prime minister. A California speaker of the house. All liquidated, either by shooting or the garrote. Often those with them died as well—it made no difference to Araña.

One more time, the assassin mentally promised, knowing the promise was empty. The exquisite pleasure of the kill was addictive—a necessity now.

She was the most dangerous woman in the world.

Slowly, carefully, she constructed the face she would wear tonight. The gray wig. Bristling eyebrows. Blue contact lenses that gave her eyes a rheumy look. She would enjoy the challenge of smoothing away her sultry model's beauty to impersonate an older male.

She feathered wrinkles around her eyes and mouth, thinking about the latest bank account she'd opened, her thirty-sixth. She had her collection of Panamanian bank accounts, one for each hit. Fortunately, her husband, Tomás, never asked too many questions about her "modeling trips." That was the way it should be. Like the American mafiosi, it was best to keep business and family strictly separated. Of course, there had been failures too—only three, but each one had had a profound effect on Araña, each one had been a personal defeat that affected her so profoundly it bordered on neurosis. On all three occasions she had gone into such deep depression, she was hospitalized for ten days. Intensive therapy, shock treatments, and powerful drugs were needed to reverse the trauma.

She finished dressing and snorted a line of cocaine. The

surge of power and control rocked her. She was Araña! The Spider! She'd proven it—in blood. They'd *never* take her down.

Ten minutes later, she strode through Times Square, along sidewalks filled with night people—couples, kids on the prowl, junkies, tourists, whores, businessmen looking for action.

A girl wearing a black leather minidress and heavy chain jewelry elbowed by. Araña saw the way her glance didn't even focus, and suppressed a triumphant smile. The gray hair, the tufted eyebrows, the old-man eyes and gait . . . she looked like any other distinguished New Yorker hurrying to have a quick bite before the theater.

Underneath her trench coat Araña wore a black tuxedo. Strapped inside the coat lining, accessible through carefully tailored slit flaps, was a Belgian-made, semiautomatic pistol, adapted from the famous Israeli Uzi military rifle. Loaded with a fifteen-shot magazine, it weighed slightly more than eight pounds, and was less than thirty inches long. It had been equipped with a snub-nosed silencer of new, experimental design. When fired, it would barely cough. It was also deadly accurate, perfect for use in a crowded theater.

Glancing at her Piaget watch, Araña saw that it was already past seven P.M. Only fifty minutes until curtain time. She felt a shiver of excitement that threatened to become a mountain of sexual fulfillment. It was starting again . . .

Seated on a low stool in the makeup room, Valentina felt the deft touch of the liner pencil along her upper right lid. Then the left. "Close your eyes again," ordered Bev, the makeup woman.

Valentina's pulse was slightly fast, her mind sliding from thought to thought. Her unconscious was telling her that something was very, very wrong.

"There," sighed the makeup artist, stepping back from her handiwork. "Fantastic! It's Lara, but it's Valentina too!"

Valentina gazed at herself in the mirror, and smiled.

They'd worked hours for exactly this look. The makeup had
been especially designed for her by Trini of Madrigal
Associates. She was going to be a new, striking, bold Lara.

"Thank you, Bev."

Valentina hurried out of Makeup, almost colliding with
Patrick Swayze.

"Valentina. Gorgeous!" He offered her his megawatt
smile.

"Thanks, Patrick, and *you* don't need any makeup," she
complimented back.

She strode down the backstage corridor, nodding to two
female dancers already in peasant costumes.

Valentina reached her dressing room and flung open the
door, inhaling the perfume of roses from elaborate bouquets
crowding every available space. Tears filled her eyes and
she closed the door and stood trembling, staring at herself in
the lighted mirror. Were second chances really possible?

If only something doesn't come along to fuck it up. The
thought slid into her mind like a tiny knife.

Thirty minutes until curtain time.

In a rented room that overlooked Forty-first Street,
Mikhail Sandovsky stood at the old-fashioned sash window,
gazing across at the Lederer Theater.

He might have less than three hours to live.

Six foot three and built muscularly wide, he had an
athlete's square, strong jawline. Mikhail's black hair, high
cheekbones, and smoldering green eyes were identical to
Valentina's, but his disciplined, military stance was that of
the decorated Russian MiG pilot he had been.

He sucked in a deep breath, then exhaled slowly. The air
in this stuffy, shabby room tasted far better than any June
breeze over the Baltic, or crisp January wind blowing over
the Neva in Moscow.

"See anything interesting out there?" Herb Cannell said
behind him, his dry voice betraying tension. Also in the
room were two other federal agents, Jerry Kramer, FBI, and
Rosalie Greenfield, from the Central Intelligence Agency.

"No," Mikhail replied shortly. His English was flawless.

The KGB school had seen to that. He hated the KGB now, and everything the dreaded secret police stood for.

He narrowed his eyes, gazing across the street at the theater.

The marquee advertised

DR. ZHIVAGO

with VALENTINA

and

PATRICK SWAYZE

Also Winona Ryder and Orchid Lederer

In front of the theater, a TV newswoman was speaking animatedly into the camera. A crowd of fans, huddled under umbrellas, watched her. A few eager theater-goers were already arriving.

Mikhail watched as a gray Rolls-Royce pulled up, and the chauffeur handed out a handsome older couple. Even from the window, Mikhail could see the glitter of the magnificent diamond necklace the woman wore. He recognized Peaches and Edgar Lederer, Valentina's parents, who had lovingly reared both Valentina and Orchid. While he . . . he had grown up in Moscow, thinking he had no one.

Mikhail turned away from the window, glancing at the three agents in the room with him. Unconsciously he rubbed his hands along the seams of his trousers.

"Well, we'd better get down to it," said Herb Cannell. "I've got all the stuff you need. It's heavy and it'll be hotter than hell, but if there's the kind of action we think there's going to be, you'll bless it."

"Yes," Mikhail said. He turned and walked toward the bed, where they had already laid out the bullet-proof Kevlar vest, with an extender to block out the vulnerable area of his neck, and thin, helmetlike padding to wear under the white wig to give him some additional protection against a head shot.

"Well, you're going to look like the guy all right," Rosalie Greenfield remarked, holding up the wig.

Mikhail began stripping off his clothes, peeling down to his boxer shorts.

He caught the CIA woman staring curiously at the jagged scars on his back and shoulders. He didn't mind the scars. They were a badge of something—a reminder of a life he despised.

"Okay, okay," Cannell said, handing him the vest. "This goes on first, and strap it on tight so it'll cover your vital parts."

Mikhail Sandovsky reached for the Kevlar vest, his pulse rate and blood pressure beginning to accelerate, just as it had done before he started a mission in Afghanistan. Holding the heavy vest, he had a sudden image—himself caught in a red, screaming circle of pain.

It was a surprising flash of fear, momentarily shocking him. He'd been trained from boyhood not to show emotion, but the rushes of raw, strong feeling were coming more and more often these days. However, within a fraction of a second, Mikhail had concealed his emotions, his expression stony. Quickly, efficiently, he donned the bulletproof vest.

He wondered what Valentina was doing right now, what her thoughts were. His beautiful sister. His twin, his other half.

He remembered a train, winding through the Caucasus Mountains between rocky crags piled high with unstable cornices of spring snow. A boy and girl, twins, laughing. Their ballet-dancer mother.

He thought of how it began . . .

Chapter

Two

Russia
1970

A LATE, WET March snowstorm swirled heavy flakes, the myriad dots of white nearly blotting out the train that sped from Kirovabad to Tbilisi, in the Caucasus mountains of the Soviet Union. The high peaks were lost in the infinity of snow, the bulk of Mount Mtatsminda looming ahead.

Inside the overheated, luxurious "soft class" car, eight-year-old Mikhail Sandovsky was teaching his twin sister, Valentina, the rudiments of cat's cradle while their mother, a widow of six days, tried to sleep.

"See? See how it's done?" The boy held up his hands, on which an intricate, interwoven pattern of strings was draped. "Around these fingers . . . so. Then through here. And around here. Anyone can do it!"

Valentina was bent anxiously close to her brother, her black curls touching his. The little girl concentrated, following every twist of the string between her brother's hands.

Finally she nodded. "Let me do it now."

Mikhail—older than she by ten minutes—withdrew his string-wrapped hands, moving slightly away. "No, Valia, not yet. Not until you watch the string."

"I am. I *am* watching. Mikhail, I saw everything you did. I can do it!" Her emerald eyes, identical to his and reddened from crying, beseeched him.

"*Da,* then show me."

Valentina took the string from her brother and, biting

15

down on her lower lip, methodically wrapped it around her fingers and thumbs, barely hesitating as she duplicated the pattern her brother had shown her. The results were perfect.

"There!" Valentina cried, her eyes shining with triumph. "Mama! Mama! I did the string perfectly!"

Nadia Sandovska was a tall, slim, dark-haired woman with the long, swanlike neck and elegant bone structure of a Bolshoi Ballet dancer. She had been napping, her head leaned wearily back on the seat, but woke with a start at Valentina's voice.

"What is it, child?"

Valentina held up the elaborate string construction. "Look!"

"Valia, darling. It's beautiful."

Valentina moved to cuddle next to her mother, while Mikhail kneeled on the seat, his forehead pressed against the window. Nadia saw the tears begin to fall from her son's eyes, and the way he turned to hide them.

"Misha, my darling, come, sit here." She settled him on her other side, stroking his forehead, kissing his soft hair. "Let us all sit quietly for a while. You have both been very brave, and I love you very much."

Now tears filled her own eyes. What would she do without her beloved Alexandr? A physicist, he had been sent to the Gulag for making "dissident statements," and the six harsh months in the reeducation camp had taken their toll too quickly. He had developed pneumonia and died before they reached the camp. Her last embrace could only be his cold, stiff body.

Nadia blinked the hot tears away. She'd lived her entire life for Alexandr and now, despite the children, barely wanted to go on.

"Mama! Mama! I saw a bear!" Mikhail suddenly whispered.

"Hush, son," Nadia cautioned, glancing at the well-dressed official who shared the first-class compartment with them. "You will disturb our fellow passenger."

"I am not being disturbed," said the man called Vladimir Petrov, looking up from the documents he had been poring over for the past two hours. "You won't see bears out there now, my boy. The snow, you know," Petrov explained heartily. "Bears hibernate in the winter, and they don't come out until spring. Yes, indeed. Bears are very extraordinary creatures, especially Soviet bears."

The man made Nadia uneasy. He was about forty, with a heavy face deeply etched with lines, and dark eyes. He was wearing an expensive, fur-lined greatcoat, from which he produced peppermint candies, giving most of them to Mikhail, usually ignoring Valentina.

Nadia was wary of him, and the looks he gave to Mikhail, and occasionally toward her. Was he KGB? She knew better than to ask. Obviously he, like they, was returning to Moscow.

She sighed. She needed to think about getting a job when they reached Moscow, for if she was not employed within three months, she would be labeled a "parasite." She would call Madam Lubayev at the Bolshoi.

Perhaps she could teach the youngest dancers, she thought, her mind rambling. But she was the wife of a dissident . . . for her it would be almost impossible to find employment . . . But she must. She must give the children an education. Teach them what Alexandr would have . . .

The odor of tea drifted into the compartment, faintly tart. Vladimir Petrov eyed the pale, pretty widow, then his gaze traveled to the twins. They were extraordinary. The little girl, Valentina, now clutching a hand-sewn calico bear, was going to be a beauty. There was a melting quality about her huge, green eyes, and the arc of her eyebrows was winglike, exquisite.

For the thousandth time, though, his eyes were drawn to the handsome boy.

A son.

"Valenka!" Mikhail had begun to squirm in his seat, as small boys do. "Do you want to live in a cave sometime? We'll hunt and fish and shoot rabbits and make shelters out of pine branches."

"And we'll have a campfire," the little girl agreed.

"And rifles."

"And soft coverlets made of goosedown."

"No, not in a cave, silly . . ."

"In our cave we will," Valentina said firmly. The boy nodded, and Petrov could sense the strong bond between them.

Suddenly angry, he got up and stalked out of the compartment. In the narrow corridor, which swayed back and forth to the rhythm of wheels on tracks, he stood shaking with remorse and lamented the fate that had denied him what he wanted most, a son.

The snow had let up a little as the train curved to the right, entering a huge notch between the mountains, where wet masses of snow seemed about to tumble. On one side was a rocky wall, and on the other, a valley that became a gorge, at the bottom of which tumbled a tiny mountain river.

"I'm going to the *tuolyet*," Mikhail announced, getting out of his seat.

The WC compartment was plastered in white, with a sink where you pushed and held a lever to get water. There was a chain that was used to flush. Mikhail peed into the galvanized bowl, the motion of the train making it difficult for him to aim.

He took his time buttoning up, gazing out of the train window at the wonderful gorge, so huge and deep, sloping downward past the line of his sight. He pulled open the door, and stepped into the corridor, thinking about bears again, and Papa.

He heard the thunderous roar, felt the very air shudder.

Mikhail grabbed on hard to the jamb of the door, but felt it wrenched out of his grip. The train car gave a terrifying lurch, and tipped over on its side.

A massive cold whiteness flowed toward Mikhail, picked him up and hurled him out · of the toilet compartment window.

He screamed as the avalanche pushed him, sliding him along, snapping his right leg like a stick, and forcing slivers of broken glass through his wool pants and into his thigh. Fiery pain shot through him.

And then he lost consciousness.

"Mama! Mama!" Valentina shrieked in terror.

There was snow everywhere. It had broken down the wall of their compartment and half filled the car, its mass terrifyingly huge.

"Mama mama mama!"

With frantic strength Valentina pulled at the section of paneling and door that had fallen across the seat where Nadia was. She could see her mother's feet, in their neat cotton stockings, and black boots, but the rest of her body was hidden by white snow.

"Mama! Mamochka!" Desperately Valentina clawed at the snow.

Nadia stirred, groaning deeply. Frantic, Valentina dug and scooped until she managed to get her mother's face and chest free. Then Nadia stirred and began to help, pushing the rest of the paneling off herself. She was bleeding from the face and scalp.

"Valentina . . . Mikhail!" Nadia screamed.

Valentina felt an icy wash of terror so intense that she could not breathe. *Misha. Where was he?*

Vladimir Petrov found himself lying facedown, his nose badly skinned by ice crystals, snow chunked in his mouth. He lifted his head. A swooping drop into the gorge began only a foot away from where he had finally been deposited by the huge overflow of snow.

He struggled up, aware that his heavy, fur-lined coat had probably saved his life.

He swore, dazed. What had happened?

Then he looked back toward the train and saw the chain of tumbled cars, some in the gorge, others half buried in snow, eight or ten tilted crazily on their sides. Only the five at the front, and the engine, remained untouched.

Avalanche. They had been seeing small ones all day. The mountains could be treacherous in early spring.

A piercing scream attracted Petrov's attention. When he
looked to his left he saw a man crushed between two cars,
his lower legs a pulpy mass of red blood.

Petrov turned aside and vomited violently, his body
shaking with the force of the spasms. He could hear other
shouts, pathetic screams for help. People were trapped—
several in the snow, some in the train. Someone had to help
dig them out.

He coughed and choked, throwing up the meals he had
eaten earlier in the day. When he was done he wiped his
mouth and started toward the horrifyingly skewed cars.

Frantic to find her brother, Valentina slipped and crawled
among the fallen suitcases and the topsy-turvy seats, finally
finding a broken window. She wriggled her way up and out,
and found herself on top of the train car.

Petrified, she gripped the metal edge of the window and
looked around.

The train was broken! All the cars lay twisted, most off
the track, and many had fallen over on their sides. Five or
six cars had fallen toward the river a thousand feet below.
The figures of rescuers walked back and forth, digging
people out of the snow.

Valentina began to sob. Where was her twin? Was he
buried in the snow? Was he at the bottom by the river? Was
he . . . ?

But her eight-year-old mind did not have a clear picture
of death yet, and could not complete the thought any further.
She had no idea that she was bleeding from the mouth and
nose, that there was a huge bruise on her forehead, blood in
her hair. All she knew was one thing. She had to find her
brother.

She had to. She screamed out his name again and again.
"Misha! Misha!"

Two hours later, Petrov was exhausted, every muscle in
his body shrieking for rest, but he had helped rescue eight
terrified passengers.

Darkness would descend soon, rendering further rescue

operations nearly impossible. The temperature was also dropping, and many of the trapped victims would freeze to death during the night.

Panting with exhaustion, Petrov started toward the sound of yet another faint plea, and stumbled over the body of a child. The boy, wearing a familiar-looking dark green padded wool jacket, lay crumpled, half covered by snow. He was unconscious, his bare head bloody from a scalp wound, his face white, and his right leg twisted at an awkward angle.

Mikhail.

Vladimir Petrov's heart lurched. It was young Misha Sandovsky. The child had somehow been flung out of the car, and now he lay separated from his mother and sister, who were either being rescued, or were dead.

Feeling a rush of triumph, the Russian bent over, dug away the snow, and scooped up the boy. Carrying Mikhail, he started toward the makeshift hospital car a hundred feet down the track where the wounded were being taken. Several doctors who had been passengers were now laboring to save the survivors. He would put the boy in another car, he suddenly decided, and prevail upon a doctor to attend him there.

He had the child in his arms and the mother didn't know where he was.

Mikhail had regained consciousness but did not cry, except for one whimper when the doctor set his broken right leg. Petrov held him while the female doctor worked, proud of the stoic child.

"He is still in shock and must be watched," the doctor said as she prepared to go back to the hospital car.

"Drugs," Petrov commanded. "He must have something for pain, to quiet him."

"There is not enough. We have people in severe pain who were crushed by the—"

"Leave the morphine," Petrov snapped. "And do not talk of this—this is KGB business."

The doctor fished in her bag for several vials, issuing Petrov the instructions for their use. Quickly she left.

Mikhail shook his head groggily, gazing around him with bewilderment and anxiety.

"Where is my mother?" he asked for the tenth time. "Where is my sister, Valenka?"

"You must be brave," Petrov finally said.

The boy's brilliant green eyes locked on his, already growing hazy with the effects of the drug.

"There has been an avalanche, Mikhail. Do you understand what that is? Half a mountain of snow slid down from the peak. Many, many people are dead. Six cars fell down into the river gorge and your mother and sister's car was one of them."

"No," Misha cried. His eyes blazed. "No, that didn't happen. I don't believe you!"

"It did happen, little one. They died. They are at the bottom of the river gorge. I am sorry." Petrov moistened his lips, adding, "Mikhail, on the train I could not help overhearing. I know that you have no other living relatives. Your grandmother died last year, you are alone."

The boy's head rocked back as if slapped.

"You must have somewhere to live, someone to take care of you to see that you grow up big and strong," Petrov went on softly. "*I* will do that for you, Misha. I will adopt you as my son and provide for you in every way."

The child stared at him in shock and tried to shake his head no, but the morphine had taken effect, and he was only able to manage a brief movement. Soon the boy had slumped back on the makeshift train seat and was snoring lightly.

Petrov possessively watched Mikhail sleep. But what about the mother?

Leaving the compartment where his small charge now slept, he pulled the door shut and stood in front of it, guarding it from intrusion. Efficiently, he began to plan. First, Nadia Sandovska must be told her son was dead—a victim of the avalanche.

Secondly, since the woman was on her way back to

Moscow, as he was himself, he must provide protection against her accidentally coming in contact with her boy in future years.

He half closed his eyes, rubbing his frost-bitten fingers together, as he formulated what to do. He could have her terminated ''for political infractions contrary to the welfare of the State.'' She was powerless, a woman, and a dissident's widow, tainted and suspect. But no. She had given him the gift of a son. He would now give her a gift. *Her life!*

He tried to recall all the various parts of the conversation he'd heard between the mother and her twins during the two days of the train journey. And then it came to him. She was educated, had told the children stories in French.

That was fortuitous. There *was* a way—yes. He would get her out of Moscow by creating a job for her.

After spending the night huddled in a train car, the warmth of the closely packed human bodies keeping them comfortable, the surviving passengers were taken by truck back to the town of Tbilisi the following morning.

''I'm sorry,'' Petrov said. ''Your son has not been found and is believed to have been buried in the avalanche.''

Nadia stared at him, her face drained of color. ''Oh, no . . . please, please . . .''

''He's *not* dead!'' Valentina shouted, small hands clutching her blue calico bear with surprising strength.

''He is gone,'' Petrov said heavily, his eyes flicking away. ''Buried under a million tons of snow. *Mnye ochem zhal.* I'm really sorry.''

The town of Tbilisi, frosted with layers of snow, was the capital of Georgia. State buildings, theaters, cultural buildings, and statues adorned sycamore-lined streets with names like Rustaveli Boulevard, Lenin Street, and the Square of Heroes. The brooding, snowy bulk of Mount Mtatsminda dominated the ''old town'' area, with its ruins of a fourth-century castle. Despite her grief, Valentina stared curiously at several ancient, sixth-century churches as their truck hurtled down the street. The cobblestones were so old they were black.

The surviving train passengers were taken to the Hotel Sakartvelo, on Melikishvili Street.

Nadia and Valentina settled into the small, shabby third-floor rear room they had been given, their room paid for by a mysterious benefactor.

"Mama! *Mamochka*," Valentina begged, anxiously picking up the cheap hairbrush they had stood in line to purchase in a small shop. She began to comb her mother's hair. "Mama, please don't cry any more today."

"I'm sorry, my darling," Nadia said, making an effort to wipe away the weak tears that kept falling.

"Mama . . . what is going to happen to us now?"

"I don't know, Valia—but I'll take care of us, I'll find a way. I've been thinking . . ."

"Will we go back to our apartment then?" Valentina wanted to know.

"No. We can't."

"But . . . how will Misha know where to find us if we don't go back to where we lived before?" Valentina inquired, her voice quivering.

"Valenka. He is dead, little one."

"The man lied. I *know* he's alive."

"*Dusha moya*," Nadia murmured, cuddling the child on her lap, rocking slowly back and forth. The little girl's obsession worried her. "Darling, we will always remember Mikhail and love him very much. We can think about him every day, and say a prayer every night. We must never forget your brother."

On the fourth day the message came, delivered by a uniformed officer of the KGB.

As soon as he had left, Nadia opened the folded note and read it.

Telephone me upon your return to Moscow as I have a job for you which I think may please you and will utilize your language ability. I am enclosing train tickets for both yourself and your daughter. Comrade Major Vladimir Josef Petrov.

She stared at the cramped, almost illegible male handwriting, her heart pounding with horror. This note made everything crystal-clear. He intended to obligate her to him by finding her employment. Then he would expect her to become his mistress. Yes, that was how things were for an unattached woman.

She reread the note. "Utilize your language ability . . ." That must mean as a translator, perhaps for foreign tourists with some travel privileges if she were fantastically lucky. *Travel.* Her mind began to race. For the first time there seemed a small glimmer of hope.

"What, Mama? What does the note say?" Valentina asked, bringing her out of her tumbled thoughts.

"It says . . . why, it says . . ." Nadia's voice cracked, as she stared at the tickets Petrov had sent. "Why, it says that he will give me a job."

On another train, Petrov and his new "son," Mikhail, were pulling into the outer environs of Moscow. The color of the air had changed, and seemed grayer, the sky overhead full of heavy snow clouds.

In contrast to the gloomy Moscow day, Petrov was in an excellent mood. He had a son! He felt sure his wife, Irina, childless after a number of miscarriages, would be overjoyed. His son . . . their son . . . would attend the top military academy. He was obviously intelligent, already tall for his age, and as an adult would probably grow as tall as six one or six two. A beautiful physical specimen. Yes, there was no question about it!

And stubborn. A quality Petrov admired even as he found it aggravating. Fortunately, with his right leg now set in a full-length plaster cast, Mikhail could hardly run away from him.

The boy was still deep in grief, and had barely spoken to him since they left Tbilisi, eating nothing, and only drinking liquids when they were forced upon him.

Already the boy's face seemed thinner, and there were

hollow shadows under his eyes. Once, falling asleep, he had cried out the name of his twin sister.

"Misha," Petrov said, producing a sack of *ponchiki,* hot sugared doughnuts he had bought in one of the train stations, along with several expensive oranges, a real delicacy. "Please, son. Please eat something."

Mikhail sniffed hungrily but did not make a move toward the fruit.

The train was slowing up for the stop at Podolsk. Petrov glimpsed a woman standing on the platform holding a basket containing three or four part-Borzoi puppies.

Impulsively he got up and excused himself, telling Misha that he would return in a few minutes.

On the platform he pushed his way through office workers heading into the city, and families greeting each other with exuberant Russian hugs and kisses. He sprinted down the platform, already fishing in his pocket for his sterling silver money clip.

"I want those puppies," he told the peasant woman curtly. "All of them."

He pressed ten rubles, about two dollars, into her hand, and reached for the basket. The pups were about six weeks old, fat and well fed. As he handled the basket, the largest animal opened its eyes and gave a sharp, yippy bark. Petrov hurried back to the train car with his precious burden.

Stepping inside the compartment, he emptied the basket of puppies into Mikhail's lap. The puppies wiggled all over him, squealing and snuffling, one of them managing to jump high enough to lick Mikhail's face.

For an instant Mikhail hesitated. Then as the eager dog licked him again, something relaxed in the boy's face. "Are these . . . are they for me?" Misha asked in a low voice.

"If you want them."

Misha didn't answer but his eyes were no longer so full of hostility. He lifted up the fattest puppy, holding it up to his face, allowing it to lick his cheeks.

After a few moments of watching Mikhail play with the dogs, Petrov leaned back in his seat, well satisfied. By tonight, Petrov believed, Mikhail would be eating not only the oranges but a hearty supper.

In three days, he'd be talking and chattering, and in a month, he would have begun to forget his mother—and his twin sister.

Their bond was broken now.

Permanently.

Chapter
Three

"Misha! Misha! Misha!" Valentina's piercing scream cut through the air. She tossed and thrashed under the thin blanket, her knees jabbing Nadia. *"Mikhail!"*

Nadia stirred, automatically reaching for her daughter to enfold her in comforting arms. "Valenka . . . oh, my little dove . . . It's nothing, nothing . . . just a bad dream . . . go back to sleep."

"But Mama!" Tears ran down Valentina's face. She jerked to an upright position, staring into the unfamiliar darkness of the small, overcrowded bedroom they had been forced to rent in someone's apartment in an apartment block.

"Mama!" Valentina sobbed. "Mikhail is crying . . . I dreamed it . . . he is feeling so sad."

"Child, child," sighed Nadia.

"Mama?" Valentina said into the night. She twisted a little under the covers. Sometimes, for no reason at all, her right leg mysteriously hurt.

"Yes, *dusha moya.*"

"Why did we never see Mikhail after he was dead?"

"Because he was buried too deeply in the snow. Hush . . . Hush! You must not talk of this again. You must be a very good girl and study your schoolwork and learn to speak English and French, the way I've been teaching you."

"Why, *mamochka*?"

"Because!" Nadia spoke more vehemently than usual.

"But . . . what if Misha is still there in the snow? What

28

if he's cold—what if he's scared . . . ? I *know* he's scared.
I know he misses us.''

"He is dead, my little dove. You must believe it,'' Nadia
said hoarsely. "Misha's body was buried at the bottom of
the snow, under tons and tons of snow. I was told this
myself, by the officials. There is no hope, they said. Child,
more than a hundred people died in the avalanche.'' Nadia
turned wearily onto her side, coughing a little. "Now go to
sleep. I have to get up early tomorrow!''

Nadia worked as a translator with UPDK, a governmental
agency that supplied translators, as well as maids, clerks,
janitors, and chauffeurs. He was waiting for something else
to open up, Petrov told them one afternoon while paying a
call at their austere room.

"I am preparing the necessary documents,'' Petrov said.

"Thank you,'' Nadia responded in a low voice.

"You have a cough. Have you obtained medicine for it?''

"I—it is only a winter cold.''

"I will send antibiotics.'' For a second Petrov's glance
swept Nadia almost with regret. "You must practice your
French and English, eh? If I get you this appointment, you
must justify the confidence placed in you.''

That night, they sat together in the small bed, huddled
under a blanket, while Nadia read aloud to Valentina in
English. Much dog-eared, the book was *Green Eggs and
Ham* by Dr. Seuss.

Nadia put the book down and leaned back on the thin
pillow. "I was in Los Angeles twice with the Bolshoi. Oh,
Valentina, you have no idea how rich the Americans are.
There was a street called Rodeo Drive, full of clothes in a
thousand colors, silk, lace, sequins, jewelry. The TV sets,
Valentina! And the American cars! I would so love to own
a red Ford convertible!''

Valentina listened, eyes shining. "More,'' she begged.
"Tell me more, Mama.''

Nadia's face was soft. "In California the women are
very, very beautiful,'' she went on. "They are the prettiest
women in the world. But no one will be more beautiful than

you, *moy zaichik*. Your eyes, so green, greener than the *Schwarzwald* in June . . . Even in Hollywood, you will be special.''

Valentina loved to hear her mother talk like this, as if they themselves might actually go to America. She wriggled closer to Nadia, stroking her mother's sleeve adoringly.

''Someday you will be grown,'' Nadia added, coughing. ''I'll be old and decrepit and gray so you will have to do everything for me, *dusha moya*. Will you promise me?'' She gripped Valentina by the shoulders. ''Will you swear to me, Valentina, by all that is Holy, by the great Mother Russia, that you will make your mark? That you will make it all worthwhile? All the . . . the pain?''

Valentina, bewildered, did not know what her mother was talking about.

''Yes,'' she blurted out, wanting to please. ''Mama!'' She winced as her mother's fingers dug into her upper arms a little too hard.

''Sorry, my child.'' Nadia let go of her. Abruptly she turned away to face the wall, her body shaking again with the tears that still often crept up on her without warning.

By early summer, Valentina and Nadia were in Paris, where Petrov had obtained a job for Nadia with the Russian Embassy. She was a translator, working for a deputy commercial attaché, spending hours poring over dull economic reports or attending routine meetings.

They took a tiny flat on the Right Bank in the Ménilomontant area, with its narrow streets and small houses, a block away from the Père-Lachaise Cemetery. But it had three rooms and to them it seemed luxurious, with its high ceilings, carved plaster moldings, flocked French wallpaper, and even a little gas fireplace. Every morning Valentina went out and bought croissants for their breakfast, from a *boulangerie* two doors away. However, Valentina had to sit with Nadia and make sure she ate; her mother had grown thin, and moved these days with tightly wound-up energy.

''Such good bread here. But don't grow too accustomed to French food, little dove,'' Nadia told Valentina one morning at the end of the second week. She was fussing with her coat, slitting its bottom hem with a small scissors. "I have a big secret; we aren't going to be here for long."

"But where will we be?" Valentina inquired anxiously. Already Paris seemed impossibly far away from her lost brother, and she did not know how he would ever find them here.

"I can't tell you," Nadia whispered. "It's bad luck to talk about good things before they happen."

"But—are we going back to Russia then?"

"It's a secret, Valentina . . . a wonderful, wonderful secret!" She swept up Valentina in a hug. "So brush your hair, please, and be sure to wash your pretty face. We are going shopping today!"

"Again?"

"This isn't just any shopping—this is special." Nadia's cheeks were flushed. "We have a whole day, Valentina, and at the end of this day—" Mama's smile flashed with excitement. "Oh, we'll be rich, child! We'll be so rich!"

Paris! To Valentina the city was a constant, incredible delight. The soaring cathedrals, green parks, wide boulevards, and narrow, medieval cobblestone streets. The wonderful shops and boutiques, delicious-smelling restaurants, all of it awash with the lissom breezes of June.

They took the Métro to the Rue St.-Honoré, exited at the station, swept along by the crowd. Holding tightly to Nadia's hand, Valentina looked around her. Crowds jostled along the narrow streets, stopping to linger at little cafés, *crêperies,* boutiques, and art galleries. A hundred odors teased the nostrils, from the perfumed flowers being sold by street vendors, to the waft of scent from fashionably dressed women.

They wandered for an hour, passing shops like Hermès, Chanel, Alexandrine, Rémy, Amie, and Henri à la Pensée. Nadia chattered to her daughter, showing her windows full of beautiful gloves, blouses, and gowns. Then Nadia said, "Now we've looked enough, it's time to work."

They hailed a taxi on Rue Scribe and within minutes were

at the Place Vendôme, where more wonderful shops displayed sparkling necklaces and earrings in their windows. To Valentina's Slavic ear, their names seemed beautiful: Boucheron, Cartier, Van Cleef and Arpels, Chaumet. But now Nadia didn't seem festive anymore, and her features took on a pinched look. She kept touching her hand between her breasts, as if to verify that something she carried in her brassiere was still there.

The routine was the same at each jewelry store. Valentina would wait in the outer shop, while Nadia accompanied the jeweler into an inner room. Left to her own devices, Valentina paced around, staring into glass cases that glittered with diamond rings, ruby pins shaped like dragonflies, diamond-and-sapphire pendants, and sinuous gold chains. Within twenty minutes Nadia would emerge, her complexion pale.

"Not here," she would announce. "They say that the cut of the stones is too old-fashioned! These people are ignorant! This necklace was worn by my great-grandmother to a ball where the Czar and Czarina danced! I carried it for years sewn into the hem of my coat, Valia. I knew I could not get good value for it in Russia."

The shadows were growing longer as Nadia emerged from a place called Sterle. Visits to five or six more stores on the Rue de Rivoli caused Nadia's mouth to tighten to a thin line, and all the sparkle to fade from her eyes.

"I could take less, of course—but I won't!" she told Valentina wearily. They were passing a side street where a nightclub called Diables was emblazoned with neon lights that at night would pulse and throb with color. Next to it was another of the jewelry shops, smaller than the others, but grandly decorated with brass trim and European cut glass.

"Here," Nadia said, dragging Valentina toward it.

Half an hour later, Nadia emerged from the minuscule back room of the shop, her face glowing with triumph.

"Valentina! Oh, Valenka!" Nadia ran toward her daughter, scooping her up. She whirled Valentina around, then, seeing the jeweler staring, hastily pulled the girl out of the shop. "Valia, I have done it!"

They found a station of the Métro and boarded the subway again, cramming themselves among the rush-hour passengers. Nadia held on very tightly to Valentina, her shoulders hunched and arms protectively wrapped so that no one should touch her front, where she was carrying the francs.

"Now," she announced in satisfaction. "I will have to go out alone myself, in the evenings, to get what we need next. But I will get it . . . and we will leave Paris soon."

Nadia's cold had worsened. On the morning they took a taxi to Charles de Gaulle Airport, she kept coughing so much that she had to hold on to Valentina for support. She kept glancing behind them as the taxi swerved through the traffic.

"Mama?" Valentina inquired anxiously. "Who are you looking for?"

"No one!" cried Nadia nervously, although inwardly she worried that her recent illegal transactions had been reported to the Russian Embassy authorities. The KGB could be following them.

"Are you sick?"

Nadia shook her head firmly. She was pale, fragile, and beautiful in her black Dior trouser suit. "It is only a cold. I will be well by the time we are in the air."

"Should you take any more of the pills that man Petrov left?"

"I have taken them all, Valia, one each day to make them last longer."

"But—"

"I will be *fine*, Valentina. Now remember, we are U.S. citizens, Valenka! You must remember that at all times. I spent much money for our papers, and this is very, very important."

They arrived with barely enough time to board the crowded flight, and several passengers stared at the striking-looking mother and daughter as they hurried to their seats. Valentina wore a dressy robin's-egg-blue silk frock. Nadia had combed out her hair in soft, glossy, flowing curls that framed her heart-shaped face, adding a shell barrette. The girl carried her blue calico teddy bear. It, too, had been dressed up with a blue silk bow for the bear's neck.

Valentina sank into the upright padded seat of the Pan Am jet and gazed out of the window at the runway with dread. In just a few minutes, she and Mama would be flying in the air, high over the sea. Since she did not speak English well, Nadia instructed her to be careful when talking with the flight attendants or anyone else.

"Mama," she whispered. "What will Misha and Papa do when we are so far away? Across the huge ocean?"

"Child," Nadia responded. "It doesn't matter how far away we fly from them. They will be with us wherever we go . . . in our thoughts, and in our hearts."

Now a pretty lady in a uniform—a stewardess, Mama told her—was walking up and down the aisle, pushing the plastic overhead doors shut.

"Now, Valia, you must fasten your seat belt," Nadia instructed in English. "Like this . . . see?"

The plane had begun to taxi forward, and Valentina clutched at the seat-belt buckle, feeling a sudden spasm of nausea, mingled with acute loss.

She swallowed hard, pushing it away. Maybe the ocean wasn't *that* big. Somehow, someday, she was going to come back to Russia and find Misha—even if she had to wait until she was grown-up.

By the time they landed at O'Hare Airport, and had gone through customs, Nadia was shivering violently. She coughed frequently in racking gasps, and her cheeks were much too bright and red, the rest of her skin too pale.

"*Mamochka,*" Valentina said, taking their old, Russian-made suitcase away from her mother. It was very heavy. "Are you all right?"

"Tickets," Nadia said feverishly, patting her purse. "We still have to fly to Detroit, Valentina . . . another flight. I have a friend there, Sonya, who danced with me at the Bolshoi. She married a rich American and is living in a wonderful place called Bloomfield Hills. We are going to

stay with her for a few months, until I can find work.''
Nadia paused to cough violently. ''Come now, let's find the
correct departure gate.''

It was late at night when their plane finally landed at
Detroit's Metro Airport. It was also raining. Sheets of water
billowed across the runway and sprayed the window of the
plane. It all looked very gloomy and forbidding, hardly the
country of fabulous sunshine, beautiful people, TV sets, and
cars that Nadia had depicted.

Valentina looked anxiously at her mother. Nadia had
slept the entire flight, her breath labored.

''Mama?'' She prodded her mother to wake her.

Nadia stirred, groaning a little, and coughed again.

''Mama!'' Valentina begged. ''We have to get off the
plane now. We have to call Sonya, your friend.''

''*Da, da,*'' Nadia said, looking confused and lapsing into
Russian. She coughed again.

Nadia stood swaying at the phone kiosk, her face so white
that Valentina feared she was going to faint.

''I could not—the number—it did not go through,'' she
said, her strength obviously nearly at an end. ''Sonya's
telephone has been disconnected.''

Valentina tried to dial the number, too, and got the same
recorded message in a strange language. She hung up, a
sinking feeling spreading throughout her midsection. Sonya
wasn't there anymore. They were alone.

''Where to, ladies?'' inquired the cab driver, who had
skin of a deep ebony. The rain still pounded down,
glistening in the night lights outside the baggage claim area.

''Hotel,'' croaked Nadia, who had miraculously perked
up a little after Valentina bought her a bottle of aspirin at an
airport shop.

''Which hotel, lady?''

''Bloomfield Hills,'' Nadia specified.

By the time they reached the Americana Inn in Birmingham, the cab driver having arbitrarily taken them there,
Nadia knew that she was very ill.

Their room was huge, with two double beds, unheard of in Russia. There was a large American television set suspended from the ceiling, a seascape painting on the wall, and a wonderful blue shag carpet.

Nadia collapsed onto one of the beds. "Valia," she whispered. "Bring me the pill bottle. Then . . . go into the bathroom and take a nice, warm bubble bath, please. Take a long soak, little rabbit. Soak yourself well in the beautiful warm bubbles. This is American luxury—you should enjoy it!"

When Nadia heard the running of water, she weakly sat up, and reached for Valentina's teddy bear. In her purse she had tucked a spool of thread and a needle, and she took these out now, threading the needle with great difficulty. There were also small scissors, and she used these to slit the back seam of the bear, revealing the gauzy net tulle that she stuffed it with.

A cough abruptly racked her. When the spasm was over, she took out the packet of American dollars. With the expenses of the plane fare, the forged passports, and identity papers, her money had dwindled to only $11,000, but it would be enough, if they were careful, until she could locate her friend Sonya.

She took out a handful of the tulle and replaced it with $10,000 of the money, reserving $1,000 for hotel expenses, then sewed up the blue bear again. This was just a precaution, of course. In case . . .

Finishing, Nadia sank back onto the pillows of the motel bed as black and white specks danced in front of her eyes. "Valentina," she called with her last remaining strength. "Valia . . ."

The child emerged from the bathroom, cheeks flushed with scrubbing. "Mama," Valentina cried. "The bathroom is so pretty. There is colored paper all over the walls, and I counted ten towels! There was even a big white cloth for the floor, and a small bottle of shampoo, and—"

"Valentina," Nadia whispered, reaching out to pull her daughter to her.

"Mama?" Valentina inquired, alarmed by something in her mother's tone.

"Hush. I want to tell you something . . . You are in a new country now but I never want you to forget me, or Papa, or Misha . . . because we will always be with you, no matter where you go or what you do."

"Mama?" The girl's eyes grew saucer-wide, luminous with fright. "Mama? Are you going somewhere?"

"I hope not," Nadia said, exhaling with difficulty. "I want to be with you forever." Tears had begun to run down her cheeks. Her mouth was trembling, but she forced out the words. "But if I can't be . . . Valia . . ." She could not say any more.

"Mama, Mama, Mama!" Valentina sobbed, throwing herself on her mother's chest.

Mother and daughter clung together and from somewhere Nadia gathered the strength to stroke Valentina's soft, beautiful glossy hair.

"My baby, my daughter, my Valenka," Nadia murmured over and over, until finally the words became only a whisper. Words she wanted to instill into her daughter's heart forever. "Never forget. You have strength, child . . . you will find your way. You will find love. I know it. *Love, Valentina. Never be afraid to love.*"

Chapter

Four

THE RAIN WAS only a drizzle now, gray and forlorn.

The two ambulance attendants barely glanced at Valentina as they loaded Nadia onto a stretcher and wheeled her through the parking lot to their big chartreuse EMS truck.

"Hey, cutie, she's gonna be fine," said the desk man, glancing down at the girl, who stood rigidly as the wailing siren of the ambulance faded into the night. "You got somebody you can call, kid? Your daddy maybe?"

Dazed, terribly frightened, Valentina heard the word "daddy," which sounded vaguely familiar. She nodded.

The desk clerk shrugged, glad to have her off his hands. "Okay, then, kiddo. Call Daddy. He'll come and get you." He stopped to buy her a Pepsi from the machine and a Hershey bar, and walked her back to her room. "I'll leave a note for the day man," he promised as he left her.

On Tuesday, Sister Mary Agnes, of the St. Vincent and Sara Fisher Home for Children, pulled the school's battered old Ford station wagon into the parking lot of the Americana Inn. Although it was only ten o'clock, the day was already breathless with the first heat wave of June. Mary Agnes was perspiring underneath her street-length black habit.

She consulted her notes, made an hour ago after a phone call from the director of social services of Oakland County in Pontiac. A little girl, approximately eight or nine years old, had been abandoned in a motel room after her mother was taken to William Beaumont Hospital. The mother had died the previous night of complications from pneumonia and an infection of the heart lining. The night desk man had written a note about the child, but it had gotten lost, and the child had stayed in the room alone for two days, drinking tap water and watching television.

Mary Agnes sighed, getting out of the car. Another deserted child—another heartbreak. She usually tried not to let her emotions affect her, but she loved children and it was difficult to maintain the necessary distance.

Mary Agnes knocked on the door, then used the key. When the door swung open, she stepped inside, squinting a little to accustom her eyes to the darkness of the room.

A breathtakingly beautiful little girl sat curled in the center of the neatly made bed, her hair tangled about her shoulders in jet ringlets. She wore a crumpled blue dress and her huge eyes were focused on the television screen with trancelike intensity. Clutched in her arms was a blue calico teddy bear.

"Valentina?" Mary Agnes said softly.

The child looked up. There were dried tear streaks on her cheeks.

"Valentina, I am Sister Mary Agnes. I'm here from a very nice place called the St. Vincent and Sarah Fisher Home for Children. It's a place where children can go when bad things happen to them, and their parents can't take care of them."

The child said nothing, but Mary Agnes saw a flicker of understanding. She was intelligent, thank God.

Mary Agnes went over to the bed and sat down beside the tense little girl, observing the way the child tried to hide her flinch. "Valentina," she said gently. "I do have some very bad news for you."

"*Nyet,*" the girl cried suddenly, her eyes filling. "*Nyet! Nyet!* No!"

The child was speaking some Slavic language, probably Russian, Mary Agnes thought.

"I'm so sorry, Valentina, but your mother died in the hospital. The doctors tried very hard to save her but they couldn't. She had been untreated for so long—the illness had gone too far."

The child stared at her, green eyes blazing. The nun

repeated her message, emphasizing the words "mother" and "died."

She watched as realization swept over the girl, draining the blood from her face. The huge, beautiful eyes were shiny with shock.

"I'm so sorry, dear, but God is watching over her now and God is watching over you, as well. Valentina, we must pack your things. You'll have to come with me now."

The station wagon pulled through a wide, wrought-iron gate that looked as if it were set in the middle of a park. A few children played ball on the grass, running, laughing, and shrieking. There was a low, rambling building, with a big parking lot in front, in which several dozen cars were parked.

Valentina closed her eyes. She didn't want to look.

"The home is run by Catholic sisters," Sister Mary Agnes explained. "We care for children who need temporary foster care, as well as orphans." She paused. "Valentina? Do you understand what I say?"

Valentina kept her eyes squeezed shut. She didn't want to be here. She hated all of it! And she did not want to cry in front of the tall, kind woman dressed in the black habit and white veil.

"Open your eyes, Valentina," the nun firmly ordered.

After a few seconds, the child did so. She gazed down at her hands.

"All right," sighed the sister. "We're almost in time for lunch—and after that I'll take you to your dormitory wing. I have a couple of children I'd like you to meet."

Mary Agnes believed that children often did for each other what therapists, adults, and even God could not.

They pulled into the lot and parked. "Here we are," Mary Agnes said. "And, Valentina—"

The child looked at her, startled.

"God loves you, child. You'll feel much better in a week or two. I promise."

"I don't *want* to wash the stupid, fuckin', ugly old car!" The girl's eyes were blue lasers. Her carrot-red hair was a tangle of rebellious snarls, and even the green-blue shirt she wore was on backward. "And you can't make me! Do you hear? I won't do anythin'!"

Sister Mary Agnes seemed unruffled by this verbal abuse.

"Sue Ann Welch, you will not use language like that, or you will spend half an hour in the chapel, on your knees in prayer." The nun went on, "I have given you the job—all three of you—of washing the station wagon. The garden hose is over there, the bucket here, and there are plenty of sponges."

Valentina cocked her head, listening carefully, although she still had not said one word since she arrived at the home yesterday morning. Beside her Sue Ann Welch was scowling, and Paul Baggio, thin, dark, dug his hands into his pockets. He, too, was glowering.

"It is a job all the *other* children want," Sister Mary Agnes finished. "See to it that you begin—now—or I'll give it to some of them instead."

She walked away, going back into the building, and the three children looked at each other.

"*Shiiit!*" cried Sue Ann. "They all tryin' to make us work like mules in the field."

To Valentina, Sue Ann's accent seemed much different from Sister Mary Agnes's.

"But it's water," Paul Baggio suddenly said, reaching for the hose. "And water is wet!"

He twisted the nozzle, manipulating it until a knifelike, silver spray of water emerged.

Sister Mary Agnes stood in one of the corridors that connected the different dormitory wings, peering out of a window that commanded an excellent view of the school grounds.

For several minutes she watched as the three children fought and tussled, spraying each other viciously with the water hose.

Mary Agnes smiled to herself. Water play was a harmless way to release anger. Maybe afterward the three would settle down and become friends.

* * *

"Furriner!" Sue Ann screamed at Valentina, lifting the coiled hose and smacking her with it. "Stupid, stupid kid, you caint even speak English, can yer?"

"And you can't speak it either, hillbilly!" shouted Paul. The ten-year-old boy began moving close, spraying the water in her face.

"Oh! Oh, shiiit!" screamed the carrot-headed girl, twisting away violently, kicking out with her bare feet.

The game had gone beyond fun, Valentina suddenly saw, and Sue Ann's face was contorted with tears.

Without thinking, she ran up behind Paul and threw both arms around his waist, tackling him and bringing him to the ground. The hose slipped out of his grip and went snaking into the air.

Instantly Sue Ann let out a whoop and scrambled to her feet, running for the hose. She picked it up, her eyes blazing, and headed for Paul.

"In his pants! In his pants!" she screamed at Valentina.

Valentina knew the word, and began laughing. She threw herself on top of Paul and sat on him, while Sue Ann aimed the hose nozzle into the waistband of Paul Baggio's green shorts.

The more Paul writhed and looked surprised and horrified, the more she and Sue Ann screamed with laughter.

Later, Sue Ann and Valentina started back to their dormitory wing together to change their clothes.

"Hey—" Paul Baggio called, hurrying after them. "Aren't we going to wash the car?"

"*Y'all* warsh it," Sun Ann tossed back to him over her shoulder. "I'm fixin' to take a hot shower."

Valentina giggled.

"All right . . . I'll wash it then . . . and some night I'm going to steal the car keys and we'll go for a ride, but if you don't help me, you can't come with me," Paul flung back.

The girls stopped.

"I can drive a car," Paul added. "I can drive one real good."

After a few minutes the three were squeezing soap out of a spray bottle and wiping it on the venerable, much-used station wagon with a damp rag. Valentina scrubbed at accumulated road dust and Michigan bugs with energetic enthusiasm. Suddenly the world looked almost good again. She had two new friends . . . well, almost friends. Especially Sue Ann.

She'd never met a girl like Sue Ann.

By mealtime that evening, Valentina, Sue Ann, and Paul were seated together, Sue Ann's skinny arm clasped tightly around Valentina, and Valentina's around her.

When one of the girls at the table made fun of Valentina's broken Russian accent, Sue Ann jumped up from the table and poured her glass of milk on the girl's head.

"Don't y'all say *nothin'* about Val—she caint help it she don't talk good. We're goin' to learn her, you just wait! She'll talk jest like us. We'll learn her good."

Within days, the threesome ate and played together, did their chores together, and sang in church choir together. They talked, giggled, and the two Americans taught Valentina English words ranging from "Pepsi" to "fudge," "pee" and "roller skate." Valentina clung to the nearness and support of Sue Ann. As long as the feisty carrot-haired girl was around, there wasn't time to cry, or to mourn Mama, Papa, and Mikhail. Sue Ann filled an important void in her.

The school library was quiet as they leafed through a book, and Sue Ann became enthralled by a photograph of huge, purple-blue Hawaiian orchids. She refused to turn the page for ten minutes.

"Listen," sighed Sue Ann dreamily. "I'm not agoin' to be called Sue Ann anymore. Sue Ann is a ugly name—it sounds ignorant. I'm gonna be called Orchid. That's a star kind of name. A name like TV stars have. I love TV stars."

As Valentina stared at her, she added, "Yeah, from now on I'm Orchid, and someday I'm gonna be a big star . . . Elizabeth Taylor maybe."

"Orchid! That's the name of a flower!" Paul jeered.

"I'm Orchid! And if you don't call me that I'll jump all over your stomach."

Later, they walked back up toward the main building. The girls were arm in arm as always, and Orchid—for that was what Valentina knew she would now have to call her—was in that strange, new dreamy mood again.

"I wasn't lyin'," she told Valentina. "Val, you know I don't lie. I'm *gonna* be a famous star someday. I want to stand on a stage and have people laughin' and cryin' and clappin'. And you can be a star along with me."

Valentina caught her breath. Even though Mama had danced at the Bolshoi as a prima ballerina, she had never thought of such a thing for herself.

"A star? Do you mean a dancer? Oh, I don't know—"

"Val," Orchid said, squeezing her hand. "Bein' a star is *wonderful*. But I don't want to be a movie star without you."

As they reached the dormitory wing, Valentina felt the hard block of ice that had been frozen at the center of her begin to melt away. She didn't have Misha, but she did have Sue Ann . . . Orchid. And Paul too. She wasn't alone anymore.

The relief was so profound that she began to jump and skip, whirling crazily about. Valentina threw back her head until her hair tangled in the wind, and whirled until she was dizzy, and Orchid had to grab her and keep her upright again.

Sister Mary Agnes, hurrying past on one of her nun's errands, stopped at the sight, and smiled. Valentina was so bright, so beautiful—somehow she had to do something special for the girl—but what?

"Misha! Misha!" Valentina screamed out in Russian, sobbing. She had been at the home for three months.

"Val? Are you okay?" The mattress springs creaked as Orchid clambered up from the lower bunk to lie beside her.

"I didn't want to leave him! I didn't want to!" Valentina sobbed desperately, clinging to her friend.

"Leave who?"

"My b-brother . . . he was killed . . . in the avalanche . . ."

"You had a brother?"

"He is j-just like me. We both have green eyes like the
Czarina's emerald, Mama said. And our hair. Black too.
And on our shoulders the tiny star mole. Oh, Orchid! I miss
him so much." Valentina lapsed into Russian again, her
voice wobbly with tears.

"Hey! It's okay!" Orchid hugged her fiercely, pulling
Valentina so close she could feel the jutting sharpness of the
other girl's small collarbone. "You've got *me* now, Val! Is
Roosia very far away?" Orchid added, snuggling close to
Valentina.

"Oh, yes," Valentina said wistfully, remembering snow-
flakes like stars and air so cold it hurt the teeth. "So far you
can't imagine."

"But you kin go back when you grow up. You kin get on
a plane an' fly back there again and find him." Orchid said
it confidently. "*I'll* help you."

Two weeks later, Paul Baggio was gone, "'dopted out,"
as the children called it. His aunt and uncle, a dentist and his
wife from Evanston, Illinois, came to the school to claim
him.

"I don't know them," he told Valentina and Orchid,
scowling ferociously. They were helping him stuff his
collection of *Superman* and *Spiderman* comic books into
paper bags.

"But they are your family," Valentina said. "They are
yours. They're going to 'dopt you."

Paul threw a wadded-up shirt into another paper bag. "I
don't care. I'm only going to stay with them until I'm
eighteen—then I'll make them pay for college for me, and
I'll become a doctor or a lawyer or something important."

As both girls stared, Paul grabbed up several paper bags
and stalked down the corridor toward the main lobby,
looking unutterably forlorn.

Sympathetically Valentina raced after him. "Paul, don't be sad—"

"Go away, Valentina!" he snapped savagely. "Ruski! Fur-in-er!"

"Paul—"

"Go away, Val! You, too, Orchid! Go away forever!"

Afterward, Valentina and Orchid went to their favorite hidey-hole in the dormitory lounge, a narrow space located behind a shabby green couch, next to the wall.

"Don't cry," said Valentina, touching Orchid.

"I ain't cryin'!"

For several moments the little girls sat in moody silence.

"Orchid . . ." Valentina clutched her friend's arm. "Orchid . . . why can't *we* be 'dopted too?"

"We cain't, sugar," the red-haired girl said.

"Why not?"

"'Cause we don't have no damn relatives that pay us no never mind, that's why." Orchid suddenly looked angry. "'Cause nobody don't want two big girls."

Just then Sister Mary Agnes came sweeping through the lounge, her black habit rustling as she called their names. "Yes, Sister?" Valentina clambered over the couch back. Orchid followed her, angile as a small deer, and both girls stood looking up at the nun.

"Well," Sister Agnes said, hiding a smile. "I see that you two young ladies have found your own private spot."

"*Da* . . . Yes," said Valentina.

"Yes'm," said the fiery Orchid.

"Well, next week the home is giving a big dinner . . . a benefit . . . and we are inviting more than seven hundred people. The benefit will earn money for the home, girls, and we have invited some Broadway stars too. Have you ever heard of Julie Andrews and Gwen Verdon?"

Orchid gasped. "I seen Julie inna movie on TV once! She's a big, big star, just like I wanna be!"

The nun knelt down until she was at eye level with the two youngsters. "I am also asking you both to sing."

"Us?"

"*We're* gonna sing?" Orchid squealed.

"Sister Patricia says you both have wonderful voices in the choir. She'll help you. And we'll find some beautiful party dresses for you to wear."

A September sun warmed the parklike grounds of the St. Vincent and Sarah Fisher home, creating hazes of light in the big trees that bordered the property.

Music drifted out of the huge, blue and white striped tent where the Mel Ball orchestra was seated on a flower-bedecked dais. More than seven hundred wealthy Detroiters milled about, gossiping and laughing.

"I'm *so* dern hongry," Orchid whispered, nervously peeking around the corner of one of the tent's main openings. She wore a peach-colored taffeta party dress donated by one of the school's patrons. She eyed the nearest food table. "I could eat four li'l hot dogs 'n ten of them burgers. An' them tiny chocolate cakes . . ."

"Not until we sing." Valentina, in robin's-egg blue, grabbed onto her best friend to prevent her from moving in. "We promised Sister . . . Anyway, we might spill something on our new dresses!"

"*I* won't spill nothin'."

"You always spill something," Valentina said airily.

"My, but don't you young ladies look beautiful tonight." A woman in sea-green chiffon was smiling at the girls. Her smooth blond hair was swept back from her fine-boned face, and her wide mouth looked as if it smiled often. Around her neck she wore a double-stranded pearl necklace, caught with a glittering diamond clip.

"Thank you," Valentina said, smiling radiantly.

"Do you like your dress?" the woman inquired, gazing intently at Valentina.

"Oh, yes, yes," she began.

"Good. I'm Dorothy Lederer, they call me Peaches, and—" Then a woman approached with a question about microphones, and Dorothy Lederer excused herself and disappeared into the tent.

Enthralled, Valentina stared after her, thinking this must

be the woman who had given them the dresses. She looked like a princess.

Dorothy Peachman Lederer, whose nickname from girlhood had been "Peaches," watched as Orchid headed for the restrooms, and the child called Valentina entered the party tent. These were the little singers Sister Mary Agnes had promised, and they were beautiful.

Peaches Lederer felt a sharp and familiar pang of loss. She was forty years old, had weathered three miscarriages and two stillbirths, and Valentina looked like her fantasy of a daughter come to life. The child was wonderful, with her luminous green eyes, porcelain skin, and stunning prettiness.

"Peaches . . . I understand you masterminded this whole delightful affair," enthused Shirley Eder, a columnist newly signed by Knight-Ridder newspapers.

"Oh, yes, Shirley, and would you like me to point out some of our other celebrity guests to you?" She knew her duty was to publicize the St. Vincent and Sarah Fisher home as much as possible.

"Joe McCarthy and Judy will be arriving soon—he's emceeing—and also, here's Dick Purtan." McCarthy and Purtan were the two most popular radio personalities in Detroit.

She went on, listing the major contributors, while Shirley took notes. "Oh, and we do have something special tonight in addition to Julie Andrews, and our other stars. Sister Mary Agnes tells me we have a little songbird at the school, a child with an incredible voice. Actually, two girls. We're going to showcase them."

"What a wonderful idea," Shirley effused.

"We hope it will start the guests thinking about the actual children they'll be helping."

Peaches's husband, Edgar, was waving at her from the other end of the tent, where he was standing with two of the Nederlander brothers, James and Joey, who had just purchased several Broadway theaters.

She excused herself, threading her way through the

elegantly dressed crowd, greeting more of her friends as she passed. Peaches occupied a stellar position in Detroit society and knew everyone.

"Peaches." Edgar Lederer smiled, sliding his arm around her. He was fifty-two, with dark David Niven good looks. Edgar, who lived and breathed business, owned a chain of forty theaters and outdoor concert arenas. Peaches smiled dutifully and joined in the conversation, thinking about the beautiful child she had just seen.

She could hardly wait to hear her sing.

Julie Andrews, wearing a shimmering tube of white, had just come up to the mike, and had begun to sing a medley of songs from *My Fair Lady* and *The Sound of Music*.

As Julie's voice soared into the tent, Senator Charles Willingham adjusted the white canvas sling he wore, feeling pain shoot from his shoulder blade up into his head.

Damn it to Hades, he thought. It had been only two weeks since a crazy had suddenly appeared in the reception area of his district senatorial office in Mobile, and fired two shots at him.

One bullet buried itself in the side of the receptionist's desk, the other grazed Willingham's shoulder. He had only consented to attend this charitable affair because his close friend Senator Philip Hart of Michigan had asked him as a special favor.

In a small alcove of the main building, a makeup woman was bent over dancing star Ann Miller, dusting talcum powder on her face. The makeup artist had also given a token brush to the two little girls, tinting their lips pink, and adding a small amount of blush.

From here, Julie Andrews's voice sounded as pure as crystal.

"She sings so g-great," stammered Orchid, in the throes of stage fright. The freckles stood out on her face in cinnamon-colored relief.

Valentina took her best friend's small, sweaty hand in hers and pressed it hard. "You know how you like to

pretend we're real stars, Orchie? Well, we'll do that tonight.
We'll just watch Julie Andrews and do everything she
does . . . then they'll like us.''

"For sure?" Orchid asked, grinning.

". . . and now, ladies and gentlemen, we have a couple
of angels in our midst, who are going to prove to us that
good things do indeed come in small packages.''

Valentina and Orchid stood nervously at the edge of the
specially constructed stage platform just as Julie Andrews
had done only minutes before.

"May I present . . . Miss Valentina and Miss
Orchid . . . !"

Murmurs and applause greeted them as the two girls
walked forward to the shortened mike.

Valentina gazed into the huge circus tent.

A sea of faces looked up at them.

Seven hundred expectant faces.

"Migosh," Orchid blurted out into the mike, gulping.
Seven hundred people tittered, and Valentina instinctively
stepped closer to her friend.

There was a piano chord, then Valentina drew a deep
breath, searching for the first note. It emerged deep from the
center of her chest, just as Sister Patricia taught her, pure
and clear, into the air.

Orchid added her sweet harmony, but it was Valentina's
voice that filled up the gala tent with full, rich sound.

Valentina and Orchid floated off the stage and down the
wooden steps in a roar of applause.

"Wonderful . . . wonderful . . ." enthused Peaches
Lederer, who had been standing near the platform with her
husband and Dolly Rutledge, a prominent party planner.

"Nicely done," said Sister Mary Agnes, bobbing her
head.

"*Ooooh,*" squealed Orchid. "The way they all
clapped . . . it jist *rolled* up to us!"

"Girls, there is a special party tent for the children,"
Sister Mary Agnes announced. "We have hot dogs, ham-

burgers, and fried chicken, and a TV star, Soupy Sales, for entertainment. After that it's time for bed. Sister Ursula will be making sure you're all in bed, so please heed her. Curfew is nine-thirty.'' Both girls nodded, too excited to care, as they scampered across the grass.

Dusk deepened the sunset, turning it to indigo. The orchestra began to play dance music, violins and a saxophone sweetening the evening air as Sister Ursula, an ancient nun about to retire, shepherded the reluctant, excited children off to their rooms.

Valentina didn't want to go to bed yet—she couldn't. She darted past the nun, breaking away from the rest of the children to return to the party.

At the far end of the tent she saw Mrs. Lederer. Peaches's gown had little iridescent sparkles in it, and a lantern hanging on the tent pole backlighted her blond hair, giving her a glowing halo.

Valentina crept closer, irresistibly drawn.

"Well, hello, Valentina, I enjoyed your performance so much.'' Peaches excused herself from her friends to come over to Valentina. "Were you frightened in front of all those people?''

"I . . .'' Valentina felt suddenly tongue-tied.

"When I was ten,'' Peaches went on, "I had to give a poetry recitation in front of my whole school. I was so nervous I tripped on the hem of my long dress. Everyone laughed, so I just kept talking louder and louder, and finally they applauded and the teacher said I was the *loudest* poet they'd ever heard.''

Valentina giggled, still unable to speak.

"I have something for you.'' Peaches handed Valentina a shiny, printed folder. "This is the program for tonight . . . with your name in it, yours and Orchid's. This is for you to keep and save. And there's a surprise in it. Go ahead, open it.''

Valentina opened the folder and saw four or five scrawled signatures.

"These are the autographs of all the celebrities here tonight—Julie Andrews, Ann Miller, Gwen Verdon, and the others. I collected them just for you, and there's another folder for Orchid, if you would be kind enough to give it to her.''

"Oh . . ." breathed Valentina. "Do . . . do you have children?''

"No." Peaches looked sad. "I don't. I always wanted a daughter but I wasn't lucky enough.''

"Do you . . ." Then Valentina stopped, amazed at the audacious words she almost blurted out.

"Valentina, you look so pale, dear." Peaches flagged down a passing waiter, requesting fruit punch and a sandwich. "Come over here, where it's a little quieter, and you can have your sandwich. I'll make it all right with Sister Mary Agnes.''

Peaches sat with Valentina, making sure she ate all of her turkey sandwich and finished her tall glass of freshly squeezed fruit juices.

"Juice is far better for you than soda pop," Peaches explained. "It will make your pretty skin even prettier. And your beautiful eyes. Are they a true shade of green?''

She tilted Valentina's face up, and gazed deeply. "Yes, they are. Oh, they are like emeralds. Someday you are going to set hearts aflutter, Valentina. You're going to have the kind of beauty that creates a real stir.''

Valentina didn't know what she was talking about, she only knew that sitting next to Peaches Lederer made her feel warm inside, safe and special.

The sky was black now, dotted with the first stars. Peaches called to someone, and had them bring a white evening wrap trimmed with sable. She settled it around Valentina's shoulders so she wouldn't feel the cold.

"I wish . . ." the girl began. Then she stopped again.

"You wish what, child?''

"I wish . . . I wish you wanted a little girl." The words rushed irresistibly out of Valentina's mouth. She saw the shock on Peaches's face, but could not halt the passionate flow, her wish-fantasy. "No, *two* little girls, 'cause there's Orchid, and she's my best friend and if you 'dopted us both, then we could be real sisters.''

"Oh, Valentina," Peaches said in a low voice.

She looked so distressed that Valentina didn't know what to do, or what to say. But the words had been said. "Please," she beseeched. "I want to be someone's little girl and so does Orchid. We need someone."

"Oh," Peaches cried. "Oh."

"You're like a princess, Mrs. Lederer."

"Oh, my dear." Peaches reached out and enfolded Valentina in her arms. "Please call me Peaches. Dear, it's my husband, Edgar . . . he has never . . . adoption is something he's never—" Then she cut off the words, and held out Valentina at arm's length, gazing deeply into her eyes again.

"I'll try," she whispered. "I'll talk to him."

Valentina stared at her, stunned.

Chapter

Five

THE LIGHTS BURNED brightly in their expensively decorated home in Detroit's posh suburb of Franklin, Michigan, as Peaches and Edgar Lederer argued long into the night. Peaches paced back and forth, her long Scaasi silk peignoir rustling with every step.

"Edgar," she pleaded. "You aren't even listening to me! You aren't even trying to see my point of view. I gave up on the idea of having children because we lost so many. And because you balked at adopting—I gave up a whole part of myself. Now I want that part back. *I want them. I want to be a mother before it's too late.*"

"But two half-grown kids? We don't even know their background, dear. We don't know anything about them." Edgar sat at a small cherrywood desk, where a Fisher Theater's monthly profit and loss statement was spread out. He tapped impatiently on the desk's polished surface.

She shrugged. "What do we have to know? They are obviously bright, and talented, and—and they're lovely, Edgar. They are breathtaking. Both of them! Even you have to admit that."

"Physical looks, yes. But what about their temperament?"

"Edgar!" she cried. "They are only eight years old! They're still young and malleable enough for me to work with them, teach them, guide them. Just think! I can make sure they have voice lessons, dance lessons, ballet. We can send them to a good college, give them all the advantages—"

"Spend thousands of dollars on them, you mean."

"Oh, stop!" Peaches cried angrily. "Stop, stop, stop!" She crossed the room to stand before her husband. "Is it money you're worried about, Edgar? If that's the case, I'll support them with my inheritance from my mother—which is more than enough to support three or four *hundred* children, as you very well know, since you manage the fund for me."

Edgar glanced briefly away, conceding this point to her.

"I have *love* to give, Edgar . . . love in here, in my heart! I give you physical intimacy, wifely love—when that firetrap theater in Philadelphia burned down, I was there for you through all the lawsuits, through everything . . . but there's much more in me than that. I lost five infants, Edgar . . . I was cheated. God cheated me. And now I have another chance, and the girls are beautiful, and *I'm not giving them up!*"

"One of them, then," he conceded grudgingly. "If you must."

"No!" she snapped. "I want both. They love each other, there's a bond, and I can't separate them."

"I don't know . . ."

"Why not?" she demanded. "Why the hell not? I can't believe you . . ." She had started to cry.

"Peaches . . . honey . . . baby . . ." He came forward and started to put his arms around her.

"No!" Peaches whirled away from him. "Not until you let me make a phone call to Sister Mary Agnes and at least investigate whether or not we can adopt those two little girls."

"Peaches, sweetheart, give me a chance, will you? I've never been a father. I don't know how. I've only held a baby—what, once? Twice? And it urped all over me."

Peaches laughed in relief. "Well, these babies aren't going to urp. They're eight years old, well past that stage. Oh, darling, wait until you see what I'll be able to do with them."

The next morning, Peaches got up early and made a long phone call to Sister Mary Agnes.

''I was hoping someone would want them,'' Mary Agnes confessed. ''That's one reason I selected them to sing. They are simply too good to be bounced around in the foster care system, or even to be here. They deserve good homes.''

''But are they free and clear to adopt?''

''Sue Ann Welch is.''

''Sue Ann?''

''She renamed herself Orchid, probably to distance herself from her unfortunate background. She has been permanently taken away from her mother, who was a prostitute and addicted to cocaine, and is serving time in a Kentucky women's prison facility, near Paducah. The child was sexually abused by her older brothers and was taken out of the home when it was discovered she had contracted gonorrhea. She also had bruises and cigarette burns all over her body.''

''I . . . I see,'' Peaches said, feeling sick. She wondered how much of this, if any, she should tell to Edgar.

''Of course, Orchid was treated for the sexually transmitted disease, and is physically healthy now. But emotionally the child is starved for love. She seeks out attention wherever she can find it. Fortunately her IQ is high—in the ninety-ninth percentile when she was tested at school.''

''And Valentina?'' Peaches inquired. ''What about her?''

The nun told Peaches what she knew about Valentina's history. ''However, papers found with her mother indicate that the mother may have been traveling under false identification, so all of that has to be resolved before Valentina is legally available for adoption. It may get sticky and could take several years to clear up. But she certainly could be fostered out until a decision is made—''

''Edgar has the best attorneys,'' Peaches said with conviction. ''They have excellent connections in Washington. I'm sure that they can solve that problem.''

''There *is* just one other thing,'' Mary Agnes added.

''Yes?''

''These two little girls are extremely dependent on each other emotionally. They cling together.''

Touched, Peaches went on to tell the nun about her plans

to take the children to lunch at the Franklin Hills Country Club later in the day.

More than ever, she wanted these girls. And she found the bond between them touching and wonderful. She felt sure that if they could love each other, then they could turn that love outward too.

"She's here! She's here!" screamed Orchid, racing along the long corridor that connected their dormitory to the main lobby. "I saw her from a window!"

"Oh," gulped Valentina.

"She's here, and she's so pretty! Look, she's got on a yellow suit! An' a yellow hat! An' pearls on her neck!" Orchid was dancing up and down with excitement.

"Girls, you have a visitor," said Sister Mary Agnes, hurrying toward them. She gave the girls a dismayed look. "Oh, no, my dear children, you can't go to lunch with Mrs. Lederer in those untidy skirts and blouses. Go back and change into your church dresses. And Valentina, your hair is a tangle. Don't you ever wear a barrette?"

After the nun had tidied the girls to her satisfaction, she escorted them to the school's tiny main lobby, where Peaches Lederer waited to pick them up.

Valentina stopped suddenly on the threshold, awestruck. Behind her Orchid bumped into her back. By the indrawn gasp of Orchid's breath, Valentina knew that her friend was equally intimidated.

Mrs. Lederer—no, Peaches—was beautiful.

"Girls," Peaches said in her soft, warm voice. "I hope you're hungry. I'm planning the most wonderful lunch. And I hope you love flowers."

"F-flowers?" Valentina stammered.

Peaches held out a white cardboard box tied with a frilly blue ribbon. "Would you like to open this? I stopped on the way here at my florist and he suggested these."

The two girls hesitated.

"Go on," urged Peaches. "Open it. There is one for each of you."

Excitedly they tore the box lid off.

"Oh!" exclaimed Valentina, thrilled.

"Hot *damn*!" cried Orchid.

Inside the box nestled two small corsages made of frilly blue cymbidium orchids. A child-sized blue silk bow, accompanied by a tiny blue teddy bear, complemented each corsage.

"So damn great," exclaimed Orchid.

"Sue Ann Welch," snapped Sister Mary Agnes. "You watch your language or you will not be going to lunch."

But Peaches was smiling as she knelt down to help each girl pin on her corsage. "Nonsense, the three of us are going to have a wonderful time. And these corsages are to commemorate . . . well, so very much. We're going to be a family, I hope. And you girls will be real sisters."

Valentina felt a spasm of sudden guilt, as if by having these warm feelings for Peaches, she was somehow betraying Mama and Misha, Papa too. Then she felt a kind of *smiling* deep inside her and knew it was Mama, telling her this was all right. Telling her that part of Peaches's love would come from her too.

"Oh, my girls," Peaches said, pulling both of them into her arms.

"What's for lunch?" Orchid chirped.

Chapter
Six

THE YOUNG WOMAN in the black dress sauntered through the crowded Casbah bazaar, shouldering her way past knots of black-clad women haggling over prices of lemons, oranges, and strange-looking melons.

She was twenty years old, slim, dark, with melting, Byzantine eyes. No one glanced at her, so well did she blend into the surging market crowd packed almost shoulder to shoulder, where skinny, long-tailed mongrel dogs fought for scraps, and even skinnier, dirty kids with shawls over their heads begged for liras.

Smells of spices, crushed fruit, and human sweat filled her nostrils, creating a dazzling feeling inside her. She almost shuddered with the joy of it, feeling a burgeoning sexual excitement.

She had killed him. A French arms dealer, so she had been told. Maybe he had provided arms for the Turks to use against Greece in their most recent border dispute. She didn't know why they had wanted him killed nor did she care. All she knew was that he had gasped and begged, then lost control of his bladder, his face purpling as she tightened the garrote around his neck. Tight . . . tighter . . . until even his clawing fingers could not loosen it.

Ah, those gasps. The incredibly thrilling sense of total power . . . *power over a human life.* It was better than sex, better than the amyl nitrate one of her lovers had once forced her to pop.

This wasn't her first kill, of course. But this was the first killing for which she had been paid.

The Greeks were going to pay her the incredible sum of two million drachmas, nearly ten thousand dollars, an amount of money that seemed miraculous to her.

Passing a booth hung with fly-laden carcasses of slaughtered lamb, the woman quickened her steps with a growing urgency. She had to catch a five o'clock British Airways flight to London, then Argentina. But even more important, she had to get back to the room she'd rented—right away.

Before the orgasm that was building inside her exploded in a wild, tormented crescendo of ecstasy.

Motown
1979

Mercury vapor lights gleamed in the mist of a foggy April evening, setting aglow the marquee of the newly refurbished Fisher Theater on West Grand Boulevard.

Tall black letters spelled out the words PUTTING ON THE GLITZ, STARRING BLUE ORCHIDS. Edgar Lederer, who owned the theater, had given the prestigious Bloomfield Hills private school permission to hold their Senior Show there.

Valentina peeled their little red Camaro into the adjacent parking lot.

"Hot damn!" cried Orchid. "We're here . . . and in only one hour Blue Orchids will be stars! Can you believe that, Val? One tiny, tiny hour! Sixty little minutes!"

It seemed they'd lived and breathed for this night forever. For six months anyway, ever since Orchid got the idea that she and Valentina could form a singing group. They both loved the name. "Blue" for Valentina's favorite color, and "Orchids," for Orchid's own name that she'd insisted on using.

Tonight was their big chance. Barney Samuels, the vice president of "A and R" at Motown Records, would be in the audience to catch his daughter, Kathy's, jazz-dance performance, but he'd be forced to listen to the entire program, which included them.

They knew he'd love them. And . . . they harbored a delicious secret. Valentina had recently found ten thousand dollars sewn into the back of the tattered old teddy bear she'd brought over from Russia. They planned to use it to finance their rock music career.

The two girls piled out of the car and reached into the backseat, pulling out their tackle box full of makeup, and the white florist box that held twenty blue cymbidium orchids.

"Don't drop it," cautioned Valentina as Orchid juggled the florist box.

"Okay, twinkle toes, *you* carry it then, since you're so good."

They reached the stage door in a haze of giggles and elevated spirits, and pushed their way inside, where a knot of excited Cranbrook School students were milling around. Jo McBanta, the musical director, clad in a trendy black pants suit, stalked through their midst.

"Everyone! Everyone! Listen up! Is everyone in costume and made up? I'm calling the twenty-five minutes now. Do you all hear me? I'm calling twenty-five minutes. Girls? Is that Valentina and Orchid? Well, it's about time. Have the Blue Orchids finally deigned to arrive among us?"

Narrowing her eyes, Jo gave both girls a thorough inspection. They already wore their costumes, sexy deep-blue sequined sheaths.

"Valentina," the director decided. "Pull your sleeves down over your shoulders a little more, honey, like this. Yes. That's much sexier. Do you have a hairbrush with you?"

The girl nodded.

"Good. Your hair is to kill for, but it needs tousling, like Farrah's. I want you to bend over and let your hair fall forward, and then comb it backward. We want your hair to be all full . . . yes . . . yes, that's exactly right. Orchid too. Both of you. Let's get darn right sexy, huh?"

"Sure," said Valentina.

"All right with me!" cried Orchid, dipping her head and drawing the brush through her flaming red curls.

* * *

Peaches sat in the front row with Edgar, listening to the orchestra warm up. She sighed impatiently. She was eager for the curtain to go up and for the pride she had in her two beautiful daughters to be vindicated.

She'd never had a moment of regret that she'd adopted Valentina and Orchid. Orchid's adoption had been straightforward, but it had taken four years for the lawyers to work their magic with Valentina's tangled papers and forged passport.

The first years had been the hardest. Valentina had wakened them for weeks with harrowing screams, and bad dreams about her twin, Mikhail, and the avalanche. The child insisted her brother was still alive, and began to save part of her allowance for a trip to Russia.

Edgar was appalled and upset at the idea. "Go behind the Iron Curtain? Don't be ridiculous, Valentina. It's very dangerous. Only a few ever go there, and that's because they have to. And certainly not nine-year-old girls. Besides, I've already had Senator Willingham in Washington make inquiries through the Russian Embassy. Your brother *is* officially listed as one of the victims of that avalanche. I'm sorry. So let's not hear any more about it."

Valentina had wept and moped for months after that, worrying Peaches terribly. But then she had signed the child up for classical ballet, and modern dance lessons. Valentina plunged into the strenuous routine, showing a natural ability, and the nightmares gradually tapered off.

By the time she was fifteen, Valentina had the lithe, supple body of a dancer. Edgar was approached several times by modeling agencies who wanted to sign her, but he had angrily told them not to bother his daughter. He wanted his girls fresh, unexposed to what he called the "potential sordid overtones" of certain aspects of show business.

Then there was Orchid.

The girl blazed with energy, always the center of attention, attracting others as a flame draws a moth. Her intelligence was formidable, and she drew top grades at Kingswood School, a part of the Cranbrook institutions . . . when she chose.

Sometimes Orchid reveled in getting straight A's. At other times she criticized her teachers, played practical jokes on them, and appeared unconcerned with academic standing. And always, she talked about becoming a star—as if this were simply her natural destiny.

Now the student orchestra had begun a spritely overture of Broadway songs. Peaches sank back in her seat, clasping her hands nervously together. Beside her, Edgar sat relaxed.

The girls had confided their secret to her. She wondered what her husband would say when he found out that his daughters wanted to be rock stars.

The curtain slowly lifted, revealing Orchid and Valentina standing on a tiny stage the eleventh-grade carpenters had built to resemble a Victorian gazebo. The audience gasped. Under the lights, the girls' midnight-blue sequined dresses shimmered, the shoulders pulled low to expose lissom curves.

Clutching her portable mike, tapping the rhythm, Valentina drew a deep breath into her lungs. She expelled the first note of "When Will I Be Loved," the Linda Ronstadt song that Jo had selected for them. Orchid joined her in sweet, close harmony. The full sound poured into the auditorium, flowing across the hundreds of seats to the last row.

The girls sang three songs, including the currently popular "Dancing Queen," by ABBA.

As the final note died, applause thundered up across the footlights. The clapping, whistling and screaming merged into one giant crescendo. The applause didn't stop, while kids in the front row crowded down to the apron of the stage.

As they took bow after bow, a stagehand brought out a basket piled with cymbidium orchids. Orchid snatched it from him, throwing the first flower into the audience.

"Oh, oh, I love you!" she shouted, grabbing the orchids now in handfuls, hurling them as far as she could to the rioting teens. Laughing, Valentina scooped up the flowers too.

* * *

It was one-thirty A.M. An untouched tray of cookies and lemonade sat on a table in the Lederers' den. The girls were coming down from their concert "high," and their disappointment that Barney Samuels, Motown's A and R man, had left right after his daughter's number.

"I can't believe he'd be that rude. He didn't even wait to hear us sing," Orchid grumbled.

"And *I* can't believe my daughters would expose themselves onstage like that," Edgar said in his gravelly voice. "Playing to the audience like—like Janis Joplin."

"Now, Edgar," Peaches soothed. "It's after midnight and the girls are tired."

"Not too tired to listen to some sense."

"Please, Daddy Edgar," began Valentina. "Please, don't be mad."

"You mean angry, and angry is an understatement," Edgar huffed.

"Now, darling," Peaches repeated. "The girls were lovely and you know it."

"They were sexpots!"

The girls looked at each other.

"Daddy Edgar," Valentina said slowly. "We've decided we're not going to the University of Michigan in the fall—"

"—at least not full-time," Orchid joined in. "We're going after a record contract."

"What?"

Valentina was pale but she went on steadily. "We're sorry, and I guess we shouldn't have pulled our sleeves so low. But this is what we really want. We want to be Blue Orchids, for real."

"My God," Edgar said heavily. "I'm already in show business and I don't want it for my daughters. Girls . . . I'm telling you now, I *know* this business. I know how frustrating and crummy it can be, how it can squeeze the life right out of young people."

"We want it! We *have* to!" cried Orchid.

"Daddy Edgar . . . Mother . . ." Valentina agreed. "We really want to try."

The next morning there was an article by Marj Jackson Levin in the Accent section of the *Detroit News*.

Blue Orchids Singers Cause Fisher Theater Riot. The accompanying photograph showed Valentina and Orchid tossing orchids to frantic fans.

Valentina and Orchid bought copies of the *News* and started a scrapbook. With great ceremony, they pasted in the clipping.

"There," gloated Orchid, admiring the two-column, eight-inch article as if it were an Emmy. "Isn't this the best thing you ever saw?"

"We're really Blue Orchids now," Valentina said quietly. "Aren't we? That picture proves it."

"Forever," Orchid said, clasping her hand.

Riga, Latvia
1979

Mikhail Sandovsky was lonely.

In his severe, gray cadet's uniform, he stood near the second bridge of the three that crossed the Daugava River in Riga, Latvia. A hot June wind swept off the Gulf of Riga, whipping up a froth of whitecaps on the wide river.

Mikhail gazed at the sun-sparkled river, his eyes watering. In fact his whole head ached. He'd spent the night before drinking massive amounts of vodka with other cadets who attended the Alksnis Academy—a Russian version of West Point, but far more rigid and austere.

Why had he drunk so much? To escape the rigors and the stiff discipline of the academy? He had finally realized that he was being groomed for a life he did not want. His ambitious father, Petrov, had pulled strings to get him in and insisted his son had the makings of a hero of the Motherland.

Mikhail began to walk along Lenin Street, which divided the right bank into almost-equal areas, cutting across the Vecriga, the Old City. To him, the Old City with its romantic past seemed mysterious. There was a church that had been built under Bishop Albert in 1211 and had taken nearly five hundred years to complete. The Zviedru Varti, Swedish Gate, built in 1698, was the only surviving city gate of Riga.

How many people had passed through that gate in three hundred years? Peasants, priests, Jews, peddlers, soldiers, rich burghers, along with Peter the Great, who had come to Riga in 1711 and lived here for a while. Perhaps even Stalin, he mused.

Ahead of him three pretty girls strolled arm in arm, their hair secured in *babushkas* against the stiff sea breeze, cotton skirts flapping to reveal bare, sturdy, muscular legs.

One of the girls caught Mikhail's attention. Taller and slimmer than the other two, she was tugging at her scarf. She pulled it off, smiling and turning her face to catch the wind. Her hair, released by the *babushka,* blew across her shoulders in a heavy tangle of black curls.

Mikhail stopped, transfixed.

Valentina! His lost twin. He still had painful, fragmented dreams about her. Sometimes she was still the small girl he had last seen just before the avalanche, when they'd been playing cat's cradle. In other dreams, she was a young woman, tall, laughing, beautiful. She looked exactly like him—only the female version.

At 24 Skarmu Street there was a Romanesque-Gothic church dating back to the 1200s. Mikhail paused and pretended to study its time-worn and soot-blackened walls, while stifling another wave of loneliness.

His dreams of his lost twin seemed so vivid sometimes. So often he had wondered if Valentina really did die in the avalanche.

But of course she is dead, he told himself fiercely. *My father showed me the official list of the avalanche victims. Both her and my mother's names were on that list.*

He walked inside the church, breathing the sudden dampness of ancient stones. *Why do I always feel as if she is alive?* he asked himself.

He had no answer to the question.

Chapter
Seven

VALENTINA FINISHED SINGING the last bar of "Pretty Girls," giving it all she had, holding the note until it exploded the air of the small studio. Beside her Orchid stood facing a second mike. They both wore headsets.

"All right, all *right*," praised their sound engineer, Danny MacClelland, his voice coming through on the headsets. "The reverb does it. It sounds just right now." He sat on the other side of a glass window, fiddling with a lever on a big, electronic, twenty-four track console that looked like something from *Star Trek*.

The studio at Ron Rose Productions was padded with ice-blue carpeting. Small carpet squares rested on the music stands, and covered each of the double set of doors. Several spotlights blazed overhead, heating up the room that, when they entered it, had been air-conditioned cool. It wasn't cool anymore. The lights, their energy and body heat, had raised the temperature in the cramped space by at least ten degrees.

They were recording three songs—an old Dionne Warwick, a torchy Abby McKay love song from the sixties, and "Pretty Girls," the rock song Orchid had written.

"Do we really sound good?" Orchid, always insecure, wanted to know.

The engineer's response was emphatic. "Hey, would I put you on? I think we've got a great top half, but unfortunately the bottom half still needs a *lot* more work," MacClelland added quickly.

Orchid looked up, frowning. She was in Gloria Vanderbilt jeans and a Loggins and Messina T-shirt, her red hair a
frizzy, electric mass of curls. The engineer had centered
most of his criticisms on her, and each time he "suggested," she stiffened up a little more.

"You keep fluffing the lyrics, Orchid," MacClelland
went on. "Your voice is coming out a little too breathy,
especially in the first bars. You need to sing from the chest.
Deep chest."

"I am! I am!"

"Now remember, we're laying down a couple of different tracks for the vocals, and we need consistency and
harmony in both of your voices. That way, when we mix,
we can use part of one and part of another. It should all
combine nice and tight, and you'll never even notice. The
blend will be dynamite."

"Oh, great!" Orchid cried sarcastically. She was near
tears. "We're going to be like a damn patchwork quilt!"

"From the top again," ordered the engineer.

"Sure, sure, okay." Orchid hunched around her mike,
looking small and vulnerable. "This seems funny, that's all,
not singing *to* somebody."

"But I told you how many bucks you save by using
canned music as background," came MacClelland's disembodied voice through the earphones. "Sing to *me*. Pretend
I'm six hundred screaming, creaming fans."

Orchid brightened. "Yeah!"

Two weeks later, the girls played the finished cassette for
Peaches.

"Well?" Valentina demanded, grinning, when it was
finished. "This cost us twenty-eight hundred dollars, including the roll of twenty-four-track master tape. Did we
waste our money?"

"You *have* to like it," Orchid echoed.

Peaches gazed at the two girls, stunned. The sound was
far better than most of the songs she heard on the radio.

"Well, I—" She hesitated, remembering Edgar's warning, and the many stories he'd told her about the rock music

life . . . the sex, drugs, groupies, payola, politics, wild parties. If something happened to her girls—if anyone ever hurt them or took advantage of them—

"Well, *say something*," Orchid cried, her eyes blazing as she pulled at Peaches's arm.

"Yes, I did," Peaches admitted reluctantly. "I did, I really did love it. You were wonderful. *Wonderful!*"

That evening, when Edgar arrived home after a late meeting with his bankers, Peaches had carefully prepared the scene. His favorite drink, a Glenlivet sour, waiting on a tray; herself in a pale ecru negligee; the girls out at the movies with their friends.

She knew she had to play the demo tape for him as soon as possible, because if she didn't, the girls would, and she wanted the opportunity to soothe him, to help ease him into acceptance of this amazing phenomenon.

Edgar flopped down in his favorite chair, reaching for his sour. "What a day," he sighed. "We're selling a convertible debenture issue to cover the purchase of that San Francisco theater, and it's getting damn complicated with the Securities and Exchange Commission in Washington."

He regaled her with business details, until finally Peaches reached out to the stereo, punching in the tape play button.

"Edgar," she said as the first notes of "Pretty Girls" leaped into the air. "I want you to listen to something really good. No, not good, it's terrific!"

She prepared herself for a long discussion. She'd make him love the tape—somehow.

Chapter

Eight

IT WAS AN ordinary two-story house at 2648 West Grand
Boulevard, near downtown Detroit, but a sign over the front
door boasted Hitsville, U.S.A. Motown was headquartered
in Los Angeles now, but as everyone in Detroit knew, the
Detroit studio was still kept open, and Berry Gordy and
other Motown stars frequently came to town.

Inside the studio, Elijah Carmody was crossing the small
reception area to grab a hurried cup of coffee before an
eleven A.M. meeting with Berry Gordy. The distant sounds
of female voices penetrated the air, quivering with a
tantalizing sexuality.

"You playin' somethin'?" he asked Doreen, the receptionist.

"It ain't me," exclaimed Doreen, gesturing toward the
window. "It's them two white chicks again, playin' their
tape out by the car. They think we're gonna listen. They real
pests."

"Yeah?" Elijah sauntered over to the window and
glanced out. A beautiful girl in a red dress was lounging
against the hood of a red Camaro. "How long she been
hangin' out here?"

"Oh, weeks. She an' that other crazy one with the red
hair."

"Not so crazy, I'd say."

Valentina's heart leaped as she watched the handsome
black man lope toward her. He was wearing pale yellow
pleated pants, a cream shirt, and navy blue blazer. With his

light skin and melting dark eyes, he looked like a sexier, younger Harry Belafonte.

"So," he said, flashing her a grin. "You lookin' to get arrested for disturbin' the peace?"

"Please," she begged, flustered, as she turned down the volume of the player. "I couldn't get anyone to play our tape. We're Blue Orchids. We're good. I *know* we're good. It would sound so much better inside a studio . . . You'd love it. Three minutes, that's all it'd take. Then if you—"

"Okay."

"What?"

"I said okay, girl. I'll play it. But three minutes, that's all I'm givin' you. I'm in the middle of a meeting and you are one big interruption."

While Valentina waited in the reception area, Elijah played the demo tape through four more times, thinking that Valentina's voice had more honey than Diana Ross, more strength than Streisand, and the sexual energy of a Janis Joplin, or Abby McKay in her prime. The kid could break glass with her amazing power.

He stared at the photo the girl had given him, of herself and the other one called Orchid. She was a knockout too—a kitteny, sexy piece who would set the boys on fire. A real little fox! On tape she had a smoky, breathy little voice— she'd make a perfect backup. Blue Orchids, he even loved the name. It was perfect for album covers.

Berry had been looking for a sharp white female group for years, and these kids just might be it. Of course, their father was Edgar Lederer, the girl had said, and he would insist on reasonable contracts, and everything nice and legal, locked up tight. No problem!

Decisively, Elijah punched the stop button and pocketed the cassette, walking into the reception area where Valentina sat perched nervously on the edge of a chair, holding an untouched cup of coffee.

He motioned to her. "C'mon in my office, honey. I wanna rap some more."

Valentina went pale. She let out a tiny shriek of joy, then jumped out of her seat, coffee spilling onto her dress.

Elijah grinned, pleased at her excited reaction. "I'm Elijah Carmody, a vice president of Motown Records, and I'd like to talk with you an' your daddy about a contract."

Half an hour later, after Valentina left, Elijah walked to the window and stood staring out at the traffic on West Grand Boulevard. These two white girls . . . he had a feeling about them. He just hoped he was right. If they got a hit, and it just took one, they'd make *his* reputation at Motown—for sure.

"He's handsome, Val . . . I didn't expect him to be so cute."

Elijah had insisted that Orchid come to Motown to meet him, and talk to Berry, and Orchid returned from the meeting flushed and stimulated.

"It doesn't matter about cute, did he like you?"

"He *loved* me," Orchid said, giddy with triumph. "He said I have just the look they want. He has the best stories to tell, Val. He knows everyone! And he's nice."

The following week, Elijah asked the girls to return to the Motown office to sign their contract, and to meet Abby McKay, Motown's Ella Fitzgerald, who would "polish" them. Their lawyer, Steven Wilen, along with Neil Fink, Motown's attorney, would be present for the contract signing. They were amply protected in case they really did hit the jackpot.

In fifteen minutes the papers were signed in quadruplicate and the attorneys and Edgar left.

"I hope you're ready to work your butts off," Elijah announced, eyeing Orchid, who was looking very sexy in a pair of tight white jeans and a baby-blue tank top, her electric red hair frizzing around her shoulders. "You know we're takin' a big chance on you. That's why we hired Abby—she's gonna teach you the right moves an' all."

A cab pulled up in front of the studio. A huge black woman got out, clad in a long, flowing yellow gown printed with African motifs. She was massive, her tented gown covering gigantic mounds of pillowy flesh. She didn't walk toward the Motown entrance . . . she flowed.

Elijah popped his head out of his office, and hurried forward to greet her with a hug. Abby gave him a huge smack of a kiss, laughing throatily.

"This here's Abby McKay," the Motown man announced. "Abby, I want you to meet our two new little singers who we hope are gonna set a few radio stations on fire."

The girls stared. Abby McKay in the fifties had sizzled the air waves with hits like "Big, Bad Blues," and "Crying All Night." Now she had a reputation in Detroit as a patron of the arts, and even had her own music show on radio station WWJ.

Valentina remembered the manners Peaches had taught her. "Oh, we're so happy to meet you. You've been our idol for—"

Abby's glance swept from Orchid to Valentina, professionally assessing them from head to toe. "Mmm," she crooned. "You're luscious, both of you. Two ripe peaches waitin' to be eaten. But lookin' good *ain't* good enough."

"But—"

"I'm gonna take you and work you over. I'm gonna work you until you're cryin' out for mercy! And the first thing we're gonna do is listen to that wonderful tape of yours . . . and we'll see just how much you've still got to learn."

Orchid had a secret. Getting into their red car, she first dropped Valentina back home, then drove onto the Lodge expressway again, returning to downtown Detroit, and the high-rise apartment building at 1300 Lafayette, where Elijah Carmody lived.

"Baby, I waited . . . what took you so long?" he demanded as soon as he let her in the door. "You turn me on, honey . . . ever since I first saw your picture."

She giggled in shy pleasure. Elijah was so handsome and exciting. "It's hard getting away—and Val wanted to go have a chocolate sundae to celebrate over at Sander's. I had to put her off."

"Chocolate sundae? That's for babies. *We* gonna celebrate right," he told her, smiling.

They walked into his apartment, which had a bird's-eye view of downtown Detroit. On the walls he'd hung pictures of Motown stars, all of them personally autographed to him. One photo showed Elijah standing with his arms around Diana Ross and Florence Ballard. Orchid stared in wonderment at the trophies of a world that she, too, might finally be entering.

"Want some wine, honey?"

"I . . . sure."

While Elijah poured them some fruity German white wine, Orchid stood trembling, a wave of doubt sweeping over her.

Ten minutes later they were lying on Elijah's long white leather couch, and he had enfolded her in his arms for some full-length, steamy kisses. Orchid gasped, trying to relax and enjoy it. But she could feel the urgent hardness just barely restrained under the front of his trousers, a very *big* hardness, and it scared her a little. More than a little.

"You're so damn gorgeous," he kept whispering. "I love redheads, honey. I love every freckle on you."

"I don't have that many freckles."

"Well, I'm gonna find all of 'em, and kiss 'em until they cry for mercy."

Shaking, she managed to pull away a little, as vague, unpleasant memories tugged at her mind, memories that she usually repressed. "Elijah, there's something—I'm . . . I mean . . ."

He raised an eyebrow, grinning. "Don't tell me *you're* a virgin, kid."

"No! No, of course not."

Elijah handed her another glass of wine and she sipped deeply, while Elijah's fingers were there between her legs, delicately stroking her through the crotch of her bikini panties.

"Oh," she groaned, opening her legs wider.

"Baby," he murmured, slipping away the fabric and inserting two fingers deep into her, turning them until they were moistened and slick with her juices. He rubbed his fingers in and out of her, creating a hot friction that caused Orchid to arch her spine and moan.

"You like it, baby? You like this? Elijah likes it too, honey. Hey, baby, lie down and spread your legs open . . . like this . . ." His hands urged her, slipping the panties down over her legs, and then he buried his face between her legs.

Orchid at first was rigid with surprise and shock. Then the persistent, sweet, darting licks of Elijah's strong tongue sent a shuddering ecstasy through her. The sensation grew, cresting in swift, shaking climaxes that rolled on and on. She laughed and cried out, then laughed again. This was . . . *wonderful!*

"Are you ready for somethin' more now?" Elijah questioned climbing up on top of her, and lowering his body onto hers. He entered her with a long, slow, deep thrust.

"Oh, yes, yes, yes," moaned Orchid. "Oh, yes!" She locked her legs around his, gripped his shoulders, and shuddered with yet another marvelous orgasm.

Chapter
Nine

ABBY MCKAY LIVED in a small house overlooking the Detroit River, within two blocks of the Manoogian Mansion, where Detroit Mayor Coleman Young reigned supreme.

Each morning Orchid and Valentina drove downtown to Abby's house, where they worked for four hours in her finished basement, which she had had Motown engineers fix up as a recording studio, and where she recorded her weekly jazz and blues show. The afternoons Abby devoted to her work on various boards of the Detroit Symphony, the Institute of Arts, and the Montreux Jazz Festival.

Abby critiqued their demo tape until both girls' cheeks were burning, then she made a videotape of them singing.

"Girls, you haven't got any stage *action* at all. You look like sweet little wooden puppets, just like the Supremes when I first started workin' with them. Orchid, you've got a bad habit of bobbin' your head like a chicken. And Val, you barely move at all, just sway back 'n' forth a little bit. That's white singin', not black."

Abby switched off the VCR. "Now, come on, we've got to get down and boogie. We're not just foolin' around here. You've got people dependin' on you, people puttin' their money on the line for you. This here's *business,* gals, and don't you forget it."

Abby, they soon learned, was a tyrant in demanding perfection.

"Singin' is breathin'," she would exhort them. "You've gotta have good breath control, otherwise, you're going to sound like shit. But don't you worry. You should've heard Florence Ballard and Diana the first time *they* tried to belt out a real long note. Why, both of them held their breath so long they nearly passed out.

"Push your chest out!" she would shout to Valentina. "Out! Out! Don't be shy . . . you've got pretty boobs, girl, and you can't be ashamed of 'em—not if you wanta sing well."

Then Abby would turn her eagle eye on Orchid. "As for you, Orchid girl, you gotta work on getting bigger notes. Bigger, do you hear? You sound like you're gonna blow away in the first wind."

Just when both girls were getting frustrated, Abby would put on the power and pull some switches on her bank of amplifiers, speakers, and other electronic equipment. Wilson Pickett or Patti LaBelle would pour into the basement.

"Now, look here, girls, look at how you've got to move . . . You've got to be loose and sexy, you've got to be free!" Abby swayed to the beat with such supple rhythm that she seemed almost slim again.

Orchid took easily to Abby's instructions, grinding her hips and shaking her shoulders with natural sensuality. But Valentina felt tense, and had more trouble. Abby solved the problem by taking out a tall bottle, pouring some into a glass.

"Here, this is peach schnapps. Goes down like velvet."

"This is good," Valentina exclaimed, draining hers too quickly. It was another ninety-degree summer day.

"Lordy," Abby exclaimed. "Don't inhale it, girl . . . sip it slowly. Just let it get into your blood, let it smooth you out, mellow you. Now let's try that dancin' and swayin' again. Only this time we're not gonna stop until you get loose, honey. Even if it takes all day. Just let those muscles *melt.*"

Five weeks later, Abby made another videotape. She played it back for them, crooning her satisfaction. "Mmm! You gals are hot little numbers. You can sing and swing black now, darlin's. Now all you've got to do is wait for Elijah to find some good tunes for you to cut."

* * *

"The girls have hardly seen a boy all summer long," Edgar said in late August. "Let's have some college boys over here for a dinner party, Peaches. Good-looking ones, from the U of M, maybe, or Michigan State. Get the girls' minds off music, and on something else for a change."

Peaches winced. Edgar hadn't been totally pleased when the girls' persistence resulted in a record contract. He'd provided them with legal assistance—no daughters of his were going to be financially taken advantage of, he said. But he'd been very critical of Elijah Carmody, and he'd chastised Orchid several times for wearing clothes he considered "too adult."

Maybe a nice party was just what they needed to smooth things over.

A week later, the Lederers' large colonial home on Willowgreen Court across from Franklin Hills Country Club was aglow with light. Spotlights were trained on the huge blue spruces that adorned the property. Fresh-cut flowers in an antique brass tub sat by the doorway to welcome the party guests.

Peaches felt an unusual twinge of nervousness as she waited for the first of her dinner guests to arrive. She glided through the house, stopping in the kitchen to check the cook's progress. For appetizers, she planned to serve marinated red and yellow peppers, and *belons,* large succulent Maine oysters on ice, garnished with a sprinkle of caviar. The main course would be grilled pieces of lobster over angel hair pasta with sweet garlic sauce. There would also be a salad of wild greens, with a tart lemon dressing to counteract the richness of the other dishes.

Thank God her cook, Enzio, who'd been with her for six years, had everything well under control.

Satisfied, she returned to the large dining room and gave the place cards one more inspection. As befitted the highest-ranking guest, Governor Milliken would be on her right, his wife, Helen, on Edgar's right. Burt Bacharach would be on her left, Carole Bayer Sager on Edgar's left.

The Lederers had dozens of friends on Broadway, since Edgar had bought several Broadway theaters to add to his chain.

Peaches sighed, knowing that her nervousness centered around the girls. Since they'd signed the record contract, Orchid seemed frenetic, constantly talking about being a "star." She was becoming secretive, receiving daily phone calls that she didn't discuss, other than to say they were "from Motown." Peaches had an uneasy feeling they were from a boy, someone Orchid didn't want them to meet. Maybe Valentina knew who he was. But as always, the girls presented a united front.

The doorbell rang and the Lederers' housekeeper, Annie, ushered in the first guests, the Joe Dresners, whom the Lederers had known for thirty years. Joe and Edna Slavik arrived a few minutes later. There were flurries of kisses.

Peaches had invited Stuart Kallman, a young entertainment attorney with Edgar's law firm, for Valentina, and Randolph Harmon III, otherwise known as Randy, a star linebacker on the University of Michigan football team, for Orchid.

The dinner progressed as planned. Burt and Carole were a handsome, articulate couple. Talk turned to play reviewers, whose frequent sharp jabs and sarcastic criticism was both hated and feared.

"The critics have got too damn much to do on opening night," Burt claimed. "They have to review the show, the actors, the costumes, the singing, and a score they're hearing for the first time. I think it'd be great if the music could come out a couple of months beforehand, on a record or cassette, so they would have some familiarity with the work. In fact—"

He was interrupted by the front door chime. Suddenly Orchid flushed deep pink. She jumped up from the table, rushing out of the dining room.

Edgar raised an eyebrow. "What's wrong with her?"

"Now, dear," Peaches said uneasily, remembering all the secret phone calls.

Five minutes later, Orchid appeared in the dining room again—with a handsome black man on her arm.

"Hi, everyone," she chirped brightly. "This is Elijah Carmody. I invited Elijah to have some dessert and coffee with us . . . he couldn't make it earlier because they were taping."

"Well, Elijah, we're very glad to meet you," Peaches said cordially.

Edgar looked thunderous, but Peaches adroitly smoothed over the incident, asking the maid to clear the plates. "Why don't we move to the living room for coffee and dessert? Elijah, we'd love to hear what Motown is doing these days."

"Shit," Elijah muttered to Orchid as they walked through to the big living room with its valuable Tabriz rug in jewel colors, its museum-quality paintings. "I thought this was just a small family get-together, not a party. Man, that crowd was heavy-duty. Girl, what'd you do that for, without telling them first?"

"I just wanted them to meet you," Orchid whispered back.

"Oh, I met 'em, all right. Your mother was nice, but your father'd like to have throttled me."

Orchid stuck close to Elijah, nervous about the havoc she had wrought. She picked at her dessert of white chocolate mousse, served in a pool of raspberry sauce. There was hot or iced espresso and Orchid's favorite double dutch chocolate coffee. Tonight she could barely touch it.

Face it. She had invited Elijah to shock her parents, and maybe she *had* overdone it.

"I think we need to talk, young lady." During a lull, Edgar took Orchid's arm and steered her toward his study.

Inside, he insisted she sit down, and began, "You've flouted all good manners by bringing that man into our home. You're being just as rude to Elijah, using him to shock us, as you're being rude to your mother, ruining her dinner party!"

"I didn't ruin her party. Everyone is talking and having a good time. Elijah is just as interesting as anyone else."

"But it's not *interesting* that really concerns you, is it, Orchid?" Edgar accused. "You're sleeping with him, aren't you? A man fifteen years older than you, and in show business, not to mention belonging to another race."

Orchid looked down, her cheeks reddening. Then she jerked her head up.

"He's *not* old enough to be my father!" she cried. "He's only thirty-one. And he's got a college degree and he was a music major and an all-American football player! Oh, you're just jealous because he's young and good-looking and because he's in a world you don't know anything about, and can't get into, because you're . . . you're so square, your whole life has corners!"

"Well, all I can say is this," Edgar grated. "Your new friend is totally unacceptable to us and I want him out of our house—now, tonight. You take his arm and you walk with him to the door, and you tell him you're never going to see him again."

Orchid gasped. "But I—I can't do that!"

"Why not? Young lady, I'm your father. I've raised you for nine years, I've provided everything you could ever want, far more than most girls your age even dream of. And I expect some respect and gratitude for—"

Orchid began to sob. "Gratitude?" she wept. "I *am* grateful . . . that you showed me what you're really like. I'm walking to the door, all right—only I'm going *out* of it. I'm taking Elijah with me. I'm going to . . . to move in with him!"

"What?"

"I said we're going to live together," Orchid shouted. "I'm almost eighteen now—I'm an adult, I can do whatever I want!"

"But you can't move out," Valentina cried, stunned. She stood by helplessly while Orchid threw her clothes into suitcases. "I mean . . . you just *can't*!"

"Can't I? Just you watch!" Orchid swept six dresses off

the rod and stuffed them into a garment bag. She crammed shoes and jeans in on top of them.

Valentina fought not to cry. "But, Orchie . . . I mean, you don't know Elijah. You don't know anything about him. He hasn't even asked you to move in with him."

"No, I asked him, and I do so know plenty about him. Sex is a great way to find out things, kiddo."

Sex. The chasm between them grew terrifyingly wider with every word.

"Anyone can have sex," Valentina said, struggling to sound sophisticated. "But Orchie, what about common values, and a similar background, and—"

"Bull crap." Orchid stood hugging a pair of designer jeans, her chin thrust out defiantly. "There's lots you don't know about me, Val—lots. Elijah and me grew up identical . . . both of us with drugged-up mothers on welfare, and brothers that hit us and beat us . . . an'— more things happened to me that only Elijah knows about." Orchid's lip quivered. "Bad things, real bad, that I can't talk about."

Valentina stared at her sister. "But Orchid . . . we've always told each other *everything*. What haven't you told me . . . ?"

She heard Orchid continue to rationalize her move. "Now Elijah can help me with my music, and he said he'd work on a couple songs with me. I can meet all the LA people, an' go on concert tours sometimes, and—all sorts of great stuff."

"What about Blue Orchids?" Valentina managed to ask.

"This doesn't have *anything* to do with that," Orchid insisted. "Everything's gonna be exactly the same."

Ten minutes later, Elijah appeared at Orchid's bedroom door to help carry her things downstairs. He took one look at the tears on both girls' faces and threw up his hands. "Hey, sugar, you don't have to do this," he told Orchid. "It's no big deal."

"I do have to. I *want* to," Orchid exclaimed, terrified he wouldn't take her after all. "I *love* you, Elijah!"

* * *

That night Valentina's Mikhail dream returned for the first time in several years. She saw him struggling in a rushing gray river, being swept away by the heavy current toward a very icy white fog.

"Misha! Misha!" she screamed, sitting bolt upright in bed. Sobs tore out of her.

"Darling? Val, darling? Are you all right?" Peaches was in the room with her. Valentina heard the soft swish of her silk negligee, and felt her mother sit down on the bed beside her.

"Orchid's gone," Valentina said brokenly. "Just like Mikhail."

"Only for a short while," Peaches said.

"What . . . what do you mean?"

"I mean, dear, your sister is out in the world learning a few lessons of life, that's all. She'll learn them well. We'll keep on letting her know that we love her."

"I . . . I don't want her to learn any damn lessons," Valentina wept. "And she doesn't either! She just w-wants Elijah to love her, and I d-don't think he's going to for very long . . ."

"No one ever wants to learn lessons," Peaches observed quietly. "But we always do. That's part of living too."

Orchid didn't call for three long days. Valentina cried every night until her eyes burned. She sobbed and sobbed. It was hell being separated from Orchid for the first time since they'd met. They were so much closer than mere sisters. Orchid was the one who'd enabled her to go on, who'd filled up the horrible void after she lost her entire family. *Orchid was part of her.*

During the day, she tried desperately to stay busy, practicing her jazz dancing and playing so much tennis she was exhausted. Although Stuart Kallman kept calling her for dates, Valentina refused him. She was too upset to laugh and pretend she was having a good time.

That Saturday afternoon, Valentina was showering after

dance practice, when the phone rang. She raced naked out of the bathroom to snatch it up.

"H'lo?"

"It's me," Orchid chirped cheerfully. "Hey, I'm so happy, Val, I could just float right up to heaven and live on a cloud. I've got great news. Elijah decided what songs he wants us to cut for the album. 'Pretty Girls' is one. And that other one I wrote, 'Blue Silk Gowns'. Then we're gonna cover a couple of Linda Ronstadt songs and do some Donna Summer."

"We are?" Valentina said numbly. She'd been so upset she hadn't even thought about Blue Orchids in three days.

"And there is one *more* thing," Orchid crowed. "As soon as we finish the album, Elijah's gonna call up Dick Clark and see if he can get us on *American Bandstand*. Can you believe it!" Her squeals of excitement penetrated down the phone wire. "Aren't you excited? Aren't you happy? Aren't you *just so damn happy you could fly?*"

"Sure," said Valentina.

"Don't be such a wiss. What do you mean, 'Sure'?" Orchid jubilantly mocked Valentina's less-than-heartfelt tone. "Hey, girl! We're Blue Orchids! We're talking gold records here, an' fame and money and hearing our own voices on the radio. I'm gonna come over there right now, drop off my suitcases and pick you up."

"Your suitcases?" inquired Valentina numbly.

Orchid hesitated. "Sure . . . See, 'Lije and I decided it'd be better if I lived back home for a while since he's in LA so much. But we're still seein' each other! I love him, Val. I just hope . . ." Her voice went low. "Well, that Daddy Edgar wants me back."

A week later, Berry Gordy flew them both to California to cut their album at the Los Angeles studio. Abby McKay flew with them, acting as their chaperon, coach, and mentor.

In their first class seats, Orchid chattered excitedly, and kept humming the proposed album lyrics until Abby told her to button her mouth. But later, when Orchid excused herself to visit the rest room, Abby frowned. "Girl, I just hope our little Orchid isn't ridin' for a fall."

"What do you mean?"

"I mean, honey child, she is one helluva pretty kid, and she's got a voice sweet enough to charm truck drivers. But it's just sweet, if you know what I mean. Not big. She hasn't got the real quality to her." Abby gazed speculatively at Valentina. "Now *you,* sugar, you've got it. I mean *you've got it.* Only—"

"Only what?" Now Abby had Valentina's full attention.

"Val, this here is one damn tough business. There might come a time when you've got to go on your own, know what I mean? When you've got to cut loose from your ties and see what you can do."

Valentina felt a chill. She gazed toward the window, where billows of fluffy cotton-candy clouds seemed to float several hundred yards below them, brilliantly lit by the sun. Were these the clouds that Orchid happily said she was living on?

"I don't think so," she told Abby quietly. "Orchid's my sister, and that means everything to me. We'll always be Blue Orchids."

Orchid raced into their suite at the Sunset Hyatt on Sunset Boulevard, threw down her suitcase and carry-on bag, and stopped short. Two huge bouquets sat on a low table in the room's elegant sitting area. Each contained roses mixed with rare, expensive orchids. Blue satin ribbons had been inserted among the blooms, and wrapped around the vases.

"Oh!" Orchid squealed in delight.

The girls eagerly fumbled among the fragrant blooms.

" 'To Orchid, my beautiful daughter,' " Orchid read aloud from her card. " 'From Daddy Edgar. I'll always love you no matter what.' "

Orchid held up the card and stared at it, her hand shaking. "This is . . . oh, Val . . . oh, *Val* . . ." She blinked back sudden tears. "He *doesn't* hate me."

Valentina read her card, smiling. Hers said, " 'To my

gorgeous daughter, the best day of my life was when you
came into it.' ''

While Abby lumbered through their two adjoining rooms,
making sure that the TV sets worked, and ordering snacks
from room service, Orchid sneaked into the bathroom and
closed the door. Hollywood-style, even this room was
equipped with a phone extension. She dialed the Mayflower
Hotel in New York City, and waited impatiently for the
hotel operator to ring Elijah's room.

She needed Elijah's reassurances . . . needed them bad.
Besides Val, he was the only one who knew just how
nervous recording in a studio made her.

"Yeah?" Elijah's voice finally came on the other end.

"Elijah! I thought you weren't there! I was gonna leave
a message for you."

"Yeah, I just got in, I heard the phone ringin' out in the
hall. I've gotta change my clothes for dinner. What's up,
kid?"

"I . . . I just wanted to talk. We just got here. We're
goin' to start the session first thing in the morning . . . ''

"Babe, you're gonna do great. Just listen to Abby. That's
why I sent her there with you, she's gonna bolster you up,
keep you going. She thinks you're ready."

"Okay . . .''

"Look, baby, I gotta go now, I'm running late."

Orchid felt a sudden, irrational panic. "But Elijah! Don't
hang up! Not yet! Tell me . . . tell me you love me."

"You know I do," Elijah agreed affably. "You're the
prettiest little girl I ever seen, honey lamb, I love your
freckles, and I *gotta* go now. I really am runnin' late.''

There was a click. Orchid stared at the phone, and finally
replaced it in the cradle.

In New York, Elijah rolled over languidly, and caressed
the hip of the actress who lay naked next to him, her body
slicked with after-love perspiration. She had a dancer's
body, and full breasts with large, dark nipples.

"Who was *she*?" inquired Juana jealously.

''Hey, she ain't nothin' to me, baby. Just singer talent, that's all she is. Girls like her, they're a dime a dozen.'' And Elijah lifted up Juana's hips, positioning a pillow underneath them. ''Let's make a little more whoopee, honey . . . before I got to get up and go meet Diana.''

Two weeks later in their hotel room the phone rang. Abby reached out a big, heavy arm and picked it up.

''Yes? Elijah? Yeah, they did so fine today. They sang real sweet. 'Course we've got about another week of mixing, but it looks good so far.''

Orchid, who'd been lounging on the floor watching *Dallas,* and brooding about Elijah, sat up. Both girls watched as a broad smile spread across Abby's face. ''Well, I think they can handle that. They're big girls now, and they sure know how to dance.''

Abby cocked her head, listening, and nodding. ''Yeah . . . yeah, they can do that. I can take them shopping on Rodeo Drive. Get them some dresses with sex appeal.''

''What? What? What?'' Both girls screamed, jumping on Abby at the same time. ''What, Abby? What did Elijah say?''

Abby laughed richly. She spoke into the phone. ''Yeah, Elijah, and the same to you. And how is your sister? Did your daddy have his retirement party yet? And what about your aunt Maggie's lumbago?''

''Abby! Abby!'' they shrieked.

Abby hung up, smiling triumphantly. ''Well, little gals, I guess you're gonna be stars after all. Elijah just got done havin' a long lunch with Dick Clark. He managed to get you on the 'maybe' list.''

Orchid groaned.

''The 'maybe' list?'' Valentina asked, disappointed.

''That's good news,'' Abby told them. ''Sooner or later, some singer they've got lined up is gonna come down with laryngitis, or their mother dies or something. Then *you* get the phone call from the main man, the producer, and you have to fly to New York right away.''

With a single reflex, Valentina and Orchid grabbed each other and whirled each other around the room.

"Thank you, Abby. Oh, thank you. Without you this wouldn't be happening," Valentina said, overcome with emotion.

Abby brushed a hand toward her wide cheeks. "Hey, child," she said awkwardly, at a loss for words for the first time since they had met her.

Five days after the mix was set and the album completed, Berry Gordy told Elijah, who had flown to LA, that he thought *Blue Orchids,* as they planned to call the album, would spawn at least three hits.

"Hey, man, I listened to it, lived with it for nearly a week, and I think we got us a winner here . . . we're goin' platinum unless I really miss my bet. You keep those little gals in line, hear? No more screwin' around with that Orchid. *If* you been screwin' her."

"Man, I ain't done more than just look at her," Elijah lied.

"Well, lookin' is *all* you gonna do, man. We got the responsibility for those girls now, 'Lije. And speakin' of which, I'm givin' a nice barbecue on Sunday after the Lions-Rams game. You tell 'em to come on along. We'll show 'em the Motown family—an' then some."

Motown sent a car and driver, and the girls were driven in style to the party, held at Berry Gordy's mansion set on a ten-acre estate in the hills of Bel Air. Abby, who was having dinner with her old friend Ramsey Lewis, would join them later.

Both girls gawked out the windows at the stars' homes they passed, set back behind wrought-iron fencing, tall hedges, and electric gates.

As the car rounded the top of yet another breathtaking hill, Orchid said, "I've got something to show you, Val . . . something new I just got. Want to guess what it is? I'm wearing it, and you haven't seen it yet."

Valentina stared at her sister, who was dressed for

partying in a white-fringed cowgirl outfit she'd picked up at Lina Lee. "I haven't? I was there when you got dressed," she said, puzzled.

Orchid giggled, and pulled up the hem of her short white leather skirt, until her right thigh was exposed. There was something blue on her skin. "My tattoo," she explained airily.

Valentina gaped. *"Tattoo?"*

"Yesterday while you were practicing your singing, I walked across the street from our hotel right on Sunset. There was this neat little tattoo place . . . Sunset Strip Tattoo, Incorporated. 'Tattooers of the Stars Since 1971.' " Orchid showed off the mark proudly. "It's a blue orchid, Val. Get it? The guy custom-designed it for me. Don't you think it's neat?"

Valentina thought it was tacky.

"Sure, Orchid. But . . . look . . . don't go showing it off to people, okay? At least not tonight."

"Right," Orchid promised.

The Motown car dropped them off inside the gate area of the Gordy mansion, where car parkers in white jackets were running back and forth, parking Bentleys and Corniches.

The party was in full swing when they walked in the door. A stereo blasted out "Do the Boomerang" by Junior Walker and the All Stars. Crowds of people gossiped, talked business, or balanced plates loaded with barbecued pork and chicken. There were men in slacks and cashmere blazers, and the women, many beautiful, wore rainbow colors, or else dashikis in exotic prints.

"Val, over half the people here are *black*," Orchid whispered.

"Hush,'' Valentina whispered back. Then she caught her breath. Wasn't that Gladys Knight in the corner, in a drop-dead ice-green sheath?

Elijah Carmody spotted them, and hurried over from the bar. Tonight he wore baby-blue, and gold nugget jewelry. His appreciative look took in Orchid's skimpy white cowgirl dress.

"Well, you're here. Hi, Orchid, baby. Might I say, you look bodacious?" Orchid rushed up and hugged him, clinging too tightly.

"This is a lovely party," Valentina began hastily, nudging her sister as Orchid seemed about to pull up her skirt and show Elijah the tattoo.

"Hey, these are Motown folks. Best people in the world." Elijah began pointing out some of the guests to them. "That's Esther Edwards, she's Berry's sister. Over there standing with Marvin Gaye is Mel Farr and Charlie Sanders from the Detroit Lions. They just beat up on the Rams today. That's Choker Campbell—he used to play with Count Basie, now he works for us. That's Diana . . ."

Berry Gordy, their host, was two people ahead of Orchid in the buffet line, forking pieces of beef onto his plate as he talked to Elijah. Berry was a short, bearded man, his hair cut in an ordinary-looking Afro. Tonight he wore a white shirt, white pants, and several African-type ornaments. Large sunglasses shaded his eyes.

"Hey, man, these Blue Orchids," she overheard Elijah boast to the head of Motown. "Mark my words—they gonna be bigger than the Supremes. Remember I said that. And remember, *I* found 'em."

"Bet you a baby-blue Caddie," Gordy said. "Fully loaded, cruise an' all. But it's gotta happen within two years or the bet's off."

"Bet's *on*," cried Elijah.

Now Orchid was too excited to eat. She reeled away from the buffet table, the men's words ringing in her mind. *Bigger than the Supremes.* And Berry had bet Elijah a blue Cadillac . . . on them. Oh, God . . . Suddenly, deep in her gut, Orchid believed.

"Drink, miss?" asked a waitress in a caterer's uniform.

"What. Oh, yeah, sure." Orchid grabbed another glass from the tray, a mai tai this time. Jubilantly she gulped it down. And reached for another. They were *really* going to become stars!

Back in Detroit, three weeks later, Orchid came pounding upstairs, her voice a screech of ecstasy. "Val, it's all happening, it's happening, they're playing us on the radio,

I heard us on CKLW, the Tommy Shannon show. We're stars now, we're on the radio, we're getting played! I can't believe it's happened so soon!''

"Really?" Valentina rushed downstairs, where Orchid was playing the Lederers' expensive stereo system. She stopped in the doorway, transfixed. Their own voices came from the radio, singing "Pretty Girls."

"Isn't it wonderful?" Orchid yelled. "Isn't it just too, too *fantastic*?"

Valentina stood there, while sudden, unexpected tears stung her eyes and rolled down her cheeks. It *was* wonderful and fantastic. It was the best thing she'd ever heard.

Orchid hurried out of Mira Linder's, touching her new hairstyle with fascinated pleasure. The stylist had toned down her wild red to a rich chestnut, adding several hair extensions, giving Orchid a tawny mane that rippled glamorously.

She was so excited she could scream. This morning the phone call had come from the producer of the Dick Clark show. They were needed to fill the slot vacated by Laura Brannigan, who had come down with pneumonia.

Thank God they'd already bought their dresses in California. Tight. Clingy. Loaded with orchid-colored sequins. Now they'd finally get to wear them, and she could hardly wait to tell Elijah.

She trotted out to the parking lot and got into the new red Camaro she'd purchased for herself out of her record advance, a twin of the one Valentina already drove. Within minutes she was on the John Lodge Expressway, and soon she was pulling into the parking area of Elijah's apartment building.

Humming, she let herself into the twelfth-floor apartment. The acrid tang of marijuana smoke stung her nostrils. Elijah wasn't in sight, but Diana Ross was warbling on the stereo.

"Elijah? 'Lije!" she called, stripping off her clothes as she headed toward the bedroom. Her T-shirt went in a heap, followed by her Gloria Vanderbilt jeans, and lastly her black lace bikini panties. As usual, she was braless. "Elijah?"

"Orchid? That you, honey?"

She reached the bedroom and threw open the door. The room reeked of marijuana, blue smoke drifting in the air. Elijah was crouched naked on the king-sized bed, bent over a buxom blonde who'd been at the Berry Gordy party in LA.

Orchid froze, horrified, and uttered a tiny shriek.

"Hi, babe," Elijah drawled, looking up from his task. "C'mon in, hon. We already warmed up but you can join us."

"I . . . I . . ." Orchid choked, feeling a surge of bile rise up from her stomach. Clutching both hands to her mouth, she turned and fled, snatching up her clothes and throwing them on as she ran.

She cried in the elevator all the way down to the lobby.

Chapter
Ten

WEARING NOTHING BUT a pair of French-cut blue panties, Orchid leaned toward the dressing room mirror, rubbing lip gloss on her mouth with her pinky finger.

"Oh, eccch, this color is too *pale*," she exclaimed, scrubbing it off anxiously. She was a wreck from the anticipation of appearing on the Dick Clark show in front of millions.

She heard Abby's voice behind her.

"What're you doin', honey? Don't you know they're gonna put the makeup on *for* you? That's what they've got a makeup artist for."

Orchid jerked back from the mirror. Her elbow, brushing the row of makeup bottles lined on a shelf, shattered several of them to the floor.

"Let them clean it up. You've got to go to Makeup, child. Right now," Abby added.

"Sure," Orchid agreed, but made no move to pull on the model's coat that Abby handed her. She was scared. Terrified! She'd already recuperated from the shock of Elijah's betrayal. Abby had made her see that she was just another easy lay for the good-looking Motown executive. "That good-looking boy's not worth pining over for one tiny second," Abby had said.

No, this was much worse—because in a way her fear was another betrayal. It was Orchid's deep terror that people would think Val was the real star, the best singer. God, she loved Val so much, but she could never stand it if that were to happen.

"Earth to Orchid . . . earth to Orchid," Abby chuckled. "Are you daydreaming about a gold record again? Well, you're not gonna get it staying in the john."

Orchid gripped the edge of the small white sink. "I . . . I think I'm gonna be sick," she quavered.

"No, you *aren't*," Abby announced, throwing the blue cotton makeup robe around Orchid's shoulders, and urging her toward the door. "You aren't even gonna think about it—and that's final."

They'd broken for a commercial and now Dick Clark—perennially young and handsome—was in a huddle with a woman in jeans who wore a headset. Abby barely heard what they were saying. Something about *skirts too tight.*

Abby's heart sank as she realized he must be referring to the skimpy costumes she'd picked for Valentina and Orchid, featuring skirts so clingy they revealed nearly all.

But then, thank God, Clark shook his head, and gestured a "thumbs up." Abby sighed with relief. Dick Clark had given all kinds of stars a boost, from Chubby Checker to Sonny and Cher.

A production assistant walked through the studio audience, instructing the kids on where to position themselves, and choosing the few that were to be featured dancing on camera. A gaffer overhead on a dolly track was also getting his equipment into position for the close-in shot that would open the number.

The director raised his hand toward a row of windows that housed the control booth, and suddenly the rhythmic intro to "Pretty Girls" flooded the air.

"I'm a pretty girl, will you kiss me? Will you kiss me long 'n' hard? I can't think about anyone but you."

Valentina began to make love to the microphone, lip-synching the lyrics, as they had practiced for hours. Beside her, Orchid slowly undulated her body, her head thrown back as she crooned and hummed. The klieg lights winked and sparkled off their brief, tight, sequined dresses.

"My body belongs to you, baby. Kiss me long, kiss me hard . . ."

The sexy, pounding song hit the kids in the studio

audience like an explosion. As Abby McKay watched in satisfaction, the audience, ignoring their previous instructions, began to press and crowd toward the front.

"Blue Orchids! Blue Orchids!" a girl shrieked, grabbing Abby's arm and shaking her. Black mascara ran down her cheeks with her tears of hysteria. "Oh, God—oh, my God! They're so fine!"

"They're *my* girls," Abby chuckled.

"Pretty Girls" soared to the top of *Billboard* magazine's list of top hits. Within three weeks it was being played by radio stations across the country. Pleased, Elijah started things rolling for a concert tour that would hit twenty-eight cities.

"Think about this, audience," said Barbara Walters, facing directly toward camera 2. "They're two beautiful sisters, only eighteen years old, and every time they turn on the radio, their own voices leap out at them. Their songs are at the top of all the charts, their videos are seen constantly on MTV. *Rolling Stone* just did a cover story on them, they're on the cover of *Cosmopolitan* this month, the first time in its history *Cosmo* has featured two beautiful women on its cover. They've just completed a sensational European tour, which was preceded by a sold-out U.S. tour."

Wearing a deep red Saint Laurent suit, her black hair tousled into clouds of curls, Valentina sat in an easy chair facing Barbara Walters. Orchid, glorious in a black and white checked Escada suit, her red curls ablaze in the strong lights, sat in a similar chair beside her.

Three TV cameras were aimed at them, the one in the center with a red light on, indicating they were on camera.

"Girls, what's it like to be the hottest singing group of the year? How has it changed your lives, and are you happy with those changes?" inquired Barbara. Costumed in a cream Chanel suit with a navy striped blouse, she leaned forward, her hazel eyes gleaming. "Valentina?"

Valentina hesitated a split second. Trust Barbara to hurl her usual tough questions right at the beginning. Everyone assumed that, of course, they loved what was happening.

They'd become worldwide celebrities. Mostly they did like it. Who wouldn't? The glamour, the applause, the attention, the gorgeous men who popped up wherever they went.

For instance, Ben Paris, the sexy star of *Men at War* and other action flicks. He'd been pursuing Valentina for nine months, bombarding her with flowers, phone calls, and pleas for her to fly to London with him just for lunch. Ben had the reputation of being a first-class womanizer. He thought all he had to do was phone her, and she'd drop at his feet like all the others. But the idea of making love to a Don Juan really turned Valentina off. She didn't want to be one of hundreds. She wanted to be special . . .

"I see you need a moment to think about that one," Barbara prompted, boring in. "Could it be that the glamorous life isn't all it's cracked up to be? What do your parents think about this? I understand they're not too thrilled."

"That's not true. They're both very excited and happy for us."

The interview continued, with several clips of Blue Orchids concerts and videos played between segments. The cameras pulled in for a closeup of the two young women as Barbara asked her next question.

"How do the two sisters get along? Are there any rivalries . . . jealousies between the two of you?"

"Why, no," they both answered, almost simultaneously.

"But surely there must be just a tiny twinge, since, Valentina, you seem to be the lead singer, and Orchid, well, Orchid's parts are less . . . prominent."

The question caused Valentina to stiffen slightly, Orchid to flush a deep red.

"Jealousy." The unspoken word hovered in the air between them.

Valentina hurried to deny the allegation. "That's not true at all. Without Orchid, the songs wouldn't work. Blue Orchids is a duo, Barbara. And Orchid gets more fan letters than I do," she added.

"Orchid, you're a talented, beautiful young woman." Barbara smiled, looking at her, then down at her notes. "The tabloids have had a field day with your so-called

romances. One-night stands with European playboys and
Grand Prix race car drivers, even a fling with a sexy young
British royal in line for the throne. You know who I'm
talking about. Also baseball player Roman Solenski. Is there
any truth to all these stories? And is it true that both of you
had an affair with Ben Paris?''

Orchid giggled. ''No, it isn't true, Barbara—at least not a
hundred percent. Val never slept with Ben Paris. But *I* did.''

''Another break, ladies and gentlemen.'' Barbara quickly
broke in.

Chapter

Eleven

ORCHID STRETCHED OUT her arms as waves of screaming applause roared upward, absorbing the energy that flowed from the audience.

She linked arms with Valentina and they ran offstage together, the deafening roar following them.

"Oh, Lord," Valentina said. "Autographs."

Crowds of people thronged the backstage area—groupies, reporters, and local fan club members milled around. The Doug Schubots and Marvin and Nola Goldman were also there, friends of the Lederers who were in town from Detroit.

Perspiring from the exertion, both girls signed autographs until their hands ached.

Later, at her dressing room, a visitor was waiting for Orchid.

"Hey, beautiful," smiled a handsome man with deep dimples, long, glossy dark curls, and the kind of straight nose found on Italian statues.

"Roman!" Orchid shrieked.

"I caught your last half-hour—you were sensational." The famous Los Angeles Dodgers baseball pitcher opened the door for Orchid to enter, locking it behind them. "There. We've got privacy. I just got in from St. Louis. Shit, what a flight, even the stews were sitting down most of the way. Your security guy let me in—I've been waiting here for two hours, getting hornier than hell."

She wriggled into his arms, delighted to see him. They saw each other occasionally for what Roman Solenski called "sport fucking."

Orchid knew she didn't love him, and neither did he love her. Who cared? They were friends, and they laughed together and Roman knew just how to rub Orchid's back when she got tired. Of course they had great sex together too. That was the point of it.

"Mmm," she murmured happily, giving herself up to the deep soul kissing that Roman liked.

He was in a dominating mood tonight, and quickly stripped off her costume, peeling it off so fast that several seams tore. He lifted her up easily, and carried her to the makeup table, pushing aside a litter of curling irons and hair spray cans. He put her down in a sitting position, spreading her legs open so that he could put his head between them. She was already moist. He dropped to his knees.

"I thought about your hot, sweet pussy all the way across the country," he murmured, bending forward to lave her inner lips with expert, strong strokes of his tongue. Orchid moaned and arched her hips, giving herself up to his skills. Roman was the only man she knew who could eat pussy half the night, never tiring.

Within seconds, she had come in a burst of sinful wet spasms. Roman lifted his head and began kissing her again, offering her the taste of her own juices. Pure eroticism! Finally he pulled away, and peeled off his tight, much-washed jeans and silk turtleneck.

As always, Orchid gasped at the sight of him.

"Oh, Rom," she moaned, reaching out to grasp him in both hands. "Oh, God—"

Fiercely he entered her, gripping her hips with both hands to set the rhythm of their union. Orchid began to rock her hips. For long minutes they were locked in a beautiful erotic dance. They gripped each other and kissed deeply.

Finally she groaned and grabbed both of his tightly fisted balls, feeling the start of a second, powerful orgasm. For a wild instant she lost control of herself, screaming out her deep pleasure. Roman, his face glistening with droplets of sweat, cried out too, swept away by his own climax.

Afterward, Roman found a silk robe and threw it over Orchid's shoulders.

"I needed that," he told her, as if it had been an athletic workout.

"Me too. But Rom—" Orchid went on reluctantly.

"Yeah?"

"I really can't stay too much longer. There's a reporter that said he wanted to interview me, some guy from the *LA Times,* and I promised Elijah I'd talk to him. It's a drag, but Elijah won't let us trash any interviews. He says we've gotta keep our names in front of the fans no matter what."

"Sure, sure, babe." Roman reached for his clothes. "Catch you later, maybe? What hotel you staying at?"

"The Beverly Hills," Orchid told him, starting toward the shower stall.

"Want some company in there?" Roman asked, running his hand over her curved backside, fondling the second orchid tattoo she'd gotten several months ago in Copenhagen.

She giggled. "Sure . . ."

"But don't drop the soap because if you do, you might be in plenty of trouble."

Twenty minutes later Orchid was dressed in jeans and a long violet-colored silk shirt. She'd run a brush through her tangle of red-auburn, shower-damp curls and wore only light makeup. She felt fantastic.

Joe Donovan waited for her by the hall that led to the greenroom.

"Do you want to come back to my dressing room? I'll have someone bring us something to drink. I could use a beer. I'm sooo thirsty!"

She flagged down a roadie to place the order, then they walked back to her dressing room. "You have anyone special in your life right now, Orchid? I mean a special guy?"

"Not really."

"I thought I saw Roman Solenski backstage—"

"He got passes from his grandmother."

"And permission to wait in your dressing room? Come on, Orchid." Then the reporter shrugged. "Anyway, there *is* one thing I do want to ask you about. What about the rumors that Blue Orchids is having problems and splitting up? Any truth to that?''

Orchid stared at the reporter, her good mood dissolving immediately. *Splitting up?* She'd watched other rock groups split and go down the tubes and the idea panicked her.

"I've heard it from more than one source," Donovan went on, "and of course I want to get your version before I print anything."

"Splitting *up*?" she cried angrily. "Who told you such bullshit?"

"I can't reveal my sources."

"This interview is over, Mr. Donovan."

"It seems I touched on a sensitive issue," Donovan remarked, his blue eyes gleaming with interest.

"Like hell you did! You didn't touch on a fucking thing."

"Then the rumors aren't true that you're angry because you're only doing backup to Valentina's lead?"

"No! No, no, no! Of course they aren't true!" Orchid was trembling. "Blue Orchids is getting along very, very fine, thank you. And now I would like you to leave, Mr. Donovan."

Donovan took the hint and exited, Orchid slamming the door behind him. Blue Orchids *breaking up*? How had such a rumor surfaced?

Valentina is the lead singer and you're only doing backup.

The seed of doubt had been firmly planted.

Valentina finally made her escape from the autograph seekers after inviting the Schubots and Goldmans and several others to a small party in her hotel suite in an hour or so.

She saw Joe Donovan leave Orchid's dressing room, and nodded to him as they passed, but did not slow her steps. She reached her own dressing room, to find a man leaning against the door.

"If you want an interview, call Janet, our publicity

person, in the morning," she said. "She arranges all our P.R."

He laughed. "I'm not a reporter. Do I look like one? I wonder if I should be flattered. Actually, I'm Mike Duffy from the William Morris Agency."

Valentina shook his proffered hand. "I'm happy to meet you, Mike."

"To get right to the point, I have a proposal to talk to you about, Valentina, and after you hear what I've got to say, you're going to be very, very excited."

She grinned, won over by the spark of enthusiasm in the homely, cherubic agent's eyes.

"I wonder, Mike, but if you want to talk for five minutes, I guess we can have a cup of coffee. Then I have to run. I'm giving a party at my hotel." She unlocked the dressing room and entered, switching on lights.

She poured the coffee, and when she turned to hand Mike Duffy his cup, he had pulled a thick blue folder out of the briefcase he was carrying.

"This is for you, Valentina—it's the book for a Broadway musical called *Balalaika*. The book by Arthur Fleetwood Stearns, lyrics by Tony Trappista, and it might be the biggest musical to come out of Broadway in fifteen years. I'm not shitting you. I'd stake my whole damn career on it."

A balalaika was a Russian musical instrument, Valentina knew. So the play was Russian. And the names impressed her.

"A musical?" She stared at him, surprised. "But I'm a rock singer."

Duffy grinned. "I'm a visionary, and I'm a bit of a gambler, and I'm damn smart. I can spot a future Broadway star at twenty paces. Honey, you make the whole theater come alive. Sorta like Streisand or Liza Minnelli. You exude a wonderful charisma that audiences really dig. Besides which, you're absolutely gorgeous. Keith Leonard, the producer for this extravaganza, is going to love you."

Valentina stepped back, amused. The man sounded like P. T. Barnum. And yet she sensed that he was sincere.

"Let me get this straight. Are you saying that this play,

this *Balalaika* musical, is somehow for me? That you want me too . . .'' She tried to think of the right word.

"Audition. That's what I want you to do. I think this is the next step in your career, Valentina. The right step.''

The "cup of coffee" stretched on for forty minutes, as Duffy described the musical's story to her, and even made an attempt to hum some of the songs.

"Okay, okay, so I sound like a foghorn. But you see how good these tunes are. Two or three numbers are going to be hits, or I haven't been a Broadway agent for thirty years. Val,'' he went on earnestly, "you're a star now—but only a rock star. And you know what happens to most rock singers. They fade away in two or three years when the kids start creaming their jeans for some other new, more exciting talent.''

"I'm happy with my career,'' she responded.

"Yes, and it's wonderful, but Val . . . I'm talking major stardom here. I'm talking Streisand or Streep— having instant name recognition by ninety-nine point nine percent of all the people in the civilized world.''

Valentina set her cup down, laughing. "This sounds more like a Jackie Collins novel than real life.''

Duffy stared into his cup, then raised his eyes to gaze at her with blue intensity. "I admit it's a big gamble. We don't know for sure how you'll audition. The role does call for a lot of dancing, but I'm told you have a dance background— modern jazz and ballet, right? And your mother was a prima ballerina in the Bolshoi Ballet, too, right? It's gotta run in the family.''

She nodded, remembering the ten years of lessons that Peaches and Edgar had insisted she take three times a week. A strange thrill of excitement had begun to ripple through her. A Broadway musical? If it was a hit, she wouldn't have to give concerts and go on tour anymore. She could stay in one spot—become a regular person again instead of a frenetic rocker.

"Look,'' Duffy went on. "I want to represent you professionally. That's why I'm here. And auditions start in

New York in two days. I've told Keith Leonard I have a big surprise for him, and you're the surprise. I hope you don't let me down. I know it was presumptuous of me to commit you before I even talked to you, but Val . . . I have strong vibrations about this.''

''I'll think about it.''

''Fine, think. Thinking is good for the soul. But call me tomorrow morning, all right?''

''I'm not sure I can—''

He handed her the script. ''Read this, please. That's all I ask. I'm not going to pressure you—not too much anyway. But please phone me tomorrow and let me know what you think.''

In the limo on the way back to the Beverly Hills Hotel, Valentina couldn't resist opening the blue-jacketed script, and leafing through the pages. The show was about a Russian princess caught in the Revolution, and the main character, Tamara, was strong and tempestuous, a woman who fought hard for what she wanted—and got it.

By the time the limo pulled up in front of the hotel, Valentina's heart had begun to pound. Already she loved the character of Tamara. She adored the sharp, witty dialogue and the brilliant concept. And the songs had a certain quality . . . a hit quality!

Ten minutes later, she welcomed her guests, apologizing for her lateness. As she smiled and laughed and told humorous anecdotes about the tour, her mind was running wild.

Broadway!

She knew she could sing whatever songs they gave her. That was hardly a problem. But could she *act*? Could she project her personality over the footlights to a live audience? And even more important, could she dance? She'd danced some choreographed numbers while on tour, but Valentina knew that she was badly out of shape for any serious dancing.

After the last of her guests left, Valentina pored over the script until nearly dawn, finally putting it down as the first sunlight touched the drapes of her bungalow. She opened them, stepping onto a patio that gave a view of Los Angeles's fabled night lights, now slowly twinkling off.

She stared at the downtown LA skyline, unable to come to a decision. Duffy was right—the play *was* wonderful. But what about Blue Orchids? She could continue to make personal appearances on radio and television shows, and do studio sessions. Blue Orchid would remain in the public eye. And what about Orchid? What would she say . . . ?

She rubbed sleepily at her burning eyes. It was only five-thirty A.M., too early to call Duffy yet. Maybe she should try to sleep for a few hours. It might help clear her thoughts.

Sleep came to her almost at once, familiar dreams rushing in to fill the fevered spaces of her mind. She was a little girl again, riding the train that lumbered through the Caucasus mountains.

"Misha!" She screamed a warning in her sleep. *"Mikhail! Mikhail!"*

Afghanistan
1983

An azure sky arched overhead, a glowing bowl inverted over the gray-green Hindu Kush mountains that stretched to the horizon and would eventually reach the jagged Himalayas. Heat tremors seemed to crawl over the horizon.

Below the right wing of the Russian MiG jet aircraft, the village of Taloquan straddled the Fayzabad-Kunduz road. This was the northernmost sector of Afghanistan—the one nearest the Soviet border.

Mikhail Sandovsky, strapped into the canopied cockpit of his Flogger B fighter plane, gazed down at this spectacle with grim appreciation. The fierce sky and folded grays and blues of this primitive country seemed to touch some melancholy portion of his mind.

So beautiful the country, so futile the effort to control it. He was deathly tired of killing.

He banked to the right, circling for another pass at the village, where several buildings were reported to contain hidden gasoline storage tanks.

The Russian MiG was a fighter-interceptor, and was equipped with a GSH-23 L twin-barrel 23-mm gun in a ventral common pack. There were also rocket packs, air-to-air missiles, and four AA-8 Aphid missiles underneath the air intake ducts, in addition to two AA-7 Apex missiles on the underwing pylons.

He was flying a death machine and had already killed— *How many? How many?*

He briefly shut his eyes as the plane climbed toward the fierce glare of the high-altitude sun. Puffs of distant smoke rose, the smoke feathering out into the air, dissipated by the wind currents that blew off the Hindu Kush.

He wanted to become a cosmonaut. It was an ambition he could strive for—entering space—because it was clean and pure, and involved no strafing and bombing of innocent women and children in an invasion he abhorred.

But first there was this six-month tour in Afghanistan to finish. He had not had a normal night's sleep in five months, and had lost more than twenty pounds. Despite this, he had received several commendations from his superiors, which had resulted in his earning the Cross of Lenin and the Red Star, two coveted medals.

On that, they could not fault him. They did not have to know the rest—his nightmares, his recurring dreams of a dark-haired girl who screamed his name in warning, over and over. *Mikhail! Mikhail! Mikhail!*

He heard the crackle of his radio—voices of other pilots cursing about the lack of ground support troops. He only half listened. It did not matter . . . not in the long run. He did not really believe he would leave Afghanistan alive.

There was a blip of radar to his left. A small rebel-owned World War II American B-26, a Marauder, a vintage bomber that had been modified, showed high at 12:00. Mikhail banked the MiG steeply; at the same time he felt more than saw the hissing, deadly rocket flare hit his plane.

* * *

Stars pierced the Afghani sky, sharp jewels pinned on a cloak of night. They lit the black-on-black outline of the folded mountains. The cold, thin air was full of the scent of smoke, death, and dying.

Mikhail gasped in shallow mouthfuls of oxygen. A band of pain encircled his ribs, stabbing his left lung. Deep lacerations on his chest had bled profusely all over his bluish-gray flight suit. His right leg had gone from agony to numbness and he knew it was broken in several places.

He had no awareness of the time, or how he had managed to jettison his canopy and release his parachute, which had landed on a slope after his plane had been hit. *A miracle,* he thought, *if such existed.*

He lay on his back in the harsh, dry undergrowth. The cold air already leached the energy from him. At night, he knew, the heat quickly left the rocks, drawn out by the thinness of the atmosphere. He realized that he could easily die of exposure by morning.

It seemed to help his breathing if he supported himself on both elbows. Breathing shallowly around the pain of his broken ribs, he felt the huge pressure of the sky pressing down on him, the towering majesty of the Hindu Kush. An existential despair filled him. Why was he here? Was it all some gigantic cosmic joke with no real meaning—only pain?

He was only twenty-four years old. His life had been one of conformity, not rebellion. He'd had women but just as an act of taking, not as love. He had never had a real friend, just drinking companions, pilots like himself who tried to bury their feelings in vodka. Now, in the dim glow of starlight, he questioned it all.

Suddenly Mikhail heard a sound—a pebble sliding down a long, rocky scree. Then stealthy footsteps. His breath froze in his throat. An animal? Some mountain goat traversing the hills at night? Some night creature emerging to prowl?

No. Human.

Another pebble. Another step. Despite the chill, Mikhail

felt sweat dampen his skin. He slowly drew his 9-mm automatic from its leg holster.

If it was an Afghani rebel he would be dead within minutes if he was lucky. Mikhail's lips moved in a silent, forbidden prayer that the intruder was part of a Russian rescue mission.

Chapter
Twelve

IN AN ESTANCIA about twenty miles outside of Buenos
Aires, a twenty-four-year-old woman named María Cristina
Ramirez hurried through her bedroom, collecting her
makeup.

It was to be the French edition of *Vogue* this time, her
third appearance on the cover. Her sultry South American
beauty was becoming fashionable, and her husband, Tomás,
a Colombian by birth and a rich industrialist, "permitted"
her to model, provided it did not interfere with her wifely
duties.

He had no idea what she really did on her modeling trips.

"Señora?" inquired her maid, Rafaella. "Do you wish
the large bag with the wheels?"

"I want the same bag I always take and no other,"
snapped María Cristina, her nerves strung tight. "And
please, do not touch it. I will pack it myself—as always."

Her model's makeup kit always had to be carried on, for
fear it would be lost by the airline before a shoot.

The sound of children's laughter penetrated through
María's bedroom windows. Her husband was playing with
their two children on the sward of perfect green that ran
within a few feet of the rambling bunk quarters that housed
almost fifty gauchos. Munching corn out of their three-year-
old son's hands was Blanco, one of the ten miniature pet
ponies that Tomás Zetina Ramirez had imported to roam his
two thousand acre cattle ranch. He was one of the richest

109

men in the world, his family owning cattle ranches, hotels, and rubber plantations in Brazil. María Cristina eyed the scene with possessive satisfaction. Tomás, although forty and graying, was still very handsome and virile. The two little boys romping with him, one and a half and three years old, had inherited her own dark-eyed, flashing good looks.

She looked away from her family, sighing with anticipation. She hadn't slept last night, so excited was she at the prospect of her "business." It only happened a few times a year, but *Jesu Cristo,* when it did, the thrill was so deep, so complete, that it kept her going for months.

For the second time, María Cristina counted the crisp American hundred-dollar bills before she stuffed them into the hidden lining she'd had sewn into her custom-made suitcase.

Tomás knew nothing about the money. Or her real destination, when she'd finished the two-day photographic job in Paris that he thought was going to take seven days.

María Cristina picked up the telephone to summon their driver to take her to the airport. Then she walked out through the Dutch doors to say good-bye to her husband and children.

"*Mia amante,*" said Tomás, patting the tiny pony on the rump to send it away. He pulled her to him for an embrace. "Have a good trip."

"Of course I will," she murmured, smiling.

"I'm going to miss you—in our bed."

"And I you," she told him, but of course it wasn't true. He never gave her a strong climax, not like she gave herself when she was working.

She had been home for almost three months now and was anxious to be working again. She wasn't going to miss him at all. She could hardly wait to be gone.

The shoot, in Paris, went as planned, and María Cristina gave it one hundred percent of her sultry best. The photographer was so enamored of her that he attempted to lure her into his bed, an offer she coolly refused by telling him that her husband was prominently involved in the drug cartel. A lie, but she enjoyed watching the reaction on men's faces when she told them the story.

By late evening she was on a British Airways flight to Kennedy International, where she would transfer to an American Airlines flight to Honolulu, then a third, twenty-minute hop to Maui. She no longer wore the fashionable dark green silk trouser suit she'd worn to Paris. Now it was the nondescript Levi's and UCLA T-shirt of a graduate student. Even her walk had subtly changed, becoming that of a striding, slightly mannish woman student. Without makeup, her face became ordinary, and no one looked at her.

When she was a teenager in the *barrio* she'd fought her way to the leadership of a gang that called themselves Los Tigres Negros, the Black Tigers. And she'd discovered her one big talent was mimicry. She could look like almost anyone she wanted . . . almost become them. She could alter her body language so convincingly that even her own husband once had not recognized her. María had capitalized on these skills by learning how to use all the professional tricks of disguise—wigs, plastics, makeup, spirit gum, glasses, clothing, artificial moles, and other devices.

In the air over the Atlantic she leaned back in her seat, allowing her new identity to seep into her and penetrate the very pores of her body.

Araña. The word in Spanish meant spider, and the image made her think of a lethal female black widow. Much more exciting than her usual dull role of housewife, mother, and bedmate.

Assassin.

Araña checked into the Wailea Beach Hotel on Maui, using a forged passport. The luxury hotel overlooked the turquoise ocean and the rocky islets of Kaahulawe and Molokini, with the bigger island of Lanai visible as a blue haze on the horizon. But she didn't care about the gorgeous setting, except as it pertained to her purpose.

She wondered if her target, Bill Lowery, and his girl-friend, Maggie Tisdale, had checked in on schedule. Lowery was a congressman from a California district near San Francisco, and, as a ranking member of the Interstate and Energy Committee in Washington, was an avowed foe of certain Japanese business interests. He believed in strict tariffs on Japanese imports. The Japanese cartel wanted to get rid of him.

She stepped to her suitcase and, after making sure her door was bolted against intrusion by the maids, began assembling the automatic weapon she had picked up in a storage locker at the Kahului airport. It was equipped with a state-of-the-art silencer and, when fired, sounded not much louder than a drawer closing.

When she had the weapon assembled, she carefully concealed it in a shopping bag and dressed in shorts and the UCLA T-shirt. She used a reddish makeup to add the characteristic ''red lobster'' sunburn of a newly arrived tourist. Her last act was to step into flip-flop sandals of the sort available at any Hawaiian drugstore, and pick up a big, floppy straw purse.

Then she left the room, putting the Do Not Disturb sign on the door.

Time to reconnoiter.

Maybe her target would be in the bar—that was where she'd start first.

Congressman Bill Lowery and his girlfriend of two years, Maggie Tisdale, were in the middle of an argument as they left the large bar area, both of them slightly high on the huge piña coladas the hotel was famous for. He was fifty years old and somewhat overweight, his face floridly red from three days in Honolulu before arriving here. She was in her late thirties, and carefully made up.

''I saw you staring at her,'' Maggie accused. ''Those big silicone boobs were practically spilling out of that little bikini top. You ought to be ashamed of yourself, Bill. At least you could have the courtesy not to leer when I'm with you. How do you think that makes me feel?''

''It should make you feel complimented,'' Bill retorted,

slurring his words slightly. "I'm with you, so you must look pretty damn good too."

"Bullshit," wrangled Maggie. "In fact—"

Sauntering several paces behind, carrying a large shopping bag from a bathing-suit boutique in nearby Kihei, was Araña.

A few seconds after the congressman and his girlfriend stepped into their room, Araña knocked on the door.

"Who is it?" came Lowery's voice.

"Maid," called Araña.

Lowery pulled open the door and Araña swiftly stepped inside. As she closed the door behind her, she brought up the shopping bag in one, smooth motion. Maggie Tisdale was standing by the dresser, her blouse half unbuttoned.

"What the—" Lowery began.

Maggie uttered a sharp, small shriek, and lunged for the telephone.

Araña shot her first. The semi-automatic pistol emitted a tiny, metallic cough that was muffled by the room's thick carpeting. The woman collapsed, looking astonished as a red hole bloomed in the middle of her chest. A second later, Araña drilled Lowery in the forehead. Red sprayed out from his features in a gory nimbus. Then he sagged downward.

Araña had been in the room approximately seven seconds. She clicked the door bolt into a locked position. All had gone well; she hadn't been thwarted. Gloating over the bodies she had killed made her feel invincible. God, such a rush—if her husband ever knew, if he could ever see her face at times like this—

Araña dropped a small, cheap plastic spider onto the corpse of Lowery—her signature.

Then she went into their bathroom and leisurely showered, standing with her legs spread while she rubbed her body with the slick soap. Braced in the stream of warm water, Araña stroked herself to an exploding orgasm that rocked her so that she fell backward against the tile.

Still aroused, she brought herself off again, this time more slowly.

Finally, weak with the release of tension, she stepped out
of the shower, toweled off, and then strolled naked into the
room. She pulled out several articles from the shopping
bag—a leaf-green and yellow flowered beach dress, a pair
of green huaraches, a frizzy blond wig.

Within seconds, she had applied makeup, inserted a small
prosthesis into her mouth to change the appearance of her
teeth, and slipped into the hallway. She walked back to the
elevator, a blond, gaudy lady tourist with slightly protruding
teeth apparently on her way to her room to dress for dinner.

Her heart was still pounding. There was nothing better
than killing—nothing in this world. Now that she'd let
herself loose on this one, she was ravenous to do it
again—soon. In fact, maybe she'd call her brother, Jacinto,
tonight, in Buenos Aires, to see if he could get another
assignment for her from some other clique. Americans,
British, Greek, it didn't make any difference to her.

New York
1985

Valentina hurried toward the Nederlander Theater, the
old Billy Rose Theater on Forty-first Street that had recently
been purchased by the Nederlander family.

The stage door was marked Authorized Personnel Only.
Mary Martin had used that door, and Carol Channing and
John Barrymore. She felt a ripple of excitement, a sense of
joining a tradition that dated back to the days of Edwin
Booth.

The guard told Valentina where to find her dressing
room, and she hurried down a beige-painted corridor
covered with posters of former Broadway shows, lugging a
garment bag that contained the dress she'd wear, and a
supply of theatrical makeup.

She found a room filled with young women in various
stages of undress, and as she entered, the chatter stopped.

"It's *Valentina*," someone half whispered.

"Oh, just great," muttered a girl with an enormous head

of frizzy black hair. "*She's* already got the part locked . . . no sense in us even trying."

"Y'all jealous?" snapped a tall redhead. "We don't have to be rude, *do we*? What room are you looking for, Valentina? I bet they gave you the one next door . . . that's a star's room."

"Thank you." Valentina managed an embarrassed smile, backing out of the room.

The redhead followed her. "Hey," she explained. "You know how it is. Most of us would kill to get a part and things can get bitchy sometimes. I'm Jinna Jones," she added, extending her hand. "I audition for everything. I probably won't even make the first cut on this production, but who knows?" She shrugged. "Anyway, good luck to you. *You* have a great chance of making it . . . if you can dance. They say this show is heavy on the dancing and that's the big problem. They can't find any name singers who can really dance and act too."

In the third row of empty, darkened theater, six un-enthused production people sat with clipboards, making notations on the day's lineup of hopefuls for the part of Tamara. They included the director, the lyricist/playwright, the choreographer, librettist/composer, casting director, and producer—all big names in their field with a collection of twenty-four Tonys, ten Obies, and five Bessies among them.

A short girl, number forty-three in today's lineup, stood onstage bathed in one strong yellow spotlight, cradling the mike as she sang a version of Streisand's "People."

"She's not too bad," ventured Art Stearns, the small, nervous-looking playwright who had written the book, and seemed frightened because they hadn't cast Tamara yet despite four months of auditions and a number of disagreements.

"Oh, just another mediocre cunt," sighed Tony Trappista, the lyricist.

"If I hear one more singer screeching that she needs people, I'm going to fucking heave," snapped Bettina

Orlovsky, the choreographer, a forty-five-year-old former
Martha Graham dancer who was thinly attractive, her body
all angular lines. "Thanks, honey," she called up toward
the stage. "We'll be in touch."

Shoulders sagging, the singer exited the stage. Everyone
knew that "thanks," said in that way, meant rejection.

Keith Leonard, the producer, seated next to Bettina,
stifled a grin. His production staff was the best in the
business, chosen for their talent, not their charm, and
he intended to stretch them to the utmost. He'd gambled
more than a million dollars on *Balalaika,* and convinced his
backers to put up another two.

He sighed with the exhaustion born of sitting up yet
another night with his wife, Cynthia, who, at the age of
thirty-six, had suffered two heart attacks from mitral valve
prolapse, and lived in terror of a third. Poor Cynthia kept
apologizing for inconveniencing him, and when she finally
drifted to sleep, Keith had spent the rest of the night pacing
his study, worrying about the damned show.

There had to be somebody out there who could sing like
Julie Andrews, dance like Gwen Verdon, and act like Mary
Martin. All he needed was just *one.*

"Next," barked Bettina Orlovsky, with an aside to Tony,
"Isn't this number forty-four?"

A beautiful woman emerged from the darkened wings at
stage right, walking toward the stationary mike. She wore a
sea-green charmeuse sheath that clung to the lines of her
flawless figure, and her hair was a riot of black curls that
tumbled over her shoulders.

"Migawd. Is that who I think it is?" asked Milton
Comden, the composer.

Keith narrowed his eyes. She did look familiar.

"I believe this is Mike Duffy's little 'surprise,'" he
murmured as Valentina stepped to the mike and sang the
first bars of "Don't Leave Me Now."

At the mike, Valentina lost herself in the familiar,
Grammy-winning ballad. It seemed strange to sing to an
almost empty theater, but she gave it her best, half expecting

a voice to stop her momentarily and tell her they'd "be in touch."

No one interrupted her.

She continued to the end of the song, giving the last notes an extra push.

The crystal notes vibrated, stunningly pure. Jubilantly, Keith made a mental note to take Mike Duffy to lunch—no, make that dinner at the Four Seasons. Valentina Lederer, of Blue Orchids, had charisma that sizzled across the footlights.

The others felt it too. He could tell by the way they had stopped fidgeting or doodling in their notebooks, giving her their rapt attention. Even Mel Parkington, the director, gazed toward the stage mesmerized.

"Very, *very* nice," Keith called up to the stage as Valentina finished. "Come back here tomorrow, ten A.M., and we'll audition you on your acting and dancing. Bring a scene to read, and a five-minute dance number."

Valentina froze, seemingly startled.

"You *do* have something you can dance to, darling?" drawled Bettina.

"Why . . . yes."

As Valentina exited, Bettina turned to Keith with a sour, I-told-you-so smile. "She's amateur hour."

"No she isn't," Keith said.

"Hell, we all know she can sing. But can she dance and act? That's the real question, and I for one don't think she can."

"Wait and see, Bettina. This time, you're wrong."

"We'll see," Bettina said, with a knowing smirk.

Valentina flew out of the theater. They'd called her back—she did have a chance! She realized now just how badly she wanted the part of Tamara, how desperately she needed a new challenge.

It had begun to rain, and she unfurled her back umbrella and ran out into the street, trying to hail one of the taxis that plowed past in sprays of water. But as one pulled up, reality hit Valentina.

She'd only passed the easy part of the audition.

"Where you wanna go?" inquired the cabbie.

"I . . . Steps, on Broadway at Seventy-fourth," she said, naming a well-known studio for Broadway dancers.

Maybe they could help her with her dance routine. She glanced at her Cartier watch. It was only four o'clock. There was still plenty of time left in the day—and she'd be willing to work half the night if necessary. It would probably be necessary.

On the third floor of the dance studio, professional ballet dancers warmed up at the barre and a class of precocious teenagers were doing exquisitely perfect jetés and pirouette combinations. Every muscle in Valentina's body ached from the severe workout she was getting from the instructor who had agreed to coach her on the routine she had selected for the dance audition.

"You have the talent," Gail Etter, one of the more famous instructors, assured her. "And you pick up things fast, thank God." Elena Kunikova, another instructor, agreed with her. "All we can do in one night, though, is to polish you off—smooth out your rough edges. That will have to be enough."

Elena added, "If you need some extra coaching, I can probably work out some studio time with you, but not for a few days."

After two hours, Valentina took a much-needed break. At a telephone in the hallway, she dialed Orchid's hotel room.

"Yeah?" Orchid picked up on the seventh ring.

"Orchie . . . it's me."

"We've gotta make this fast, Roman is here," Orchid burbled. "An' he's *not* fast. Good lord, is that classical music I hear in the background? Where are you calling from, Val?"

"I'm at Steps now. I'm working on my dance routine. Orchid, I have the most wonderful news—"

There was a moment of silence. Valentina had tried

several days ago to tell Orchid about the Broadway play but her sister had refused to listen. Now Orchid said, "I *told* you, I don't want to hear about it, Val."

"Orchid—"

Orchid's voice shook. "This is going to change everything. Don't you care about Blue Orchids? *Don't you care at all?*"

"I'm not doing this to hurt you, or to hurt Blue Orchids. I'll do the next album, there'll be plenty of time for studio sessions, and we can work out a schedule for personal appear—"

"Bull*shit* you will! What about concerts? How can you go on tour if you're stuck in New York doing a stupid musical? Val . . . please . . . don't do this. Please! I *need* Blue Orchids," Orchid pleaded pitifully.

"Oh, Orchie," Valentina began, about to give in. Her sister's distress tore at her. Was being in a Broadway show worth hurting someone she loved so much?

"Anyway," Orchid interrupted, "if you keep on with that silly, stupid idea, I'm gonna make you sorry . . . you just wait! I'll—I'll get a lawyer or something. I really will, Val!"

"What?"

"You heard me," Orchid snapped. "Remember your committment to Blue Orchids, Val . . . or you'll be very, very sorry." She slammed down the phone in Valentina's ear.

"Valentina, we're ready again."

"What? Oh . . . oh, yes." Cheeks burning, Valentina set the pay phone back in its cradle, and walked back into the studio again. How could Orchid say such a thing?

But as she worked harder, straining on the strenuous combinations, something hardened inside Valentina. It *was* time to take the next step.

She decided to go ahead with the audition.

She'd do her best to smooth Orchid's ruffled feathers later.

By the next day, a pelting rain had turned into a real storm. Heavy winds, sweeping down from Canada, had battered the city all night, and there were sporadic power outages, causing New Yorkers to remember apprehensively the mammoth blackout of 1965.

Emerging from a cab in front of the theater, Valentina clutched her Burberry trench coat shut against the wind, and fought an umbrella that wanted to turn itself inside out. Every muscle in her body groaned from the hours of rehearsal last night, but she'd downed three cups of coffee and felt ready.

A sudden crash sent her reeling backward.

Her bent umbrella had collided with another umbrella—one of the hazards of rainy days on the crowded city sidewalks.

"Hey, are you all right?" She heard a burst of warm male laughter. When she lowered the black silk, she found herself looking into the smiling face of a man in his late thirties.

"Sure, but I think my umbrella has had it," she said, holding up the umbrella, which had a long rip in its fabric.

"Here, have mine."

"Oh, no, I couldn't—"

"Of course you can. I have at least six of them in my closet at home, maybe seven. I seem to get another one every year on my birthday."

He pressed his umbrella into her hands, and looking down at the handle, Valentina noticed that it was handcarved in some deep, rich wood, far more expensive than her own. It was still warm from his touch.

He wasn't handsome—not exactly—but he had deep-set blue eyes and a soft accent. His features were Marlboro Man rugged, his mouth generous but firm, and his full head of glossy brown hair had a few attractive strands of gray at the temples. "Are you going into the theater . . . Valentina?"

She laughed. He'd recognized her all along and had been gently teasing her. But who was he? They entered the door together, and when she signed the register, Valentina saw his signature: Keith Leonard.

"Oh!" she cried involuntarily. "You're— That is, you're—" She had auditioned for him yesterday but the theater had been so dimly lit that she hadn't been able to see any faces.

"One of your greatest fans."

Onstage Bettina worked with eight female dancers, warming them up, including Valentina, teaching them a set of rather basic routines, then watching carefully to see how fast they could pick up new material. Later, each dancer would perform her own five-minute routine to backup music.

Leaning back in his third-row seat, Keith inspected the eight women, discovering that his eyes were constantly drawn to Valentina Lederer. It wasn't just because she was the most beautiful. Her stage presence was so strong that she made the other dancers seem faded by comparison.

And she had a lovely smile, he remembered from their encounter outside the stage door.

Impatiently he watched as the dancers began their individual routines. One, dancing to "Dry Bones," was amusing and light, and he thought she might make a good second lead. But when Valentina began her fiery takeoff on a Russian cossack dance, he leaned forward, his heart beginning to pound.

She commanded the stage with her physicality, just what he was looking for. She'd light up *Balalaika* and make it blaze.

"She stinks," Bettina flared up, later that night. "I mean, Keith, she just can't cut it."

They'd been arguing for hours, taking time out to consume some takeout from Pongsri Thai, at Broadway and Eighth.

"She was wonderful," he insisted. Mel Parkington nodded agreement. "She has it, Bettina . . . the quality I want. She lights up the whole damn stage. I couldn't keep my eyes off her, and I know damn well I wasn't the only one who felt that way."

"She does look like Tamara," agreed Art Stearns. Loren

Gray and Bruce Rosen, two of the important backers, who had wandered into the theater for the audition, nodded.

"But she stumbled around like Topsy," snapped Bettina. "Dammit, I've got my reputation on the line here too. I *need* this production, Keith—and I don't intend to fuck it up by bringing in a rock star who thinks she can be a dancer. High school ballet," she sneered. "I mean, really! This whole production swings on dancing and now you want to compromise that."

"But she does have presence," put in Parkington. "And her name. We can't forget her name. People will come just to see her, and they don't give a fuck whether she can dance or not. I like her—a lot."

"Mel is right," Keith began, thinking about his prerogative as final authority. He knew in his gut how right Valentina was for the show. She had touched him in some way he couldn't describe. It was better, though, to have them see it on their own. Mel's support was important.

"But she isn't a terrific *dancer*," the choreographer insisted stubbornly, puffing on a menthol light. "Dammit, I want terrific, and I'm going to get terrific, or I don't stay with this production."

A silence fell around the table.

"You admit, Bettina, that she does have presence."

"Well, yes."

"That she has a name."

Bettina blew out a long curl of smoke. "Yes."

"How did she do on the combinations you taught her?" Keith persisted.

"She was quick, but—"

"*Very* quick?"

"I'd say yes, but that doesn't mean—"

Keith pounded his fist down on the tabletop, rattling their coffee cups. "All right," he cried triumphantly. "Mel and Bettina, will you buy this? I have a proposition. I think Valentina will make this production and I want her—bad. Give me four weeks prerehearsal time. I'll see that she gets intensive coaching in dance and acting. If she can't hack it by then, she's out and another actress gets Tamara."

There was another silence. All seven faces were now riveted on him. They all knew a name like Valentina's would insure advance box office appeal for the show.

"You're a crazy son of a bitch," Mel finally said.

"But a smart one," Keith said, grinning.

His good mood continued on the train to Connecticut, where he and his wife, Cynthia, had a large home in the village of Wilton, not far from Stamford and Darien.

He'd tell Valentina himself, he decided. He could hardly wait to hear the excitement in her husky-sweet voice as he gave her the news. He hoped she'd be willing to take the gamble.

At the train station in Norwalk, he exited the train and walked across the track to the nearly deserted parking lot to pick up his dark blue Mercedes convertible. Without an umbrella, the rain pelted on his face, dampening his collar.

He drove home. Even at night, the Connecticut woods, with their meandering old stone fences, were lovely. Within an hour's commute from New York, the area catered to CEOs of major companies, ABC and NBC network executives, big-time attorneys, arbitrageurs and junk bond dealers, and wealthy entertainers such as Dave Brubeck, George C. Scott, and Regis Philbin, who had lived in Wilton for years.

His home was off Wolfpit Road, near the South Norwalk Reservoir, a Georgian-style mansion with two wings that had been recently assessed at four million dollars.

"Is that you, Keithie?" Cynthia inquired as he entered their bedroom. A hardcover book was on her lap. A long-time insomniac, she only slept three or four hours a night, and spent the rest of the time devouring novels by Danielle Steel, Judith Krantz, and Janet Dailey.

"Yes, hon. Got tied up in a production meeting—but I got my way," he told his wife with satisfaction.

She didn't ask how he had gotten his way. The ins and outs of theatrical productions seldom interested Cynthia. She gazed at him, smiling vaguely, a petite woman with beautifully styled blond hair and elegant skin that was beginning to show the effects of ten years of illness.

"Well, at least you're back," she crooned, patting the empty place on the bed beside her. "Maybe we can cuddle up for a few minutes before you go to sleep. I need my cuddling."

Keith nodded. He knew "cuddling" was not a euphemism for making love, but meant a few minutes of rather dry hugging before both of them turned over and tried to sleep. Even on their honeymoon, Cynthia's passion had been lukewarm, and now they only had sex once a month or less. But Cynthia loved him and depended on him . . . and he loved her too. Perhaps not passionately, but there was a deep connection and he never forgot that.

He began to undress. "Your shirt collar looks damp," Cynthia remarked.

"I—forgot my umbrella," he told her.

"I'll call Bergdorf's and order another one for you then," she said comfortably.

Keith climbed into bed, switched out the bedside light, and dutifully offered his wife the requisite hug.

The next morning, Valentina phoned Mike Duffy to tell him how the audition had gone and to feel him out discreetly about Keith Leonard.

"Honey lamb," Mike Duffy said. "Keith Leonard is a fireball who's been setting Broadway back on its ass for the last ten years. He's got so many Tonys crowding his shelf that there isn't any room for the bric à brac. He has the reputation for making stars. But you know all that. You're from a theater family too."

"Is he . . . that is . . . is he . . . ?"

"Spit it out, girl," Duffy said, amused. "Is he straight? Hell, yes. He's also very, very married. A lot of women have tried to tempt him but he's loyal to Cynthia, which is pretty damn unusual in this day and age. A classy guy," he finished.

"Wonderful," she said, stifling a pang of disappointment.

Half an hour later, Keith himself called. He outlined his proposal, emphasizing that it would be hard, grinding work for only Actors' Equity scale, and she could still end up losing the role of Tamara to another actress.

"You mean that I'm to be on probation . . . that I might work my crackers off and still not get the part?" she repeated.

"Think of it this way. If you do make it, you have a chance to become a great actress and a Broadway star of true magnitude. Isn't that worth a four-week gamble?"

"Of course," she said after a slight hesitation.

"Yes, but I don't hear real enthusiasm in your voice," Keith probed. "Are you able to do the work that's going to be necessary? I told you, it's going to be a stiff regimen. It will be a total bitch."

Valentina laughed. "Anyone's who's done a rock tour of forty cities is used to a stiff regimen."

"That's the kind of answer I like," Keith said, his voice lowering slightly.

"Fine," she agreed, feeling a new thrill. Keith Leonard was definitely exciting. But she knew she had to put him out of her mind . . . *that* way, anyhow. She had no intention of being hurt.

Valentina hurried into Cafe San Martin, a Basque-inspired Spanish restaurant on First Avenue between Seventy-fifth and Seventy-sixth streets. Her heart was pounding fitfully.

She'd arranged to meet Orchid here . . . they had to talk.

She nodded to Ramón, the owner, and allowed herself to be shown to a table. Several of the other diners looked up as she entered, admiring her in her elegantly shaped Anne Klein textured wool jacket in a subtle shade of tea leaf.

The air smelled deliciously of the restaurant's specialty, paella a la Valenciana.

Her Perrier was finished and she was impatiently reading the menu when Orchid breezed in, thirty minutes later. Heads turned as Orchid strode to the table. She wore a bright teal Perry Ellis jumpsuit that made her frizzy auburn hair look almost Lucy red. A teal-blue headband, almost matching the color of her eyes, completed her look.

"I was shopping," she announced. "I'm getting some new costumes made—really smashing with lots and lots of black sequins and beadwork. I think it's time for a change with Blue Orchids, Val. Sexier costumes, more revealing. Also, I'm thinking about getting silicone implants. I like the rounder look in boobs."

"If we get any more revealing we'll be naked," Valentina murmured, watching as Orchid settled herself at the table in quick, nervous motions.

"Orchid—" she began, just as her sister said, "Val—I hope you—"

They both stopped.

"You first," Orchid mumbled.

"Orchie . . ." Valentina struggled for the right words. There were areas of difficulty between them now, little land mines, around which both had to tread carefully.

"Yeah, yeah, yeah," Orchid prompted. "Go on, say it. You took the fucking part, didn't you? You're going to play Tamara." The way she said the name, it was almost a sneer.

"Yes. I am going to take it, if I can. But first I have to put in four weeks of—"

Orchid sprang up from the table. Her face was beet-red and her eyes blazed fire.

"So you've really done it! Well, don't think that you're going to get away with it, Val—because you're not!"

"Orchid—please . . ."

"I don't *need* you!" Orchid shrieked. With a violent gesture, Orchid picked up the edge of the table and tipped it toward Valentina, sending glasses of water and the remains of her Perrier flying into her lap.

As Valentina gasped, and several waiters came running, Orchid yelled, "Blue Orchids is broken up, dammit! You're a lousy traitor! I don't ever want to see you or talk to you again, Val!"

Orchid swung away from the table and hurried out of the restaurant.

"Are you all right, miss?" inquired a horrified waiter.

"Yes," Valentina haltingly whispered, staring after her sister with tears in her eyes.

By the following morning, the news of Blue Orchids' split-up had made all the tabloids and the evening news. Several of the diners in Cafe San Martin had been coaxed to give their versions of the quarrel. *Star* and *The National Enquirer* ran full-length photos of Orchid and Valentina in their sexiest costumes—faced away from each other.

Valentina's phone began ringing off the hook with phone calls from reporters, columnists, and friends in the record business, as well as officials at Arista Records, where they now had their recording contract. To all of them Valentina insisted that it was just a routine quarrel, a disagreement that would be smoothed over. She wanted to leave the door open for Orchid if she should change her mind.

Early in the afternoon Peaches phoned to ask what had happened. She and Edgar were in LA, where Edgar was completing one of his many theater deals. The Lederers had bought a second home in Bel Air.

"It's only temporary," Valentina insisted, her voice hoarse with crying.

"Is it, dear?" Peaches sounded troubled. "Maybe you don't realize, Val, just how much Blue Orchids means to your sister. Somehow she's found her entire identity in it, and now you've taken that identity away."

"*I* took it away?" cried Valentina, beginning to sob. "She's the one who broke it up, not me. My being in a play wouldn't have hurt Blue Orchids—I was still planning to make records, and do some concerts—" She broke down.

"Oh, honey," said Peaches softly. "I know how much this must hurt you. But look on the bright side—now each of you may have the opportunity to see what you can do on your own."

"I don't want to be on my own, not without Orchid," Valentina wept.

But she knew she had no choice. Blue Orchids was finished, at least for now!

Chapter
Thirteen

Moscow
1985

SNOW WAS FALLING on the seven-story headquarters of the KGB building in Dzerzhinsky Square. It dusted the crenellations of the ornate, wedding-cake rococo building, and whitened the ugly windows of the multistoried extension to the original building, built during World War II by political prisoners and German POWs.

For a few hours, the new-fallen snow would remain white and pure, but soon the soot of Moscow's wood fires and smokestack industries would blacken the snow, turning it as foul and insidiously dark as what went on inside this building.

"*We* are among the very few privileged to use this main entrance," Petrov boasted to Mikhail as they walked briskly toward the entrance of the original building, where there was now a large bas-relief of Karl Marx. "Only important officials can use this door—the rest of the staff has to use the six side entrances."

Mikhail gazed at his father. Comrade General Vladimir Petrov wore an official's black wool coat with sable collar, his once thick black hair now thinning and grizzled with gray, deep lines scoring his face. But Petrov was still as ambitious as ever, as determined that Mikhail should accomplish in the KGB hierarchy what he himself could not.

Petrov had used his influence to have Mikhail admitted to the KGB training school. The injuries he received in

Afghanistan meant he could never become a cosmonaut—that dream, nourished for years, had been destroyed along with the lacerated flesh of his body.

In a field hospital in Afghanistan, he'd swung between life and death for several days as his body battled painful wounds on his torso, a severe wound infection, and the fracture of four ribs and his right leg.

He'd known then that he could never be a cosmonaut, and he hadn't wanted to live. Why should he? Life was as dirty as the snow that now lay in the streets of the Kremlin, and he wanted no part of it. The rocket that hit his MiG fighter had killed something far more important than his body—it had killed his spirit.

He'd pulled out his own IV several times, and once had gone into cardiac arrest, revived by an angry woman doctor, who had screamed at him and cursed, "Live, live! You must live! You are a Soviet hero!"

Somehow his body hadn't listened to his mind and had healed. He was now in the worst possible place for him, KGB Headquarters. But he didn't feel much of anything these days. He was anesthetized—numbed to his emotions now. It was safer that way.

At the building entrance, Mikhail's face was stony as he presented his KGB visitor's permit to a guard, who scrutinized it for several minutes, then stamped the time. Guards, Mikhail knew, would be stationed every twenty yards throughout the building. Each check would be time-stamped, and so would his departure. No unexplained gap would be allowed in this security procedure that ran like clockwork.

"Ah," his father kept saying as they passed each checkpoint. "Ah . . ."

Their footsteps echoed hollowly in the hallways, which were high ceilinged and dark. Heavy wooden paneling, installed before 1939, had blackened still further with the passage of time.

They paused in front of a door marked with the name of Arkady Lessiovsky, head of the GRU, the Glavnoe Raz-

vedyvatelnoe Upravlenie, a spy and assassin branch of the
KGB.

"Remember," Petrov whispered. "This meeting is just a
formality. Everything is set for you to go to 'Department V.'
I have used my influence to get you this position and you
must not let me down. You are the cream of the Soviet
young men—the wave of the future."

He knocked and almost at once the door swung open. A
male assistant ushered them inside to an anteroom furnished
in heavy oak furniture made in Siberia. Windows looked out
toward Levoforto Investigations Prison, a nearby building
even more dreaded than the one they were in.

They were taken to an interior room, big and overheated,
where a man sat behind an enormous desk, behind framed
pictures of Lenin, Andropov, and Khrushchev. He was
about fifty-five, heavy looking, with an impassive face and
a knobby, once broken nose. His mouth was thin and cruel.

"So you are Comrade Major Mikhail Gregorivich Sandovsky."

Mikhail nodded, keeping his own face as stony as
Lessiovsky's. He wore his army uniform, freshly pressed
and resplendent—the garb of a hero—and his posture was
superb. His leg had healed perfectly and there was no sign
of a limp.

"You are much decorated, I see," Lessiovsky said,
turning a page in a thick report he had opened on his
desk. Mikhail could see several official photographs of
himself, his fingerprints, various stamps, and lines of
closely spaced type. "The Red Star, among others. And a
glorious war wound."

"Yes."

"Pfah! That is nothing—that was easy!" Lessiovsky
suddenly jumped to his feet, pounding on the desktop with
a fist. The sound echoed in the huge, high-ceilinged room.
"Any good man can be decorated in battle, under the heat
of passion—that stands for nothing! What we will ask of
you is harder. We will ask the ultimate—we will ask your
total, unmitigated devotion. You will become a machine . . .
our machine. You will do as we ask . . . when we ask. Are
you prepared to do that?"

Mikhail hesitated. A sick feeling welled up from his stomach, sour acid spilling up into his throat.

"Well?" Lessiovsky barked. Petrov was looking at Mikhail in alarm, waiting for him to speak.

"I am prepared." Mikhail heard the words issue from his mouth as if coming from a very far, very cold distance.

Loathing himself, Mikhail left the KGB headquarters and declined his father's offer of a ride in his black Zil. "I need to walk," he told Petrov.

Blindly he strode down the Marx Prospekt toward Sverdlov Square, hurrying by other passersby, mostly Kremlin office workers, without seeing them. The snow was falling harder, feathering his eyelashes and tasting vaguely metallic.

With a shudder Mikhail remembered that other snow, the day of the avalanche. That was the day his life had changed forever. Perhaps he should have died then. How sweet it would have been to lie peacefully dead, free of these impossible demands.

"Mikhail!" He heard his name called. Startled, he turned to see Georgi Kazakov, one of his old comrades at the Frunze. "Mikhail, you old dog, you! Where have you been? Wait—wait up for me!"

Vodka. It was the national drink of Russia, the anesthetic of millions, and Mikhail drank more than his share that afternoon, as he and Georgi exchanged war stories and made the rounds of the few bars that were open. By nightfall, fortified by a meal of Ukrainian borscht and *guruli,* a chicken dish with walnut dressing, he and Georgi took a taxi and found themselves in front of the Bolshoi Theater.

The massive white columns of the theater, visible from any point on Sverdlov Square, were surmounted by four rearing steeds harnessed to the chariot of Apollo.

"Let's go inside and find us some sweet, young ballerinas," suggested Captain Georgi Kazakov, already very drunk. "That's what I want, some tight-assed dancers." Jovially, he jabbed Mikhail in the side.

"Now?" Mikhail laughed. He was nearly as drunk himself.

"*Da, da,* why not now? We'll watch 'em dance and show us their legs. Women! Bring me women! And afterward," Georgi said, leering, "we'll go backstage and meet some of the prettiest ones—eh, would you like that, Comrade Major Sandovsky? My fine friend?"

Tonight they were dancing *Paquita* and *Le Corsaire*.

Beautiful young bodies flashed through the air, twirled in exquisite lifts, turns, and jetés. The red and gold interior of the Bolshoi Theater, with its multitiered boxes, its rococo gold leaf, gold-encrusted pillars, and huge chandelier overhead was breathtaking enough when the viewer was sober. But when seen through drunken, hazed eyes, it took on a warm and roseate glow. This was where Mikhail's mother, Nadia, had once danced.

Mikhail's eyes kept being drawn to one ballerina, a slim, fiery girl with a long, delicate neck, whose arms and extended leg formed a graceful arabesque. Her glossy blond hair was parted in the center and pulled back from her face, and her eyes were slanted and mysterious.

"See any?" Georgi inquired several times during the applause, nudging Mikhail. "See any? Women you like, I mean. You know what they say about ballet dancers—"

"Shut up," Mikhail snapped.

Afterward, at Georgi's insistence, they went backstage. They were not the only men who had come backstage after the performance. Heavyset men in dark winter clothing strode down the narrow old corridors that smelled of analgesic balm, greasepaint, mold, ancient fixtures, and the faint whiff of perfume. These were Kremlin officials, Mikhail knew . . . important men, probably here to seek new mistresses.

"Here, this way," Georgi said, tugging at Mikhail.

The soft sounds of female laughter and chatter drifted from the end of a long, grimy corridor.

The door stood ajar, and Georgi pulled it open with a grin at Mikhail. "Which one do you want?"

Mikhail gazed inside. Fifteen or twenty slim young girls were changing out of their filmy costumes, crowded into a space barely large enough to contain them and the long racks that held their clothing and costumes. Some still wore tulle or white body suits, others were half-dressed or in street clothes, combing out their long hair as unselfconsciously as preening birds. None looked older than twenty, and all had the same kind of long-necked, long-legged, swanlike bodies. The length of their necks and legs were actually measured as children, Georgi had told him, to assure that they met the high Bolshoi standards.

A girl in white tulle with one strap slipped off her shoulder was staring at Mikhail, her melting blue eyes intense. She lifted her pale arms upward, and removed the clasp that bound her streaked blond hair. The thick hair tumbled downward on her shoulders almost to her waist in a silky fall of dazzling golden petals.

She turned slightly, gazing at Mikhail over her shoulder, a provocative half-smile on her lips. The smile wasn't so much seductive as it was challenging.

"Which one? Which?" Georgi inquired drunkenly. "Point her out to me, my handsome friend, and I will get her for you. You can get any of these women . . . they'll love you in your uniform with all the medals you wear on your chest!"

"I want none of them," Mikhail said.

But the golden-haired dancer walked up to him, offering him a small tulle flower she had snipped off the hem of her costume.

"Here," she said in a soft, breathy voice. "Take this."

He stared at the girl, not the flower. Seen up close, the heavy stage makeup seemed almost garish, dark lines drawn around her eyes and lengthened at the corners of her eyes, red circles painted on the high part of her cheekbones. But even that could not dim the girl's dewy, flowerlike beauty.

"For you, a remembrance," she told him.

Numbly, he took the blossom. For a brief second her hand brushed his. All the vodka he had drunk surged inside his veins, combining to make this a moment of magical, almost electrical portent. There had never been a dancer this beautiful, a moment this strong.

"My name is Yulia," she said, smiling.

Even her inviting smile was mysterious.

Holding the tulle flower, Mikhail inhaled the fragrant, musky aroma of her body and fell in love.

Chapter

Fourteen

YULIA POPOVNA PULLED her stylish white sable coat closely around her slim shoulders as Mikhail hailed a passing taxi. She gazed sidelong at the handsome young officer whom she had picked up tonight, wondering just how well he would perform sexually. What was his name? Mikhail something—ah, yes, Sandovsky.

She was angry at her regular lover, a powerful man who had given her many gifts, including the coat she wore, and her three-room apartment. Big Bear was what she called him, because of the size of his belly and the growls he made in bed. However, Big Bear had slighted her for three weeks, and she suspected he'd been playing around with someone else.

Yulia was angry with him. Let Big Bear wonder where she was tonight—she would show him she was not just a pretty toy kept on a shelf for his occasional pleasure.

"Where shall we go?" Mikhail said, handing her into the cab as if she were as fragile as a Fabergé egg.

She gave him her prettiest smile. "I know a club . . . a supper club called the Volga, that serves Georgian food and caters to important people."

He only looked at her, his eyes yearning for her.

Yulia's laugh rippled. She loved it when men became puppy-eyed for her . . . it was a feeling of power like no other. And ballet dancers had to use their power while they could. Most dancers were seventeen to nineteen years old. A female dancer was finished professionally by age twenty-seven or twenty-eight . . . sometimes thirty if she was very fortunate.

''Come, come, you'll love it,'' she urged, cuddling up against him. ''There is a wonderful chanteuse too—a friend of mine.''

The club, located on Gorky Street, was small, dark, and smoky, its tables jammed together, lit by candles. It was one of the most expensive eating clubs in Moscow. The air smelled strongly of burning wax, cooking meats, and the heavy perfumes and aftershave worn by its patrons, mostly high officials and their mistresses or wives. Mikhail breathed deeply. The odor was unexpectedly erotic.

Yulia said she was hungry . . . ''Starving!'' . . . so they ordered a selection of the piquant Georgian dishes, various shish kebabs roasted over burning coals, and *Khinkali*, meat cooked in dough. Yulia drank Gurdjaani wine, while Mikhail continued to drink vodka— Yubileynaya, a very good brand. He did not know how much he had drunk now, but like most Russians, he had an enormous capacity for it.

Yulia began to chatter about small intrigues in the ballet company, and Mikhail told her that his mother had once danced too.

''Ah. Was she very beautiful?'' Yulia wanted to know.

''Oh, very. Or so she seemed to me.''

''As beautiful as I?''

Mikhail flushed. ''You are the most lovely.''

''You are handsome too,'' Yulia said, favoring him with one burning look before lowering her gaze to the tabletop.

The chanteuse was a woman named Sophia, about thirty-five years old, with white-blond hair and a full bust, who entered the small stage to the sound of thunderous applause.

''Sophia is almost a queen here,'' Yulia whispered. ''Without her, this club would be nothing.''

Sophia had a voice like liquid smoke, and such magnetism that even the drunkest and merriest of revelers paused to listen, entranced. She sang a selection of ballads, some in French, others in German and Russian language.

Seated next to Yulia, his hand touching hers, Mikhail lost himself in the plaintive words that reached into remote corners of his heart. The room shimmered around him, its candlelight vivid. For a brief second he had a wild fantasy . . . himself as owner of this small club, creating a world small and safe, his boundaries that of soft, lilting music, not war and the killing and maiming of people innocent of politics.

"Come," Yulia said, squeezing his hand. Her blue eyes were intense. "Come, let's go now—it's going to be dawn soon . . . I have to sleep."

Mikhail shook himself, glancing in bewilderment at his watch. Had three hours passed?

"Come," the dancer urged. "Take me home, handsome Mikhail, and we will make love—if you haven't had too much vodka."

Yulia's apartment was in an old building, and had very high ceilings, and wallpaper from France, extremely expensive. There were 33 rpm records by Western rock groups like the Rolling Stones and Chicago—priceless possessions in the Soviet Union. Mikhail, his head fuzzy from all he had drunk, did not stop to ask himself how a young ballet dancer could have acquired an apartment that most Russian families waited years to get, if ever.

A silver samovar sat on a table in one corner, and Yulia began to prepare tea for him, boiling the water in the samovar. The room was heated to about seventy-five degrees, and when she came to serve the tea, in glasses as many Russians preferred, Yulia had taken off her dress. She wore only a flimsy cotton slip, its fabric so thin that it revealed the pout of her perky breasts, tipped by pinkish nipples.

Mikhail stifled his pleasured shock. The light blond fluff of her pubic thatch, visible underneath the sheer cotton, was the most erotic sight that he had ever seen.

"Drink your tea quickly," she breathed, coming to sit on his lap. The cotton rode up, revealing inches of slim, muscular thighs. Her bare feet, he noticed, were the only part of her that wasn't pretty. They were large and strong looking, bunioned, the toes callused and deformed from dancing *en pointe*.

The tea was very strong, mahogany-colored, served with lemon and well sugared. Mikhail took a few hot sips that burned his tongue, then set the glass down and reached for her.

"No . . . no . . ." Giggling, she held him off.

"Please. I must have you."

"Make *love* to me, you mean. I only allow men to make love, never to use me. They must love me or they cannot have me."

"I will love you," he promised recklessly.

"But only for one night," she warned. "I must tell you I already have a protector, a very important man. He is the one who pays for this apartment. But he isn't here now, and he's not as handsome as you either. In fact, he is not handsome at all."

Mikhail barely heard the words, only the erotic tension in them, the unbearably sexy combination of submission and aggression, of precocious sexual knowledge.

"Oh . . . God . . ." he said, burying his face in her breasts.

"One night," she insisted. "That's all I will allow you."

"Yes, yes, yes," he whispered.

Yulia was a voracious lover, ministering to Mikhail with her hands and her soft mouth, in a manner as skilled as any courtesan. With her greedy tongue she licked and sucked Mikhail into erection, flattening her tongue to run it down the sides of his hugely thickened cock, before taking him deliciously full and deep into her mouth. He had never been so iron-hard.

He felt himself begin to surge and throb, but tried to hold himself back—he didn't want to climax this way. He pulled her to him and they rolled over, their bodies pressed together. Kneeling astride the tiny Yulia, whose legs were spread to receive him, Mikhail entered her soft moistness. He began moving slowly, just enough to maintain his erection but not to orgasm.

He didn't want to come—not yet.

He wanted this to last forever.

"Oh! Oh! Oh!" Yulia cried out, writhing under him, her back arched, perspiration sheening her piquant face. "Oh . . . please! Please!" she screamed. "I love you, I love you!"

Mikhail thrust deeply, precariously close to the edge. But he still held himself back, ripples of exquisite pleasure spiraling through his body as he played Yulia like a balalaika. She was multiorgasmic, and also a screamer, and he glorified in her abandon, drawing climax after climax from her.

After her sixth climax, he finally allowed himself to break free. He could feel the exquisite pleasure down to his toes, the orgasm that exploded through him so powerful that it seemed for a few seconds he had died.

But as Mikhail sank back on the bed beside the dancer, so surfeited he could hardly move or even think, Yulia suddenly jumped out of bed, grabbing a cotton robe that was flung over a chair.

"You have to leave now," she announced.

"What?" he repeated stupidly.

"I said you have to leave. One night . . . remember, that's what I told you. I already have a lover and sometimes—not often, but sometimes—he comes in the morning, and I want to clean up this room in case he comes today."

"But—"

"Here," she said, handing him his sharply creased uniform pants.

Sober now, Mikhail wandered the streets. It was below zero, the air crisp, and the sky was pearl-gray, a few stars still visible, dotted over the spires and rooftops of Moscow. His breath exhaled from his lungs in puffs of white smoke.

He felt stunned and angered by what had happened. How could she demand that he "make love" to her, and scream in such rapture—and yes, cry out that she loved him—then

dismiss him from her room as if he were a stranger, a man
who had used a whore?

Who was the important man who was her permanent
lover? Why had she yelled out "I love you" if she had no
feelings for him? If he went back to the Bolshoi tomorrow,
he might be able to get some answers.

"Go away," Yulia said that night after the performance.
She was dressed in her fur coat, a sable hat pulled down
over her light hair, hiding its beauty. "Go *away*."

"No," he said. "Not until you tell me why."

She shrugged angrily, licking her full, red, moist lips.
"What is there to tell you? You are a pretty man—you
appealed to me. We used each other. What is so exciting or
new about that? And now I want you to leave me alone!"

"But you said—"

"I said nothing. I felt nothing. Can't you get that through
your head? Now if you don't leave *immediately* I will call
Dmitiri . . . he will throw you out—forcibly."

Mikhail stared at her for a long moment, burning with
frustration. He still believed she loved him. Something must
have happened—perhaps her other lover had beaten her or
threatened her.

"I doubt that, but if that's the way you want it, very well
then," he said curtly, and turned on his heel.

He was not scheduled to begin the course at the GRU for
another month. It would, he knew, be a grueling schedule of
expert rifle and pistol shooting, the use of automatic and
semiautomatic weapons, boxing and crippling tae kwon do.
Later he would be transferred to a large country dacha at
Kuchino, just outside Moscow. Here he would learn the use
of poisons and drugs that dissipate in the body minutes after
being administered, giving the impression of death by
natural causes. He would be taught to fire gases from special
ejector guns, so lethal even to the firer that he would have
to take a special antidote first, before firing the gun. He
would be taught the use of special, battery-operated guns
concealed in cigarette cases or pens, as well as plastic

explosives, and the fine points of organized sabotage and subversion. Also courses in the use of the knife and garrote.

Mikhail did not want to think about that yet. Yulia was on his mind, not a course in professional killing.

He began haunting the Bolshoi, attending the performances every night. He no longer went backstage but waited inconspicuously in the alley outside, hoping to catch a glimpse of the dancer leaving with her important lover—whoever he was.

During the days, he sometimes took the Metro to the apartment building where she lived, and waited outside hoping to catch a glimpse of her, or even better, a sighting of the man who had given her the apartment.

On the third day, the temperature dropped to ten below zero and Mikhail was forced to don a heavy fur overcoat and layered clothing beneath, along with a fur hat. These hid his face, making him look as anonymous and bundled-up as all the other pedestrians in Moscow in December.

He saw her several times, but she was always alone or with several other girls. Once she seemed to glance briefly his way, but he could have been mistaken for she gave no indication of recognition.

Then, early one morning, a black Zil limousine pulled up in front of the building, a uniformed driver at the wheel. A man in a black coat with a fur collar got out, his breath puffing in the extreme cold.

It was Vladimir Petrov. His father.

"Now I want to take you from behind," Petrov ordered, reaching for the full glass of Stolichnaya, flavored with hot pepper, that Yulia always kept waiting for him. He downed a long swallow of the fiery liquid. "Go on," he insisted. "Get down. Kneel, Yulia. I know you love it."

Both of them were naked in the overheated apartment, and Yulia was drunk, too, laughing and throwing back swig after swig of the expensive vodka.

"Not yet," she protested, lifting her glass. "I want to drink . . . more, Big Bear. Pour me more."

"Now," he demanded. "Do it now, Yulia, the way I like."

"Oh, very well," she said with a pout, kneeling down on the bed so that her beautiful, slim rump was high in the air.

He used the lubricant she kept for him, and entered her with a strong, forceful push that rocked her forward. Grunting, he thrust again and again.

"Oh . . . oh . . ." she cried out in obedient passion, her voice thick, her hands clenched on the coverlet. Sometimes she came this way, but mostly she did not—which didn't matter to Petrov one way or the other. He continued to thrust until he reached his brief, quick orgasm.

He pulled out of her. Yulia immediately rolled over, and reached for a tissue with which to wipe herself. She then reached out to clean him, too—a process he always insisted on as the last act of their lovemaking.

While she was washing him, his eyes flicked to Yulia's carved, ornate dressing table, lined with bottles of perfume he had brought her from a recent official trip to Paris. On it stood a wine bottle layered with colored candle wax drippings, and had a white candle in it.

"That," he said, pointing. "Where did you get that?"

Yulia's eyes were dark pools. "Oh—Sophia gave it to me."

He recognized the candle holder. And he knew who Sophia was—the chanteuse at the Volga, the supper club where he had taken Yulia several times. But he knew the manager of the Volga, Ivan Korolev, and he would never have allowed his employees to give away such an item. Therefore, he speculated, Yulia must have gone there without him and taken it as a souvenir . . . she had probably gone there with another man.

"Come here," he said roughly, pulling the girl toward him. Surprised, Yulia complied.

"Lick me," he ordered. "Suck me hard—I want to do it again. And this time you will swallow everything, and beg me for more."

Yulia began a protest, but when she saw his face, she

stopped. Her eyes were bright with fear. *"Da,"* she whispered.

Thirty minutes later, when Petrov left the apartment, sated yet angry, he took with him the few shaving things he had left there for his own use. He was finished with Yulia.

He had a telephone call to make.

"Why?" demanded Mikhail. He was in a rage of betrayal, so hurt and furious that he'd gone back to the Bolshoi again that night, and blocked Yulia in the corridor as she was leaving.

"Why him? Why? Did he hurt you? Did he threaten you? My God, Yulia . . . he's my father!"

"How was I to know?" she responded sullenly. "I knew him long before you came into my life." The light seemed quenched from her pale face, and her eyes were hooded. Were they bruised? He could not see clearly in the dim light.

"You couldn't love him—he's almost sixty years old, Yulia, that's thirty-five years older than you!"

"What does it matter how old he is?" she spat at him, eyes flashing. "The point is, Mikhail Sandovsky, that I'm twenty-five years old, not seventeen! Do you know what that means for a dancer? It means I'm *old, old, old!* It means that I might have only a few more years to dance. *I have to take care of myself while I can.*"

He was stunned. "But that doesn't mean—it shouldn't mean—"

"It means that you are a stupid, silly fool!" she cried, pushing past him. "Go away, Major Mikhail Sandovsky! You are an idiot and I don't need you or want you!"

"You want *him,* then?" In two strides Mikhail caught up to her. He spun the girl against the green-painted wall of the chilled backstage corridor. He forcibly pinned her with his hands to hold her quiet.

"You want this old man—Petrov? Tell me you don't. Tell me the truth!"

"Now you *are* a fool," she snapped. "I want no man. Did you ever think I did? I like women better, you jackass!

Women! So go away, will you? I never want to see you or your ugly father again—ever!''

The following day Mikhail, enraged with jealousy, went back to the apartment to try to talk with Yulia again. He banged on the door loudly. It was opened by an older women with fat cheeks and shoe button eyes, dressed in a sagging gray wool sweater and shapeless dress.

''Where is Yulia?'' he almost shouted.

''She does not live here,'' the woman said in a Ukrainian accent.

''She does live here! I was here only yesterday!''

''This is an apartment belonging to an important official and there is no Yulia here,'' the old woman repeated.

''But there has to be! She was here—she is here . . . she's told you not to let me in.''

''There is no Yulia,'' the woman told him sadly.

The next day, a child who lived in the building told Mikhail that last night he had seen some men take Yulia away in a shiny black Zil.

Chapter

Fifteen

New York
1985

"ONE! TWO! HIGHER kick! Head turned! Keep smiling! And keep that back arched!"

Elena Kunikova, Valentina's dance instructor, stood near the studio mirror, shouting out instructions and watching critically as Valentina performed a difficult combination for the twelfth time—or was it the twentieth?

"Yes . . . yes . . . that's better, Val. Much, much better. We'll make a Broadway dancer of you yet," she added. "That's it, head for the showers, you've earned it."

But instead of leaving, Valentina sank down on the floor and clasped her knees, her breath heaving. Her leotard was soaked with perspiration after the three-hour workout, and even her hair was wringing wet. After two weeks of the rigorous training schedule, her entire body screamed with exhaustion.

"Too strenuous?" inquired Elena.

"Oh, no," lied Valentina, lifting her head slowly.

"We *have* to get you back in shape, Val. You've got years of practice to make up for. Dancing is a bunch of hard work. No pain, no gain."

"I know, I know." Valentina sighed, getting to her feet.

"Hey," said Elena, grinning. "You've come a thousand miles in two weeks, young lady. But . . ."

"I just have another thousand to go, right?"

"Maybe eight hundred and ninety-nine."

Valentina laughed as she headed for the locker room.

Elena was a great teacher—the best. She felt sure that tomorrow Keith would be pleased.

She stripped off her damp leotard and tights and stiffly trudged toward the showers, glancing at the big clock on the wall to see how much time she had. In twenty minutes she had to jump into a taxi and race to her two-hour drama class at the Neighborhood Playhouse on East Fifty-fourth Street.

After a hot shower, she toweled herself dry and headed toward the dressing room.

"How's it going?" asked a stunning redhead in the locker room, a tall woman wearing only bikini panties as she propped a long leg on a bench, slathering it with cream. She spoke with a slight southern accent.

"Just great." The woman looked familiar and Valentina looked again. "Didn't I see you at the audition?"

"Yeah, I'm Jinna Jones."

Jinna was a regular at Steps, and they talked about their classes for a few moments. "I'm working every damn day," Jinna confided. "I'm gonna make it, honey, just you wait. But I'm twenty-eight now and all I hope is that it happens before I'm too old to hoof it." Then Jinna casually asked, "Are you still seeing Keith Leonard? Rumor has it that you two are an item, and he's coming over tomorrow to watch you dance."

Valentina blushed. Then her blush turned fiery. She'd been afraid this would happen. "No, we're only spending a lot of time together because he's giving me a crash course in acting—we go to a lot of plays, some university productions, some off-Broadway, and he critiques the performances with me."

Jinna raised an eyebrow. "So that's what it's called." But her tone wasn't offensive. "Look, Val, could I give you just a tiny piece of advice?"

"Sure."

"Well, it's like this. When people work together on a production they get kinda close. Their hormones start raging, you know what I mean? That's why so many movie stars marry each other; they meet on the set. But those kinds

of relationships don't always work very well . . . things
kinda fade after the show is over.''

"I . . . see,'' Valentina said. She reached for her bag in
search of her hairbrush. "I got hurt once, a few years back
when I was on a concert tour and a married man—well, he
decided to stay married. I don't intend to have it happen
again.''

"Mmm-hmm,'' drawled Jinna.

Looking in the mirror, Valentina thought about Jinna's
warning. She *was* attracted to Keith Leonard. His slow, easy
smile, his way of looking straight into her eyes as he talked
to her. There was a goodness about Keith that went far
deeper than mere sex appeal. He was basically, decently
genuine. A man who could be tender. Honest.

That made him definitely dangerous.

But only if I allow him to be, she decided.

"Well, what did you think?'' Keith said as they left the
Roundabout Theater, after seeing *The Price of Fame* with
Charles Grodin. On the sidewalk, hundreds of theater
patrons were jostling for the cabs lined up two deep. The
atmosphere was muggy and it felt like rain. "This way,
Val,'' he added. "I told the limo to pick us up on the corner
of Irving Place rather than at the theater. It's not quite so
congested there.''

As he said this, he gave her a warm smile and took the
crook of her arm. His touch sent an arc of electricity through
her.

The black stretch limo was waiting on the corner. Keith
told the driver to take them to the Foxy coffee shop on East
Fiftieth Street near Madison. He liked the shop because the
booths were huge, and private.

Excitedly they went to "their'' booth and sat down, to
begin hashing over the play in detail—a process that
Valentina was beginning to find more and more enjoyable.
She loved his sense of humor, and his enthusiasm. Whatever
Keith did, he did it one hundred percent. He was nearly
forty, but he had the exuberance of a man in his early
twenties, and the energy of one too. She'd already learned
that Keith was a skilled horseman, an experienced polo

player and respected bronco buster, who occasionally made trips back to Houston where he rode in rodeo exhibitions. He skied Aspen, played a reasonable game of golf, had even tried hang gliding once.

Two hours later, as the shop had begun to empty, Keith leaned back, smiling. "I think that's enough for one night. Tell me, Val, what's happening with Blue Orchids? Did you two really split up for good?"

Valentina frowned. "I hope not. I've been trying to call my sister for days, and I've had my agent doing the same thing. Orchid hangs up on both of us. She won't give an inch—and now I've committed myself to this," Valentina admitted. "Sometimes I do feel very guilty about it."

"Don't. There's no point to it. You've offered to continue making records and appearances, and she won't buy it. A hiatus of a year or so won't hurt Blue Orchids in the long run. Look how long the Rolling Stones go between albums, or even Bob Seger or Huey Lewis and the News." He went on. "If you could have anything on earth, Val, what would it be? Be honest, now."

She stared at him, shaken.

"Stardom?" he persisted. "Is that what you really want? Fame, glory, the whole bit?"

She hesitated. "I think I just want to *work* and to know I'm one of the best, you know, like Barbra Streisand. And—"

"Yes?"

She blushed. *Love.* But how could she say that to Keith?

Fortunately, the owner of the coffee shop was coming toward their table, signaling them that he wanted to close for the night. With relief, Val said, "Ooops, I think he's closing. Damn, and I wanted to see if I could reach Orchid again."

"He'll let you use the phone in the lounge," Keith suggested. "Anyway, Orchid's so damn stubborn, she probably won't talk to you even if she's home. Give her a few more days. She'll come around."

"No," Valentina insisted. "I want to talk to her tonight if I can."

* * *

"Shit!"

Orchid heard the trill of her telephone while she was still outside in the hallway fumbling with her key. She'd been out cruising the discos, especially Régine's on Park Avenue, which featured live music. Her feet ached from hours of nonstop dancing, and she was also a little drunk.

"Damn!" she cried again, fumbling with the key as the phone pealed again and again.

She rushed into the room, and made a grab for the receiver.

"Yeah!" she snapped.

"Orchie," came her sister's voice. It had that muffled, phone-booth sound. "You're home, thank God. I've been trying to reach you for a couple of weeks to tell you. My rehearsals are going great, and I've already arranged a recording session for Blue Orchids with Cloud Nine studio, in Detroit, and—"

"I *don't* want to talk to you."

"Orchid," Valentina begged. "Listen to me. Please, just listen—"

But Orchid slammed the phone down. She snatched up a crumpled package of Benson and Hedges Menthols and her new, thin gold Dunhill, and lit a cigarette, her hands shaking violently. Tobacco would toughen her vocal cords but at this moment she simply didn't give a shit. Tears seeped from her eyelids.

She didn't want to be a has-been . . . a failure . . . a backup. She *needed* Blue Orchids, to make her feel like a whole person again.

Valentina slowly hung up the phone. Keith was waiting for her near the door. As they left the coffee shop, sheets of rain began to pour down.

Valentina retreated to the awning of the Tatou Club next door, which served as very little protection, and within seconds, water had plastered her coat to her body, and flattened her hair.

Keith followed her, soaked, his hair plastered to his head.

"The limo probably pulled around the block," he told her. Rivulets of water ran down his face and neck.

"You're a tad wet," Valentina remarked, grinning.

"You're a drowned rat."

"Oh, no, not half as drowned as you."

The limo arrived, and Keith's shoes made sloshing noises as they waded through a flowing stream of rainwater.

"I sound like Charlie Chaplin in hip boots," he remarked, doing a little soft-shoe step.

Valentina giggled. All his dignity was gone. He looked adorable. She began to do her own tap dance in her ruined Jourdan pumps, humming a bar from *Singin' in the Rain*.

They were laughing hilariously as they climbed into the limo.

When the stretch pulled up in front of the New York Fitzgerald Hotel, where Valentina was staying, she made a split-second decision. "You can't go home with your clothes that wet. Why don't you come up to my room and dry off? We'll call Valet Service, maybe they can press your coat and suit while you wait."

"I haven't heard a better offer all day. But I'll have to phone my wife, of course," he added.

"Of course, I understand."

They sloshed through the hotel lobby, as two bellhops standing by the bell captain's stand eyed them suspiciously. Valentina giggled. "I wonder if they think we're street people."

"I hardly think so."

She threw back her head and laughed. "I wouldn't be too sure. Your shoes, Keith . . . they're flapping like wet laundry!"

They clutched each other, swept with renewed waves of hilarity as they entered the elevator. Even with her hair soaking wet, Valentina looked beautiful to him, her skin glowing. He could not get enough of her smile. Despite the rock star life she had led, there was something completely unspoiled and natural about her. She was gorgeous and warm, and Keith knew damn well he'd better put a rein on his emotions . . . now . . . before it was too late.

The elevator was hung with mirrors edged in polished brass. Valentina took one look at their bedraggled reflections and once again burst out laughing. When Keith saw his own nose, with a droplet of rain still hanging from the end, he began to roar too.

They collapsed against each other, still giggling. When he touched her, it seemed only a few inches between his mouth and hers.

They crossed those inches as sweetly as if they were children. Keith tasted the soft rain on her lips, and felt a rush of pure feeling that left him shaken.

Then he groaned and pulled her close. He pressed his mouth on hers, and their lips parted. Then all rational thought vanished from his mind. All he could think was, he had to get closer to her, he had to get closer.

As they walked into her suite, Keith could smell the scent of several huge bouquets of roses, mingling with the subtle aroma of her clothes and perfume. It sent a shock straight to his insides.

"I . . . I'm not sure whether I should . . . that is, I don't think—I can't . . ." Valentina stood with her arms folded across her chest, looking suddenly anxious.

"Of course," he said, pulling away too.

They stood uncomfortably silent. This wasn't supposed to happen and both of them knew it.

"I'll just phone my wife, if you don't mind," he told her quickly. "No need to call Valet Service. My clothes will dry in a jiffy, I'm sure."

"The phone's over there," she said, pointing.

While Valentina was in the bathroom freshening up, Keith quickly dialed Cynthia and told her he would be saying in town.

"Fine," his wife agreed. "I'm reading the most wonderful book, Keithie . . . a new historical by Ruth Ryan Langan. I just love her, she's so romantic . . ."

As Keith hung up he felt a deep spasm of guilt. His wife received romance from novels, not from him.

"Maybe we should talk," Valentina said seriously, coming out of the bathroom. She had changed to a long ice-blue satin bathrobe embroidered Japanese-style with dozens of blue orchids, and had combed her damp hair back from her face. She'd washed off the remnants of her makeup, and looked about eighteen, young and fresh.

"Of course," he said, his heart twisting ask he looked at her.

"I mean, I don't think either of us are looking to have just an affair. At least it's not what I want at all. I could never do that to another woman and I know you feel the same way. But . . . maybe we could talk for a while, just as friends."

They sat in the room's sitting area, she on a love seat, he on an adjoining chair, and they talked about their pasts.

He told her about his boyhood in Houston, his days at the University of Michigan when he had played tight end for the Wolverines, his marine tour as a rookie second lieutenant in Vietnam and Thailand. The dreams he sometimes still had of a buddy wounded by a grenade. There'd been a girl in Thailand, too, Mei Ling . . . He had never told anyone about her, even Cynthia. He suspected Mei Ling might have had a child by him, but she had refused to tell him. For many years he had sent her money, until one day his letter was returned marked Deceased. It had torn him apart.

He told Valentina about how, after he had moved to New York, he met Cynthia at a Museum of Modern Art benefit ball. Her ethereal blond beauty had intrigued him. Her beauty reminded him of Grace Kelly, but she was physically fragile.

"Her first heart attack just wiped me out," he said in a low voice. "She was so young and really loved life so much. We had planned a large family, but often plans . . ."

"You love her," Valentina interrupted softly. Her eyes sought his, searching for the truth.

Before replying, Keith hesitated for a long moment. He looked at the heavy jacquard drapes, drawn tight against the heavy rain that continued to pound the window. He knew that many men in his position, alone in a hotel room with a beautiful woman like Valentina, would have said the convenient thing. That their marriage was just duty now, that they'd grown apart and hadn't really made *love* in many years.

But he couldn't say those things. They wouldn't be lies, but only partial truths. A marriage was composed of many complex feelings.

"I won't mislead you, Valentina, I do love my wife, although perhaps not in the way you might think. She has been loyal to me and I've returned that loyalty. It's not her fault that we couldn't go ahead with our plans because of her poor health. Many see us as an ideal couple," he explained with difficulty. "I'm sorry. But I can't lie to you."

She looked away, her graceful head held very straight. He knew his words had hurt her.

"Do you want to hear about me?" she finally said.

"Of course. Of course I do."

He listened, entranced, as she told him about her father, who had been sent to a labor camp, her ballet dancer mother, the train wreck in the Caucasus mountains of Russia. The story of the eight-year-old girl screaming in the snow, searching for her twin brother, moved him considerably. Few knew this but, as a child, he had lost an older sister to leukemia. Keith felt a lump fill his throat.

"Twins," he remarked. "They have a special relationship, don't they? Almost psychic. Attached to each other by more than just genes."

"I often dreamed about Mikhail," Valentina said. "Especially in the months after the avalanche, when I felt so lonely and had only my mother to depend on. I would see him being lost, swept away from me . . . in danger, always in danger. Occasionally I still dream of him, and he's still in jeopardy, Keith. Sometimes I wake up crying. The dreams seem so vivid sometimes . . ." She sighed.

Keith glanced at his watch. "My God," he exclaimed. "Do you realize it's four-thirty in the morning?"

They stared at each other. He saw a ripple of concern

cross Valentina's face. "That late?" she said haltingly. "Tomorrow you're going to see me dance." Her eyes lifted to meet his, and instantly he was drowning in them.

"Val," he whispered hoarsely.

"Please," she whispered. "Don't—I can't—"

Her pupils were dilated and he could see the beautiful green and gold colors in her irises, hear her soft breathing, smell her wonderful spicy, female scent.

He knew what he should do right now. Get up and take off for his apartment for a few hours of sleep. He did have a wife. But this time he couldn't stop himself as he reached for Valentina again.

She breathed out a long, shaky, yet contented sigh.

With shaking hands, Keith pulled the satin folds of the bathrobe off Valentina's shoulders, sliding the fabric down and following it with kisses. She moaned as each sweet kiss sent tiny electrical shocks through her.

When he had bared her shoulders, kissing every inch of her skin, he reached for the sash and pulled it apart, so that the satin fell open, revealing the fullness of her breasts, the dark shadow of her silky, black triangle.

"My God," he whispered, staring at her as if she were a goddess. "Oh, God, Val . . . Jesus . . ."

She slid out of the satin robe. After she was naked, he caressed up and down her skin with his warm hands, as if taking possession of every inch of her, every delicate fold and crevice.

She gasped with desire, impatient to have him enter her quickly—take her!

"Slow," he muttered. "Slowly, darling."

Valentina curbed her fierce longing. She reached for his shirt buttons and unfastened them one by one, taking his shirt off slowly, as he had done for her.

Keith was hard bodied and muscular, his chest covered with a thatch of silky black hair in which a few silver hairs glistened. Now he wore only narrow low-rise briefs, blue silk that felt deliciously slippery to her fingers. Beneath the silk he was already urgently erect, straining at the fabric.

"I want you—I need you," Keith gasped, gripping her arms so hard that she could feel the imprint of his fingers.

He was very male, tremendously desirable.

He lifted her up and carried her to the bed, lowering her onto the expensive floral duvet.

"I can't wait," he choked. "I can't wait—I have to be close to you, Val."

They wrapped their arms and legs around each other, suddenly frantic to have skin touching skin, to taste the other's breath, to feel, to smell. Burrowing closer to him, Valentina felt rushes of sharp, contradictory emotions. It was such painful ecstasy, such mad, loving joy. She could live forever here in Keith's arms.

His mouth found hers and he began kissing her deeply. His tongue explored the warm cave of her mouth as if taking possession of that, too, and she kissed him back, possessing him in the same passionate manner. They kissed frantically, their breath heaving, hands caressing, bodies thrusting blindly—trying to get inside each other any way they could.

And then—raucous voices from the outside hall as a man and a woman returned to their rooms after nightclubbing, laughing loudly. Reality came crashing back. Valentina froze in shock, her body stiffening. They'd both said they wouldn't get involved—and now they were doing exactly that.

"We can't!" she choked, pushing him away. She sat up, shaking. "Oh, God—what are we doing? Oh, Keith . . . oh, God!"

His face was twisted with regret. She knew he felt as stunned by their encounter as she did.

"I'm sorry," he whispered. He held her gently, his ardor gone. "I know you told me how you felt, but . . . you are so beautiful and I haven't loved in so long."

She felt as if her heart had been lacerated. He hadn't *loved. He loved her.*

"Keith, if we were different people . . . maybe I could see this happening. But . . ."

"But we are who we are," Keith agreed, beginning to dress. "Val, you don't need to tell me we shouldn't do this.

I know it. It's just that it's so damn difficult." He turned to her and she could see the diamond glitter of tears in his eyes. "*So* damn hard, Val."

"I know." she said, her own eyes flooding.

The next morning, Valentina danced the jazz routine she'd been working on for two weeks, before Keith and Elena, her instructor. The sleepless night had lent her fire, and it was the best performance she'd ever given.

"Val, you knocked me out," said Elena as Valentina left the floor, still breathing heavily. "You gave it everything, and it worked."

But Valentina's eyes were only for Keith. He had risen, walking over to one of the long windows that looked out on the street.

"Well?" she said, walking over to him in her soft black Capezio jazz shoes.

He turned. He wore a Turnbull and Asser tweed jacket with a yellow turtleneck and jeans, and she wondered fleetingly if he kept a supply of clothing at his apartment. His eyes glowed as he looked at her. She could sense the deep feelings he held back, his sorrow mixed with pain.

"Valentina, you were superb. And I love you so much that I'm ready to explode. God help me!"

Another class had entered the studio and was doing their warmup to the Pointer Sisters. Under cover of the loud rock music, Keith and Valentina spoke in low voices.

"Me too," Valentina choked. "But I can't make myself happy at the expense of someone else. I know people do it all the time, but I'm not one of them."

"That's why I love you."

"What are we going to do?" she whispered.

"What can we do, except be very dear friends? Val . . . I don't have any other answer. Cynthia's condition is medically serious. The stress of a divorce could kill her, and I'd never forgive myself. I—"

She touched her forefinger to his lips. "It's okay," she forced herself to say. "I could never have a friend more wonderful than you—ever."

She stood rigid, her body shaking, afraid she was going to break down.

"Go on with your life, Val," Keith said dully. "It's really the best thing for both of us—don't think about me anymore."

They looked at each other. Both of them knew it wasn't going to work that way.

Buenos Aires
1985

María Cristina—Araña—lay back as her husband, Tomás, stroked in and out of her, sweat pouring from his body. The sound of his lusty panting filled the room. His hands had been all over her the instant he greeted her at Ezeiza International Airport. Now they were in the condominium penthouse he owned close to the Plaza Hotel, overlooking beautiful San Martin Square and Florida Street.

"Are you—? Are you—?" he demanded.

"Oh, yes, yes . . . Tomás . . . oh, yes!" South American men were macho, and she knew he wanted to believe he was the all-powerful male who could bring her to multiple orgasms.

"God . . . give it to me! *Are you? Are you?*"

"Yes!" she sobbed, and allowed her body to thrust and buck, orgasmic cries ripping out of her.

After uttering his own hoarse cries, Tomás collapsed on top of her, nearly unconscious with satisfaction. María Cristina sighed and lay back, staring at the ceiling. She'd faked her orgasm—as usual. Her mind began to drift away from her sleeping husband, imagining herself with utmost power over another human being—the absolute power of death.

Moscow
1985

Mikhail was frantic to find Yulia. He took a taxi back to the block of apartment flats located in the "Garden Ring" of the city, near Vosstaniye Square, its ground floor occupied by a food shop and a cinema. It had been his home for almost fifteen years—at least while he was not in the military academy or on duty.

He still couldn't believe it. His own father had been Yulia's "important man," the one who had provided her with the apartment. But obviously, Petrov had guessed that Yulia had someone else. Did he know it was him? Probably he'd already beaten it out of her. Mikhail held few illusions about how she would have been treated.

He reached the fifth floor and waited impatiently while the elevator doors slowly lumbered open, then strode down the hallway, breathing in the familiar atmosphere with a feeling of despair and futility.

He used his key and flung open the door, striding inside. The luxurious apartment had fourteen-foot ceilings with elaborate carved wooden moldings, and tall sash windows that looked out on an inner courtyard. Busy flowered wallpaper covered the walls. Every inch was crowded with antique furniture, lace doilies, cutwork embroidery, photographs, memorabilia from summers on the Crimean Sea, and a collection of Lithuanian folk dolls.

His mother, Irina, was seated in a rocking chair, watching a movie on a VCR—a device so rare in the Soviet Union as to be priceless. The movie, Mikhail saw dully, was the American film *E.T.*

"Where is he?" he demanded angrily. "Where is my father?"

"Why, I don't know," Irina replied disinterestedly, not removing her eyes from the set.

"Where is he?" Mikhail nearly screamed.

"Why, Misha, I suppose he is in his study. Must you be so loud? I think—"

Ignoring her, Mikhail pounded down the hall to Petrov's study. The fourteen-by-seventeen-foot space was another luxury unknown by most ordinary Russians, who usually were forced to cram four, six, or even eight people into two rooms. He knocked loudly on the door, then pushed it open.

Petrov looked up, startled, as his son burst in. He was

seated at a big desk, studying a thick, mimeographed report full of densely printed tables of statistics marked Top Secret. Behind his father stood a large, ornate, claw-footed safe that dated back to before the Revolution. Petrov always kept his most important documents in it.

"Where is she, dammit!" Insane with rage, Mikhail rushed over and grabbed Petrov by the shoulders, yanking him to his feet. "Where is she, you bastard—tell me!"

Petrov didn't react, but gazed coldly at his son. For the first time Mikhail saw his father as he really was.

"Let me go, Mikhail," Petrov ordered. "There is no need for this fuss over a whore."

"Chort vozmi!" Mikhail yelled as he shook Petrov violently. "You took her away, didn't you? You were the one with the Zil. You took her somewhere! *I want to know where.*"

Petrov shook himself free. Mikhail let go, and sank back against the edge of the desk. Had he gone mad? Yulia had nearly driven him crazy with jealousy.

"Why should I tell you where? I'm very disappointed that you have behaved so badly over a cheap tramp."

"Because I need to find her. *I* caused this, didn't I? You did it because of me. I don't want her to pay for something I did."

"If anything was done, she did it to herself, that dancer whore." Petrov uttered each word with sharp emphasis. "I have had her sent to Murmansk to work in a fish-processing factory. The Bolshaya Collective."

"A fish-processing factory!" Mikhail stared at his father, stunned. On the Arctic Circle, hordes of hard-working women staffed huge fish factories. Some worked in the holds of fishing trawlers. Others, their hair tied back in kerchiefs, stomped around on water-soaked floors in rubber boots and aprons, lugging ponderous slabs of frozen fish, or cutting off the heads and tails of herring, cod, or sea perch. He couldn't imagine the fragile Yulia performing such heavy work—it would kill her.

"You can't!" he cried. "She is too small for such work!"

"Ballet dancers have legs like iron," his father snorted. "She'll love it—and if she spreads her legs for the manager of the factory . . . why, she'll love that too. He's a big fellow!"

Mikhail felt the blood rush to the veins in his head and neck. He knew he was within millimeters of losing control of himself again.

"Calm down," his father ordered evenly. "You have made a mistake, Mikhail—a big one. You have allowed *pizda*, pussy, to interfere with your thinking. I did this to bring you to your senses. Your future lies with Mother Russia and the KGB, not with some little *prostitutka*."

"She was no whore," Mikhail whispered. "Though you used her like one, didn't you?"

Angrily he turned and left the study.

After three weeks he had to admit the truth. There was no fish-processing factory called the Bolshaya Collective. Yulia Popovna had simply disappeared!

He turned his anger inward, keeping his face set and stony, refusing to speak to either of his parents in more than polite monosyllables.

He thought about retaliating against Petrov for what he had done to Yulia but decided that he could not do that either. After all, the man was his father. He would have to think about it some more.

The KGB training school was located in several four-story brick buildings in the forests about twenty-five kilometers outside Moscow. The grounds were patrolled by KGB officers in civilian dress, at night accompanied by watchdogs. The students were forbidden to reveal their surnames . . . he was known only as Misha. Surrounded by six-foot walls topped with barbed wire, Mikhail felt as if he were incarcerated in a prison, one that he had signed himself into for a life sentence.

The KGB also placed great importance on physical fitness and he joined Moscow Dynamo, a soccer team that played with fierce intent to win. Mikhail played with murderous skill, releasing his anger through the sport.

Butting heads and vicious body checking were ways of dealing with the pressures of being a gentle man forced into the KGB standard mold of an elite killer.

One day in March, when the snows had begun to thaw, Petrov picked Mikhail up at the school and drove him back into Moscow to KGB headquarters.

A brass samovar steamed in Petrov's office, the smell of rich, freshly brewed tea filling the air. In an anteroom, a heavy young woman pounded on a manual typewriter.

"How is the training progressing?" his father wanted to know.

"Very good," Mikhail said shortly.

"I am told that they never saw a sharpshooter like you. And that you are feared in the boxing ring," Petrov added, laughing. He seemed jovial today, as if he'd completely forgotten about their dispute over Yulia. "Perhaps we should send you over to America and you could fight Muhammad Ali, eh?" He pronounced the name the Russian way, chuckling at his own joke.

Mikhail stood rigid, not replying.

"Mmm, ahem," Petrov said, the laughter dying away. "Perhaps you need to learn a little lesson, eh? I have arranged a special demonstration for you—something to sharpen your techniques and give you an advantage over your classmates."

"I do not need an extra advantage over them."

"Don't be a fool. After you graduate, you will be one of thirty thousand KGB members all over the world. You must stand out from the rest or you will never be noticed. Meet me here in my office tomorrow morning at eight o'clock exactly. We are going to pay a visit to the Detention Room. You will see how things happen in the *real* world."

"What do you mean, the real world?" Mikhail was startled at his father's pronouncement.

Petrov glanced out of his office window, which faced a courtyard, and grim-looking brick walls with barred windows. "A Chinese pilot has been shot down over Soviet air space. Tomorrow we will interrogate him—it will be most educational, I assure you."

* * *

Guards at frequent checkpoints demanded to look at their special security clearances as Petrov and Mikhail walked deeper and deeper into the bowels of Lubyanka Prison, a massive hulk of a building that most Soviet citizens dreaded even thinking about, so stained was it in blood and infamy from Stalin's reign of terror. In the 1930s, it had been a notorious extermination center. Thousands, perhaps millions of the cream of the revolutionary intelligentsia and armed forces had been shot here.

Even Petrov didn't talk as they continued to walk down the musty, grim corridors that led deep into the warren of interrogation rooms and dank prison cells.

The Chinese prisoner was about twenty-two years old, thin and wiry, with a narrow face and slanting black eyes that seemed to spit hate as they began the interrogation. He was naked, strapped to a chair, bound at wrists, ankles, and chest with heavy metal collars. An interpreter stood by, stony-faced.

"What air group were you with? What was the strength of the group? Isn't it true that you were photographing Soviet military installations?" Petrov kept repeating. A technician had been called in to operate an electrical apparatus on a cart that was attached with electrodes to the prisoner's penis and testicles.

Petrov uttered a deep grunt, then turned toward Mikhail as if to see his reaction.

"No," muttered Mikhail, starting toward the torture apparatus. He yanked out its plug, then, continuing the motion, he shoved the flat of his hand into the technician's chest.

The man collapsed backward, spittle bubbling from his mouth.

"What—you—" Petrov sputtered.

"Have you never heard of drugs and serums to extract this type of information?" Mikhail snapped. "It is far more effective and the information will be useful instead of something the prisoner merely screamed out so we would leave him alone. Obtain the drugs for me, and *I* will interrogate him myself properly.''

Petrov nodded, a flare of pride lighting his eyes. Mikhail felt a deep chill. He realized this had been the real purpose of the interrogation all along—not to get information but to see and judge Mikhail's own reaction. He'd passed a test he didn't know he was taking.

As they left the prison, Mikhail made a final decision about something that he had been thinking about for months now. He didn't want to be a KGB expert in interrogation, part of an elite killer group. The screaming of the Chinese pilot had convinced him of that.

He must leave Russia forever!

Chapter

Sixteen

New York
1985

KEITH LEONARD WAS the first to arrive. He entered the theater from a side door, and walked down the aisle, between rows of empty seats.

It was Valentina's day to prove herself. Keith could feel the tension tighten his neck muscles. Since Valentina came into his life, he had not been sleeping well.

"If Tamara's fabulous, then everything else will fall into place," the choreographer kept repeating. "If she's not, it's a disaster. And I'm not bullshitting you, Keith. I'll drop out if I can't pull this off right. I don't do mediocre," she'd insisted a few days ago.

Now he heard heel clicks and turned to see Bettina, wearing a thin black jumpsuit swirled with silver studs, and a new hairstyle that was shaved on the back and sides of her head, and tufted in a high crest on top. A chunky hammered sterling silver pendant completed her ensemble.

"Well, today's the big day," she said to Keith in her gravelly voice.

"Yes."

"I just thought you should know. I have Jenny Trillin on standby. She's prepared to dance either Tamara or the second lead. She's been a prima ballerina with Sadler Wells in London for years now, and she even danced for Martha Graham—I've worked with her a number of times and she's brilliant. She can sing too."

"We'll still use her, but for second lead," Keith said. "It'll give the production depth."

Bettina shrugged. "Well, in twenty minutes we'll know, won't we?"

"Yes," Keith said, more calmly than he felt. "We certainly will."

Backstage, Valentina was applying the last of her makeup, sweeping lines of black at the corners of her eyes to give them an exotic look. Odd—her hands weren't trembling at all, although she'd barely slept last night as her mind kept going through every step of the difficult dance routine.

She slithered into the silver bodysuit she'd found in a little dance shop in Greenwich Village. Transparent scarves embroidered with silver threads and sequins were layered over it. There was a wonderful dream sequence in *Balalaika* and Valentina had decided her routine would follow that sequence.

What the hell, she thought. Although special effects weren't generally used at auditions, she'd had a long meeting with the lighting man at Mike Duffy's suggestion. Lighting could work wonders. In return, she'd promised to give his daughter the last Blue Orchids album if he'd do her this one favor.

Adjusting the scooped neck of the suit, she gazed at herself in the mirror. She looked like a long, shimmering tube of silver.

The production staff and several of the financial backers of *Balalaika* filed into the third-row seats, Keith hurrying from a breakfast meeting, the playwright leaving his word processor for the occasion, and one backer, Larry Gaynor, wunderkind cosmetics millionaire, flying in from Bloomfield Hills, Michigan, in his company jet. Their ranks were augmented by the costume designer, the set designer, as well as several wives who "just wanted to see Valentina in person."

Word had spread. Today theater history might be made.

Keith sat next to Mel Parkington and Bettina, hoping that Valentina wouldn't be too unnerved.

The stage gradually went dark. Pools of blackness created a heavy, poignant depth. Exotic sounds of uileann pipes, violin, electric guitar, and a computerized synthesizer filled the theater.

As the music surged and throbbed, the lighting subtly changed, transmuting from black to violet, then becoming a deep, nacreous pearl. Gradually revealed in the center of the pearly light, seeming to grow out of it, was a long, silver column. Valentina arched her spine, beginning an arabesque of sensuous, silvery movement, gossamer scarves swirling, reflecting the light.

Keith gasped, enthralled, as the spot went through the color spectrum to hot red. Now the iridescent bodysuit became glittering scarlet, and Valentina a dancing flame.

"Jesus God and Mary," he heard Bettina mutter beside him.

The music ended some several minutes later in a climax of drums, and sudden darkness that quenched the brilliant flame.

Spontaneous applause rang through the empty theater as Keith grinned from ear to ear, feeling rushes of love for Valentina so intense that his chest felt tight.

"I think we have ourselves a star," Bettina whispered to Tony.

The following day, rehearsals began.

To Valentina's shock, playing opposite her was the star who had once bombarded her with phone calls and flowers, Ben Paris. He had been pushed on them after Continental Studios had become a financial partner in the Broadway production. But that was all right since Keith wanted some Hollywood glitz to insure box office success, and already had a movie sale in mind.

"Surprised to see me?" he said to Valentina. In worn jeans and a white sweater, Ben Paris looked even handsomer than Valentina remembered.

"Well, it's something I never expected," she responded warily. Was he going to come on to her again? She hoped not. "I had no idea you could dance . . . or sing."

"I can't sing too well, but only a few people know that I

have a fifteen-year background in modern jazz and tap. I toured with Martha Graham for almost two years—that's where I met Bettina. Of course, I danced under my real name, not as Ben Paris.''

"Your real name?''

"If I tell you will you keep it a secret?''

"I'll try.''

"It's Benito Prazzo,'' he told her, grinning. "I was born in Sicily, if you can believe it.''

Fifteen people had speaking roles, five of whom also danced, and there was a chorus of twelve men and women, plus ten more walk-ons who would do crowd and fight scenes.

The long, slow process began. Mornings were spent reading their lines aloud, "walking" through their parts, going back to the author for rewrites or clarification. In three weeks all would be expected to have their parts memorized.

In the afternoons, they worked on the musical numbers.

"I've worked with Bettina Orlovsky before and she's sheer hell,'' remarked Jenny Trillin, the superb dancer playing the role of Lena. She and Valentina had become good friends. "Bettina will work and rework a combination until you think you're going to scream. She'll try new things a dozen different ways, and she'll expect you to stay with her through all of it—and to get it right the first time, or else.''

"I've noticed,'' said Valentina.

Jenny explained, "She'll stop at nothing to get just the effect she wants. But it's worth it—that's why we all put up with her. The woman is a genius, Valentina. She'll make us all look fabulous.''

As three weeks segued into four, and the production slowly began to take shape, Valentina realized that Keith was avoiding her. He seldom spoke directly to her, and when he did, his words were strictly business.

He showed up every day, usually sitting in the third row,

observing, then left early. His face was grim, his eyes deeply shadowed. It was obvious something was on his mind.

Leaving the theater one cool September evening, bone tired, Valentina felt a surge of loneliness. She missed the closeness she'd felt with Keith during those wonderful four weeks they'd worked together, the feelings they both had shared.

The setting sun had imparted a golden dazzle to the glass windows of Manhattan. She decided to walk the twenty blocks back to her hotel, but had gone only two when she saw a familiar figure ahead of her—Keith.

She broke into a run, catching up to him. "Keith— Keith!"

He turned and saw her, his face lighting up. "Are you walking home today?"

"I thought I would. The weather . . ." Almost touching, they strolled along sidewalks teeming with the usual eclectic mix of New Yorkers.

"So we are friends, but only friends from a distance, right?" Valentina inquired at last.

His face looked ashen. "Val. God, I'm so sorry, but I—well, there are problems.

"Has something happened?"

"Yes, Cynthia hasn't been doing too well. She's going to have to have a coronary bypass. The prognosis is good, but she's very frightened."

"I . . . I see."

"Her surgery is scheduled for next week."

"Of course," Valentina murmured. "Oh, I hope everything works out for her. I know it sounds strange but I wish I could send Cynthia my best wishes."

"You can. She loves your music, Val . . . she is a very trusting woman, and I suppose naïve. She has no idea of what's happened between us and she's told me she wants to meet you when she's fully recuperated. She says she's your greatest fan."

"Oh," said Valentina, pleasantly surprised.

"I didn't know what to tell her."

"I'd like to visit her in the hospital," Valentina said after a long moment.

Valentina rapped twice on the half-closed hospital room door, and then pushed it open, stepping into a private room flooded with sunlight and bouquets of flowers.

"Nurse, would you— Oh! Oh!" cried Cynthia, who was lying propped up with a book on her chest. "It's you, Valentina . . . Thank you for coming."

Cynthia's beauty appeared fragile, her skin translucently bluish.

"How are you feeling, Cynthia? Keith said the doctors predict a full recovery. That's wonderful! I brought you something to read."

Valentina put down her bag from Doubleday Book Shops, which held several best-sellers and a selection of Blue Orchids CD's. It seemed to take all of Cynthia's strength to reach for the bag and open it.

"Oh, thank you so much . . . it was so thoughtful of you. But please sit down, Val. It's so good to meet you finally. Keith talks about you all the time. He says you'll be Broadway's newest star!"

With a pang of guilt, Valentina pulled up a bedside chair.

"How are rehearsals going?" Cynthia wanted to know.

Relieved to have something to talk about, Valentina launched into an account. The original set designs were being scrapped, and they were starting from scratch again. Four new songs were being written to replace three that the lyricist and composer had junked. There'd been major arguments between the author and the set designer, and between Bettina and the director. Ben Paris's female fans kept sneaking into the rehearsal theater and extra security had to be hired.

Cynthia seemed to lose interest halfway through. "Lovely," she said, sighing, laying her head on the pillow. "I suppose . . . I suppose you enjoy working with my husband."

Valentina froze.

"Why, yes, I do, he is very professional," she said quickly.

"Keith is so special," Cynthia went on. "I know I'm not exactly the most exciting person anymore. I don't share much in his world. I can't. I pretend I don't care, but I do. It hurts me to see him so vital and active while I've become a semi-invalid."

"I'm sorry," Valentina whispered.

Cynthia sighed, closing her eyes. "I envy you so, Valentina. Do you know I saw Blue Orchids' first New York concert? I'd brought my niece and I caught one of the orchids you threw across the footlights. I still have it somewhere, pressed in a book as a keepsake."

"Oh, Cynthia." Valentina could not stop the tears from falling. "Oh, oh," she repeated, her eyes filling up again, and overflowing down her cheeks.

Cynthia opened her eyes and gazed softly at her. "My husband wants a hit so badly," she finished. "And I want it for him too. Please give it to him. For me."

"Again! Again!" shouted Bettina. "Dammit, Ben, get that positioning right this time, will you? Hit your marks! You're not playing Captain Hook, you're supposed to be a romantic lead. I want those ladies in the audience to swoon. Piano player! Are you with us? You're playing a little too slow. We need—"

"One dose of rapture coming right up," Ben quipped, giving Valentina a smoldering look.

Ben had the same lithe, muscular build as Alexander Gudonov, emphasized by the sleeveless black unitard he wore during rehearsals.

"The rapture's supposed to be onstage, not off," Valentina responded, smiling.

"Val . . . Val . . ." Ben sighed. "Relax, will you? I'm not going to jump your bones. I've changed, can't you see that? I've grown up over the past few years."

Valentina kept back her laugh of disbelief. Even now, standing in the wings was a pretty young woman in jeans and a tweed jacket, her eyes yearning toward Ben.

The piano began to play again, and Valentina assumed her position for the first combination. Ben positioned himself beside her.

"As long as we dance well together, that's *all* that matters," she told him as they glided onstage.

Orchid let herself in the stage entrance of the theater, showing the press pass she'd wangled from one of her lovers, a reporter for the New York *Daily News*.

Wearing a mousy brown wig, no makeup, and granny glasses, along with a shapeless long skirt with boots, she hoped her Annie Hall look would prevent Valentina from recognizing her.

She *had* to see if Val was as good as rumors said she was.

"She's a natural," her reporter boyfriend had told her. "It's all over Broadway. That girl will kick some kind of ass before the season is over."

God . . . could she really? Orchid's heart hammered as she slipped into the darkened theater and found a seat in the back row. She sat down, her eyes riveted on the stage, where a dance rehearsal was in full swing. Valentina, Ben Paris, and ten other dancers clad in a motley collection of old dancewear were rehearsing the dream sequence.

Orchid watched as her sister was lifted up by a muscular Ben Paris and draped over his shoulder, her back arched with supple grace.

"Jeez," she muttered to herself. "It isn't fair . . . Val has so much talent," she thought dazedly.

Orchid stumbled to her feet, feeling like the wicked stepmother in Cinderella, and fled into the lobby.

Monumental advance publicity generated sellout crowds at the Boston tryouts in early October, but the reviews came in mixed. Not bad, but not sensational either. Alarmed, the production people sat up late, filling the room with blue cigarette smoke as they argued about what could be done to give first aid to the production.

There were frantic rewrites. Extra hours as Bettina revised the choreography. Valentina had to memorize more than eighty new lines of dialogue, and learn two new songs to replace two that had been cut.

"It's tough making big changes at the last minute," Keith told the assembled cast when they were back in New York for more rehearsals. "Rewrites are hell. That's Broadway, folks—a little patching here and there, a hell of a lot of hard work—but somehow it all comes together in the end."

Afterward, as the cast was filing out of the meeting room, Ben Paris pulled Valentina aside. "How about some dinner, sweet girl?"

"I've made plans."

"Sure you can't change them?"

"These are plans I can't break."

His eyes begged her, but Valentina turned away. She'd felt the onstage chemistry blazing between them, but she wasn't interested. She just couldn't get Keith out of her head.

"Darling," exclaimed Peaches, surprised to see Valentina show up unexpectedly on her doorstep in Franklin, Michigan. She drew her daughter to her for a warm hug. "It's so great to see you, Val—but I thought—I mean, isn't your play opening in two days?"

"Yes, and I just flew in for a couple of hours." Valentina flushed. "I want to go visit Nadia's grave, Peaches. My Russian mother. I feel I have to."

"Of course," Peaches said, after only a brief pause.

"You don't mind, do you?" Valentina said. "Peaches, I love you so much, I always will. And I do want to spend some time with you first and share all our news. But then—"

"I understand completely," Peaches said warmly.

At White Chapel Cemetery in Troy, where a gravesite had been marked with a small white headstone, Valentina sat on a bench, staring at the lush plantings of mums, her mind picturing the beautiful woman with wings of black hair, who had loved her so much. Her eyes moistened as she tired to formulate the right words to say.

"Mama . . . *mamochka* . . ." Even the Russian words came with difficulty to her tongue now.

"*Mamochka,* without your sacrifice I could not be here right now. I hope—I hope you'll be there somewhere when I go onstage. Will you watch over me? Will you . . . ?"

Then the words failed her, and she merely sat in silence, soaking up the feeling of peace that seemed to surround her. After an hour, she rose to leave, feeling drained, but happier. She had a flight to catch back to New York.

Opening night. Valentina felt the cast's contagious excitement; they were high with anticipation of a hit. Warming up with the other dancers at the barre that had been set up in a rehearsal room, she tried to control the rapid pounding of her heart, the slight stomach twinges of stage fright.

Peaches and Edgar had come in from Detroit, and even Jo McBanta, the girls' old dancing instructor from Detroit, had sent word she'd be flying in. Valentina's agent, Mike Duffy, was bringing a theater party of twelve.

But Orchid was not coming to the opening night.

Valentina had called and begged her to attend, but Orchid stubbornly refused. "You don't need me—and I don't need you," she'd insisted.

"*Of course* I need you, Orchie . . . I do! *Why* are you so angry at me? What have I done?"

"*You know what you've done,*" Orchid said, ominously hanging up.

Now Bettina Orlovsky walked into the room. "Listen up!" she called to the dancers. They obediently stopped their stretches and turned to face the choreographer who had made their lives miserable for the past two and a half months.

"Tonight's going to be a tough night. You'll be dancing routines that are relatively new and you haven't had nearly as much rehearsal time as we would have liked, or as you needed."

There were murmurs among the dancers.

"But let me tell you this!" Bettina snapped. "I worked damn hard to choose the best and I picked you. I know goddamn well what you're capable of, because I've pulled it out of you inch by sweating inch. You can do it. You're . . .''

Bettina's face suddenly filled with emotion. ''You're wonderful dancers, every one of you,'' she finished, rushing out of the room with streaming eyes.

As soon as the door closed behind her, there was a hubbub of surprise. Jenny Trillin turned to gaze at Valentina. ''My God, even that old bitch has a soft spot.''

Valentina had just left Makeup, when she bumped into Keith in the corridor. He looked even more handsome in evening dress, his dark hair cut in the new, fashionable short style. Electricity crackled from him tonight—as if the triumph were already theirs.

''Val,'' he said, stopping. ''You look beautiful. You're— wonderful.''

They gazed at each other, and Valentina again felt the electricity leap between them. By his intent look, she knew he felt it too.

''You're so important to me,'' Keith said intensely. ''More important than is right. I want to be a part of your success tonight. I want to be with you . . . in your thoughts. Any way I can.''

''You will be,'' she whispered. ''You always are.''

''Val, this has been tormenting me. I can't believe it. My life has been turned upside down since I met you. I think about you constantly. I don't know the answer, I don't think there is one, but, God—''

He broke off as Ben Paris emerged from his dressing room.

''Break a leg, Val,'' Keith told her briefly, squeezing her hand and then breaking away. He strode down the corridor, toward backstage. Valentina stared after him, her hands clenched to her chest.

Ben Paris raised an eyebrow, and Valentina spun, hurrying away.

The first, plaintive notes of a balalaika rose over the

first-act set, a pleasant village near St. Petersburg, Russia, buried deep in snow.

The production jelled from the very first scene.

When she finished singing "Sometime, Somewhere," the major love ballad, applause thundered for a full five minutes. Valentina felt a thrill of the purest happiness she had ever known. She was suffused with love not only for her audience, but also for Keith Leonard.

Sardi's, at Forty-fourth Street and Broadway, reeked with Broadway tradition. The paneled walls in the main dining room were hung with hundreds of celebrity caricatures and signed cast photos depicting such luminaries as Laurence Olivier, Vivien Leigh, Katherine Cornell, Bert Lahr, Gertrude Lawrence, Yul Brynner, Ezio Pinza, Rex Harrison, Patricia Neal, Henry Fonda, even a young and gloriously handsome Marlon Brando.

The cast and crew had assembled about one hour after the curtain's closing. Stars didn't always appear—sometimes they met to wait out the reviews in the producer's suite—but tonight both Valentina and Ben Paris knew they wouldn't miss the traditional wait for the first reviews to come in.

"Wow," breathed Ben to Valentina, impressed despite his Hollywood fame.

They had reserved a room upstairs from the main dining room, and ordered huge plates of shrimp and lobster salad, along with platters of baby lamb chops, mixed salad, and different kinds of fancy sandwiches. Supervising the festivities was Vincent Sardi, who had seen it hundreds of times over the past fifty years.

"Oh, Val—oh, darling!" Peaches hugged Valentina for the tenth time. "Honey, you were so wonderful, everyone loved you. I had to hold on to Edgar to keep him from jumping up and yelling out, 'That's my daughter!' The applause went on and on and on. Six curtain calls. Unbelieveable."

"You set Broadway on its ear," Edgar raved, hugging her tightly.

"I can hardly believe it yet," Valentina exclaimed, smiling at the two people who had reared her so lovingly.

"Oh, darling, we're just so happy for you. If only—" Peaches hesitated. "If only Orchid had been here too. Then it would have been perfect."

"She just didn't want to be here. She hates me," Valentina replied quietly.

Edgar had wandered off to say hello to David Merrick, one of his oldest friends.

Peaches hesitated. "Do you think you might try to see her again? Talking face-to-face is so much better than a phone call, and maybe that's all she needs."

"I've tried a dozen times."

"Then try once more, will you?" Peaches begged. "I love both of you and it hurts me to see you like this. If she won't see you this time, then I'll get the two of you back together. And Daddy Edgar can't understand it. To him, family is family."

Valentina agreed to do as Peaches asked, just as the assistant stage manager returned with the first armload of newspapers. With a flourish, he set them down on a table. The cast crowded around. Abruptly the chatter stilled. The atmosphere became strained.

Keith Leonard flipped through the thick *New York Times* to the theater section. The room became deathly hushed. He held it up and began to read aloud.

" 'From the first, plaintive notes of a Russian balalaika, to the rousing second-act reprise of "Sometime, Some-where," *Balalaika,* touted as the year's best new musical, lives up to its reputation as a heartwarming, show-stopping extravaganza. It's in the same class as *My Fair Lady, South Pacific,* and *Funny Girl.*

"One reason the production succeeds so brilliantly is that the producers brought in some big-time names. Valentina Lederer, formerly of Blue Orchids, absolutely set the show ablaze with her fiery dancing and powerful voice . . .' "

There was more. Ben Paris was hailed as "a stage star of major proportion," and the dancing was touted as "strikingly brilliant and innovative.'' Keith Leonard was again described as ''Broadway's wunderkind.''

Keith's voice was drowned out by a whoop from Ben. There were screams of excited delight from the clustered dancers and actors. They surged forward to grab the papers, reading aloud bits and pieces from various reviews, laughing, crying, jumping up on the tables to whirl wildly about.

Dancer after dancer came up to hug Valentina, and Ben lifted her up for a bear squeeze, roaring, ''My pretty! My wonderful partner! God, I love you! I want your body!''

News people from WABC, Channel 7, showed up with minicams, and interviewed Valentina, Ben, Keith, the director, and several of the actor/dancers, in particular Jenny, who had attracted favorable reviews as well. Bettina got loaded and had to be half carried out to a cab, laughingly crying out as she went, to everyone's vast amusement, ''I'm notta bitch, I'm notta bitch!''

Later, when they'd all had a chance to read the papers, Keith whispered quietly in her ear, ''Val, you're a star now, a real one. I knew you could do it. Did you think about my words?''

''You know I did.''

Balalaika played to packed houses. Valentina continued to try to contact Orchid. But on the following Saturday, Peaches called and said that Orchid had left on Val's opening night for Amsterdam.

''Amsterdam?'' Valentina was stunned.

''Yes, dear, she said there were new music groups forming over there and she thought she'd check it out. She did give me her hotel, though, if you want to call her.''

''Fine,'' Valentina said, shifting the conversation to other topics. She felt sure Orchid wouldn't answer her calls in Amsterdam any more than she'd answered them in New York. Her heart felt heavy with her sister's rejection, and she was also beginning to be angry. Orchid was behaving like a spoiled, jealous brat.

Orchid's room at the Amstel Hotel in Amsterdam, one of Europe's smaller grand palaces, reeked with the rich, musky odors of sex. Sunlight streamed through the windows, bringing with it traffic sounds from a city of charm and decadence. Windmills, tulips, tree-lined canals, and rows of three-hundred-year-old gabled houses drew tourists to the fabled Dutch city. But in the infamous *walletjes,* the red-light district, kimono-wearing prostitutes sat in street windows, beckoning customers. Any imaginable drug was openly available. If you wanted to lose yourself in a round of continuous, heavy-duty partying, Amsterdam was the place.

On the bed, straddling a huge, bearlike man with a pelt of golden fur all over his body, Orchid was building toward orgasm.

She gasped and moaned as the man lying underneath her gave violent thrusts upward, gripping her at the hips. Piet Vanderkloot was a Dutch construction worker, twenty-four years old, with a grizzled beard and mustache, nearly six feet six inches tall. He fucked like a wild bear. They'd tried at least five different positions already, and his imagination seemed endless.

Just as she was about to begin her first, convulsive shudder, Piet suddenly stopped his frenzied bucking. He looked at her with his deep blue eyes and then gave her a push, swiveling her around on his huge cock so that she faced the other way.

The sensation caused her—at last—to tumble over the brink. Screaming, pulsating with one explosion after another, she lost herself in the burst of ecstasy, the only time nowadays that she was happy at all.

Piet was snoring gently. Completely satisfied, Orchid began to relax and let her mind drift. She knew she'd run away to Amsterdam . . . to escape Val's success, the almost daily magazine and newspaper articles that served as a torturing reminder of her own failure.

Amsterdam, where Europe's drug culture congregated, offered everything. Orchid had plunged right in, sampling everything except the hard drugs. It suited her self-destructive mood. She'd even joined a new, all-female rock group—in Dutch their name meant "Sexual Flowers." But when she showed up late for two or three of the rehearsals, they'd kicked her out.

That night in her hotel room, she'd finished a whole bottle of wine and gotten morosely drunk, feeling exceptionally sorry for herself. *Nobody needed her!*

Maybe she should just take a handful of the red pills Piet had given her the previous week. Swallowed down with a whole bottle of wine, they'd knock her out all the way . . . permanently. But halfway through the first handful, her gag reflex took over, and she vomited uncontrollably.

"God!" she wept, lying on the floor, gasping. "God, are you there? Why did you do this to me. *Dammit!* All I want is to be like Valentina. That's *all* I want. Why can't you give me some talent too? Why?"

But there was no answer.

She moaned, retching again, knowing her sickness was deep within her, and finally she got up and staggered to the bathroom, intending to wash her face.

Halfway there, she heard another sound through the thin walls of her hotel room. It was familiar and reassuring—the tap-tap-tap of the keys of a typewriter. The guest in the room next to hers was typing something.

Orchid wobbled back to her bed, and flopped down on it, passing out until the following morning.

At dawn she woke up, feeling oddly refreshed, despite her crashing hangover. She dressed and went out on the streets again, browsing around on Elandsgracht Street until she found a pawnshop that had some electric typewriters for sale.

She bought one.

She already had twenty pages written now—a screenplay she intended to call *Rock, Lady, Rock.* It was going to be a "kiss and tell" based on Valentina's vicious betrayal of Blue Orchids.

The insistent pealing of the phone brought her thoughts back.

"The damn hotel desk," Orchid gasped, rolling off Piet. "I *told* them to hold my calls today." She glared at it.

It rang four more times, and finally Piet reached out a beefy hand and picked up the receiver, handing her the telephone. "Here, baby," he said in his thick Dutch accent. "I hate the sound, so you answer."

Annoyed, Orchid snatched the receiver from him. "Yeah?"

She was greeted by the unmistakable reedy hum and long pause that signified a transatlantic phone call.

"Shit," she exclaimed, ready to hang up.

"Orchid," came her sister's voice, thinned by the wire. "Please, I beg of you—"

"*I don't want to talk to you!*" Orchid snapped.

"Will you please come back to New York so we can talk?" Valentina begged. "Or I'll take the Concorde and meet you in London . . . please? I can do it on Monday, the theater is dark then, I'll fly over for just a few hours. Orchie, we can't go on like this. We're sisters. Don't you remember at the children's home when we first met, we—"

As Valentina began to talk about when they were eight, Orchid shrank. She knew Val was trying to get to her with sentimentality—remind her of their wonderful years together—and it was working.

She was almost ready to agree to the meeting, when her eyes, darting around the room, hit the Olivetti, which still had a sheet in the roller from *Rock, Lady, Rock.*

"Orchid? Are you still there?" Valentina said.

"I . . . I can't talk," Orchid gasped, setting the phone in its cradle.

She jumped out of bed, flinging on a bathrobe, and rushed over to the typewriter where she began frantically to type. The *real* story of Blue Orchids . . . and when people read it, they'd all know how *she* had suffered.

"Still got a hot pussy?" inquired Piet, emerging from the john.

"Get out of here," Orchid snapped, bending over the keyboard. "Can't you see how busy I am?"

Hollywood
1986

A year later, Orchid was seated on a Pan Am jet to LA, flipping restlessly through a copy of *Vogue*. From the cover, Valentina's smiling face looked up at her, stunningly beautiful. She'd been on the cover of almost every European magazine, too, so that Orchid couldn't walk down a street without seeing Val's face.

They airbrushed the hell out of those fashion photos, she told herself, tossing the magazine aside. Her sister wasn't all that gorgeous!

The elderly American woman seated next to her picked up the copy of *Vogue* and opened it to the article about Valentina, which also featured a photograph of Blue Orchids. "Oh, my God," the woman gasped, looking at Orchid. "It's . . . you're Orchid! You're . . . Blue Orchids! My grandson bought all your albums. Good heavens, I can't believe I'm really sitting next to you!"

Orchid's annoyance faded away. It soothed her battered ego to have someone recognize her.

"Are you going back to the States to make a record?" the woman inquired naïvely.

"Yes," Orchid lied. She added, more truthfully, "And I've written a screenplay and tomorrow morning I've got an appointment with a big Hollywood agent who's interested in it."

ICM agent Conn Danson was on the telephone in the bathroom issuing orders to his stockbroker.

"Now don't forget," he finished. "I want ten thou on it. And maybe we'll take a breakfast meeting next Friday at Jan's, right off La Cienega on Beverly, near the Beverly Center. Seven o'clock, all right? I want to talk more in depth about real estate limited partnerships."

He concluded the call, hung up, and walked into his bedroom, opening up one of the scripts on his nightstand. The little gem he'd selected today was entitled *Pit Bull,* the story of a Cujo-like dog that rampaged through a small town killing everyone in sight.

Conn made a face and tossed it to the floor. Glancing at his reflection in the mirrored walls, he stood tall, sucking in his gut. Not too bad for forty-six, he assured himself. Or . . . did he need a little liposuction along his slightly bulging love handles? Shit, he didn't think he needed plastic surgery yet, but he knew that when he did, he'd sign up for the program in a heartbeat.

Appearance was everything in LA, and his current mistress, Raven Gregory, had made it very clear just what she required in a man. It was imperative that he be part of the Hollywood power structure, but he must also be a hunky-looking stud who could go like a goddamn pistol for hours on end . . .

So far he'd managed, but there were nights when he worried about it.

Still naked, he moved to the vanity cabinet and opened the top drawer. Inside was a small plastic bag filled with white powder, the very best, provided for him by Raven, a sometime actress who'd dubbed herself "coke supplier to the stars." Next to that was a mirror, a small silver spoon, and a folded hundred-dollar bill.

Conn stared at them longingly for several minutes, but decided to wait until tonight when Raven came over, before treating himself to the high-grade cocaine. He was no coke head. No way. All he did was use a little before making love, to give him that extra boost he liked so much . . . and maybe needed.

Half an hour later, Conn was seated behind the huge white marble-topped desk in his office at ICM's office on Beverly Boulevard. Everything was white—the carpet, the furniture, the walls, the tables, the telephones, the row of cabinets that held the stacks of screenplays and back issues of *Variety, The Hollywood Reporter,* and *Billboard* that Conn deemed inappropriate to have in plain view. He even insisted that his secretary, Magda Boynton, wear white, just for the effect. In fact, the only spot of color in the office was the huge painting that hung in his private office, depicting Conn's own face airbrushed onto the stylized drawing of a pouncing leopard.

He'd had it specially commissioned.

"Mr. Danson," said his secretary through the intercom. "Your eleven o'clock appointment is here."

"What? Who?"

"Orchid Lederer. Remember, Edgar Lederer set up the appointment."

"Oh, yes, yes." He owed Lederer several favors over the years, Conn remembered. He sighed, wondering just how awful his daughter's screenplay would be. Bad, worse, or downright horrible? Fortunately, he'd only scheduled her for twenty minutes, long enough to give his usual pep talk, and a recommendation for the Michael Hague screenwriting course at UCLA's Continuing Education Center.

But when Magda ushered the girl in, Conn was pleasantly surprised. She was a little beauty, wearing a tight baby-blue leather pantsuit trimmed with fringes and studs, and three-and-a-half-inch heels that made her look like a high-class hooker. Her glorious hair flowed over her shoulders, and she had a heart-shaped face with a feline prettiness, and enormous blue eyes. Her walk undulated.

"Well, hello there," he said, much more warmly than he'd intended.

"Hello." Orchid grinned at him, her smile revealing white, perfect teeth.

"How was your flight from Amsterdam?"

"Oh—turbulent." She gave him an intense look, turning the reply into something sexual.

Conn decided to seat the girl in the chair immediately beside his, rather than across his desk. He lifted the screenplay in its classy-looking blue jacket. "In one sentence, tell me what this is about."

She didn't even blink. "It's the story of two girls who form a rock group and how one betrays the other."

"Nothing personal in this, hmm?" he inquired. He remembered reading about Blue Orchids' split a few months ago. "Anything that'll get us in deep legal shit?"

"I've changed all the names and places and I've added some new characters."

He nodded. "Well, I'll take a look at it. I have to tell you, though, that more than five hundred scripts go through my office each year and four hundred and ninety of them are dreck. Everyone in America thinks they can write for the silver screen, and most of them can't even get the mechanics right."

"I can," she told him, those blue eyes blazing. "And—and I can do lots more too."

Goddamn, she was hot stuff. And she'd lived in Amsterdam, where everything hung very loose, mucho uninhibited.

"Look," he suggested. "I'll tell you what. I don't usually do this for beginners, but how about if we take a dinner meeting tomorrow night? We can talk more about, well, your screenplay and other things then."

She nodded excitedly. And Conn felt a frisson of excitement too. She would make a nice change from the intensity of Raven.

"More," his mistress demanded that night, writhing under him, her black hair, dampened with perspiration, spread across the pillow. "More, Conn! Harder!"

Raven's "thing" was issuing orders. He did his best, but was starting to go a bit soft after his first climax a few minutes ago. Apologizing, he pulled out, and reached for the mirror he'd placed by the bedside stand. Laying out two thin lines of white powder, he rolled up a hundred-dollar bill and snuffed up the cocaine, waiting for the first, sweet rush.

"Can't you get it up again without that?" Raven complained.

"I take a little coke, you get the benefits," he told her, manipulating himself into rock-hardness again. "Anyway, you sold it to me, remember?"

They went back at it again, and this time Conn easily brought Raven to several more climaxes, pleased when her loud screams of abandon echoed through the room.

"Hey," Raven said sharply. "You're thinking about something else, aren't you? I can tell."

"I'm not," he lied.

"You're *mine*. You belong to Raven . . . you're Raven's little bear," she cooed, as she strode over to her clothes and began to get dressed. She was a tall brunette who said she was thirty-eight, which meant she was probably at least forty-four, but she had a slim, elegant body and was great in bed.

He watched her. That remark about other women . . . Raven was growing far too possessive. Maybe she'd served her purpose. Of course—He stopped to think. If he dumped her, who would he buy his coke from?

Over dinner at Jimmy's, on the corner of Moreno Drive and Little Santa Monica Boulevard, Orchid could scarcely contain her excitement. Two tables away, actress Teri Garr was dining with Amy Heckerling, a writer and director who looked like a star herself.

Everything was going exactly the way she wanted it, from the delicious *coq au vin* with *duxelles,* to the attentive man who had told her to call him Conn, and hung on every one of her stories about Blue Orchids.

Finally she could stand it no longer. She summoned up her courage to ask Conn the question that had been burning in her mind for the past twenty-four hours.

"What . . . that is, what did you think about *Rock, Lady, Rock*?"

"It's wonderful."

"Migod, migod, migod," she sighed.

"It's great. Fabulous, Sensational. What more can I say?" Conn said, enjoying her spontaneous pleasure. "Your story line is fantastico, and I'm going to put together a complete package for your script, from director down to the lead stars. We're gonna make this thing fly, Orchid. We're going to take it all the way. I've already got my secretary typing up our contract."

As she stared at him, stunned and bedazzled, Conn snapped his fingers for the waiter, who came scurrying over. "Champagne," he ordered. "Cristal. We're going to celebrate."

They finished the bottle of bubbly, and by the time they got up to leave, Orchid was feeling deliciously woozy, the best she'd felt in years. At last! she thought jubilantly. At last she was going somewhere again.

"Would you like to stop by my place for a nightcap?" Conn invited as they got into his white Silver Cloud Corniche.

"Would I!" She didn't even hesitate. He was older than her usual studs and besides . . . if she was required to sleep her way to the top, she'd do it. It would be a small and easily paid price for what she wanted.

Chapter

Seventeen

CONN DANSON'S BEDROOM was a Hugh Hefner fantasy. Orchid ran in, crowing with delight, to inspect the king-sized four-poster waterbed with mirrors set in the canopy, the massive Bang and Olufsen stereo system, a wide-screen TV, and a collection of hundreds of pornographic videos. Sheepskin rugs were spread in front of a big fireplace, and the huge mirrored bathroom was equipped with a Jacuzzi, and lined with cupboards containing Conn's collection of sex toys.

"I never saw so many vibrators in my life!" she gasped, pawing through a selection of battery-operated dildos of all shapes and sizes, massagers, and even a "butterfly" vibrator.

"Want to test-drive some of them?" Conn asked, grinning.

"Sure." She reached for him and began to massage him through his clothes, kneading his buttocks in her strong, firm fingers.

Reluctantly Conn pulled away. This one was a firecracker and he didn't intend to screw it up by being impotent.

"Just a sec, hon. I've got something that'll really put us through the roof. We'll do a couple of lines before we get started."

"Um." Orchid looked at the small plastic bag filled with white powder. "I used to do coke but I don't anymore. I'm straight now."

"Oh, just one line," Conn urged. "It'll make everything that much better."

She frowned. "I spent a whole year in Amsterdam partying myself crazy, but now I'm back in LA and I don't want to do that stuff anymore."

"Well, if you don't mind . . ." Conn laid out two lines for himself. He sniffed deeply, inhaling every speck of the expensive powder. Then, breathing a sigh of contentment, he reached for Orchid, pulling her sweater down over her shoulders.

Laughing, she helped him peel her clothes off. Within seconds, they were both naked, rolling around on the sheepskin rugs.

Orchid Lederer was simply the best lay he'd ever had.

Several weeks passed, and Orchid was delighted with the turn her life had taken in Hollywood. Conn Danson was a man of his word. He'd offered her a fair contract, she'd had Edgar's lawyers check it out, and he actually *was* putting together the elements of a package to make her film.

One of his other clients was Jette Michaud, the sultry star now on location in Acapulco making a picture with Mickey Rourke. He'd sent the script to Jette and the star had agreed to read the screenplay.

"Oh, lordy," Orchid enthused to Peaches long-distance. "Jette Michaud! Can you believe it! She's so cool. And he's getting me a director and producer . . . like Lou Rudolph. He's even got three or four stars on his client list who could play the male lead. Don't you think it's absolutely, totally incredible?"

"What's this screenplay about, Orchid?" Peaches asked. "You never did tell me the plot."

"It's . . . it's about rock singers," she explained evasively.

"Well, I'm sure it's a very good script. What else are you doing, honey? Have you met any interesting men?" Peaches always asked that, in the increasingly diminished hope that Orchid might actually settle down sometime.

"Just Conn."

"Conn? You don't mean the Conn Danson who's your new agent, do you?"

"Oh, it's nothing," Orchid lied. "He just takes me out to dinner once in a while."

She wondered what Peaches would think if she knew

about the sybaritic delights in Conn's bedroom. Seated naked, munching popcorn, they watched movies with titles like *Games Couples Play, Stiff Competition,* and *Debbie Does Dallas.* Then, as the story onscreen grew more torrid, they created a few hot scenes of their own.

He had a problem with his erections sometimes. But Orchid knew what to do to get him turned on, or he'd snort a couple lines of cocaine.

She was even starting to have some feelings for him. Not any sort of major love, but she did like him, and *loved* the fact that he was actually developing *Rock, Lady, Rock.* He was saving her ass, and for that Orchid was willing to overlook a lot. This definitely was an exciting relationship for her.

Raven Gregory screeched her little Fiat to a halt, and finger-waved at the night guard who manned the gatehouse on the private enclave in Brentwood where Conn Danson lived.

She'd been coming here several times a week for nearly three years, and the guard waved her through without question.

Her heartbeat was still racing from the sight she'd just seen through one of Conn's windows while driving past his house—a brief but telling glimpse of her lover striding into the kitchen, stark naked, with someone else, equally naked, standing next to him, both of them raiding the refrigerator. She'd suspected it for weeks, since several people told her he'd been seen dining out with some little cupcake.

The damn fool, she thought, trembling with fury. She parked and sat fuming in the car for several seconds, before switching off the motor, grabbing up her big shoulder bag, and getting out.

She'd warned him.

She found her way to Conn's entrance, and let herself inside with the key he had given her several months ago.

She paused inside the foyer, hearing the sound of the Playboy channel coming from the bedroom. A trail of female clothing lay strewn across the rug, leading in that direction. Raven eyed it in furious revulsion. A large Gucci purse had been dropped on the floor near the couch.

Raven smiled to herself. She walked over to the purse and rummaged in it until she found what she was searching for, a mother-of-pearl compact containing translucent facial powder. Raven dumped the cosmetic from the compact into the base of a nearby tropical plant, and replaced it with several ounces of cocaine that she took from a small baggie. She'd added a hefty dose of heroin to the white mixture—a regular chemical rollercoaster.

Swiftly she walked to the lower liquor cabinet where, she knew, Conn kept his own supply. The four baggies she'd sold him last night were still there. She took them out and replaced them with the new, stronger mix.

She was going to send that fucker Conn Danson and his whore girlfriend orbiting to the nearest star.

"Hey . . . I don't suppose you'd stay the night," Conn murmured, hugging Orchid close.

"I guess so," she said.

"I mean, you don't have to." .

"Oh, I will," she agreed.

He cuddled up next to her, snoring lightly like any husband, and she held him, staring into the darkness. Conn really did like her, she sensed. And she liked him. She could even marry him, she supposed. They were well matched in many ways.

Then she sighed, a wave of sadness flowing through her. She'd *never* found any man she'd seriously consider marrying, and she doubted if she ever would. Was it because of her childhood, the abuse, her essential distrust of men? Who really knew?

She allowed her eyes to close and her breathing to drift off. She'd better get some sleep, because she knew that in the morning Conn would awaken with renewed lust.

Mornings were when he was horniest.

"Baby . . . baby . . ." Conn kissed her awake, nibbling at the lobes of her ears.

Orchid moaned, burying her face in the pillow. She always slept nude and his hands were straying to the cleft between her legs.

"Baby . . . Orchid . . . I've got something for you. Something real, real nice . . ."

"Wanna sleep," she protested.

"Something *real* nice. But first I gotta go in the living room for a second. Be right back." Conn climbed out of bed and padded naked through the condo, returning with one of the baggies, his mirror, and other paraphernalia.

"This early?" Orchid mumbled, struggling awake. "You're gonna toot this early?" She glanced at her watch. "Jeez, it's only eight o'clock!"

"Just a couple of lines, babe. I've been awake for two hours waiting for you to come alive." He laid out the lines on the mirror, then began to stroke himself, his hand moving rapidly up and down until he was erect.

"Let me put it in," he said, panting. "Then I'll snort . . . would you like that? I want to get high when I'm already in you. That'll really prime my engine. That's high octane, premium fuel."

She wasn't feeling very sexy—night was her preferred time to make love—but Orchid willingly accommodated him, opening her legs so he could enter her. Kneeling astride her, Conn began to pump and thrust, moaning with pleasure. Then he stopped and balanced the mirror, manipulating the rolled-up hundred-dollar bill.

She could see the rush hit him at once.

"This is the greatest—" he began, sucking in great gasps of air as he often did after snorting. But then his breathing became an odd, choking gasp.

"Hey," Orchid began.

Conn stared unseeingly down at her, his eyes wide and blank, his face turning an ugly shade of ashen red. Beads of sweat had popped out on his forehead, and his mouth had fallen open. Spittle was forming at the sides of his lips.

"Conn?" she cried. *"Conn, Conn, are you all right?"*

He wasn't. Suddenly all two hundred and ten pounds of him collapsed on top of her.

"Conn!" she screamed, trying to struggle out from underneath his dead weight. "Oh, no," she sobbed. "Oh, God . . . God . . ."

Orchid finally managed to squeeze out from under Conn's inert form, and she began to shake him wildly, slapping his face.

Then she grabbed the phone to call the Brentwood police.

The Brentwood police station was classier than most. They treated her with courtesy, making sure she had a cold Pepsi, and a comfortable chair in a vacant office.

"Tell me," said the handsome detective, after he had read Orchid her rights and questioned her to make sure she understood them. "Tell me everything from the beginning. Where did you get the drugs in your compact? Were you the one who supplied drugs to Conn Danson?"

Orchid stared at him dazedly. She hadn't touched her Pepsi. She was still immobilized with the shock of Conn's death—he OD'd, the ambulance attendant told her. While he was on top of her . . . *inside her.* The horror of it still overwhelmed her, and she'd barely been functioning by the time the police took her to the station.

They'd found drugs in her purse. They thought she gave them to Conn—that she, personally, had OD'd him.

The horror of learning that fact had nearly unhinged Orchid.

"I didn't!" she screamed, frantic to clear herself. "I never would have! I didn't even do any myself! I'd stopped—I don't do drugs anymore! I liked him! Conn was good to me. He treated me well. He was my—my—"

She collapsed in wild sobbing.

The detective stared at her, unmoved. "How much did you sell him per week?"

"I *told* you . . . nothing!" Orchid swallowed, regaining control of herself. "I want to have a lawyer, please. I want to make a phone call. I want to call my father, and you have to let me."

Peaches answered the phone. "Is anything wrong?" she immediately asked, recognizing the fright in Orchid's voice.

"Yes. Please. Daddy Edgar," Orchid croaked.

"I think he's just leaving for a lunch meeting at Franklin Hills with Harold Beznos. Let's see if I can catch him."

Orchid waited, shaking all over, for several minutes, but finally her father was on the line.

"Honey? Orchid? What's wrong, baby doll?" Her father's voice was both warm and anxious, and it unhinged Orchid. She began to cry again, her sobs rolling out in a torrent of despair.

"I—they—they think I—he's dead . . ." she blurted out between bouts of anguished weeping.

"Now, honey, I can't understand what you're saying."

"I said . . ." she choked. "I said Conn D-Danson died, he OD'd and they *say* they found cocaine and heroin in my p-purse, Daddy Edgar, but I never put it there. I swear it, *I swear it*!"

Two weeks later, chastened and miserable, Orchid sat beside Edgar on an American Airlines plane back to Detroit, trying to read a copy of *Vanity Fair* she'd bought at the airport newsstand.

Rock, Lady, Rock, had fallen on hard times.

Nobody was interested in promoting a "package" for it now. She was anathema in Hollywood—the girl who'd been in the sack with Conn Danson when he died. The girl who'd been *questioned* about his death. The devastating publicity was almost as bad as being judged guilty.

"You are coming back to Detroit, young lady," Edgar told her when they received word that Raven had been arrested and charged. The crack team of hotshot criminal lawyers Edgar hired had found enough facts to convince the court of Orchid's innocence. Judge Cohen granted the motion to dismiss, but only after Edgar had spent nearly $25,000 in legal fees and expenses.

"You are going to come home, and you are going to forget all about this stardom crap."

"But—" she'd started to say.

"There aren't any 'buts' about it," Edgar had snapped. "You're not star caliber—that's already been proven conclusively. I told you that the life of a rock star was a sordid one, but you refused to listen, and now we're all paying the price. You can just thank your lucky stars that you have a family that loves and cares about you, and will stand behind you.''

Now the flight attendant came around handing out headsets—they were going to show a Sigourney Weaver flick, *Gorillas in the Mist*. Orchid shook her head. She didn't want to watch a movie. She wanted to disappear from the face of the earth.

She dreaded facing Peaches when she got back to Detroit. What would she tell her? That she'd wanted to be special so badly that she was willing to do anything? Orchid had begun to hate herself, and it was not a pleasant feeling.

''Breakfast is being served,'' Peaches said enticingly. ''Belgian waffles with strawberries and fresh-squeezed orange juice, your favorite.''

There was no response.

Peaches felt an anxious twist of her heart as she stared down at Orchid. The girl lay curled up in a ball underneath a light blanket on her big, untidy bed. Only her tangled mop of auburn hair stuck out from underneath the covers, hair that hadn't been combed in more than a week.

She took a step into the bedroom, flooded with late August sunlight. It smelled shut-in and stale. Orchid had barely left her room in two weeks. Sometimes she played old Blue Orchids music, or FM radio, but mostly she just slept, as much as eighteen hours a day. The horrible incident in LA had drained her of all life.

Something had to be done—and fast.

''I'm not hungry,'' Orchid mumbled, squirming deeper into the pillows. ''Go away.''

''*Fresh* strawberries. I sliced them myself,'' Peaches said, trying to tempt her.

''No,'' Orchid groaned.

''You have to eat, honey! You've hardly touched any food in two weeks. And you haven't left your room. There's a whole world out there, Orchid! You can't just lie here in bed all day. It isn't healthy."

"I d-don't care about healthy."

"Honey, you're terribly depressed."

"Oh, whoopee. I'm so glad you noticed." Orchid grabbed the pillow and folded it over both of her ears, blocking out the sight of her worried mother.

"Dammit!" Peaches swore, unusual for her, and grabbed the pillow away, tossing it onto the floor. "Are you just going to roll over and die? That'd really be giving in, wouldn't it? I can't believe you'd act like this. You're the fighter in this family, Orchid. You're the one I'd depend on if I needed someone to stand up for me no matter what the odds."

Orchid passed a hand wearily over her eyes. "It isn't that simple. I did fight. I fought a lot. And what did it get me?"

"It got you home to me," Peaches cried. "It got you a second chance. Honey . . . I've made a few calls to George Pittman Falk, he's the new dean of Northwestern University's School of Speech. They're willing to waive some of their usual entrance procedures and let you in right away—all you have to do is drive down for an interview." She hesitated. "Your appointment is—tomorrow."

"Tomorrow?" Orchid jerked upright, staring at her mother.

Peaches blushed. "So we've got a lot to do today, don't we? I'll take you to Mira Linder's and we'll have your hair done—a facial—the works. You want to look terrific. They'll fit you in, I've already called."

"But—but—" Orchid shook her head. She seemed stunned at Peaches's temerity in doing such a thing without her permission.

"You have to do *something*, Orchid," Peaches went on firmly. "Look at it as therapy. Anyway, I did choose the program I thought you'd love the most."

"Drama? Do you think I can act?" Orchid unconsciously touched the reddish tangles of her hair.

"Orchie, I'd guess that you can act like a trooper. And we already know you write like one. Even if your screenplay

didn't get developed, the fact that Conn Danson liked it is a
wonderful sign. I think you should take all the screenwriting
courses you can get, and acting lessons too. I think Daddy
Edgar was wrong, darling. You *can* become a star if you
still want to. But you'll have to work at it.''

As Peaches was talking, a series of emotions flashed
across Orchid's face. Disbelief, hope, fear. Peaches felt a
stab of misgiving. Maybe this was only going to drive
Orchid further back into her shell of apathy and depression.

Then Orchid lunged out of bed and headed for Peaches,
throwing her arms around her. ''Northwestern! I can't
believe you did it. Exactly where I would have picked. Oh,
Peaches . . . I love you.''

''I love you too,'' Peaches murmured, wondering if this
impatient and flawed daughter of hers was ever going to
find happiness.

On sunny days, the buildings of Northwestern University,
in Evanston, Illinois, overlooking the sparkling blue ex-
panse of Lake Michigan, looked more like a resort than a
university.

Within days, Orchid's brief notoriety had faded, and she
was accepted as just another student. She settled into the
drama program with a feeling of homecoming. Best of all,
there was Studio 22, where students wrote, staged, and acted
in their own, original productions.

In October she joined the Kappa Kappa Gamma sorority, where many of the members were part of the drama
school. At the cocktail party to welcome the new sorority
sisters, there was a student jazz quartet, and three tables
laden with the best hors d'oeuvres that campus restaurants
could provide.

The hostess, a pretty senior named Jan Rasmussen, had
even provided a handpicked selection of men from the
medical, law, and dental schools. ''They're guaranteed
sexually straight,'' she promised. ''Doctors and lawyers!
The cream of the crop.''

The clean-cut embryo doctors, destined for huge incomes
in suburbia, didn't interest Orchid in the slightest. Wander-

ing through the party holding her drink, she wondered if she'd turned to stone or something. She hadn't even thought about sex in two months.

"You look very familiar," a sexy male voice said in Orchid's ear. "Haven't I seen you before?"

She turned to see a tall, dark young man with fine-hewn, handsome features, and a square jawline, good-looking enough to be a male model. His name tag said Paul Jensen, but his smile seemed strangely familiar. That slight gap between his front teeth . . . Actually he was just the type of faintly dangerous-looking hunk she used to go for. But couldn't he have picked a more original opening line?

"I doubt if you've seen me—in person," she told him, eyeing him over the rim of her wine glass.

"Orchid, don't you really recognize me?"

Orchid shrugged. Half the men she met said things like that and every one of them thought it was some kind of new, exciting line.

"Your real name was Sue Ann Welch."

Sue Ann Welch.

"How . . . how did you know that?" she quavered.

"My real name is Paul Baggio—but now I'm Paul Jensen. Now do you remember me?" he added as Orchid shrieked and threw her arms around him. She whirled him around so violently that he laughed and stepped back. "Hey, don't knock me over. I'm real glad to see you too."

"Paul! Paul! My God, the last time I saw you you were crying and mad as hell because you were being 'dopted by people you didn't even know!"

"Well, now I've just finished med school. Remember, I always said I'd do it, didn't I? I'm an intern now at the University Hospital."

Oblivious to the others, they hugged each other over and over again. "I can't believe it. I just can't believe it," Orchid kept repeating. Paul was from her past . . . he was practically part of her roots.

"I believe it. It's fate," Paul declared. "Fate brought us together."

* * *

The campus coffee shop was crowded with students, some studying as they ate, others chatting in low voices.

"Medical school is organized poverty," Paul told Orchid over coffee and croissants, as they caught up on their lives. His straight brows had drawn together in a slight frown. "Especially in my case. My parents——the people who adopted me—lost most of their money when my father had to go into a nursing home. So I've had to swing most of it myself."

He sighed ruefully. "My debt load is staggering. I mean, I owe more than thirty-six thousand dollars already."

"But you're a doctor," Orchid enthused. "That's wonderful!"

Paul took a bite of his ham and turkey croissant. "I'm not going to be poor for very long . . . I'm going to be an orthopedic surgeon and specialize in sports medicine. Yeah, that's where the big money is, and I've got plans to open a big sports medicine clinic—maybe in California."

"California," Orchid repeated, thinking of her experience in Beverly Hills.

"But that's enough about me. What about you and Blue Orchids? I remember what a frizzy-haired little brat you were, always fighting. God, I can't believe how pretty you turned out. I could start really liking red hair if you gave me a chance."

She gave him a long, assessing look. Her old look. "Ohhh?"

"Red hair like yours . . . auburn, whatever color it is, really turns me on," Paul declared.

The waitress laid down their check in front of Paul. Orchid picked it up.

"I'll get this," she said.

Paul was exhausted all the time from being on an intern's rotation shift. Sometimes he just came to her room and fell asleep in her bed, while Orchid snuggled next to him, studying for her Renaissance Drama class.

"You're different from the others," Paul told her.

"You're more sophisticated—you just brim with life, Orchid. Valentina was crazy when she split up Blue Orchids like she did. What a mistake. I'll bet she regrets it now."

They went for long walks, or attended movies on campus, paying the bargain rate. Once, when Orchid impulsively bought herself a leather bomber jacket at a campus boutique, Paul acted shocked.

"You just spent three hundred and fifty dollars on a jacket that looks like something a pilot would wear."

"Leather is an investment," she told him.

"Well, maybe someday I can afford to 'invest' too," he said, eyeing a man's jacket in buttery soft, deep brown leather. "But not now. For today it's my old corduroy jacket—it still has plenty of wear."

She admired his attitude. She loved being with him. And she'd recovered most of her zest for life. It was all due to Paul, she knew. He had no idea of just how down she'd been when she first arrived on campus. She'd even allowed herself to daydream . . . Well, Peaches had hinted more than once about her settling down.

Paul's birthday was in January, and Orchid thought long and hard before finally giving him a check for a thousand dollars. It was far too much money to give a man she had only been close to for three months, but her allowance from Edgar was huge, there were residuals from Blue Orchids' early hits, and Peaches had also given her a big check for Christmas.

"I can't take this," Paul said.

"It's only money. I want you to buy one of those leather jackets you liked."

"I couldn't."

"Sure you can," she said, giggling. "All you have to do is walk over there, go into the shop, take one of the jackets off the hanger, walk up to the sales person—"

"All right, all right," he agreed, laughing. "I'll buy it. But I want you to know, Orchid, I'll just consider this a loan. Someday I'm going to pay you back with interest."

Paul looked wonderful in the leather jacket. He'd had enough left over to buy several sweaters and some new pleated pants too. That night they splurged for dinner at an Italian restaurant that had just opened on campus.

In a month, Paul became so bogged down with work at the hospital that he was forced to quit his job waiting on tables, so Orchid wrote him another "loan" for two thousand dollars to cover his fixed monthly expenses. She wanted to do it.

"So you and Paul are a thing now, huh?" asked Jan Rasmussen one evening before a meeting of the sorority, which was putting on a special drama evening featuring Milan Stitt, a playwright who had written *The Runner Stumbles*.

"Oh, yes," Orchid responded eagerly.

"I see he bought himself a sharp new leather jacket."

"Yes, isn't it sexy? I love it."

Jan smiled sourly. "Yeah—I love it, too, especially since I paid for it."

Orchid stared at the other girl, bewildered. "No, I bought it for him—at least I gave him the check—"

"No, I gave him the check."

Both women looked at each other.

"You mean—?" Orchid began.

Jan nodded. "I think we've been had."

"I can't *believe* you did such a cheap thing!" Orchid stormed.

"Did what? What's so bad about accepting a couple of loans from two friends?" Paul exclaimed, pacing up and down the small interns' lounge. A hospital PA system blatted in the background.

"Two *friends*? Is that what they call it nowadays? Some *friend*!" Orchid shouted. "She told me she gave you nearly six thousand dollars!"

"Don't yell, Orchid, this is a hospital," Paul said. "Her family is rich, she can afford it," he added, shrugging.

"And me? Is my family rich too? Is that why you've been sleeping with me, Paul—because my family is rich? *And taking my money too?*"

Paul's eyes flashed. "What is your problem, Orchid?

What's the big deal? I'm poor, is that such a big crime? I didn't rip you off or anything like that. I accepted a couple of loans which I absolutely intend to pay back when I have a rich medical practice, at ten percent interest.''

Orchid laughed bitterly. ''You accepted *two* loans from *two* women, you used both of us!''

''No matter what you might think, it was not a major crime, Orchid. Now if you wouldn't mind leaving, I have a postop patient I've got to look at.''

Orchid never spoke to Paul again.

She was tired of men, weary to the soul with the way they'd all treated her. From her two brothers who had raped her in the barn, to Elijah Carmody who had broken her heart for the first time, to all the men who'd screwed her and left her, to Conn Danson who'd gone and died on her. And now, Paul. *The supreme user!*

From now on she was going to concentrate on just one thing—getting through school. Because the world hadn't heard the last of her yet. Somehow, some way, she was going to become famous on her own—the star she'd always wanted to be.

And she would use *men* the way they had used her.

Chapter

Eighteen

New York
1987

THE LATE-NIGHT SUPPER party in the private upstairs dining room at La Grenouille was finally breaking up.

Valentina broke away from an amazingly rich Citicorp banker who wanted to fly her in his private jet to "a little seafood place I know" on Cape Cod for lunch.

A wave of weariness washed over her. The day had been overfull, with studio time in the morning to try to work on a new album, a costume fitting, a dance rehearsal, two interviews, and then the usual evening performance, which always left her feeling ragged after the initial rush of adrenaline. This party, hosted by designer Bill Blass, had been the final straw.

She decided to catch a taxi and go home and give herself an avocado and cucumber facial—something a little special that she whipped up in her blender when she had time.

"You look like a woman who'd like nothing better than a long, hot bath," someone said.

She turned to see Ben Paris, resplendent in evening wear.

"Oh, Ben," she sighed.

He raised an eyebrow. "Is that all I am to you, Valentina? Just 'oh, Ben'?"

She laughed. "I'm sorry, I didn't mean it that way."

"You don't like me very much, do you?" he added, accompanying her as she descended the stairs to the main level of the renowned French restaurant. Gathered outside the door were seven or eight paparazzi who rushed forward, snapping photos of the couple as they emerged. Ben gave them a cavalier wave, Valentina simply smiled.

She said to Ben, "I never said I didn't like you."

"Well, you never said you did either. You still think of me as being this major Don Juan, don't you?"

"Well, aren't you?"

"Come on," he said. "We'll share a cab—or you could come up to my apartment if you want."

"And look at your 'etchings'?" But her tone of voice was kind.

"Men don't keep etchings as bait anymore," he told her, laughing as he waved down a taxi. "Now it's more likely to be a collection of Peruvian artifacts or porno videos—of which I do own several, I must confess. Do you prefer a little light bondage? Or—"

"Hush," she said as they jumped inside.

Ben gave the driver only his address, so she gave hers to the driver and settled back into the seat. She glanced at Ben. He was considered one of the handsomest men in the world, a man whose role in *Balalaika* had made him seem warmer, more accessible to the masses, and had increased his star quotient considerably.

The cab jerked away from the curb. Valentina was thrown against Ben's shoulder, and he steadied her with his arm.

"Val," he said, "you know I'm mostly words, don't you? Plain hot air and a little bullshit. I talk far too much, but my heart is warm. And I no longer screw around the way I used to—I swear I don't."

"I'm happy for you," she said.

"Then . . . ?"

"I still don't want to go back to your apartment with you, Ben. You . . . we . . . we're just not compatible," she finished awkwardly.

"You mean you're still in love with Keith Leonard."

"Who told you that?"

"Nobody had to tell me. It's a lost cause, Val. You're wasting the best years of your life waiting for a man who'll never divorce his wife in a million years."

"I know that," she said stiffly.

"Then why are you being so stupid, when you have me
to take up the slack? Do you realize I've had a mad crush on
you for years now? All those flowers I sent. I've done
everything but stand on my head to get close to you. I even
took the part in *Balalaika* because of you."

"What?"

He shrugged, grinning impishly. "Sure. Bettina Orlovsky
is my second cousin, didn't you know that? She told me
about that neat little four week tryout that Keith Leonard
gave you before rehearsals started, and after I found out,
well, I asked her if I could audition too."

Valentina sank back against the seat, surprised. "You
never told me that."

"You never asked. Val . . ."

"No," she said firmly. "Ben, no. I'm sorry, but no."

At home, Valentina felt suddenly restless as she hurried
into her quiet apartment. It was small, but exquisite. She'd
decorated it herself with Oriental rugs, and a few jewel-
colored paintings and art objects. An amethyst-colored
Lalique vase that Keith had once given her occupied a place
of honor.

Lamps set on timers greeted her, along with a radio preset
to a light rock station. She switched off the radio, which was
tuned to a station she and Keith often listened to, on the rare,
precious occasions when he visited her here. They didn't
make love, of course. They just talked. But in a way it was
a sharing far more intimate than lovemaking.

She decided not to bother with the cucumber facial, but
just to take a long, quiet soak in the tub. Ben Paris's remark
had disturbed her more than she wanted to admit.

*You're wasting the best years of your life waiting for a
man who'll never divorce his wife in a million years.*

It was true. Even Peaches had scolded her, saying that she
had "put herself on hold," while Jenny Trillin had advised
her to find another, more available lover. Jenny said,
"There's nothing like a new man to erase an obsession
about another."

Maybe that was one reason she'd jumped at the invitation

to attend Keith and Cynthia's garden party tomorrow in Connecticut, she reflected. Maybe if she saw Keith in his home surroundings, he'd look less desirable to her, and she could begin to move on with her life.

The phone rang. She reached out an arm dripping with foam for the extension she kept in the bathroom. "Hello?"

"Valentina." Keith's voice was low, tortured. "Val, are you really coming tomorrow?"

"Yes, I am."

"In a way I wish you wouldn't."

"Why not?" she inquired, her voice going sharp. "Cynthia issued the invitation, and she'll be disappointed if I don't show up. I told her I'd sing, and she's looking forward to it."

"I know . . . ah, God, Val . . ." He stopped then, not saying the words. They were star-crossed lovers, and it was becoming more and more painful to both of them.

"Oh, did I tell you," Keith said, changing the subject. "I've had a nibble from Hollywood about *Balalaika*. Laddie, you know, Alan Ladd, Jr., at MGM, is interested—he thinks it would make a terrific movie. I'm flying out there next week to 'take a meeting' with him, as those people call it."

"A movie?" Valentina stifled her shock.

"It's a natural," Keith said. "The country's just in the right mood for another *Flashdance* or *Grease*." They continued their conversation for several more minutes, then Valentina made an excuse and said good-bye. Weariness from her long day was beginning to sweep over her.

She toweled off, threw on a robe and went to the window, and opened the drapes. The skyscrapers of Manhattan twinkled and sparkled in the clear night air like stacks of jeweled boxes. Keith, she knew, had never meant to hurt her and felt great guilt that he had placed her in this limbo. But she allowed him to do this to her. She loved him so much, far too much. Sometimes she wished she had never met him.

In her elegant bedroom, Cynthia Leonard could hear the voices of the caterers' staff as they finished setting up the tables for two hundred guests outdoors under the huge green and white tent.

She stood in front of a rack of designer dresses and wondered if she was going to faint. Or worse, fall down on the carpeted floor and die of a heart attack right here and now.

No, you will not, she ordered herself, taking deep breaths, forcing the fear back.

She pressed her hands to her chest for a moment, massaging herself. This past week her doctor had told her that another bypass, a triple one this time, was going to be necessary. Keith didn't know yet; she dreaded telling him.

Daily, a terrible question nagged at her. If she was completely well, would he still stay married to her? Cynthia was afraid he wouldn't. In fact, her psychiatrist had hinted as much, implying that might be one of the reasons she couldn't seem to shake her condition—to keep Keith under control. Cynthia wasn't at all pleased.

She knew that they didn't have a real marriage anymore, they hadn't in years. That's why she read her books, to forget. *If you love something, set it free. If it comes back, it's yours.* Hadn't someone said that once? It sounded too dangerous for her.

She frowned at the selection of dresses. It was a garden party, of course—her garden was the prettiest in Wilton, and she always gave a party every July to show it off.

For the occasion she'd purchased a simple but elegant Adele Simpson cotton dress in a small, fuchsia flower print, with wide white piqué bands at collar, cuffs, and waist. With it she planned to wear an enormous, floppy white hat. Now she stared at the outfit in dismay. It looked too much like Princess Diana at Ascot.

She wanted to look sexy today, not royal, she decided impulsively. Maybe even a trifle naughty.

She flipped through the clothes in their garment bags, settling on a one-shouldered short dress by Adele. The dress revealed plenty of still-creamy skin, and as much leg as a Connecticut hostess dared show and still keep her decency.

She was finishing her makeup when there was a knock at her door.

"Cynthia, are you decent?" It was Dolly Rutledge, her professional party planner, who had recently opened a New York branch of her business.

"Come in, Dolly."

"I just wanted to let you know that everything's going fabulously," Dolly began.

Cynthia nodded, barely listening as Dolly went through her checklist. The party, she felt sure, would take care of itself. She had other, more important, things on her mind. Like Valentina. She'd taken a huge chance, and invited her husband's lover to the party.

She hoped it wasn't a fatal error.

Chapter

Nineteen

VALENTINA'S LIMOUSINE DROPPED her off at the Leonards' front door.

"It's terrific that you could make it, Valentina, on your one day of rest." Cynthia Leonard greeted her, looking stunning in an off-one-shoulder dress. Careful makeup covered up any signs of exhaustion or illness. She wore a startlingly beautiful gold and diamond necklace.

"So wonderful of you both to include me," Valentina responded, smiling nervously.

They spent several minutes in the usual small talk, and then Cynthia said, "I should go and check out some last-minute details. Keith tells me just to relax, he's so considerate, but I want to supervise it all, so if you'll excuse me . . . Take the door to the left, that leads to the garden."

Stepping onto a bricked patio, Valentina drew in a gasp of astonishment.

The party looked like movie clips that she had seen of Britain's Royal Ascot. Nearly every woman wore a fabulous hat, and the men had shown up in a variety of trendy, casual jackets in light summer colors. A big green and white striped tent, hung with pennants that rippled in the summer breeze, held long tables of hors d'oeuvres, and tables for the guests. Everywhere flowers blazed color, not only in the magnificent garden beds, but also in huge tubs and planters. Beyond a hedge could be seen the turquoise sparkle of an Olympic-sized swimming pool and cabana area.

"Valentina . . . Val." Keith left a group of guests and came over to meet her, a smile breaking over his rugged, healthy-looking face. He wore a pale cream blazer, navy slacks, and a blue shirt, with a white tie. His dark hair shone glossily in the sun.

"Hello," she cried. "Oh, this is lovely!"

"Isn't it? Cynthia's pride and joy is her garden. She's put in a sundial this year."

They gazed at each other, trapped in platitudes, and painfully aware of the others surrounding them.

"You look very beautiful," Keith added in a low voice.

Valentina flushed. She had chosen a low-necked slate-blue Missoni print dress with a tight, shirred bodice that showed off her full breasts. It had a cropped jacket in a variation of the same print. She had braided her magnificent hair into a thick coil at the base of her neck. In her ears, she wore long, dangling antique earrings of canary-colored diamonds.

"Would you like me to get you something to drink?"

"White wine, please."

As he went to get it, she looked around, feeling slightly out of place. Many of the guests were wealthy neighbors of the Leonards, or women with whom Cynthia lunched. Several members of the cast and staff of *Balalaika* were present, along with various producers, directors, and Wall Street bankers. She glimpsed tall, dark Tommy Tune standing by the bar. Kathleen Turner was just arriving . . . she'd worked with Keith on several of his early projects.

She quickly decided that she wouldn't stay long. She'd greet everyone, sing her four agreed-upon songs, and leave.

Keith returned with her drink, accompanied by his wife.

"White wine," he murmured, handing Valentina a fluted glass.

Cynthia's smile was bright and pretty. "Keithie loves these parties I give," she murmured, touching the necklace she wore. Its wide gold "leaves" were lined with diamonds, centered by a huge, glittering cluster of diamond "blossoms." The kind of necklace a man gave to an adored wife.

Valentina forced herself to nod and smile, as Cynthia began to talk about her new Japanese gardener who had recently moved to Connecticut from Los Angeles. So that's what today was all about, she reflected. Cynthia rubbing it into her face that *she* was the wife, with all the rank and privileges thereof.

When one of theater's top composers joined their conversation group, Valentina made her escape, fleeing to the hors d'oeuvre tables.

"Valentina—I just *loved* you in *Balalaika*." One of Cynthia's neighbors cornered her, effusive with compliments. As Valentina made conversation, she noticed that Keith and Cynthia had gone back toward the house, Keith's arm around his wife.

Dolly Rutledge came hurrying up to Valentina.

"Valentina, if it's all right, I've scheduled you to sing in about twenty minutes. I've got a man checking out the mike and the sound equipment now."

"Fine," Valentina agreed with relief. All she wanted was to sing and leave. "But I do need to freshen my makeup."

"That way," Dolly indicated. "We've set aside a lovely powder room for you to use, just off the herb garden door."

Valentina found her way along the beautiful brick garden path.

Stepping into a breakfast room hung with Laura Ashley wallpaper, she saw the huge kitchen on one side and only a few feet away, standing in the doorway, were Keith and Cynthia. Cynthia's pale arm was wrapped around her husband's waist, and she nuzzled her head against his shoulder.

"Keithie," she was complaining in her low, musical voice. "Oh, honey, I *am* so tired. These parties wear me out so."

"You do too much," Keith murmured gently.

"I know . . . I do it for you . . . would you take me upstairs and rub my shoulders or something? I have such a nasty kink in my neck."

Embarrassed, Valentina was about to back away, when she saw Keith slide his hands over his wife's back, and start to massage her muscles.

"Right here?" he murmured.

"Mmm. A little bit further down. Keep rubbing. Oh,

Keithie, that feels so good. Keithie, I know we haven't been—well, you know what I mean. But I wore this dress today for you. Do you like it?"

"It's gorgeous."

"And there's something I wanted to tell you too."

"Is there, honey?"

"Oh . . . maybe it can wait."

Valentina felt faint. How *close* they sounded. How intimate! A couple who'd been married for years and years, each knowing the other's every mood and thought. Which, of course, was exactly what they were.

Almost as if she knew she were being watched, Cynthia arched herself up against Keith's stroking hand like a cat being rubbed. She murmured, "Do you love me, Keithie? Do you?"

"I lo—" Keith began, but Valentina didn't stay to hear any more. She spun around and ran blindly away, back the way she had come.

Valentina was furious as she was driven back to the city, barely seeing the scenery as it flashed past her window, gradually changing from clean New England villages, to grimy brick buildings. She'd barely been able to sing her medley, and begged off an encore, despite the enthusiastic calls.

She couldn't believe she'd been fool enough to visit Cynthia's own turf. Cynthia had known exactly what she was doing. She'd wanted Valentina to see her beautiful home, the pampered lifestyle that Keith gave her, the brilliant diamond necklace, the little loving, husbandly touches, and the murmured "I love yous."

Cynthia was still beautiful and clever, and she was fighting to keep her man. And who could blame her? Keith was her husband . . . he was her man at least legally. Valentina lapsed into despair.

Back in her apartment, the tears that had been welling up in her eyes for the past two hours finally burst out, spewing over her cheeks.

She'd have to talk to Keith, and settle this one way or another. She didn't see any other choice.

A loud buzzing of the house intercom disturbed her sleep late the following morning.

It seemed to echo down a long, dark tunnel. She'd cried most of the night, falling into an exhausted sleep in the early morning hours.

Valentina struggled awake, squinting against the ray of sunlight that crept between the drapes. "Jesus Christ, who could that be at this hour," she mumbled, glancing at her digital clock. "Twelve . . ."

She got up, stretched catlike, and padded naked to the front hallway where she punched the intercom button. "Yes?"

"Miss Lederer," said the desk security man in the lobby. "You have a visitor, a Mr. Leonard. Shall I send him up?"

Keith. Her heart gave a thump. She moistened dry lips. "I . . . all right. Tell him to wait ten minutes."

Like a woman possessed, she rushed into her bathroom, brushed her teeth, and added a few dabs of translucent powder, a quick brush of violet eyeliner, and peach-colored lip gloss. Then she whirled to her walk-in closet, where she stepped into a glamorous-looking kiwi-green jumpsuit.

As the door buzzer sounded, she ran her fingers through her hair, then sauntered to the door.

"Valentina!" Keith stood in the hall, looking anxious and concerned, and she saw that he'd cut himself in several places while shaving. "Can I come in?"

"No," she snapped, putting her hands on her hips.

"What?" He looked as if he hadn't slept at all. There were dark circles under his eyes and a weary cast to his skin. She felt a stab of renewed fury and betrayal.

"No, dammit!" she cried. "No, you can't come in, 'Keithie.' I don't want ever to see you again—which was the whole purpose of your wife inviting me to that garden soiree yesterday, wasn't it? To scare me off! To blow me off good! To show me that you and she have a wonderful marriage and there's absolutely no room for me or any other woman.''

Keith looked ashen, anguished. ''Val—Val—Do we have to speak out here in the hallway? Please, just let me in. We have to talk.''

''I don't want to talk!'' She'd started to cry. ''Just—go away!''

She started to close the door but he caught it with his hands, and then he was inside. He locked the door behind them and took her in his arms. His arms, the familiar feel of him, the clean yet musky odor of his body only aggravated her painful hurt.

''Dammit!'' she yelled, fighting him. Wildly, out of control, she slapped at his chest, hitting his chin. ''No! No! You bastard! Go away! Go away!''

He locked her arms behind her back and she butted him with her head, uttering a strangled cry that changed into a hollow sob.

''Val . . . Val . . . ah, God, what have we done to each other?'' Keith held her until the worst of her sobs were spent, and her weeping had changed to an anguished quiver.

''I . . . I c-càn't be the other woman,'' she sobbed into his shoulder.

''Val . . .''

''I can't. I won't. I just damn well fucking well *won't*! Keith,'' she tried to explain. ''Cynthia isn't some loathsome creature—she put me through that because she loves you. *I'd* have done the same thing to keep you . . . Oh,'' she cried, lapsing again into deep melancholy. ''Oh, shit!''

''We have to talk,'' Keith said in a low voice.

They lay on Valentina's bed, wrapped in each other's arms, not making love, but just touching, as if that human, physical contact was a lifeline to their two souls.

''Val, I have tried to keep my thoughts away from you, I've tried not to love you. I've tried to keep it just friendship, but that's like asking me to stop breathing. The more I try to push back my feelings for you, the stronger they get. I don't know. Maybe we've gone about this all wrong.''

"And what about Cynthia?'' Valentina's voice cracked. "Keith, I heard you saying you loved her. *I heard that.* Dammit! Don't tell me you don't love her because I know you do!''

Keith held her close, and she heard the rapid in-out of his breathing as he thought about what to say.

"I do love her,'' he admitted at last. "But Val, there are so many different kinds of love in this world. Everyone loves more than one person, and each love is different. The love I have for her is—more of a caretaker kind of love. I'm not sure how to say it.''

She sat up, pushing away his arms. "Oh, you sound just like all the married men!'' she snapped. "Doesn't she 'understand' you, Keith? Is that the problem? You just want to have your cake and eat it too!''

He sat up with a violent motion that made her fear she had gone too far. His face was etched with grim pain. "That's not fair, and you know it. Valentina, I'm not saying I'm the perfect man. I was thinking about this all last night. What you and I have, the emotional connection between us . . . even if we haven't actually made physical love, it still is a betrayal of Cynthia.''

"I know,'' she said miserably.

Keith turned to her, his eyes wet, shiny with tears. "But Val, God . . . I may be damned, damned to hell, but I still want you and I still love you and nothing, *nothing,* is going to make me feel any different, not ever. I always will care about you, Val, to the end of my days, even if we never see each other again, if that's what you really want . . .''

They fumbled blindly for each other, as sobs racked out of Valentina. "I didn't mean—Keith—'' she wept.

He cried too. "Oh, God, oh, Val. Maybe we should just grab . . . grab it while we can . . .''

They came together like a storm, clutching at each other, crying, talking incoherently.

"I love you,'' Valentina tried to say but her words were kissed away by Keith's hard, seeking mouth. She kissed him back. He tore her clothes away, and she tore at his, and as soon as they were naked, he entered her violently.

They rocked together, fiercely needy, both of them climaxing almost at once. Valentina's cry of pleasure and passion filled the room, while Keith's groan was low, deep in his throat.

He didn't pull out of her, growing hard again almost at once. But now his lovemaking was tender, almost worshipful. His kisses adored her, as if drinking in every particle of her. His tongue gently probed between her lips as he sucked their rims, then plundered her tongue. He planted rows of kisses along the curves of each breast, then tantalized downward to the delicacies of her rib cage and navel. Below that was the tender bud of her innermost core.

After she'd cried out with several small, exquisitely perfect orgasms, Keith moved upward and entered her again. She lifted her hips to meet him. They moved together, joined not just physically but by every fiber of their beings.

"I love you so much it hurts." Keith whispered.

"And I love you back," she whispered, full of the guilty joy of being with the man she adored most in the world.

They made love for hours, while Valentina let her answering machine take her phone calls. She had to leave for the theater at six P.M., so around five they sent out for Chinese food. She threw on a robe and went to the door, returning with the fragrant cardboard tubs. They picnicked naked on the bed, greedily devouring Peking duck, shrimp rolls, and seafood chow mein with pork fried rice.

"I should call my service," Keith said, as they were finishing. As she nodded, he phoned his answering service and listened intently as the messages were relayed to him. Several times he jotted down phone numbers. Then his expression changed.

"When? When did she call?" he said sharply. "Doctor who? Are you sure that's what she said?" Then: "Thank you." He hung up, gazing at Valentina with a tense expression.

"What was that all about?" Valentina inquired in a low voice, although, of course, she already knew.

"It's Cynthia. Apparently she's been keeping a little secret from me—she needs another bypass operation. The doctor has had a cancellation in her surgery schedule and wants to move Cynthia up. She couldn't reach her, so she called me. My wife is going into the hospital for preliminary tests tomorrow."

"Oh," Valentina said in a small voice.

Keith rose from the bed, reaching for his clothes, which he had flung onto the floor in the frenzy of their lovemaking. "I've got to go back to Connecticut and be with her, Val. She gets hysterical at the thought of doctors and shots, she's not a very good patient at all."

"Of course you must," she said woodenly.

Valentina went through her performance that evening in a haze of anguish. What a fool she'd been. What a lovesick, utter fool. Married men didn't leave their wives—the pull of the wife was just too strong. When was she going to "wake up and smell the coffee"?

"Anything wrong?" asked Ben Paris as they were waiting in the wings to start the famous second-act dream sequence that had received such rave reviews in the trades, and was the subject of much controversy on all the talk shows. It was an exceptionally complicated and hazardous but spectacular routine.

"No," she snapped.

"Val. Hey, we've danced together every night for almost a year. I know you, kid, better than you know yourself. You've got a major-sized worm burrowing in your gut. You're doing a fantastic job of hiding it, but I know it's there. Want to talk about it?"

"Not really," she said as their musical cue sounded.

However, later, after the performance, when Valentina left her dressing room, Ben Paris was waiting in the corridor outside. In his arms he cradled an enormous bouquet of at least five dozen deep red roses. His dark hair was slicked back, still shower-wet, and there was a new light in his intensely blue eyes. A single diamond stud gleamed in his earlobe.

"Hi," he said softly.

Valentina stared at him. In the past months she'd grown familiar with his astonishing handsomeness and, for the most part, had ceased to notice it. But tonight his looks struck her with fresh, full force. The man was gorgeous.

"Here are the flowers I always wanted to give you," he told her as he put them in her arms.

"Ben—no—" But her protest was weak.

"Just let me try to love you, Val. I swear I'll be good to you. I'm not half as bad as the press says I am."

Chapter

Twenty

Milan, Italy
1989

Strains of sexy Brazilian music drifted out from the runway, mingling with the frantic, high-pitched cries of models who had lost earrings or ripped hems.

As a crew of dressers struggled to zip, button, and fasten eighteen models into Gianni Versace's fall collection, the designer himself strolled about, plucking at hems and capriciously changing accessories. Backstage at a fashion show was always mass confusion.

Naked from the waist up, María Cristina leaned toward the mirror, as a hairstylist hurriedly retouched her hair. Behind the stylist, the dresser assigned to her waited to zip her into the long bridal gown she'd wear for the finale in fifteen minutes.

"Getting too thin?" inquired the dresser, her professional eyes studying the model's long, lean body.

"No, of course not," María snapped.

She knew there was something wrong with her, though. Her stomach was knotted, clenched with tension. Every time someone shouted, she jumped, and for the first time in her life, she was getting frequent headaches.

She hadn't been on an assignment in six months now, and her body craved the release it would provide her. She felt incredibly tense—needy. She glared at her offending reflection, then suddenly leaped up from the stool. Over her dresser's protests, she hurried out to the hallway.

She bent over the wall telephone, dialing first the country access code, then the number of her contact.

When he came on the line, she spoke only four words. "I need another one."

Los Angeles
1989

A sky the color of a Hopi turquoise arched over the northbound Hollywood Freeway, as morning sun poured down on the windshield of Valentina's red BMW.

Getting off at the Lankersham exit, she pulled up to the gate at Continental Studios, waving to Scotty, the guard on duty. The driveway still glistened from its morning hose-down, and tropical flowers bloomed in tubs.

Valentina drove her BMW past sound stages 18 and 22, into the maze of driveways and parking areas provided for the more than five thousand people who worked in the complex. In front of her teetered two black women dressed as hookers in spandex and leather boots with four-inch heels. They were drinking Pepsis and laughing.

To her left, the executive office building known as the Red Tower caught the morning sun. To her right stood the huge, hangarlike buildings that were the sound stages. Currently, more than six TV shows and three feature films were being shot on the lot, including *Balalaika*, which Keith had put together after a year of wooing production executives and the studio.

Parking behind sound stage 20 near her luxury Winnebago trailer, Valentina shut off her motor and sat drawing a deep breath. She hadn't slept well last night. She'd awakened with her heart slamming and sweat pouring down her body. She hadn't been able to get back to sleep.

They were filming the big dream sequence this morning, the one that the *LA Times* reported had "1940s MGM musical glamour buzz-sawed together with 1980s frank sexual statement." There were so many expensive special effects that it was reputed to be costing over one million dollars for these stunning ten minutes of footage. Keith had urged her to use a stunt woman for some of the more difficult portions but Valentina had refused.

Keith. She closed her eyes, picturing him for an instant. The familiar, dear lines of his face, the laugh wrinkles that fanned out from his eyes, the full, mobile mouth so ready to laugh. He would be there to watch, she knew. He'd already told her that he would not miss this for anything.

Oh, stop thinking about him, she told herself violently. *What good is it?*

But she knew that she couldn't, any more than she could stop breathing.

She got out of the car and started toward her trailer.

Joe Donovan, who now wrote for *People*, clicked on his microcassette tape recorder, made sure the tape was rewound properly, and placed the mike on a table where it would catch every word that Valentina uttered.

"There," he announced. "All ready."

He glanced at the star, who sat opposite him in her deluxe Winnebago trailer. Even without makeup, she looked sensational. Her uninhibited mane of jet hair tangled below her shoulders, augmented by hair extensions into a smashingly "wild" look. She wore an almost transparent silver bodysuit glimmering with sequins and beads that made her look breathtakingly sexual. Only a scattering of beads preserved her essential modesty.

As usual, he planned to start with the standard, innocuous questions first, then work around to the more sticky, personal ones—like Ben Paris and Keith Leonard, her two famous "friends." His readers wanted to know every detail.

"So how do you feel about *Balalaika* finally being made into a film?" he began.

"Of course, I'm very, very excited. Patrick Swayze is just fantastic. He's a joy to work with."

Donovan knew that originally Ben Paris had signed to play the male lead, but something had happened—no one would really talk about it—and he'd been released from his contract. He now was in Rome making a picture with Jette Michaud. Swayze was being paid 4.3 million dollars and Valentina a cool 8.2—the largest contract ever for a female star.

Artfully Joe probed, getting Valentina to talk freely, and finally he cut to the question he really wanted to ask.

"Is there any truth to the rumors that you and Ben Paris . . . well, that you had a major quarrel and he left the production in a huff?"

A flush colored Valentina's cheeks. "No, there's no truth to that whatsoever."

"Well, why did he leave?"

"You would have to talk to him about that."

"Is it true that you fought because he's having an affair with Jette Michaud?"

Valentina pulled back a little, recrossing her long, slim legs. "No comment," she snapped.

By the way she lifted her chin, Joe knew he might have only a few more seconds before she lost patience and terminated the interview. "Val," he went on quickly, "how do you feel about working with Keith Leonard? I mean, scuttlebutt has it that you and he were once very, *very* close. Now he's the executive producer on a picture with you and you're in the position of seeing him every day. Which, I hear, Ben Paris didn't like."

"Again, no comment," she said, rising. "And Mr. Donovan—I realize you have readers to consider, but please consider me too. I'm one of those rare stars who likes to keep at least some of her personal life personal."

"Sorry, Valentina," he replied slowly. "The truth is, a star of your magnitude doesn't have a personal life anymore."

Valentina left her trailer at a fast walk. *Damn,* she thought, ruffling her hands through her hair. Joe Donovan had only been trying to do his job. But he'd really hit a sensitive area.

She thought about her breakup with Ben. Yes, they'd had a few glorious months after she first decided to accept his affections, but then it began to sour. He was egotistical enough, *normal* enough, to want her exclusively for himself. One day just after filming started Ben had seen Valentina and Keith talking closely on the set, and he'd blown up.

"I may be old-fashioned but I want my woman to look at *me* with love in her eyes, not someone else!"

Valentina hadn't known whether to take him seriously, or to make light of it instead. "Ben, is this you talking? The great stud of the Western world who has broken up marriages and romanced half the female stars in Beverly Hills and Malibu?"

"It's not funny," he'd told her, glaring at her. "I'm in love, Val . . . I've gone crazy, I'm not my normal self, and I don't want to share you, especially not with a prick like Keith Leonard who didn't love you enough to go after you when he had the chance."

"That's not fair!" she exclaimed.

He pulled her to him. "Who cares if it's fair? It's how I feel. You kept me hanging for years, Val, and now I want you all the way. I want you to marry me."

She'd stared at him, shocked. "You are wonderful, Ben, and you are unbearably handsome, and I'm so fond of you. But marriage? I don't think so."

"Dammit, Val!"

But she'd refused to budge, and the following morning Ben stormed off to Rome to join Jette Michaud on a shoot—and, well, she didn't want to think about it now.

Now she headed into Makeup.

"Good, you're here," said Tina Borman, the professional attendant who usually worked with Valentina. She looked harassed. "We're running late."

Valentina sank into one of the makeup chairs, allowing Tina to fasten the plastic drape around her shoulders.

"Your makeup looks great," Bettina Orlovsky remarked, lighting up a cigarette that she immediately stubbed out again in the one, token ashtray Valentina kept in her trailer. "Okay. I realize you know the dream sequence like your own face, but let's go over it just one more time. That set is too fucking complicated. I want to pound those combinations into your head, *and* the marks you have to keep on, because if you make one mistake— Well, let's just say that we don't want you to make one."

"Bettina," Valentina pointed out at last, gently. "It's going to be wonderful—everything will work."

"Of course it will—*I* choreographed it."

"And *I'm* dancing it," Valentina added, smiling for the first time that morning.

Keith Leonard hurried onto the closed set, his nerves jangled from a fender-bender on the Hollywood Freeway that had delayed him in traffic.

Damn, he hated being late, and this was something he wanted to see—no, had to see. The brash, hot young set designer had gone all out with his incredible moving staircase that opened up like a giant seashell.

The red light on top of the sound stage door hadn't yet been lit, signifying it was safe for him to enter. He pulled open the door, striding inside. The sound stage was big enough to park three or four jumbo jets and still have room for the loading gate. Dominating it, towering thirty feet high, was the dream-sequence set that had taken six months and nearly $800,000 to construct. Valentina's and Patrick Swayze's stand-ins stood posed on one of the ramps as the lighting men adjusted the spotlights. Male dancers in Cossack costumes milled around, waiting for the cameras to roll.

Keith joined a few Continental studio executives, along with representatives from the press who were there to cover the spectacular sequence.

He recognized two uninvited observers, Joe Donovan accompanied by a young female photographer. "Do you have permission to shoot pictures in here?" Keith asked sharply, walking over to them.

"Peace, peace," Donovan said, raising both of his palms. "The studio gave me the okay. How many times do you shoot a sequence like this? Not since some of the great Fred Astaire and Ginger Rogers dance numbers back in the fifties."

"Okay, fine," Keith consented grudgingly.

There was a murmur as Valentina entered the sound stage, followed by Patrick Swayze.

"First team, please!" came the amplified voice of the director through a bullhorn. This meant he wanted the actors, not the stand-ins, on the set. "Hit the mark. From the top, please. Rolling!"

The first two run-throughs had gone reasonably well, Valentina thought. She'd managed to conquer her slight fear of heights, and had landed on every one of the marks placed on the steps by Bettina during rehearsal.

Now, during a rest break, the director and choreographer stood near the back of the set, arguing about the final sequence—something Bettina wanted to change.

A makeup girl hovered in front of Valentina, dusting her face with translucent talc from a big powder puff. The powder made her sneeze twice.

"God bless you," said Patrick Swayze, standing next to her, giving her the lopsided, sexy grin that had mesmerized millions of women in *Ghost*.

Valentina glanced up as the director's voice reverberated through the bullhorn again. "Let's do it again, people. Places. From the top, please."

Valentina quickly lost herself in the complex choreography, whirling down the staircase, being lifted and thrown from the arms of one gorgeously handsome Cossack dancer to the next. Her supple spine was arched, her knee bent, in a style reminiscent of the high-stepping forties and fifties, except that this dancing was infused with a hip-grinding sensuality.

Valentina had loved the choreography from the first time Bettina walked her through it, but being tossed from one man to another was strenuous and dangerous.

"Easy!" muttered one of the dancers, as he passed her down the line. Then Patrick set her on her feet where she began an energetic series of hip thrusts, while the Cossack dancers crouched to begin their leg-thrusting kicks. As this was happening, red smoke began to roll upward from the smoke machines and the staircase began one of its metamorphoses, the stairs moving higher and fanning outward, opening up into the seashell effect that had cost so much to produce.

Valentina felt a thrill of sheer, exuberant joy. Everything was working. Every movement felt right. She was twenty-five feet high!

Then one of the Cossack dancers on the level above Valentina kicked too wide.

He compensated, but he had still moved too wide for the narrowness of the stair treads at that point, and the toe of his shoe gave Valentina a sharp, glancing blow.

She might have caught herself if she'd had both feet on the ground, but she was in the midst of one of her beautiful, soaring leaps. The blow knocked her balance slightly "off." She did not land on the wide lip of the seashell, as was choreographed.

She kept on falling.

Fear caused her to clutch the air, her arms flailing. There was time for her to see a brief flash of klieg lights, of staring faces, of a grip starting to run forward, of Bettina Orlovsky's shocked, horrified face.

Then pain smashed all the way up through Valentina's body exploding inside her brain, swallowing her scream of agony.

There was a second of astonished shock. Then everyone began yelling, and running, and screaming.

Keith uttered a cry of rage, pushing his way through the packed bodies.

"Val . . . Val . . ." Keith shoved someone aside. He glimpsed Joe Donovan, also fighting his way through the crowd of frightened dancers and crew, dragging his photographer along by her arm.

He reached the center of the milling crowd of dancers and crew. "I'm a medic, I'm a medic. Give her some air," one of the dancers was shouting, crouched over Valentina.

Keith looked down and felt all the hope drain out of his body. His beautiful Val was lying sprawled on her back, blood pouring from her mouth, soaking her black curls, her arms and legs rag-doll loose. Her skin was bluish-gray in color. In the distance, he heard the wail of a siren.

"*Val! Val!*" he shouted. He threw himself down beside her, grasping one of her hands, trying to find a pulse. He was racked by the most violent grief and shock that he had ever known.

"Get back!" snapped the medic/dancer, suddenly an authority. "Don't touch her! She may have a back injury."

Keith drew back, fighting the tears that burned his eyes. The wail of the sirens ground to a stop just outside the sound stage, and a couple of uniformed EMS attendants came running in carrying a stretcher and bags full of medical supplies.

Val, Keith thought numbly, looking at the pale face of the woman he loved.

In New York, Orchid was having telephone sex with her sometime lover, Roman Solenski, who was in Houston to play the Houston Astros in a doubleheader. Roman gave great phone sex. He should have been hired by one of those kinky 900 numbers.

"What are you doing, Roman . . . talk to me . . . tell me . . ." she asked breathily, becoming excited, moving her panties aside, and allowing her new vibrator to create delicious thrills of sensation. She was getting wet and very slick just fantasizing about his nude body touching hers.

"I'm rubbing myself . . . I'm just throbbing thinking about you," Roman said huskily, his breathing rapid.

She moaned and closed her eyes, about to start the first of several tiny climaxes, when she heard Valentina's name on the television set. Something about a network news flash.

"Are you . . . ?" groaned Roman. "I can't hold back much longer, Orchid . . . are you . . . ? I want us to come together . . ."

"Wait," she said, switching off the vibrator and fumbling around for the remote. "Wait—there's something I want to hear."

She flicked up the sound volume, just in time to see Connie Chung's familiar face appear on the screen.

". . . critically injured in a fall in a sound stage at Continental Studios, in Hollywood. Valentina was rushed over to Cedars-Sinai Hospital in Los Angeles and immediately placed in the intensive care unit, where doctors have not yet issued any bulletins as to her condition.''

Orchid froze.

The voice of the popular female news anchor continued, "Bystanders on the scene reported that Valentina appeared to be in critical condition. Others say they observed flutters of her eyelids and movements of her hands—''

Orchid let the telephone slide out of her bloodless fingers, clattering to the floor.

In Detroit, Peaches was on a conference call, discussing arrangements for the annual benefit party at the St. Vincent and Sarah Fisher Home. Her housekeeper of twenty years, Mary Abbott, came hurrying into her study without knocking.

"Mrs. Lederer! Mrs. Lederer! You gotta come . . . oh, Jesus, Mary, an' Joseph . . . you gotta come.''

Peaches looked at the woman, whose usually ruddy complexion was ashen. She experienced a deep sense of alarm. "Mary? What is it?''

"It's Valentina . . . on the little TV . . . she fell . . .''

"I have to go,'' gasped Peaches. She dropped the phone into the cradle. Forgetting that there were three other television sets in the house, she rushed off to the kitchen, to watch the screen of the housekeeper's small set.

A series of still photographs with white arrows showed Valentina's actual fall from the thirty-foot-high staircase set.

"Oh, no . . .'' she breathed. "God, no.'' Mary put her arms around her, holding her up.

The avalanche had caught Valentina in its vast, crushing white power. It swept her along like a tiny chip caught up in eternity. She tried to scream, but no sounds emerged. When she opened her eyes she saw nothing but white. She must have fallen on something, for jagged spears of pain pierced her spine.

The pain kept changing. Sometimes it was like a red-hot barbecue fork, sometimes it was a dragon's tooth, biting into her flesh. At other times she was being crushed beneath a train car, while her mother screamed, and Mikhail sobbed.

She moaned, begging them to lift up the train car so she could breathe, pleading with them to stop her from being crushed.

"Valentina, can you move your . . ." queried a voice that faded into other voices and split into fragments, and became cold and white. Then the train car shifted, and fell over on her again, darkening everything.

In Moscow, Vladimir Petrov hung up from a phone conversation with the KGB desk at the Russian Embassy in Washington. His military attaché had given him some astonishing information.

Valentina Lederer, a few hours ago, had just had an accident at a movie studio and was near death.

Petrov got up from his desk and stalked to the door that separated his office from the anteroom, slamming it shut. Alone with his thoughts, he rubbed both hands together nervously.

Then, opening the official safe, he reached for a thick manila file. Dog-eared from years of handling, it contained typed reports, articles, and photographs clipped from Western magazines.

A *Rolling Stone* cover shot by Richard Avedon stared up at him.

Mikhail's twin sister. He'd always known where she was.

Did that pretty ballet dancer actually think he would have let her escape to America with her little daughter if he didn't want her to go? It had served his purposes well.

He thought for several minutes, then reached for his private phone again, dialing a series of numbers. After the delays of going through a complicated security system and the activation of a scrambler device, he was finally speaking to his personal Washington contact at the Russian Embassy.

"I want to be kept informed of every aspect of this woman's life," he ordered. "In more detail than ever. Leave *nothing* out."

"*Da, da,*" came the expected agreement.

He had always given Petrov everything he asked for.

Cedars-Sinai was total bedlam, with reporters, TV camera crews, paparazzi, and fans spilling out onto the front portico and lawn, many carrying signs saying Val, We Love You and Valentina, You're in Our Prayers.

A white-coated doctor emerged from an unmarked door, accompanied by two security guards, one carrying a portable mike. The hospital was accustomed to dealing with all the hullabaloo connected with stars' illnesses and traumas.

Immediately there was a rush toward him. TV cameramen carrying minicams on their shoulders tried to position themselves for the best shots.

"Ladies and gentlemen," began the physician, a Dr. Richard Feldman, who had a California suntan and was very handsome. Joe Donovan taped it all as Dr. Feldman read from a prepared statement, telling the assembled group that Valentina had a vertebral burst fracture of the mid-lumbar region and needed immediate surgery. A team of doctors would go in and straighten out the deformity caused by the severe blow from the thirty-foot fall.

"While operating, we plan to examine the *cauda equina,* the sac of nerves that—"

Before he had even finished the sentence, the clamor rose. "Will she be able to walk?" shouted a woman from NBC-TV.

"What are her chances?"

"Will she be a paraplegic?"

"Is she breathing without a respirator?"

"Is she conscious?"

A security guard stepped forward, raising both hands to silence the crowd. The doctor consulted the typed sheet and continued. He finished by listing off the names of the specialists who had been called in on the case, naming their credentials and his own.

"We will issue hourly updates on her condition," he concluded, as the reporters rushed off to file their stories and the TV cameras whirred.

Paul Jensen had mapped out his career, and Cedars-Sinai Hospital was the first step. He'd hoped, prayed, and pulled every string he could think of to do his orthopedic surgical residency here, where celebrity patients were commonplace, and sports injuries received a high priority. From here it was only a matter of a few years, he hoped, until he headed up a wealthy Beverly Hills sports clinic.

He spotted Dr. Feldman striding down the hall, having finished his news conference, and hurried to catch up with him.

"Rick, how's she doing—I mean really?"

"We won't know the full extent of the spinal-cord damage until we get into surgery, Paul."

"I'm off duty right now. Can I scrub and observe?"

"If you want," Feldman said, stopping in front of the elevator.

Valentina. Paul wondered if she would remember him. He felt sure she would. He'd followed her career from day one and, especially after meeting Orchid, had always intended to contact her.

She was floating at the bottom of a deep black well. Above her, disembodied voices talked and chattered. She couldn't catch their exact words.

"Valentina . . . Valentina . . . can you hear me?" repeated Peaches a number of times. "Valentina, wake up. Wake up, dear. You're in recovery."

Valentina shook her head, which seemed to be tied down with gossamer cables that made weird, yawing noises, sucking at the inside of her skull, when she tried to move.

"Valentina. Wake up, Valentina. You're all right. Everything's fine. You're in recovery now."

Recovery? From what?

"I can't move," she gasped.

"You're bandaged and restrained to the bed, Valentina.

That's why you can't move. The doctors say you're doing fine, honey."

Bewildered, terrified, Valentina shook her head, feeling a knifelike stab of pain somewhere in her legs as she did so.

"Don't try to move. Dr. Feldman will be in in about ten minutes, and he'll talk to you."

"Doctor?" Valentina tried to moisten her dry, cracked lips. Her throat felt sore and raw. She heard a blip-blip-blip sound. Odd. Was she in a hospital? Brief flashes flicked through her brain. Something about Cossack dancers.

Then huge waves of exhaustion billowed over her, drawing her back into unconsciousness.

"Valentina, don't go back to sleep. Wake up, dear. You have to wake up now. You're going to be fine."

"No, no, I'm so sleepy, let me sleep," mumbled Valentina, retreating into the safe darkness.

"If she's paralyzed, what will we do?" Peaches verbalized her fears, clutching Edgar's hand.

They were in a VIP lounge set aside for the families of celebrity patients. A television set had given them the hourly updates, along with reruns of the horrifying fall scene. "Honey," Edgar assured his wife for the fourth time. "Nobody's told us she's paralyzed. We have the best doctors in the country—in the world. And they got her in time. There's all sorts of new techniques now for repairing ruptured discs . . . we can thank God a million times over that her spinal cord wasn't severed—only damaged."

"But doctors aren't infallible, they aren't God," Peaches fretted.

"Baby, they're the best there is."

"Mr. and Mrs. Lederer?"

"Yes, yes, yes," Edgar barked, jumping up.

Dr. Feldman strode forward, smiling heartily. "The news is excellent, Mr. and Mrs. Lederer. Valentina is conscious now, and we've stabilized her condition. Preliminary tests show that she does have some feeling and movement in her limbs—she can move them slightly."

"Oh, thank God," Peaches wept.

"Hands *and* feet?" Edgar queried sharply.

"Yes, both. We'll keep her immobile for about a week or ten days, and then she can start to move around a little, with some support for her back."

Edgar looked horrified. "But Dr. Feldman, Valentina is a dancer."

"She can still do aerobics in time, if that's what she wants, but there will be a long period of physical therapy. It really depends on her body's healing process. We just can't make any further prognosis at this time."

When the doctor had left, Peaches sank back onto the couch, and gazed at her husband in shocked horror. "Edgar! Do you realize what he just told us? He said 'aerobics.' She might never be able to dance professionally again."

"As long as she's okay," Edgar said hoarsely. "That's the important thing."

Outside the window, Keith Leonard watched the hundreds of fans who milled restlessly on the lawn, waiting for the news of Valentina. Security guards kept shooing them away, but they returned anyway.

He looked down at Valentina, lying pale on the hospital sheets, her hair plaited into two braids. She wore a lightweight plastic "body jacket" over her surgical dressings. Her cheekbone bore a huge, bluish-yellow bruise from her fall and her whole face was bruised and swollen.

He pulled up a bedside chair and cautiously touched her right hand, afraid even the slightest pressure might hurt her.

"Val," he whispered. "It's me, Keith. I'm here."

"Hi, darling," she murmured sleepily. "Sorry . . . they just gave me a pain shot . . . it makes me float . . ."

"It's okay. I just want you to know that I love you so much, Val. And I want to assure you that *Balalaika* is safely in the can," he went on. "We were able to splice together those first two takes of the dream sequence—it came out beautifully. And we'll use a double for a couple of the stunts. No one will ever know the difference."

"Good. That's really good," she whispered. "Hold my hand, Keith. I never thought . . ."

Within seconds, her eyelids fluttered shut and she drifted

off. He stared down at her, agony squeezing his chest. How fragile she looked, her skin almost transparent. She looked so completely helpless.

What have I done? Keith wondered miserably. *I've hurt two fine women.*

A passing orderly turned to gawk as Orchid strode down the hospital corridor. She wore black snakeskin boots, a pair of tight black leggings, and a tweed jacket that was several sizes too big for her. Underneath the jacket, a chestnut-colored silk camisole revealed inches of cleavage. With her wild red mane of long hair, she looked as sexy and audacious as a *Cosmo* cover girl.

"Orchid—Orchie!" Peaches hurried forward, intercepting her flamboyant daughter.

"Well, I'm here," Orchid announced in a defiant manner. "I had an appointment with an independent film producer to look at my work, and maybe give me a job, but I broke it to come here. At your request. Are you satisfied?"

"Aren't you even going to ask how she's doing?"

"How's she doing?"

Peaches grasped Orchid's sleeve, and pulled her into the nearest lounge. "I've *never* seen anyone as stubborn as you!" Peaches snapped. "If you want to be angry at Val, fine, be angry, but not when she's so ill and needs your love."

"But she's—"

"Dammit, we nearly lost her! Doesn't that mean anything to you? And she came within a sliver of being paralyzed. Don't you even care, Orchid? Doesn't that bother you just a tiny, tiny bit?"

Orchid's defiance sagged out of her, and her shoulders slumped. She lowered her eyes. "I . . . I do care," she rasped in a quivering voice. "I don't want anything to happen to her. But I still hate her."

"That's the most preposterous thing I ever heard," snapped Peaches, driven beyond her customary sweetness by the pressures of the past two days. "You love her a lot . . . a whole damn lot. Otherwise why would you be

acting like such a total fool? Now, I want you to go down
to the hospital gift shop and buy her some flowers or a book,
or *something* to carry in your hands. I want you to go in
there, and give her lots of hugs and kisses, and tell her you
care about her. If you don't do that, and make her believe it,
then you'll be doing her more harm than good—*and I damn
well hope you'll mean it!*''

"I . . .'' But then Orchid saw the implacable look in her
mother's eyes and swallowed her protest. "All right,'' she
meekly agreed.

Orchid arrived just before the scheduled pain shot that
would smooth away the hot, raw edges, and allow Valentina
to float for an hour and a half or so.

"Here,'' Orchid said, plopping a bouquet of flowers on
the nightstand.

"Did Mom tell you to come here?'' Valentina moistened
her lips.

"What if she did?'' Orchid mumbled. "I came, didn't I?
I gave up some important business in New York to do it too.''

Sudden pain shot up through the center of Valentina's
spine. She stiffened into a rigid column of pain, forgetting
her sister until the flare of agony was finished. Drops of
sweat appeared on her forehead.

"What's wrong?'' asked Orchid anxiously.

"The . . . it hurts.'' Valentina glanced up at the wall
clock, then reached for the call button. "Could I please have
my pain shot?'' she asked the desk nurse when she
responded on the intercom.

"As soon as we can get it to you, Valentina,'' responded
the nurse.

"Pain shots?'' Orchid asked, looking slightly shaken.
"Does it hurt a lot?''

"Imagine short zaps from a flame thrower,'' grunted
Valentina, her anger at Orchid fading, to be replaced by one
of the sudden waves of despair that frequently overwhelmed
her.

"*That* bad? Oh, God,'' Orchid said in a small voice.

"Oh, Orchie—''

* * *

After Orchid left, Valentina rang several more times for her pain shot, and was assured she would have it soon.

She gritted her teeth together and tried to count backwards from one hundred. But when she reached fifteen, tears began to roll down her cheeks. She still couldn't believe she'd been caught in this nightmare. The pain, with its force just barely dented by the shots of morphine. The fear of not getting better, of being a semi-invalid, unable to pursue her career or have a child.

A knock at her door roused her from the spasm of self-pity.

"Val? Are you up and awake? You look beautiful." It was a resident she hadn't seen before. In his green hospital coat and slightly funky hairstyle, he looked like a young, sexy doctor on one of the afternoon soaps. He had a cleft chin, and his mouth somehow looked very familiar to Valentina.

She forced a smile and impulsively said, "I guess I'm feeling mighty sorry for myself—a new bad habit."

He came into the room smiling. "Want to talk?"

It all came spilling out. "I've been lying here with too much to think about, and they haven't brought my pain shot, and I need too many pain shots, and I'm worried about never dancing again, and I *hate* just lying here, and—" Her voice began to shake. "God, listen to me," she managed, stopping herself. "I'm rattling on and on."

"You're just going through a natural and expected shock reaction," he assured her. He touched her hand, and she felt the warmth of his skin radiating into her palm and up her arm. "Valentina, don't you remember me?"

She shook her head.

"I would have thought you, of all people, would have remembered. Think back. All the way back. Remember a day when three kids were assigned to wash one of the rattiest, oldest, rustiest station wagons ever seen in Michigan. There was a certain brat of a boy who kept spraying you with the garden hose, and he sprayed water all over you—and in your—"

"Paul!" she shouted. *"Paul! Oh, Paul!* My God!" She stared at him, amazed and pleased. "No wonder you looked so familiar. Is it really you? I can't *believe* it. This is just so—"

"In the flesh," he admitted, smiling. "I'm Paul Jensen now, though. I gave up the name Baggio when I was adopted." He added, "I see you're due for a pain shot. How about if I see what happened to it?"

She sagged onto the mattress, limp with gratitude.

"And so," Paul finished, bringing her up to date on what had happened in his life. "I did run into Orchid down at Northwestern—didn't she ever tell you?"

"No. Well, maybe she told our mother; we haven't been very close."

"Well, it was just a quick dating thing. That was all I had time for when I was an intern. I had to prop my eyes open with toothpicks most of the time, I wasn't much fun to anyone. I was always going to contact you, but the one time I tried, they said you were in Europe on tour."

Within two days, she and Paul felt like long-lost best friends. Maybe it was her enforced confinement, but Paul attracted her tremendously. Soon it seemed as if Paul had always been there, cheering her on, bringing her small gifts, teasing her, encouraging her, making sure that the nursing staff never neglected her.

She loved the way Paul shared things with her, especially his dream of building a huge sports-medicine clinic in Beverly Hills that would showcase the best orthopedic surgeons in the country, drawing famous athletes from all over the world, and major celebrities as well as children in need of special operations.

"I suppose I dream way too big," he said, laughing to cover the fact that he really meant every word.

"No," Valentina cried, flattered that he'd confided in her. "That's a wonderful dream, Paul, and I know you can make it happen."

"In about twenty years, maybe. But I'm not going to forget about it."

As the bedside phone rang, he jumped to answer it. "Yes, this is her room. Tell him to come on up—yes, room two forty-four."

"What's going on?" Valentina said, laughing in spite of herself.

"Just a little surprise from Spago. One of their special pizzas, all slathered with peppered Louisiana shrimp, sun-dried tomatoes, and leeks. And how about some angel-hair pasta with sautéed wild mushrooms, garlic, and glazed shallots?"

As she uttered a squeal of surprise, Paul laughed. "I love pampering you, sweetheart. You make the whole thing fun."

He sat down on the edge of her bed and stared intently into Valentina's eyes. "I realize you haven't known me very long, other than when we were kids, and now you're under a lot of stress. But I just want you to know something. I—"

A rap at the door interrupted him. "Hi, kiddo, it's never-never land," said a nurse, coming into the room with her medication tray.

Valentina looked startled. "But I still have an hour to—"

"Take it," advised Paul. "That's another thing I did for you, got the bastards to ease up on you a little bit. No sense putting you through torture just to satisfy some silly six-hour rule."

A few days later, after examining the dressings on her back wound, Dr. Feldman said she had developed some spinal fluid leakage in the operative region. It wasn't terribly unusual or even dangerous, *but* they were keeping an eye on the condition. If fluid could get out of the wound, Dr. Feldman said, then bacteria could get in. It might necessitate some additional surgery. They just weren't sure at this time.

Later that day, a star-struck member of the housekeeping staff brought Valentina a crumpled nine-by-twelve hospital transmittal envelope, into which had been stuffed a sheaf of clippings from tabloids like *Star* and *The National Enquirer.*

"You're real popular, honey, even more than Liz, when she was here."

Valentina pulled out some of the clippings. WILL VAL WALK AGAIN? screamed one headline. VAL CRIPPLED FOR LIFE, yelled another headline. VAL WEEPS AS PATHETIC INJURIES TAKE THEIR TOLL, said a third.

"You can keep those," said the housekeeper magnanimously, unaware of the blow she had just dealt. "I can get lots more of 'em—every week they have articles on you."

"Please. I . . . I have enough. No more articles," Valentina protested, shuddering. But the damage had been done.

During the times when her pain shots wore off, and she was able to think more clearly, she pondered the inescapable questions: would she have full recovery, would she dance again, would she be able to become pregnant? She already knew one thing about herself . . . much as she loved the joys of stardom, she wanted more in her life than just that. She wanted a home life and a family too.

Three days later, Dr. Feldman told her they wanted to operate again, to reclose the leaking hole in the spine sac with a few more stitches.

Valentina's heart sank. "Is this necessary?"

"We need to prevent an infection from developing in the wound. Don't worry—generally the operation is a very easy one. Within a few days you'll be well on the way to recovery."

That night Valentina refused her eight o'clock shot, and lay in bed thinking. Those awful tabloid headlines. She wished she could phone Orchid and unburden herself to her sister—just to have someone to share the worry with. But Orchid had gone back to New York after visiting Valentina only twice. The sight of all the reporters, the masses of flowers, the fans camped out in the hospital lobby, had unnerved and angered her.

No, she couldn't depend on Orchid.

Finally Valentina reached for her bedside phone and dialed the number of Keith's answering machine, which he kept in his Manhattan apartment.

"You have reached the answering machine of Keith Leonard. I am sorry I cannot come to the phone right now, but your message is important to me, so at the sound of the beep—"

She clutched the phone long after the beep sounded, unable to speak. When would she face reality? Keith was not free to be with her, and she did not have the kind of selfishness that would break up a man's marriage to satisfy her own needs.

Which left her where?

Alone.

Slowly she hung up the phone without leaving a message.

An hour later, when Paul came into the room, she told him that she'd decided to go ahead with the surgery.

"Oh, Val, I'm sure they'll take care of the problem in no time. Feldman is a top man—the best."

"I guess I don't have any choice," she added miserably.

"You do have choices—we always have choices." He hugged her. "Val, I'll be with you in the operating room, I'll scrub and observe everything, I'll be only a few feet away from you." His voice suddenly broke. "I know it's only been a week or so, but I care about you, Val. I more than just care. I . . . I live for these moments when I can come to your room and talk to you, touch you."

Paul leaned toward her. It was a soft, tender, gentle kiss. But gradually it deepened, and he gently parted her lips with his tongue.

There wasn't the deep rush of emotion she'd experienced with Keith, nor was there the exuberant physical lust she'd felt with Ben Paris. It was just . . . sweet. But so caring, she reminded herself, reaching up her arms to slide them around Paul's neck. He smelled of some expensive, faintly musky aftershave.

"Yes," he murmured. "That's better . . . so much better, Val. I want to be with you. I'll make sure that you

never have pain again, darling—ever. I want you to be the
best that you can be, and I'm going to help you.''

Orchid raced into the narrow, old-fashioned office building on West Forty-fifth Street, between Sixth and Seventh
avenues, and punched the button for the fifth floor.

As the elevator jiggled its way upward, she ran her
fingers through her frizzy hair, bouncing her foot impatiently. Mort Rubick, the independent film producer who'd
shown interest in her writing, had hired her as his assistant
and gofer.

Today was her first day of work.

The elevator stopped, its doors shuddering open directly
into an incredibly tiny anteroom. There was just barely
enough room for a battered old wooden desk, which
supported a telephone, fax machine, and desktop computer.
The one grimy window looked down on a Chaldean market
on Forty-fifth Street. The walls still bore the original
lead-green paint, now cracked and peeling. Didn't the man
believe in remodeling? Orchid thought in annoyance. She'd
probably get lead poisoning just from breathing deep.

Despite his lack of decorating ability, however, Mort
Rubick represented the best chance she'd had in years. He
was a growing legend in New York—an ''indie prod'' who
was as creative as Woody Allen, and as stubborn as a pit
bull. In fact, his latest project, a love story about two
construction workers, had played in fifteen hundred theaters, and Marty Grove of the *Hollywood Reporter* said it
was ''an artistic triumph.''

''Well, well, there you are,'' Mort Rubick said, hurrying
out of an inner room. The smell of coffee and Brut
aftershave drifted out with him. ''Nothing I like better than
a girl who's right on time.''

Orchid looked at her new employer. She'd been so
nervous during the first interview she'd barely remembered
his appearance. Mort was all of five-two, with a head too
large for his body, and a slightly crooked spine, so that the
expensive dark suit he wore fit oddly. To complete his

homeliness, he wore dark horn-rimmed glasses with a flesh-colored hearing aid in his right ear.

He gazed at her and made a wry face. "Okay, you done looking?"

"I—" She blushed. "Sorry."

"Hey, sweetie, Robert Redford I'm not, but most of the people I deal with aren't Clint Eastwood or Raquel Welch either. I look nice and comfortable and it relaxes people, it deludes them into thinking they can dick around with my mind. Then . . . poof! I surprise the living bejesus outa them."

As Orchid laughed, Mort gave her a wide smile that revealed his best feature—white, evenly spaced, good-looking teeth. "You'll provide the beauty in this place, Orchid. I provide the chutzpah. Hey," he added, "don't sit down yet, baby. I've got a package that needs delivering to a literary agent on West Twenty-sixth Street."

Orchid took the manila envelope he handed her and headed for the elevator again. She'd been on the job less than five minutes.

As she exited from the building onto the sidewalk filled with hundreds of scurrying pedestrians and the blazing sunlight of a hot August afternoon, she felt a thrill of hope. Maybe—finally—her luck was turning around.

Peaches decided to throw a small party for Valentina in her room on the night before her second surgery, to cheer her up. Running over the guest list beforehand, she spoke her mind on the subject of Paul Jensen.

"I'm not telling you what to do, Val, I'd never do that. But at least consider Paul. He has wonderful prospects, and I think he is a very kind, good person. He might be very good for you."

"But I haven't—I mean I've known him only a week or so. Except when we were kids."

"Darling, don't you think it's time you asked for something for yourself? You have a whole life to live, not half a life, shared with another woman, which is all that Keith Leonard gave you."

"No, Mom," she whispered. "You're wrong. Keith gave me everything."

But later, after Peaches left, Valentina closed her eyes, drifting off into a haze of painful memories about Keith. Their talks, the feel of his body. His smile. The agonizing moment at the garden party when she'd seen him embracing Cynthia.

After Keith, other men paled by comparison. She didn't even want to be with them. That's why Ben Paris had left her—because he knew he was such a faraway second. Peaches was right. As long as Keith was in her heart, she would never be free to go on with her own life.

A single tear rolled slowly down her cheek. *Keith, darling,* she whispered. *Forgive me.*

The guest list was tiny—just Jenny Trillin, who'd flown in from New York, Abby McKay, Peaches, Edgar, Mike Duffy, and of course, Paul Jensen.

"You gonna show 'em all," Abby announced in her rich voice. She had just bought a condo in West Hollywood, and her radio program was now being syndicated on one hundred and eighteen stations. "You've got the spirit and drive, girl—you're gonna be dancing in another six months, mark my words."

The group quickly added their vigorous assent.

"Oh, I hope so, Abby," Valentina said.

They spent the time laughing and chatting, and watching an old Cary Grant movie on the VCR that Paul had rented for the occasion. But at ten o'clock, Paul broke up the party with a genial announcement.

"I've got to ask you all to leave now . . . our beautiful Val has to get her beauty sleep. Five A.M. comes darn early."

There was a hubbub of good-lucks and I-love-yous.

"I'll be here first thing in the morning to be with you," Peaches promised.

After the room was empty, Valentina released her breath in a long sigh. "I know they love me, Paul, but I'm almost glad they're gone."

"Why?"

"Because—I need some thinking time. Paul, I want to be well again. I want the surgery to be over and done with."

"Baby, trust me, you're on the homestretch." He sat down next to her and slid his arms around her, pulling her close.

She gazed into Paul's eyes, seeing the variations of their color from deep blue to a dark slate-gray. He had such sincere eyes, she found herself thinking. So loving.

"Val, I don't know how to say this. I'm not sure there is any good way. I just want you to know I'm in love with you. All it took was one look at you and I was totally smitten— I'm yours."

"Oh, Paul," she repeated, drawing back a little in startled shock.

"I know it's sudden. I—well, what can I say? I could give you such a good life. I want to see to it that you're happy forever."

She felt a rush of stunned shock that turned into amazement. "You're not—" She cleared her throat. "Paul, you're not . . . asking me to . . . oh, no, you couldn't be."

"I am. I'm doing exactly that, Val. I know it might be premature but I wanted you to carry the knowledge into your surgery tomorrow that I love you and adore you and want you to be my wife."

"But we haven't even—I mean, we're not—"

"Not sexually intimate? Not yet, no. But we will be, and I'm sure it will be wonderful, Valentina. I haven't had a relationship in more than a year because, frankly, there hasn't been anyone I could give my feelings to. Now there's you, honey, and . . ." Paul pulled her close, pressing his face against hers. "I love you so much, Val. I'm afraid of how much. Please give me a chance."

"But it's so soon. I never thought of anything like this," she replied weakly.

"Then think about it now. Marry me. I'll give you children, Val, as many as you want. I'll keep you safe—I'll adore you as no woman has ever been adored."

She and Paul just held each other, while Valentina tried to recover from the stupefaction of his proposal.

"Well?" he whispered at last. "What about it, Val?"

She whispered the answer.

Nine days later, Valentina sat in the hospital lounge. She was wearing a "chairback" brace, about halfway up her back, designed to keep her back immobile so it would heal normally. Dr. Feldman was pleased with her recovery.

"Val . . . dear Val." Keith Leonard, suntanned after a recent trip to Houston, strode into the room, looking fantastic.

"Darling." He hugged her, pressing her close. "I'd whirl you around and call you beautiful, and declare my undying love for you, but that might shake up your bones too much."

"I'm not that fragile anymore," she declared, smiling. "Look—I've been walking! Well, for a few minutes at a stretch anyway. Then I have to lie down again. And it hurts plenty. But I'm going to recover fully."

"I'm so happy," he told her warmly.

They sat down in the lounge area and spent half an hour sharing their news. Keith was involved in a deal for a thirty-five-story office building in Houston, and had several new Broadway projects he was trying to get off the ground.

"Keith," she finally said in a low voice, lifting her left hand. As if cooperating, the sun streaming in the window seized the small but perfect diamond Paul had given her.

"My God," Keith breathed, seeing this. "Val?"

"I'm getting married," she choked, but instead of telling him who her fiancé was, she put both hands over her face and burst into tears.

"I can't believe this." She'd never heard his voice sound so strained. "This—this is a nightmare, Valentina. I'm dreaming. I'm not hearing this."

"It's true! I can't put my life on hold for you," she wept. "We agreed on that, Keith! We both agreed!"

There was a long silence that tore at Valentina's heart. It was obvious that Keith had only given lip service to the idea that she should go on with her life. In reality, he'd wanted to continue to think of her as his. And she could have been his! That was the horrible thing! If only their timing had been different. If only there hadn't been Cynthia. But there was Cynthia.

"Val, Val." He seemed numbed, too shocked to react. "I'm sorry. That's all I can say, I'm sorry I put you through this. I want you to be happy."

He jumped up from his chair and started toward the door.

"Keith—" she called after him, but he was halfway out of the room, his steps echoing on the polished floor.

It was over. Finally—after how many years? Forever.

"I'm sorry, I'm so sorry," she sobbed. "Keith, I . . ."

But he was gone, taking life and joy with him. Now what she had left was Paul. Her fiancé.

She sat for a few minutes, clenching her hands together so tightly that the hard edge of the diamond cut into the flesh of her finger. Finally she got up and walked slowly, painfully, back to her room.

"I'm not sure I love you enough," she told Paul that night. "I mean, I *love* you, but . . . maybe we should wait a year or so before actually getting married."

"What? Val!"

"We've only known each other for a few weeks, really, Paul, maybe we're rushing too much."

"Honey," pleaded Paul. "I can wait a few more months, but I just love you too much to wait a whole year. Baby, what's the real problem? Why the cold feet? You need me, Val. I can help you through this. I'll love you. I'll pamper you. I'll . . . I'll stop work here at the hospital, I'll take a year off and just take care of you. I can always finish my residency next year."

Gently she said, "I don't want to marry a man just to have someone to take care of me. Mom is here, she can—"

"Your mother has a husband, darling. She has a life of her own. *I* love you. *I* want to be the one in your life—the one you turn to. Please let me be that one. I need you."

She gazed at Paul. She did love him, in a quiet, gentle

way. He was bright, handsome, ambitious, and talented. He could give her a child. Surely her love for him would deepen.

"You are that one," she told him, smiling. "You really are, Paul. And I—"

"I want you, Val. I'll always want you. You're perfect for me—the only woman I'll ever want for the rest of my life."

Wearing a Hard Rock Cafe T-shirt and a coquettish short blue jean skirt, Orchid sat in front of the IBM, rapidly typing up a letter to Detroit Pistons owner/billionaire Bill Davidson, whom Mort was trying to interest in his latest project, a Broadway musical called *Big, Bad, and Beautiful*.

She snatched up the telephone on the first ring. "Good morning, Mort Rubick's office."

"Orchid? Is that you? You sound exactly like a real receptionist." It was Peaches, phoning from LA.

"I am one—well, kind of. I make killer coffee and I've been thinking about getting one of those messenger bikes." Orchid glanced toward Mort's door to make sure it was closed, before lifting her feet, clad in blue snakeskin boots, to the desktop. After three weeks with Mort she actually felt half human again.

"Dear, I've called with the most terrific news," said Peaches.

"This doesn't have anything to do with Val, does it?"

"Now, honey, listen before you start getting so negative. First, she's feeling so much better—"

"I knew it! I knew she'd be fine. Her luck always comes up roses! I don't even know *why* you were so worried."

"There's something else, too, Orchid. Val's getting married, to—"

"Married? Val's getting married!"

"It's Paul Jensen, darling. It's so nice they were able to connect again after all these years."

"P-Paul?"

"Yes, dear, I'm sure I told you, he's one of the doctors on Val's case. Even Daddy Edgar admits he's been wonderful to her. We're planning just a small ceremony on December twelfth at the Bel Air Hotel, honey. I hope you'll fly out for it. Please, will you try to be there? For us?''

"I . . . I can't . . . Please don't ask me to fly out—"

"Now, Orchid, can't you put aside your—"

"I won't go!" snapped Orchid, slamming down the phone.

The phone rang again. "All right, all right," Orchid muttered. She put the call, from a London playwright, through to Mort.

After her boss picked up, she sat scowling at the blue monitor of her computer screen. *Valentina is getting married.*

To Paul. She closed her eyes in an agony of indecision. Then she blinked them open again. She'd behaved like such a bitch to Val already. If she did tell Val about Paul, would she even believe it?

The yellow light on the phone line went off.

"Orchid, my little flower," said Mort, pushing open his office door and coming into the anteroom. "I want to take you out for a little lunchie."

Lunch? She stared at her boss in surprise. "Let me get my purse," she agreed.

The Cafe Pierre in the Pierre Hotel, at Sixty-first and Fifth Avenue, was jammed with power lunchers. The cuisine was French, and Mort ordered for both of them.

For forty minutes he entertained her with outrageous stories of his days working as a producer on the lot at Universal Studios. Then he got down to business.

"You know the walls aren't all that thick in the office, chickie, and you did talk kind of loud today when you were on the phone to your mother."

Orchid froze.

"Honey, I couldn't help overhearing about Valentina— how she's pretty much back in action, or will be soon. And now she's getting married and you're going to the wedding, right?"

"Not right," Orchid said sullenly. "I'm not going."

"Yes, you are going," Mort said. "I want her."

"What?"

"She's a natural for the lead of *Big, Bad, and Beautiful,* and her presence in it would guarantee a hit because of her accident and all the publicity. I tried calling her agent but he says she's not considering any new projects right now. You're her sister, you can talk to her."

"Mort." Orchid pushed away her chocolate *pots de crème,* her appetite abruptly spoiled. "In the first place, I barely *speak* to her. In the second place, *I* screwed her fiancé before she did. Third, I wouldn't be caught dead going to her wedding if you paid me a million bucks."

"Maybe not a million bucks," Mort said, giving her one of his hard-businessman looks. "How about a chance to get your old script *Rock, Lady, Rock* produced? Would that be enough of an inducement for you, sweet Orchid flower? I haven't forgotten that's really why you came to work for me, you know."

"You'd do that?" she breathed.

"To get Valentina Lederer in my show, I'd package ten movies for you, babes. But you've got to come through for me. I want Valentina signed, sealed, and delivered. I'll rework the contract I want her to sign, I'll write it all out for you. You can type it up before you leave."

Orchid half jumped up from the table, reaching over to give Mort a huge hug. She squealed, "Oh, Mort . . . oh, Mort . . . All I need is a chance, just one chance—my script is wonderful—I know it is—it really is—"

"Hey, this is business, honey. *Business,*" he emphasized. "You better sign her—or your script stays right where it is, in my bottom file drawer."

Valentina started up the hill, walking fast despite her pain, tears of frustration filling her eyes. She'd been spending *hours* in rehab every day, painfully working her back muscles to strengthen them. Thus far the results hadn't been sensational. She was still living on pain pills. She could only ride upright in a car twenty-five minutes, and after that she had to lie down in the backseat.

Making matters worse was the way her mother hovered around her, anxiously trying to do everything for her. Only Paul kept her going right now. His cheerfulness, his daily phone calls or visits, buoyed her.

She reached the gate of the home Peaches and Edgar had bought in Bel Air on Bellagio Drive, and slipped through. A little red Jaguar with Avis rental plates was parked in the circular drive.

Peaches came out onto the front veranda, wearing a yellow sunsuit that showed off her still-glamorous legs. "I have a wonderful, wonderful surprise, darling. It's Orchid. She's out by the pool, honey, taking a swim."

Valentina caught her breath, uttering a little shout of joy that turned into a gasp of pain as she tried to walk too fast toward the pool.

"Hi, Val— Geez, I'd forgotten how good it feels to jump in a swimming pool. This water is perfect—like blue Jell-O."

Orchid pulled herself out of the water, and shook her head, spraying droplets. She wore a black bikini that hugged her tiny, perfect figure, revealing the two small blue tattoos shaped like orchids on her right thigh and left buttock.

"Orchid, I'm so glad to see you," Valentina exclaimed joyfully, ignoring her back pain to rush forward with her arms out. "God, it's so fabulous you're really here!"

"Oh, don't hug me, I'm wet," Orchid said, stepping away and throwing herself down into a lawn chair, beginning to towel herself off.

Valentina froze, hurt by the rejection. She lowered herself onto a chaise. The lying down position eased the worst of her back pain, but soon she was going to need one of the Percodans Paul had prescribed. She forced herself to say politely, "Did you just get here? How was your flight?"

While Peaches went inside to ask the cook for refreshments, the two sisters talked awkwardly about Orchid's plane flight, the weather in New York, and the latest exploits of Los Angeles Dodger pitcher Roman Solenski, Orchid's lover.

"You look great," Orchid finally said, eyeing her in a

speculative, assessing manner. Valentina wore shorts and a Detroit Pistons T-shirt.

"I'm making progress."

"I mean, you look *really* great, and I imagine you're ready to jump right into things again. You know what they say when you fall off a horse," Orchid went on.

Valentina frowned. "You mean get right back on again? But that's impossible right now, Orchid. I still have six more months of therapy, and I can only sit up in a chair for a little while—how would I ever go onstage or even play a scene in a movie. I couldn't."

The color drained from Orchid's face. She leaned forward, her face earnest and intense. *"But you have to!"*

"I know, and I'm chafing at the bit myself, but the doctors say—"

"To hell with the doctors!" Orchid burst out. "Val, you have to come to New York. You just have to. Mort is doing a new musical called *Big, Bad, and Beautiful.*"

"Who is Mort?"

"Why, he—you know, *Mort Rubick!* The independent producer. I'm working for him, now, Val, and he's just so creative and he has this absolutely wonderful part that would be *so* perfect for you—"

Valentina stared at her sister, stunned.

"I'm sorry, Orchid," she said coolly. "Why didn't he call Mike Duffy? Mike would have told him that I have a long recuperative period ahead and I can't sign for any new projects right now—maybe not for a long while."

"But you have to!" Orchid repeated.

Valentina drew back, unnerved by the intensity in her sister's voice. "Talk to my doctors, then," she said, wincing as she lifted her body out of the chair and started toward the house.

"Wait!" cried Orchid, running after her. "Wait, Val— you can't just walk off. Not when I've come all this way! You're so incredibly selfish—"

"You're the selfish one," Valentina snapped, opening the patio door. "Ya don't care about anyone but yourself."

Chapter

Twenty-one

PAUL JENSEN PULLED his black BMW into the parking lot of the Powerhouse Gym off Hollywood Boulevard. It was his haven, where he went when he wanted to think. And he sure as hell needed to think right now.

There were only two days left until he'd be a married man, tied, chained, and bound. With a few compensations, of course . . . He'd have to concentrate on that, not the feeling of claustrophobia this whole wedding thing was giving him.

He reached for his gym bag and slung it over his arm, starting toward the club.

"Paul . . . Paul! Wow, it is you, isn't it?"

He turned to see Orchid Lederer jumping out of a little Jaguar, wearing a pair of skin-tight jeans and a cropped T-shirt that left nothing to the imagination. She carried a designer gym bag made of yellow parachute material, and looked even hotter than she had at Northwestern.

"Orchid," he greeted her warily. "My beautiful sister-in-law."

"Not until the wedding, I'm not," she said, grinning as she brought one hand up to push a mass of curls out of her eyes. "Peaches told me you work out here all the time, so I thought I'd say hello." Her eyes challenged him. "And now you're marrying my very own sister. Amazing."

Paul masked his alarm with a smile. "You're as sensational looking as ever," he told Orchid as they walked into the high-tech club lobby.

"Aren't you going to ask me what I'm doing these days?" Orchid began.

"So what are you doing?"

"Well, I'm in New York working for an independent producer—and I'm finally going to hit it, I think. And you? Been borrowing any more money lately?" she drawled.

"Hey," he protested. "I told you I'd repay the loan with interest and I intend to keep my word."

"I'll write that down. Or would you rather I talked to Val about it . . . you know, a nice sister-to-sister gabfest?"

"No, no, no, no. Look, Orchid, can we keep this between ourselves?"

"Maybe." Her eyes teased him. "*If* you do me one, tiny favor. Talk to her for me, will you? I have this wonderful screenplay, and Mort Rubick will package it for me, if I get her to sign a contract for a musical called—"

Paul listened, nodding, as Orchid told him all about it.

"I'll do my best," he promised her, knowing he wouldn't. He wanted Val dependent on him, not out on her own. "Now, babe, let's go and pump a little iron, all right? How much can you curl and how many reps?"

"Enough to keep you happy," Orchid quipped, grinning. As they parted for their respective locker rooms, she gave him that smoldering look again. Paul felt the stirring of an erection.

The next morning was Sunday, and Edgar insisted on taking them all to the Rib Joint in Beverly Hills for one of their famous champagne brunches.

Valentina, however, only picked at her food. Across the table, Orchid was on her third glass of champagne, as she and Paul laughed about Orchid's apparently comic efforts to keep up with him at the gym a few days ago. Somehow it appeared they'd hooked up at the body-building club.

"Are you all right, darling?" inquired Peaches quietly.

"Of course I am, Mom."

"You seem so quiet, honey. Are you in pain again?"

"No, Mother, I'm not," lied Valentina. Her hand moved to the purse in her lap, where she'd placed a bottle of the Percodans that blunted the stabbing back pain that she'd been forced to live with.

She needed another one. Murmuring excuses, she got up from the table and walked across the sawdust-covered floor to the ladies' room.

Orchid made small talk with Edgar, but inside she was seething. Paul's promised talk with Val hadn't worked out. They weren't staging *Big, Bad, and Beautiful* for five more months, which was plenty of time for Val to get herself back in shape.

She renewed the argument with Val when they arrived back home again. "You don't care, do you, Val? I mean, Mort has promised me he'll package my screenplay and I need that, Val, can't you understand? *I need some success. I really, really do.*"

"Orchid, I'm afraid if I go back to work too soon I'll be permanently damaged. I don't want to be a permanent invalid."

"Oh, bullshit. You're just doing this to hurt me—that's the real reason you won't go back to work. I need you and you won't even try."

"Will you stop?" Valentina begged. "Orchie, will you just stop for two minutes and listen to yourself? You just want to use me. You know that's what this is about. Mort Rubick has promised you—"

"Oh, stop!" Orchid cried, spinning around and starting toward the hallway that led to her bedroom. "I'm hot—I'm going out to the pool. You're jealous of me, Val. I can do things now and you can't. You'll be sorry!"

All that day Orchid kept drinking. Mimosas out by the pool. Then wine with dinner. By evening she was royally smashed. She'd tried her best and failed. Tomorrow morning she had to fly back to New York.

Valentina went to bed early, and Peaches and Edgar announced they were turning in too. Paul said he had some medical periodicals to catch up on.

Her body still on New York time, Orchid wandered outdoors to the pool again. She sat staring glumly at the glimmering bowl of turquoise.

"Hey," said a soft voice behind her. "I wondered where you'd gone to."

She looked up. Paul Jensen had changed to a pair of loose black silk lounging pants, and was bare-chested. His chest, rippled with gorgeous pectoral muscles from hours of working out at Powerhouse, looked magnificent.

"If I said you had a beautiful body, would you hold it against me?" she murmured.

"All night long," Paul responded, grinning.

She rose. "Your room or mine?"

"How about mine? It's at the other end of the house."

Paul's technique had improved only slightly since Northwestern. He had no real lovemaking "soul." He was like some warm, breathing robot, programmed to mechanical fucking.

But what did she care? she thought, opening her legs to allow him entry. This was purely revenge!

Valentina awoke from smothering, terrible dreams in which an avalanche of snow swept her downhill and broke her legs like matchsticks.

She sat up, gasping, and then sank down on her pillow again to fight the spurts of pain in her back and legs.

She tried to calm herself. Tomorrow was her wedding day. She'd be Mrs. Paul Jensen, and she'd be safe.

She fumbled on the bedside stand for the bottle of pills, and within a few minutes, the pain had faded, and she slid out of bed, starting for her bathroom to shower. A knock on her door stopped her, and she grabbed for a light bathrobe.

"Darling? It's me . . . can I come in?"

Peaches was carrying a heavy white wicker tray, on which had been arranged a complete breakfast, and a pink rose in a sterling silver bud vase. "I just wanted to give my beautiful daughter a special treat," her mother said, sliding the tray onto the bed. "And maybe to talk a little. Val, you just don't seem yourself lately. In fact—"

Another knock sounded. "Are you decent, darling? Can I come in?"

Paul entered the room, jauntily dressed in dark pants and white shirt for the hospital, his hair still damp from his shower. He immediately walked to the bed and gave Valentina a long, lingering kiss.

She clung to him, grateful for his attentions.

"See the wonderful Spanish omelette Mom brought me?" she murmured, when they pulled apart. "It's her specialty."

"Lovely. Darling lazybones, did you know I dropped off a demo tape to Orchid in her room last night after you dozed off on me? Howie Emmer works out at Powerhouse, and his wife Rebecca is trying to break into the music business. He asked me to get Orchid's opinion. And yours, too, of course. Will you play it?"

"I'll listen to the tape, of course." Valentina began to pick at the delicious omelette.

"Eat it all," Paul advised. "You need the extra calories. And, honey . . ."

"Yes?"

"Maybe I'd better prescribe some B-12 for you too. It'll perk you up a little. I can't have my beautiful bride all draggy for her wedding. Did I tell you I finally got the beach house I wanted to borrow in Carmel? The owners said yes. You'll go crazy when you see it. The view is fantastic! Are you happy, darling?"

Peaches had discreetly left the room, leaving Paul and Valentina alone.

"Of course I'm happy, Paul. Only I hope I can be a good lover to you," she blurted out. "I'm—I mean, my back—I don't know if I can—"

He smiled and took her hand. "I know what you're talking about, and there won't be any problem, darling. That's why you're marrying a doctor—so there won't be."

The lush tropical garden at the Bel Air Hotel had been the scene for many celebrity weddings, its velvet lawn, with deep green foliage and blazing flower beds, so perfect that it looked more like a movie set than a real garden. A Victorian-style gazebo, threaded with lilies and white roses, was where they would say their vows.

Valentina wore a magnificent Scaasi wedding gown. Its long lace sleeves, deep sweetheart neckline, and tiered flounces with a six-foot train gave her a romantic, ethereal look. She wore the same filmy veil Peaches had worn, forty years ago, to marry Edgar. In her bosom she carried a cream-colored embroidered handkerchief that Nadia had brought over from Russia.

Long forgotten, Nadia's last few, gasped words now came flooding back to her. *You have strength, child . . . you will find your way. You will find love. I know it. Love, Valentina. Never be afraid to love.*

Valentina stood in front of the mirror in the bridal suite, tears rolling down her face. Why wasn't Orchid with her? They used to fantasize about being each other's bridesmaids. And where was Keith? She fought a panicky urge to run to the telephone and call him in New York.

Peaches hovered over her, touched and worried. "Are you all right? Are you sure your back isn't hurting?"

"My back feels fine, Mother, I just took two more pills. As long as they don't stop making Percodan, I'm all right."

"Here . . . let me freshen you up with some more powder. Darling," her mother added. "Are you sure? I mean, it isn't too late. People have been known to change their minds before at the last minute. Honestly, darling, your happiness is the most important thing to both Daddy Edgar and me."

Valentina hesitated. When she looked into Peaches's eyes she saw the worry there. She was just having an acute attack of bridal cold feet, that was all.

Dolly Rutledge was knocking at their door. "Two minutes," she called.

"Val?" Peaches persisted, looking deeply into Valentina's eyes.

"I am happy, Mother," she said, forcing a smile. "I . . . I love Paul very much."

"Are you *sure*?"

"Very, very sure," Valentina insisted.

She took another pill just before she left the suite, and its warm fuzziness helped her get through the ceremony in a soft daze.

Four hours later they were in Paul's car on their way to Carmel along the Pacific Coast Highway. Valentina rode most of the journey lying on her back in the backseat, to ease the persistent gnawing pain in her spine.

The "beach house" turned out to be a mansion near Point Sur, with eighteen rooms and two swimming pools, and a stunning view of the Pacific. It even had a ballroom, along with two tennis courts. It was for sale, the asking price fourteen million dollars, but had been loaned to them by its owner, a wealthy physician who practiced at Cedars-Sinai. There were three full-time servants.

"Isn't this fantastic?" Paul kept saying. "I mean, this is the way to live, Val."

Valentina changed out of her traveling suit into a white negligee. She brushed out her thick masses of jet curls from the upsweep she'd worn them in for the wedding, and washed her face, adding only a dab of peach lip gloss, and a brush of violet over her eyes.

God, what if they weren't sexually compatible?

"Honey?" Her new husband was tapping on her dressing room door. "Baby? I've ordered us up some champagne . . . I think it's exactly what we need tonight, don't you?"

"You're beautiful, my own movie star," Paul kept saying as he smothered her with kisses, while expertly caressing her. She moaned, giving herself up to his skills. Paul was like a virtuoso, kissing sensitive parts of her body that sent erotic messages to her brain. The backs of her knees. Licking her toes and each finger. Sucking the silken inside of her arm at the elbow.

He was a love machine.

But after her second orgasm, Valentina lay spent and tired. The pills were starting to wear off, and she felt an arrow of pain shoot down her spine and legs. She wondered why Paul's whispered I-love-you's seemed so mechanical.

"Was it good?" Paul queried, raising himself up on one elbow. "Was *I* good?"

"You were wonderful," she murmured.

"Was it wonderful enough to try again?" He was already moving toward her.

Valentina closed her eyes and tried to give herself up to the pleasure of sex with her new husband, but the mood was gone.

After he rolled away and fell asleep, Valentina lay awake, staring toward the windows that overlooked the pounding surf.

Keith. Somehow she knew he would have been different. He would have held her more tenderly, he would have blended his feelings and emotions with hers. Keith would have *loved* her, not just had sex with her.

Then she rolled over, burying her tear-stained face in the pillow.

Valentina awoke the following morning feeling a burst of renewed cheerfulness. The sun, streaming in the windows of the huge master bedroom, along with the music of the clock radio, somehow gave her a new hope.

Paul had already risen, and she could hear the distant ponging sound as he practiced his serve on one of the tennis courts. She stretched out luxuriously, and decided she wouldn't take another pill this morning unless she really needed it. She was tired of being in a perpetual vague, light-headed daze. She wanted to get back to normal again!

She got up and went into the shower, then soaked in the Jacuzzi for twenty minutes. So what if their lovemaking hadn't pleased her one hundred percent. It *had* only been their first time. There would be many, many more times, and she could begin to show Paul how to be really tender—she could train him in the things she liked.

Dressing in tight-fitting white Ralph Lauren jeans and an oversized white crocheted sweater, she walked out onto the balcony that overlooked the ocean. The house had been built on a spit of land that overlooked a tumbled causeway of rocks. Spumes of lacy spray jetted up fifteen feet high. The perfect honeymoon setting.

For the first time she allowed herself to relax. This was only the beginning, she assured herself. Marriage wasn't just one night—it was forever.

"Honey? Are you up so soon?" Paul came out onto the balcony and slid his arms around her waist, drawing her close to him. He was wearing tennis whites and smelled of fresh air.

"The view . . . it's everything you promised," she said, smiling.

He hugged her, then pulled away. "Good, I'm glad you like it. And I'm glad you're up and happy. I've got a physical therapist driving out from San Jose this morning, Val. I don't want you to miss even a day."

"A therapist? But it's our—"

"I know, I know, it's our honeymoon." He kissed her lightly. "But we can't have you backsliding, can we? It's only an hour, babe. And I've brought you another kind of pain pill that I think might give you relief without making you so drowsy."

She shook her head. "I'm going to try to get along without it."

"With all the therapy you're going through? No way, honey. You know how pain tightens the muscles—you'll ruin everything we've set out to accomplish."

"But I really don't think—"

Paul went into the enormous marble bathroom, returning with a glass of water. He waited while she obediently swallowed the pill. "Now let's go down to breakfast. Then I want to show you the hothouse porch—it's absolutely fabulous, right out of the Victorian era. There's twenty different kinds of orchids, can you believe it? And antique wicker furniture that's outa sight."

They returned after two weeks to a home in Holmby Hills, a wealthy community that was almost an annex to Beverly Hills. Edgar had pulled strings for them to stay in the house for a year while its owner, a stage star, was appearing on Broadway. It had a small but exquisite swimming pool, and a mirrored workout room equipped with the latest Nautilus equipment and free weights.

"The weight room is really why I wanted this place,"

Paul told her. "It's perfect for your rehab, Val . . . I want you to promise me you'll do the exercises every day."

Three weeks later Paul became certified as an orthopedic surgeon by the board and went back to work at the hospital, where he again became absorbed in his medical practice and worked late hours.

"Honey," he pleaded when she complained. "Please bear with me. You know I don't want to depend on your money, or your father's generosity. I'm chauvinistic enough to want to be the one who supports us. And of course, there are my loans. God, I've hocked half my life to become a doctor."

"But couldn't you spend at least a little time with me? I'm so—" With effort, she cut off the word "lonely."

But when a whole week went by without her and Paul sharing dinner together even once, Valentina couldn't hold back her feelings.

"Most doctors get *some* time to themselves," she accused on Friday night when Paul arrived home after midnight.

"Not this one," he told her, shrugging. "It's different in Beverly Hills, honey."

"I'm tired of eating alone, Paul. I've seen every movie on cable and I've read every best-seller on the *New York Times* list."

His mouth tightened. "You're not a prisoner here. Call Peaches, honey—or invite one of your friends to go out with you. Call Jenny Trillin. You girls can go out to the Bistro Gardens or L'Orangerie just as often as you want."

"The girls? I don't want to go out with the girls all the time, Paul. I want my husband."

"You have him, babe," Paul said. "Really. I mean that. Just be patient." He came forward and slid his arms around her, nuzzling kisses into her neck.

The weeks melted one into the other, and Valentina did not make the kind of progress she had expected.

"You might have to resign yourself to chronic pain," Dr.

Feldman told her one afternoon after she had burst into tears of frustration in his office.

"Chronic? But I thought it was all just a matter of therapy," she protested.

"Val, we've done all we can do, medically, for your problem. Pain is a very complex phenomenon, and we don't understand it fully yet. Stress, emotions, our personal thresholds . . . they all play a part in any discomfort we feel. I'm going to refer you to a chronic pain clinic. They use biofeedback and a lot of other stress reduction techniques, and might be able to help you reach a level you can live with."

She stared at him, flushing. "You're saying that the pain is all in my head, aren't you?"

The young, handsome physician shook his head. "Val, I told you, pain is such a subjective thing."

Still, she left the doctor's office in an angry mood, pausing only to dry-swallow two of the Talwin Paul had prescribed for her.

By the time she pulled into the hilly parking lot of Spago, where she was to meet Peaches, the medication had taken effect.

"Darling, you look white. Are you feeling all right?" Peaches inquired as Valentina was shown to a window table overlooking Sunset Boulevard.

"I'm fine."

"But you seem a bit light-headed, darling."

"Peaches, I'm fine!" Valentina snapped. She never called her mother Peaches unless she was angry.

"Very well then." Peaches picked up the menu. "What are we in the mood for? Would you like some nice grilled tuna, or some roast Sonoma lamb?"

"Not lamb," Valentina said, feeling a wave of dizziness.

"The roasted Alaska salmon in Cabernet butter sounds good."

"Too rich. I—"

When she excused herself to go to the ladies' room, and rose, the room suddenly spun. She stumbled forward, half falling across the table.

Peaches jumped to her feet, both arms around Valentina as she supported her. From a long, spinning distance, Valentina heard her mother's anxious voice. "Are you faint, Val? Would you like to go lie down? I'm sure they have a place where you can stretch out for a little while."

"No," Valentina choked. "I want to go home."

"All right, darling." Discreetly Peaches motioned for a hovering waiter. "Would you please help us, my daughter is suddenly feeling a bit faint."

The following week, a tidbit about Valentina's collapse appeared in *Star*.

Valentina cleaved through the azure water, executing a flawless crawl. Swimming was the one exercise that made her feel wonderful.

When she had finished ten laps, she climbed out, reaching for a terry robe to dry herself. The maid had left lunch on a tray, along with the *Los Angeles Times* and *Variety*.

Beginning to munch, Valentina picked up the *Times* and leafed through to Calendar, her favorite section.

The item in Jack Mathews's column jumped up at her.

Young and Restless star Anni York, on the mend from a motorcycle wipeout last month, was spotted in Chasen's this week with a handsome doctor newly wed to a gorgeous Broadway and rock star. Is he good medicine, Anni?

Valentina gasped, and read the paragraph again.

No, she told herself. He couldn't be. They'd been married only three months. There were any number of reasons why Paul might have been out with Anni, an important patient who could refer other celebrities to him.

That evening Paul dashed home to change for a dinner meeting of the Los Angeles County Medical Society.

Valentina went into his dressing room and sat in a chair, watching as he selected an Armani suit and a silk jacquard tie. She noticed that his eyes sparkled with nervous excitement.

"Isn't that just a little elegant for a medical meeting?" she remarked.

"What? Oh, you know the style around here. LA casual. Everyone has to look like a fashion plate."

"But for a medical meeting?" she persisted. "Paul, I—"

"Are you grilling me, Valentina? I suppose you read that stupid item in Jack Mathews's column."

"As a matter of fact, I did."

"Well, it was just a business meeting, Val. You know Anni can send all her friends to me. I want that kind of referral. Trust me, Val. I'm in a highly visible profession, dealing with screwed-up stars and the temperamental wealthy. You're going to have to give me some slack, that's all."

"All right. I do love you. Do you love me, Paul?"

"I'm with you, aren't I? Of course I love you."

She wrapped her arms around him, leaning into his embrace and thinking how vulnerable she had become. Her life had begun centering around Paul and she realized she needed more. It was time to think about cutting another album, or even going back to work in a new play.

Valentina began looking for songs to record. She placed a call to Bonnie Hayes, who had written "Have a Heart" for Bonnie Raitt, and began playing the dozens of demo tapes that her agent, Mike Duffy, and Arista Records kept sending her.

A month later, Mike called with news. Cy Coleman was trying to put together a new musical, *Dream, Ladies, Dream.* Could she come to New York and do some songs for the backers' audition, arranged by the Schubert organization? They were dying to get her.

"Oh, Mike, I'd love to. I think I need to work again. God, I need it in the worst way."

"You all right, cookie? I mean, you have the green light from *los medicos,* right?"

"Oh, yes, for singing anyway. I don't think I'm up to major dancing yet, though. But that's okay, isn't it?"

"Baby, they're gonna love to see your face . . . you're a shoo-in for this part if you want it. I'll be there at the audition too. I can't wait to see you knock 'em dead."

Bemused, Valentina hung up. A sudden joyous burst of energy spun her across the room in a crazy little dance.

That night she told Paul.

"You're not ready yet, Val," he told her, frowning.

"Of course I am! I need this—as therapy."

"I don't want you that far away."

She sighed. "We'll make it somehow. I really want to try."

Then Paul seemed to brighten. "Well, all right . . . Val, baby, I'll miss you while you're gone."

"I'll miss you too."

Valentina checked into the Plaza. The flight from LA had been turbulent and they'd circled in a holding pattern over Kennedy for nearly forty minutes. Now her back ached with a deep, steady throb.

The middle-aged bellboy recognized her at once. "We're glad to have you back in the Big Apple, Valentina—we've really missed you."

Valentina scribbled an autograph, feeling absurdly pleased at the welcome. As soon as she reached her room, she swallowed several of the Talwin. While waiting for them to take effect, she wandered to the window. Her tenth-floor suite looked out on the green of Central Park, beyond which could be seen the gray ranks of skyscrapers on the other side. New York! Noisy, crowded, and dangerous as it was, she'd missed this place.

And Keith, who had always been part of it. She'd read in the trades that he'd backed a production that had closed after two nights, losing more than three million dollars. Broadway's magic man had flopped.

Keith, Keith, she thought longingly as she picked up the telephone.

He was waiting for her in one of the back booths at the Foxy coffee shop, and jumped up awkwardly as she hurried toward him. He was wearing his sideburns shorter now, and there was more silver at his temples. He wore a simple white cotton sweater and slacks, and looked unbelievably handsome.

"Keith?"

"Honey." He pulled her to him and they embraced, clinging to each other. Valentina breathed in the familiar scents of this man she loved so deeply, and felt unabashed joy.

"Your perfume," he choked. "I've missed it."

They sank into the booth, instinctively choosing to sit side by side so they could be closer. The owner approached them and Keith ordered cheese danish and a pot of Kona coffee—their usual order.

"I can't believe you're here," he said, at the same time she was saying, "I can't believe I'm seeing you," and then they both laughed, holding hands.

"LA is too damn far away," Keith said, squeezing her fingers over and over.

"Oh, God, I'm just so glad I'm here now."

They shared their news. Cynthia was feeling better than she had in years.

"She's a trooper," Keith said, "and she's even started taking more of an interest in my work."

"I see."

"Honey, oh, honey." Keith tightened his grip on her hand. "I'm just glad that she's feeling better. She's my obligation but you're my heart, my life's essence. *I swear it.*"

She stared deeply into his eyes, seeing only honesty.

"Let's not talk about Cynthia any more. I accept that part of you, Keith. There's no other choice for me."

She began to tell him about the new album she wanted to cut.

"How are you feeling, Val? Really."

"I'm improving. I'm learning to accept the pain."

"And Paul? How are you getting along with him?"

"He—I— We're managing."

"But not so well, I hear."

"What do you mean?"

"Well, for one, darling, you were seen collapsing in Spago."

She swallowed dryly. "I just felt a little dizzy. And the tabloids blew it all out of proportion."

"Honey, listen to me. The word on the Coast is that Paul is overmedicating you. That he's been seen with Anni York, and other beauties, and you're too spaced out to care. He hasn't bothered to hide his tracks."

"It's only business," she whispered. "Paul is very ambitious, and he wants to have a celebrity practice, and a sports clinic . . ."

Keith looked skeptical. "Sweetheart . . . please don't be upset. I didn't say it to hurt you. I'm worried about you. You've got to do something about that medication you're taking. You've got to—"

But Valentina didn't want to listen. She jumped up from the table and pushed her way out of the coffee shop, holding back tears.

The huge, white-carpeted living room of Cy Coleman's Park Avenue triplex had a magnificent view of Central Park treetops, and was hung with original Chagalls and Picassos. Near the bank of windows stood a white grand piano, where a pianist waited to accompany Valentina.

Gathered around a marble coffee table were eight men and one woman, most of them billionaire players in New York's financial clique.

"Valentina, you look just gorgeous," Cy said, eyeing Valentina's slim jersey dress with its daringly low-cut neckline. She had brushed her hair to the side into a wild ponytail secured by a huge pearl-studded bow.

There was a flutter of eager male attention as Cy escorted her to the gathered group, introducing her to the assorted backers.

"Ladies and gentlemen," said Cy, coming forward. "I hate to break this up, but could you all take your seats? And now may I present a woman whose beauty has electrified the entire country, and whose voice is legendary—the incomparable Valentina!"

* * *

By the time she had finished the second ballad, Valentina knew the audition was a disaster. She'd given the backers a rehearsal-quality performance, and slurred some of the lyrics, fluffing one of the lines so badly that the pianist had to stop.

Glancing at Mike Duffy, she saw the expressionless set of the agent's face. She felt moisture spring to her eyes, but she forced herself to continue.

When her last note died away, she stepped away from the mike to the sound of polite applause.

On her way to the door, Mike caught up with her. "Val, don't go yet. We have to talk."

"I blew it, didn't I?" she choked.

"Look, maybe we pushed too hard and too soon, Val. Why don't you go back to LA, soak up some sun, maybe see a voice teacher, get those high notes back under control again, huh? Meanwhile I'll keep looking for something for you—but not too soon, okay?"

"Okay," she agreed dully.

She stumbled onto the sidewalk, feeling another wave of dizziness from the Talwin. Self-hatred overwhelmed her. It was the pills that had fuzzed her brain, causing her to fluff the lyrics. Oh, shit, she hated them and she hated herself.

Valentina had planned to do some shopping after the audition, and leave early the next morning, but instead she rushed back to the hotel and packed, phoning American Airlines for the first flight back to LA.

By ten o'clock that evening, her mind in turmoil, she was pulling into her own driveway. She used the remote to slide open the wrought-iron gates that guarded the property. She parked in her usual space and noticed that Paul's BMW was there. The house blazed with lights.

"Paul? Paul? Darling?" She dropped her purse on a table and hurried through the living room toward the master bedroom. This room, too, glowed with light, but it was empty. He must be swimming, she decided. Maybe she'd join him. It'd be a great homecoming, and she needed the exercise after the hours of being cramped on a plane.

But as she started to take off her clothes, she stopped short at the sight of a small pile of women's clothing crumpled on a slipper chair. A black tank top, faded jeans torn with parallel rows of fashionable rents. Tossed on the floor were a pair of minuscule hot-pink bikini panties, and a pair of women's black leather biker boots.

Not hers. She'd never worn biker boots in her life. Nor did she wear torn jeans.

Her heart thudding in her throat, Valentina walked to the sliding door that opened onto the pool area. Stepping onto the bricked patio, she gazed through the screen of tropical shrubbery.

Paul and Anni York.

The actress's wet hair streamed darkly over her round, silicone-augmented breasts, and her skin glistened whitely in the light. Paul gripped Anni tightly, supporting her as his hips thrusted.

As Valentina watched in mute horror, Paul flung his head backward and began to shudder in a climax. She could hear his groans of satisfaction—the same groans he uttered when making love to her.

Valentina stumbled back into the bedroom again, frantic to get away. She ran through the house and out to the garage and jumped in her car, backing it out with a loud screech of tires.

"It was nothing, just an isolated incident . . . an accident," Paul told her when Valentina returned later, exhausted after driving around for hours.

"*An accident?* How could something like that be an *accident*?"

"Val, why are you getting so damn bitchy about this? I told you, Anni is only a—"

"You fucked her to get ahead, didn't you? What a sleaze ball you are!"

"You're calling your husband a sleaze ball? When you

can't get through one damn night without being spaced out on pills?''

"Pills *you* gave me . . . literally forced me to take."

"We hardly ever have sex anymore, Val, or haven't you even noticed? And when we do have it you're daydreaming about that asshole Keith Leonard! So if I found a little empathy somewhere else, can you really blame me?''

"How dare you," she screamed, jumping up from the table with a hot flare of back pain. "Are you justifying yourself by blaming me for all this?''

"If the shoe fits, wear it," Paul snapped. "Now if you don't mind, I've got to get some sleep. After all, one of us has to work tomorrow.''

Valentina got through the night with the aid of four Talwin. She lay next to Paul, with her hands clasped over her mouth to keep back her sobs of grief. She'd married a man she barely loved. Now she was paying the price.

The following day, Valentina had an appointment with Dr. Feldman.

"Well, Valentina, how are you today?" Dr. Feldman said, entering the examining room with a smile.

"Terrible," Valentina said.

"More pain?''

"Yes, but that's not it . . . I mean, I do have pain, but I—" She crumpled up a corner of the paper gown and used it to blot her tears. "Drugs . . . I'm hooked on the damn pills," she finally blurted out. "Talwin, Percodan, Tranxene, Valium, you name it.''

"Hooked?''

"Paul gives them to me.''

"I see." A flash of anger crossed Feldman's face, but quickly was replaced by his usual professional demeanor. He sat down on the stool and gazed at her thoughtfully. "Well, let's do a thorough exam, and then we'll talk in my office.''

* * *

"P-pregnant?" Valentina cried, stammering over the word. She stared at Dr. Feldman over the surface of his large, pecan-wood desk. "*Pregnant!* But I can't be. We were using the diaphragm."

"You're two months along, is my guess, but you should visit an obstetrician right away. But Valentina, what concerns me is the fact that apparently you've been on very heavy doses of medication."

"Oh, my God."

"You need to see a specialist right away, and we also need to get you off those drugs immediately. I'm going to give you the phone number of the Meadows Clinic, in Prescott, Arizona."

"My God," Valentina repeated, swaying. *What if the drugs hurt the baby? She'd carry all the guilt—she'd blame herself for the rest of her life.*

"Valentina? Lie flat now, and the blood will go to your head again." She heard Dr. Feldman's voice from a long distance, then the sound of a buzzer. A nurse hurried into the office, and assisted her in lying down on the couch. Hands briskly rubbed her own.

"I can't," Valentina was crying quietly. "I can't have a baby. I can't. I can't."

"Do you want me to call your husband?" queried the young nurse.

"No!" Valentina sobbed. "Please—no! I have to think. Please."

She let herself into the house, grateful that Paul wasn't at home. She walked into the bedroom and entered the master bathroom, going straight to the shelf where she kept the supply of drugs. Six bottles, and scribbled prescription slips, guaranteeing an endless supply. Revulsion gripped her.

What had she done to her innocent unborn baby? What had they done?

Sobbing, Valentina emptied all the bottles and then tore the prescription slips into tiny pieces, flushing them down the commode, sending five months of her life swirling away.

I didn't mean to do it, she told the tiny fetus inside her. *Please, please be all right.*

Finally, shaking, she went to the phone and punched in the number of the Meadows clinic.

Chapter

Twenty-two

New York
1990

IT WAS SUMMER again, and the air-conditioning in the building at New York University was on the fritz once more as the city suffered from its traditional hot weather brownouts.

Orchid ran into the classroom and threw herself in her usual fourth row seat, thumping her briefcase, which contained the new screenplay she was writing, onto the floor. She had overslept again and was out of breath and perspiring.

"Well, you finally deign to join us, Miss Lederer," drawled the instructor.

"I forgot to push the alarm button."

"Join the adult world, Miss L. I sure don't appreciate people who aren't interested."

"I *am* interested!" she protested, as the class giggled nervously.

She squirmed on the hard, wooden seat, thinking that despite Moishe Silverman's sarcasm, his class on playwriting was the only good part of her life right now. Her year had thudded to a halt when Mort Rubick fired her after she couldn't deliver Valentina for him. She'd auditioned for a few walk-on roles, and actually gotten a ten-line part in an off-Broadway production that folded after two nights.

Then it had been a succession of temporary jobs. Shitsville, as far as Orchid was concerned. She knew she'd never starve—she still had residuals coming in from the Blue

Orchids albums, and Daddy Edgar would always help too. It was the principle of the thing.

There wasn't a real place for her in the world, that's what the problem was. Nobody really gave a shit if Orchid Lederer did or did not show up anywhere, and the knowledge was eating away at her insides like a cancer.

She wanted to be a star again—somehow. It was the only hope that kept her alive these days . . . that and her hatred for Val.

She realized that the instructor was now critiquing the scenes she'd turned in for classroom discussion.

"*Dr. Zhivago,* hmm? A nice little contemporary remake? Don't you think y'all are being, well, a little ambitious?"

The class tittered as Silverman targeted her for his daily baiting.

"No, I don't," Orchid said. She'd reread the Pasternak novel and fallen in love with it again.

"Y'all will require a cast of thousands, I presume . . . not to mention Julie Christie and Omar Sharif. Well, as I've told you people, a cast of four to six characters is easy for a small company to produce—not endless dancers and kicking legs by the gross. Besides, the movie's already been done, sugar—a long time ago. Now it's filed away in video heaven, sprouting angel's wings."

The class again laughed.

"*I* think it could be a wonderful musical," Orchid persisted. "And you would, too, if you'd sit down and read it instead of using it to practice your lame witticisms! It's one helluva lot better than the *Biloxi Picayune,* or whatever old newspaper you have a column in."

"Oh, oh, touché," muttered the boy behind her, but Silverman was grinning.

"Okay," he said, eyeing Orchid's legs in her short skirt. "See me Monday after class, Miss Lederer. I'll tell you what I think—and I won't spare your feelings. My days of southern chivalry are over."

The following week over spaghetti at a little Italian restaurant, Moishe Silverman dropped his sarcastic facade.

"Sugar, there're people on Broadway who would kill for some of these roles—but, of course, it'll be prohibitively expensive to produce," he added in a more negative tone. "Three, four million at least. Maybe more depending on the casting."

"But it's good?" she persisted.

"Good? Maybe I didn't make myself clear. It's fantastic. Let me show it to a few people I know, and see what they think of it."

Orchid stopped herself from swooping over the table to him, and sucked in a cautiously deep breath. She'd been disappointed too many times.

On the plane to LA for a quick visit to her parents, Orchid found a copy of *Newsweek* in her seat pocket. She glanced through it, reading about the surrender of drug lord Jorge Luis Ochoa, arrested for smuggling fifty-eight tons of cocaine into the United States.

"We're going to dry up the flow of coke to the U.S.," Senator Charles Willingham was quoted as saying. "I will spend the rest of my life making that happen."

The article went on to say that because of his hard line on drugs, Willingham received hundreds of telephone threats as well as letters and bomb threats. Orchid had met him several times and remembered him as a feisty, cornpone extrovert with baby-blue eyes and a wicked sense of humor. He was also filthy rich, she recalled. His family fortune had been founded on cotton in the 1840s—they'd been southern royalty.

Could she interest Willingham in several million to back *Dr. Zhivago*? He wouldn't be crazy enough to do that . . . would he? She slumped into her seat, depressed. Moishe Silverman was right. Why had she written something so expensive to produce?

That night, after she arrived, Peaches gave her all the news.

"You mean . . . *Val is getting a divorce*?" Orchid exclaimed, staring at her mother incredulously.

"It seems we all made a big, big mistake with Paul

Jensen. He was even pushing Daddy Edgar to invest in his sports clinic . . .''

"Paul always was a user," Orchid said in a way that caused Peaches to stare sharply at her.

"Your sister is in a clinic in Arizona getting rehabilitated from all the drugs she was taking . . . and she's pregnant."

"Wow," Orchid said, drawing a deep breath.

Peaches looked tired. "We talked about her getting an abortion but she didn't want to do it. I went with her for a few days during the indoctrination period," she went on. "It's a pretty tough regimen. Constant individual and group therapy, and she can't leave the premises for six weeks."

"But her baby," Orchid whispered, horrified. *Damn, damn,* she thought.

"It's in God's hands, dear. Val hasn't told Paul about the baby yet. That's our secret for now. I'm afraid he's furious and fighting the divorce and it's going to get ugly. He's a vindictive man."

In her room after dinner, Orchid went to the telephone and stood scowling down at it. Within seconds she could be talking to Val.

She reached out her hand, then stopped.

What would she say, after all this time? *I hated you. I was jealous of you and tried to use you. I even screwed your bridegroom two nights before you married him.*

Back in New York, depressed and irritable, Orchid trudged into her apartment, threw her suitcase on the floor, and pushed the message button on her answering machine.

The first voice she heard was Moishe's. "Are y'all back yet, Orchid? I was thinking about dinner. Oh, and I did pass the word out and I had nibbles. I'll tell you about it when we meet, sexy lady."

There was the click of the hang-up, then another message.

"Sweetie, pick up, will you? Pick up." It was Mort Rubick. "Okay, okay, you're not answering. This is Mort, baby, remember me? I want to talk to you—seems you've been a naughty girl and written something that old Mortie really can do something with. Give me a call at—'' He listed his home number and his office number, then added his girlfriend's number for good measure.

Orchid stared at the answering device, transfixed. Her heart had leaped into her throat and was clogging her breathing. This had to be about *Dr. Zhivago*!

She grabbed the phone and dialed.

Mort took her to lunch at Le Régence in the Hôtel Plaza Athénée, on East Sixty-fourth Street, a baroque Louis XIV setting that made Orchid feel as if she'd wandered into the wrong century. She knew Mort reserved such splendor for people he truly wanted to woo.

Over a scrumptious meal, Mort talked enthusiastically about the *Dr. Zhivago* manuscript, which Moishe had passed on to him. He loved the new, modern twist she'd given it. "It's contemporary in a very historical way. And the lyrics you've written for the tunes are sensational."

"Really?"

"In fact, they're so good that I want Valentina to sing them. With her, I can put together a package that will make the entire Western world sit up and take notice."

Valentina.

"You're her sister, aren't you? You've got the magic access, kid."

"Not Val," she repeated.

"Why not, babe?"

"For one thing, she's pregnant!"

"A minor consideration," Mort said, shrugging. "It'll take six, eight, ten months just to whip the book into shape and start casting. I mean, you know that certain scenes will have to be rewritten . . . and also maybe we can get Burt Bacharach or some other heavy to write the music. By then she'll have taken the cake outa the oven and be ready."

"Women don't take their *cakes out of the oven,*" she snapped. "Besides, she's still not well—she's in a clinic in Arizona right now, getting detoxed!"

"So? Another minor problem. She'll lick it in no time like dozens of others have. Look, cookie, can I speak frankly? Nothing in this world comes without strings. You've got talent, yes, but so do a thousand other kids in the Big Apple. What they *don't* have is Valentina Lederer for a sister. Get her for me, girl. *I don't care what you have to do!*''

Valentina strode down the flight ramp from the Northwest jet, wearing a Navajo-print pants outfit, scads of turquoise jewelry, and a golden Arizona suntan. Her hair was pulled back, and enormous sunglasses shaded her face.

She wasn't being met because she hadn't told anyone when she was arriving. She wanted a little time to air-lock back into her normal life.

It felt fabulous to be walking through an airport—striding along at a fast clip. *With no pain.* The clinic had accomplished a miracle.

The hours of group counseling had been hell. Eight of them sitting in a room sometimes crying, sometimes laughing. Letting go of their frustrations by striking an oversized chair with a baseball bat wrapped in heavy padding. More than once Valentina had run sobbing out of the room, vowing to fly back to LA.

Each time, one of the group members or therapists had brought her back.

They'd fought it out, day by day. She'd learned meditation and biofeedback techniques to reduce the stress that negative emotions wreaked on her back. Tea! Sun tea, that's all she had drunk for six weeks. She never wanted to see another cup of tea as long as she lived.

Now, as she hurried down the corridor toward the baggage claim area, her mind went over her plans. First, she'd call Paul and ask him to meet her for dinner. They'd talk . . . maybe what she'd learned in therapy could help them have an amicable divorce.

She'd also place a call to Orchid. At the clinic she'd come to see that the emotional trauma caused by her relationship with her sister had created much of her physical pain. She wasn't letting it go on any longer.

The downstairs baggage claim area was crowded with

passengers from eight or ten arriving flights. Valentina scanned the announcement board looking for the luggage carousel for her flight.

"There you are," cried a breathless voice behind her. "I was waiting at the gate but you just kept right on walking—you didn't even see me!"

"Orchid?" Valentina cried, spinning around. *"Orchid?"*

"I called the Meadows and they said you'd checked out, so I called the airline and got your flight number."

Valentina looked at her sister. Orchid was dressed like a Frederick's of Hollywood sex kitten, in a short leather skirt, a jeweled halterlike top, and a motorcycle jacket. But she'd lost weight, and her face was much thinner, making her blue eyes seem huge and intense.

"Orchid . . . God, I'm just so glad to see you. You don't know." She rushed forward to hug Orchid, but received only a lukewarm hug and peck. Bewildered, she stepped away.

"I *had* to talk to you and I just couldn't wait," Orchid blurted out.

Valentina turned, alerted by the anxiety in her sister's tone. "What about, Orchid?"

"I can't talk here. Can't we stop on the way home for a drink? You are going to Peaches and Daddy Edgar's, aren't you?"

Valentina saw the way Orchid's mouth was tight, and the defiant look in her eyes. The joyousness drained out of her.

"No, let's talk now," she said heavily. "You had an ulterior motive for meeting me here, didn't you, Orchie? I want to know what it is."

"I *didn't* want to talk like this," Orchid said desperately. "Please, Val . . ."

"Let's be honest with each other just for once. What are you after this time, Orchid?"

"Okay. It's—another play. That's all. A play you're perfect for, Val. A musical that would make you—"

Valentina spotted her first bag and ran forward, scooping it up as it sped past. In a few minutes her second one appeared and she grabbed it up.

"Let me carry that," Orchid insisted, reaching for it.

"No, dammit! I'll carry it. Orchid," she began, "I'm not going to be used or manipulated anymore, that's one thing I learned at the clinic. Not by you, or by Paul, or by anyone. I can't be in a production just to please you or to make your career easier. I have to do it for me. Because it's right for *me*."

"I know, I know. Oh, Val—" In the crowded public setting, Orchid had begun to cry. "Please," she begged. "I know you're going to have a child to raise—maybe a handicapped child."

Valentina's face drained of blood as her worst fears were spoken aloud.

Orchid went on, "You're going to need the money, the work."

"I'm not ready to work right now, Orchid. I'm pregnant. I need time."

"But this play is wonderful. I wrote it myself. It's called *Dr. Zhivago*. It's—"

"I'm sorry," Valentina said heavily, starting toward the taxi stand.

"Val!" cried Orchid, running after her. "Val—please—" She thrust a bound folder into Valentina's hand. "This is the script— Please, Val—just read it tonight! Just read it! That's all I ask! I know you hate me and I don't blame you, I don't blame you a bit, but *please just read it*!"

Valentina sat up late reading the script for *Dr. Zhivago*. It was wonderful. She laughed, she wept, she found herself reading sections of the witty dialogue aloud. Then she cried again. Orchid had written this!

But, oh God, what was she going to do? The brilliance of the play forced a decision on her, a decision she didn't feel quite ready to make.

Valentina put on a robe and wandered through the house, finally ending up out by the pool. She found a bathing suit in the small pool house, and plunged into the warm, shimmering water. She began to swim laps, pushing herself hard. At the end of the thirtieth lap, she paused at the edge to catch her breath. It was one of California's breathtakingly beautiful nights. The breeze tasted of tropical blossoms, and overhead, a million stars were dusted across a canopy of black velvet.

Orchid needs me, the thought came.

But didn't she need to work also? The divorce was going to be messy, and Paul was demanding more than one million dollars as a property settlement. Even if he got half of his demands, she would need some immediate cash.

She sprang out of the pool and dried herself off, going back into her bedroom. Finally at three A.M., she dialed the number of the Four Seasons Hotel, where Orchid had taken a room. Her sister picked up on the first ring.

"Orchid, the play is everything you said it was, and more. It's brilliant. It's funny, it's touching, it's modern, it's—I just love it."

"You do? Oh, God you do? *You love it?*" Orchid screamed into the wire. *"Oh, my God, my God,"* she repeated. *"Oh, sweet Jesus!"*

Edgar insisted on finding Valentina a Los Angeles obstetrician who specialized in difficult pregnancies. Dr. Molly McIntyre was a graduate of Harvard Medical School, with a practice in nearby Westwood, and had an outstanding reputation among her peers.

"Valentina, the ultrasound shows that the infant is developing normally, which is very, very good news."

"Oh, thank God," Valentina breathed.

"But the battle isn't over yet. I have to warn you, there could be other complications—I don't want to scare you, I just want you to be aware. Please, *no* alcohol, cigarettes, or other medication, even aspirin, during this pregnancy. We've got to give the little one every possible chance. As it is I think she's got a fifty-fifty chance of having no complications."

A fifty-fifty chance. Valentina's swallow caught in her throat. *The fates just had to be kind to her now.*

"Krista," she managed to say. "That's what I'm going to name her."

"Very pretty," the doctor said kindly.

"I think so," Valentina said, rubbing her hands along the soft curve of her abdomen, trying to hold back the waves of anxiety.

Paul and Valentina met for lunch at Monty's in Westwood. They spoke stiffly, sharing what had happened to them in the three months of their separation. Finally Valentina cleared her throat. "Paul, there's something you should know. I'm pregnant, four months along."

His face turned a pasty gray. "You can't be," he said stupidly. "We used a—we used birth control."

"Paul, you're a doctor, you know the percentages. And you also know what can happen when an expectant mother is drugged up on Percodan, Talwin, and Valium . . . have I forgotten anything? My medicine cabinet bulged at the seams."

"Jesus Christ." Paul shook his head in distress. "Val . . . are you sure about this? Have you gotten a second opinion?"

"I certainly have. Dr. Feldman told me that you had no business pushing drugs on me without his knowledge, it was medically unethical. I'm filing a suit against you for malpractice, Paul. And if our baby is born with any defect at all—*even a birthmark, Paul*—I'm going to hold you personally and financially responsible. How does five million dollars sound, for openers? You've almost ruined my career and could have seriously affected our baby at the same time."

"Jesus," he choked. "Val—I sure don't want to be stuck with support payments for the rest of my life. I'd like to give up any parental rights—"

She rose, pushing back from the table. "If I have my way, you won't be stuck with anything. You won't even see the baby. Incidentally, I've already felt life," she snapped. "They've also done an ultrasound. It's going to be a little girl. I hope you like what you've done . . . and we'd better pray to God that she's born normal, daddy."

In a maternity waiting room at Brentwood Hospital, Peaches and Edgar Lederer stood hand in hand, gazing out of the window.

"Fifteen hours," repeated Peaches, clutching at Edgar's hand. "This has been going on for *fifteen hours,* Edgar . . . a difficult labor on top of—all the other problems."

"She'll make it, honey. You know how strong she is. She's survived a lot worse than just a little childbirth."

"But the baby . . ."

"She'll be all right too," consoled Edgar hollowly.

Dionne Warwick was being piped over the PA system in the labor area, her song punctuated with terse announcements.

In her private birthing room, Valentina stiffened as another contraction racked her body. Her hair was matted with perspiration and her lip was bloody where she had bitten through it. She hadn't known labor would be so rending. Every contraction pulled on her back muscles, tripling the agony.

"Pant," ordered Orchid, gripping her hand. "Pant, Val . . . remember what that nurse said. Practice your breathing!"

"I can't . . ."

"You've got to, Val! Please . . ."

Valentina, exhausted, tried to pant. Then, as the pain finally receded, she sagged back against the mattress.

"You're doing great," Orchid encouraged in a muffled voice.

Valentina glanced down at the fetal monitor strapped to her abdomen. An ultrasound device was recording the fetal heart rate, while another device recorded the uterine contractions. A nurse popped in every two or three minutes to check her.

She closed her eyes in a brief prayer that was interrupted by another spasm. This one arched her violently upward. Valentina tried, but could not keep back her piercing scream.

"Are you all right?" Orchid gasped.

Instead of diminishing, as the others had done, this pain

solidified itself with crushing force. Valentina uttered another sharp scream.

Orchid looked appalled. "V-Val, should I call the doctor?"

"Yes, yes, yes, yes," Valentina cried through gritted teeth. "It's coming . . . now . . . oh, God . . . hurry! It's splitting me apart!"

Orchid lunged up and stumbled toward the door, then suddenly her face drained of all color. She folded to the floor in a faint.

"Orchid!" Valentina screamed.

Terrified, she fumbled for the call button on her pillow.

Krista Dorothea Jensen came into the world with a piercing cry that filled the sterile delivery room with sudden life.

Valentina couldn't stop weeping. "Is she all right? Is she all right?"

"She looks great, Val," said Dr. McIntyre from behind her surgical mask. "She's eight pounds, two ounces. An excellent birth weight. I'm giving her to the pediatrician now and he'll run the usual tests but she looks beautiful to me."

Valentina moistened her cracked, bleeding lips. "I want to know as soon as possible."

Fifteen minutes later, as the nurses were cleaning up Valentina after expelling the afterbirth, the neonatal pediatrician approached her. "Mrs. Jensen, the Apgar test we gave the baby shows a very good score, well within normal range. We'll need to do other tests later, but all signs are optimal."

She cried again—from sheer joy.

Washington

Senator Charles Willingham hurried out of the Dirksen Senate Office Building, hitting the long front steps at a half run. He knew a crowd of reporters and photographers was lurking outside and he hoped to bypass them if he could.

"Senator Willingham! Senator Willingham!"

"Yes, yes, yes," he replied in his southern drawl as they surrounded him. Flashbulbs popped. "All right, all right."

Their questions bombarded him.

"Senator Willingham, is it true that the Colombians have threatened your life?" "Senator, are you going to push for Senate bill number 4388?" "Senator, are you still swinging your support behind Harrison Lovell for Russian ambassador?" "Senator, did you receive a secret bomb threat yesterday?" "Senator! Senator! Are you engaged to Jinna Jones, the Broadway actress?"

He positioned himself on the steps in a way that would photograph well. Everyone in his home state of Alabama, and sixty percent of the people in the rest of the country, could recognize him instantly, with his mop of snow-white hair, his expensively tailored white sharkskin suit, cream shirt, and black string tie. Willingham had been around Washington for more than thirty-five years. Consummate politician that he was, he loved being in the thick of it all.

"Well, well," he began jovially. "I'll answer everything if you'll just give me some breathin' room."

The reporters grudgingly moved back a few paces.

"To start with the most important thing, my engagement. As you might have read in the papers . . ." He winked. "We're havin' a big party next week at the Jockey Club. My beautiful Jinna's gonna be there, of course—I don't go anywhere without her, and when you get to see her, you'll know why. She is gorgeous."

"The bomb threat!" shouted a woman. "Senator, what about the bomb threat?"

"Well, now," Willingham drawled. "Every holder of political office gets a little of that kind of harassment, now, don't he? Or she," he added. "I leave that business up to my staff and they do very well at it . . . we ain't been blown up yet, have we?"

"Is it because of the Medellín cartel?" persisted the woman.

Willingham never passed up a chance for fiery oratory, especially when he believed in it as deeply as he did this cause.

"Honey, I've got a vendetta against them. I'm cleanin' up those sons of B's who're stranglin' our nation with their damn drugs and makin' it real clear to them that they can't come in here and terrorize us anymore. That's my mission, it's been my mission for the past fifteen, twenty years, long before anybody ever heard of Medellín, Colombia, or Pablo Escobar. *I want to rid this country of those nefarious criminals and send them back where they came from.*"

"Senator—Senator—"

"That's it for now, folks," he said, indicating the interview was over. There were groans as he trotted down the steps where his driver had pulled up in his dark blue Fleetwood Cadillac.

The flashbulbs continued to pop as he approached the car.

"Senator!" cried a weedy young man, breaking out of the crowd and racing toward the car. "Aren't you afraid for your own life?"

"I'm gonna live to be a hundred an' eight," Willingham told the neophyte, as he got into his car. "An' don't y'all forget it. My young fiancée made me promise."

Valentina searched her closet, pulling out a selection of short evening gowns, lithe tubes of spandex, lace, and beads that would show off her new, sleek figure to perfection.

She settled on a royal-blue Nina Ricci, off-the-shoulder with a swirly, asymmetrical hem.

Carefully she packed the gown into a carry-on garment bag for the trip to Washington, where she had been invited to attend Senator Willingham's engagement party. The nanny would accompany her with the baby, so Krista would not miss a feeding.

She'd agonized for several weeks, then finally selected her agent as her escort. He was presentable, polite, and wouldn't climb all over her—the three main qualifications she required in a man right now.

"Miss Lederer, the baby is crying for her feeding," said Mrs. Davies, the British nanny.

"Fine, I'll feed her right now before we leave."

Nursing Krista, Valentina sat contentedly, feeling the exquisite tug that seemed to travel all the way through her chest straight to her heart.

"Krista," she whispered, gazing down at the baby's milky skin. "You're a little beauty, did you know that? I love you so much, my baby. Betcha don't know how much you mean to me. And I'm going to get a father for you someday—a real one who'll love you more than anything in the world."

On the plane, while Mrs. Davies pacified Krista, who didn't like the pressurized takeoff, Mike Duffy outlined for Valentina his plans for the next two months.

"First, kiddo, you gotta get yourself back in top physical shape—dancing, the whole bit. Second, I'm arranging just a little comeback tour for you—ten cities, not that many, in Europe. It'll ease you back into performing, and you can use the bucks."

"Europe!" She stared at her agent. "But you know I have a baby."

"So we'll bring her. Val, those people in Europe are clamoring for you. We'll call the tour 'Valentina Sings Again' and HBO wants to do a live concert via satellite from Moscow."

"Moscow?" She stared at him as if he'd gone mad.

"Honey, the Russians adore you, and HBO likes the whole feel of it. You're Russian, singing from Russia—hell, they're putting you in the Bolshoi Theater where Nadia danced. Millions of people will watch that special and it will really get you back among the world of the living—fast."

Russia. The country where she'd been born and where so many ghosts existed for her. Valentina felt a thrill run through her.

"But I do want to bring Krista," she insisted.

"It can be done, but more importantly, I'm coming along

too. I'm going to keep you out of trouble, kid,'' Mike added affectionately.

The engagement party at the posh Jockey Club in the Ritz-Carlton Hotel, on Massachusetts Avenue, was a crush of wall-to-wall bodies. At one end of the room, Senator Willingham and Jinna Jones were shaking hands in the long receiving line that snaked nearly to the front entrance of the room.

The Miles Davis orchestra played, battling an almost deafening hubbub of laughter and conversation as Washington regulars talked shop, conducted business, and formed alliances. Secret Service men mingled among the guests, wearing earpieces and carrying walkie-talkies. There were two former Presidents and one current one, along with assorted Kennedys, and so many important senators and congressmen that there would be an international crisis if this room happened to be bombed.

Felix Guerra, heavily built with dark, sad eyes and thick lips, a member of a Cuban trade delegation, couldn't have cared less about all the celebrities. He was getting paid to be here and mingle, and most important of all, to keep his eyes and ears open.

Still, his eyes focused on a beautiful woman in blue who entered the room on the arm of a rather ordinary-looking man. Someone said it was the movie star Valentina. He felt a shiver of lust.

She was some piece of work, all right.

Valentina and Mike moved through the receiving line.

"I wonder if it hurts to shake three hundred hands," Valentina remarked as she saw Willingham pump yet another hand in cordial greeting.

"I'd rather kiss than shake," quipped Mike, eyeing Jinna as she pecked Ralph Gerson, a well-known Washington lawyer, on the cheek.

Jinna was delighted to see her. The attractive redhead leaned forward, her smile dazzling. "Hey, I finally got a part—I'm going to be in the chorus of that new musical, *Dr.*

Zhivago! Charlie pulled a few strings for me. I'm so excited! And I heard your sister, Orchid, has a small part too.''

Valentina added, ''We'll get to know each other even better. I couldn't be more delighted.''

''I can't believe I made it. I still don't know why they picked me—maybe they got tired of saying no all the time—but I've been dancing on cloud nine for the past two weeks! Getting that part is almost as good as getting engaged.''

''Don't y'all listen to her,'' Willingham said jovially, clasping both of Valentina's hands before giving her a warm bear hug. ''It's better. Gettin' picked for that musical is what my honey's lived for . . . and I'm so damn proud of her I could spit Liberty nickels.''

Felix Guerra made the rounds, doing the obligatory networking expected of him. Finally he excused himself from his bored date, and shouldered his way through the crowd, entering the ornate hotel lobby to telephone the boss.

The lobby was crowded also, filled with the overflow from several concurrent parties going on in the other banquet rooms. He saw a placard set up on a metal easel, something about the Organization of American States.

At a bank of phones he waited impatiently for one of the phones to be free. A dark-haired man of thirty-five with hard good looks was hunched over one of them, talking in rapid-fire Spanish. Apparently he was arguing with someone, for his voice had risen.

As he stepped backward, giving Guerra a full view, the Cuban felt his insides freeze. He was standing only a few feet away from Carlos Manuel, a Colombian drug lord.

Guerra listened carefully a few moments longer, then casually moved away, crossing the lobby to the phones on the other side, where a booth had just become free.

He dialed the access code for Cuba and waited while the antiquated Cuban phone system routed him. What he'd overheard tonight was political dynamite. After ten minutes, he was finally speaking to Fidel Castro.

* * *

Champagne had flowed for two hours when Senator Willingham finally took Jinna's arm and ushered her to a microphone set up near a speaker's dais. The senator looked flushed, and his blue eyes gleamed with excitement.

"Friends . . . friends . . . everyone, listen up! I've got an announcement to make.

"First, I want to introduce the beautiful woman in my life, Jinna Jones, the lady who's won my heart and who I love even more than I love politickin' and drinkin', and that's sayin' one *hell* of a lot!"

There was a ripple of expectant laughter.

"I just want to say . . . oh, heck . . ." The senator's face suddenly contorted with emotion. He pulled Jinna close to him, encircling her with his arm. "She's gonna be my bride, folks . . . we're gonna get married at Christmas!"

Spontaneous applause filled the room.

A waiter appeared carrying a huge bouquet of deep red roses, and handed them to Willingham, who presented them to Jinna with a southern-style flourish. A dozen photographers had been lurking, and now ran forward, encircling the couple.

Flushed with the pleasure of the moment, Willingham grabbed the mike again. "One more thing, folks—and you're hearin' this straight from the horse's mouth. My gorgeous Jinna just landed herself a part in a new Broadway musical, *Dr. Zhivago.* She's gonna be fabulous and I can promise you this . . . I'm gonna be sitting in front row center come opening night. This is one opening night I wouldn't dare miss, or she'll have my tail in a sling."

Chapter
Twenty-three

THE OFFICE WAS high-ceilinged, its paneling made of dark oak hewn in the forests of Byelorussia. Flags of all the Soviet republics were prominently displayed, along with the obligatory portrait of Lenin. A massive credenza held a display of American folk and ethnic gifts given to Soviet President Mikhail Gorbachev by President George Bush during a recent summit meeting in Helsinki.

Today Gorbachev looked harassed and angry. Vladimir Petrov felt a worm of dread crawl through his stomach. Why had he been called here?

After a minimum exchange of pleasantries, the Soviet President got straight to the point. "I've just received word that the Colombians are planning to assassinate the American Senator Charles Willingham."

"What? The southerner with the big voice?" Petrov stifled his loud burst of nervous, relieved laughter.

"I'm very anxious to prevent this execution."

"Da, da," Petrov agreed eagerly.

"Willingham is the staunchest supporter of Harrison Lovell, the nominee to become the American ambassador to the USSR. We need Lovell. He is a man we can talk to, and seems to understand our problems better than the average American politician. Further, if we prevent this assassination we will win enormous favor with Bush, an opportunity that cannot be neglected."

Petrov listened, amazed, as Gorbachev explained that an informer had told them that the Colombians wanted to make

290

the killing very public and visible, in order to instill fear in other public officials. "We don't have a name or description yet for the assassin, although we believe it could be one of four that other foreign powers have used in the past for similar situations. And we don't know where or how the termination is to take place, which makes matters much more difficult. Warning Willingham will be of little use. He already receives weekly death threats and tends to discount them."

"Yes, yes, yes," said Petrov, nodding as the President handed him a thick dossier.

"Take this—it has personal and political information on the American senator. I want you to organize a counterattack on the assassin. Send someone—do whatever is necessary."

Gorbachev stood, indicating the interview was finished, and Petrov backed out of the office, his mind reeling. Whoever succeeded in preventing this assassination would return as Gorbachev's hero. What a chance for Misha! And his own prestige would be greatly enhanced by his son's new glory. If, of course, there was some kind of "insurance policy" guaranteeing Mikhail's performance.

Later, back in his own office, he was deep in the Willingham dossier. He came across a clipping cut from the *New York Post* about a dancer called Jinna Jones, who was Willingham's fiancée. A photograph showed her in costume for a road company production of *Cabaret*.

Thoughtfully, Petrov studied the pretty dancer. He remembered similar clippings in Valentina Lederer's file— and a recent entry, faxed to him from his contact in Washington, stating that Valentina was embarking on a ten city foreign concert tour, and would appear in a few weeks in Moscow at the Bolshoi Theater.

Triumphantly he shoved aside the KGB dossier and leaned back in his chair, reaching for the bottle of Stolichnaya he kept in his desk drawer.

He'd possessed the "insurance policy" all along— Mikhail's twin sister, supposedly dead, whom he could

fortuitously bring back to life again with just one word to
his son.

The steam radiator in Petrov's office had filled the room
with heat. Waiting for Mikhail to arrive, Petrov poured
himself a glass of pepper-flavored vodka, and downed it in
four stinging gulps.

"I have news for you," he began when Mikhail arrived.

"What sort of news?"

"You will see."

He launched into the story of the avalanche again,
informing his son that he had found new information about
his family.

"Without our knowledge, a separate truckload of survivors was taken to a small peasant village near Tbilisi and
was not properly recorded as part of the survivors' list. Your
sister was among them."

Mikhail's face whitened. "She is alive? *She is alive?*"

Petrov nodded, pleased with the impact his news was
having. He pulled out a copy of *Life* magazine and shoved
it across his desktop toward his son. For Russia, the picture
was shockingly graphic. It showed Valentina, barefoot and
bare-shouldered, seated on a rock at the beach wearing a
filmy, off-the-shoulder white cotton dress that was drenched
with sea water. Her intense, emerald-colored eyes gazed at
the camera.

Mikhail scowled, contemptuously throwing the cover
down. "What's this for?"

"That is your sister, comrade son."

"I have no sister. This is a lie. You show me a portrait of
an American rock star and expect me to believe she is
my . . ." Mikhail was gazing at the cover, his face paling
again. "She can't be my . . ."

A shoulder of the white dress had slipped downward,
revealing a small strawberry mole. Mikhail's eyes were
riveted on that mole. He bore a similar one on his own body.

"There is more," Petrov said, grinning with deep satisfaction as he saw that his son had begun to believe. "I'll
pour you some vodka and then we will talk at length."

* * *

Mikhail left KGB headquarters, and strode unseeingly through Red Square. His temples pounded with a clanging headache and his war wounds had begun to ache. Sitting in his father's office, he'd held his anger back. If he'd stayed in that hot, close room one more second, he would have attacked the man and squeezed his throat until he choked.

Finding out he had a sister, and then being told to meet her and use her as a cover for a KGB assignment was not only a horrible shock—it was also entirely too coincidental. Did his father think he was that stupid? *Petrov must have known all along that Valentina was still alive.*

Yes, Petrov had known, had deliberately lied. Tears began to roll down Mikhail's cheeks but he was unaware of them, of anything but his terrible grief.

The shouts and wild applause lasted for more than ten minutes as Valentina took bow after bow. Young Russians jumped up and down, screamed, whistled. Flowers rained down on her, covering the stage in a carpet of roses and lilies. TV cameras captured the tumult for the more than twenty million who watched on HBO. Finally, hoarse and choked with emotion, Valentina ran from the stage.

"Fantastico! You were fabulous!" congratulated Mike, who had been waiting in the wings, along with the nanny and Krista.

"I can't believe it!" Perspiration was pouring down Valentina's face, and the white Bob Mackie gown she'd worn for her finale was drenched. "I just can't believe they could love me so much!"

The baby was wide awake, and in the early, whimpery stages of needing to be fed. Valentina leaned down and kissed Krista's face. "Guess what, sweetie. This is where your grandmother danced too . . . Oh, Mike, I just can't believe I'm really here in Russia. It's all so incredible, it's just like a dream."

"Well, there's a reception afterward given by the American Embassy and you're going to meet several important

Russians firsthand. Ambassador Howe, who has just announced his retirement, is putting on some fancy wingding, sort of like his 'swan song.' They say maybe even Gorby and Raisa might be there briefly, and that's real enough. It ain't no dream.''

Valentina nodded, knowing she would not come down from this postconcert high for many hours. "Mrs. Davies, please take Krista back to the dressing room, and I'll come and feed her.''

The reception, held at the Tsentralny Hotel on Gorky Street, was jammed with American dignitaries and Russian officials and their wives.

Valentina circulated among the guests, who included diplomats, generals, Bolshoi officials, and of course the host, Charles Howe III, the American ambassador and his lovely wife, Andrea.

"Do you own a car?'' "Do you know Madonna?'' "Do you get mugged often?'' "Do you eat McDonald's hamburgers?'' were some of the questions she was asked. While she remembered a few phrases of Russian from her childhood, she was not fluent in the language.

"All this Russki stuff—it sounds like Greek to me,'' complained Mike after an hour. "I can't wait to get back to New York where I can get mugged any time I want, by good old Americans.''

As they were returning to the hotel, the Intourist guide assigned to them announced, "There is a problem with your papers. You cannot do your second scheduled concert tomorrow night until you meet with a security official.''

"What?'' Valentina stared at the woman in shock.

"I have been asked to tell this to you,'' she repeated.

"But—but we've signed a contract to do the concert! The record company and me. All of our papers have been cleared, our visas, everything! It's all been taken care of!''

"You must meet with a KGB official before you can perform,'' repeated the guide.

* * *

The following morning at eight o'clock, she and Mike—for he'd insisted on coming along—were picked up by a driver in a black limousine. The guide went with them.

What had they done wrong? Valentina wondered anxiously. Fighting tears, she chided herself. They hadn't done anything—none of them had. Of course they were perfectly safe.

"This car is like a damned hearse!" Valentina whispered to Mike.

"Yeah," he whispered back. "But what I'm worried about is where the fuck are they takin' us?"

"I just hope they don't keep us all day—Krista needs her feeding."

Finally they stopped in front of a tall old house located near one of Moscow's large parks. The ornate, seventeenth-century gate was decorated with statues, and the wavy, hand-blown windows were made of three-hundred-year-old glass.

"We have reached our destination," announced the guide.

"No shit," said Mike.

"I am General Vladimir Petrov," announced a man in a vintage Russian business suit, as they entered the library.

But Valentina only saw the handsome man who stood near the windows, his arms crossed over his chest. He was tall, more than six-one, and his face was lean, with chiseled cheekbones.

There was something hauntingly, eerily familiar about him . . . a quality that stopped Valentina's heart, causing her to draw in her breath. She'd seen him before, but where? He looked so familiar! He looked like . . . who *did* he look like?

Those eyes . . . deep green, the exact shade of her own.

"What the hell," Mike muttered beside her, catching the resemblance too. She barely heard Petrov making some kind of an introduction in heavily accented English. Her eyes were riveted to the tall, dark man as shivers ran through her body.

Valentina shuddered under the waves of recognition.

"I don't believe . . ." she began, taking a tiny step forward.

"You are not . . ." He dropped his defensive stance and started toward her.

"Just what the *hell* is going on here?" demanded Mike.

"Misha," Valentina yelled, and threw herself forward, into her twin brother's arms.

At first Valentina was so overwhelmed that she could only sob. She clung to Mikhail, her body shaking violently. "You're here, you're alive! You didn't die!" she cried, pulling back in an ecstasy of delight to look at him. God, he had her own hair—it even curled back from his forehead in a widow's peak, the same way hers did.

"My sister," he said gruffly. Even Mikhail's voice, deep, masculine, seemed familiar and she realized it was the same as their father's. She started to cry again. All the old ghosts poured back with such force that it left her reeling.

"Come," he said in English, his accent barely perceptible. "We must go for a walk now, to get to know one another."

Petrov nodded approvingly.

As they walked, they exchanged stories, and the more Mikhail told her about his background, the more fantastic it all seemed to Valentina.

"I can't believe this! I can't believe it! Oh, Mikhail—I've dreamed of you so often!" Valentina kept exclaiming as they walked along streets lined with houses once occupied by important members of the czar's court. Of course they had to walk, she belatedly realized. The house they'd been in was probably wired for sound. Only in the open air could they have any sort of privacy.

"And I've had dreams about you," Mikhail admitted. "But what about our mother? Were you with her when she died?"

Haltingly, Valentina told the story of their trip to America, of Nadia's illness, her last words, her own terrifying two-day wait alone in the motel room.

Mikhail's chest heaved several times, and then he started to cry. His tears were silent and agonizing. "So futile, so futile," he choked. "All these years. If I'd known, I would have found you somehow. I would have come to you. I would have found a way."

"But it isn't too late! You can come to the United States . . . can't you? You can visit me! Oh, Mikhail! Maybe you could even move there—emigrate to America. Do they allow that now in Russia?"

But as soon as she issued the invitation, his face changed, closing down to the expressionless mask he'd worn when she first saw him.

"No," he muttered. "I will not let them use us this way."

"Use us how? Oh, Mikhail, I have to give my concert tonight and then tomorrow morning we're flying to Helsinki, then home. It's not enough time! We can't catch up on a whole lifetime that fast. Please—please— They'll let you visit, I know they will. Otherwise why would they have brought us together when they didn't have to?"

"Why else," remarked Mikhail sardonically. "I'm sure I'll find out within the next few days. *They* don't do anything without a reason."

"Well, this is a story to end all stories," Mike said on their way back to the hotel. "Do you really believe that guy is your brother, Valentina? How do you know?"

"Oh, Mike . . . he remembered all kinds of details about the avalanche, he even knew that we were playing cat's cradle right before it happened. And—he's my *twin,* Mike. It's a psychic pull . . . I just know it's him."

"Okay, okay, I'll take your word for that. But sweetpea, he's one of them, don't you realize? The KGB! And you're inviting him back to the good old U.S. of A.? Get real, honey. It's no coincidence that they introduced him to you, and now he suggests to you that he visit you in the States."

"The idea was mine. He didn't suggest anything," Valentina said hotly. "Anyway, I don't care what his background is—he told me all about how he was raised—he was forced into a mold."

"Val, baby—"

"I don't want to listen! He's my family. He's the only natural family I've got. I don't care how far away we are, or how long it's been since I've seen him, nothing has changed between Mikhail and me—and it never will."

Medellín, Colombia

In Medellín, Colombia, six men lounged on the veranda of a large plantation home half buried in luxuriant foliage. The sextet accounted for more than forty percent of the world's cocaine distribution. Tumblers of golden Glenlivet whisky sat on tables. Tina Turner's hit "Steamy Windows," playing on a portable CD player, vibrated through the moist air.

Juan Arrinda suddenly flicked off the CD player.

There was a murmur among the men, Fernando Quintas, Jorge Cardona, Augusto Linares, Julio "El Gordo" Costas, "the fat man," and Pablo Salir, the Bogotá drug lawyer.

"Enough! Listen," Arrinda declared. "We must decide and decide now—who we're going to use for this hit."

"Carlos Navarro!" suggested Linerio.

"Shit, no," Arrinda said. "He's too recognizable. The FBI or CIA would make him in two minutes flat."

"Vasquez isn't recognizable, and he can do a motorcycle hit . . ."

"No, no, no," disagreed Arrinda impatiently. "That kind of thing happens on American highways all the time. People might think it's just a gang shoot. We want terror. We want to make these ugly-faced *gringos* shit in their pants. I want Araña."

"Araña." They all sighed. Araña was the most expensive assassin they had ever worked with, and the most secretive, a killer who worked through a middleman. Payment was made to a numbered bank account. Rumors were that the infamous "spider" killer was really a beautiful, high-born woman. Others said Araña was a forty-year-old male and a former member of the French Secret Service who had retired and hired out for the money. No one really knew for sure.

"But Araña fucked up in Israel last month," objected Salir. "The target wasn't killed—only a double for Begin."

"Regardless, some *hombre, muy tristo,* still has tubes coming out of his nose and dick, and is a vegetable," Arrinda pointed out. "Enough! It is decided. I myself will call Pedro, the contact man. I will do it tonight."

"It will be public?"

"So public the whole fucking country will know," Arrinda shouted, pounding the table. "Girls! Bring more whisky! Come out here, all of you! And turn the music on again. Immediately!"

Washington, D.C.

The Northwest jet plunged through a layer of heavy grayish cloud cover, and landed with a slight bump of wheels on runway 6 at Dulles Airport. The engine brakes roared as the aircraft rolled to a stop.

No one even glanced at Araña as she claimed her luggage and then went out to the taxi stand, where she took a cab to the Greyhound bus terminal.

The blue gym bag was in the locker, exactly as promised, and she hefted its weight with a feeling of satisfaction.

Later, in the Library of Congress, Araña switched on a microfilm machine and began running a film of the *Washington Post.* It was only a few seconds before she found what she wanted, coverage of a speech Willingham had given three weeks ago before the Senate Foreign Relations Committee.

"Extradition of the nefarious drug lords to the U.S., so we can try them and put them away for two hundred years," was his battle cry.

Almost every issue of the *Post* contained at least one item about the man, she discovered. There were photographs too.

Willingham in his white suit and black string tie, standing
on the steps of the Senate Office Building, one arm raised.
The senator receiving some sort of plaque from President
Bush. Araña made a few mental notes, but frowned. This
wasn't what she was searching for. She wanted something
more personal. Something that would reveal the man's
habits, predilections, regular social activities.

She fed in another square of film, and found an article
about Willingham's engagement to a dancer called Jinna
Jones. A photo showed the white-haired senator, grinning
broadly, his arm tightly wound around a slim, pretty young
woman.

Growing more excited by the moment, she read the fluff
piece about Jinna's aspirations as a dancer. She'd just gotten
a role in a Broadway play called *Dr. Zhivago,* at the Lederer
Theater.

Willingham was quoted as saying, "This is one opening
night I won't miss."

Araña smiled. She'd been told to produce terror. *Public*
terror!

A theater was very public.

"Charlie, are you mad at me because I'm in New York all
the time now?" Jinna crooned to her fiancé, as they lay
sprawled across his king-sized bed in the Watergate complex.

"Honey, I could never be mad at you for anythin',"
Willingham sighed, running his hand over her breast.

Jinna smiled to herself, digging her fingers into his back
just deeply enough to excite him. Charles Willingham was
the kindest, gentlest, most decent man she had ever known.

Inside the Russian Embassy on Sixteenth and K Street,
guarded by two fully armed Russian soldiers, several
television sets and radios played.

"This is—very nice," Mikhail murmured.

The contact, the military attaché for naval affairs, a fifty-
year-old KGB agent named Boris Talinov, provided Mikhail

with a huge dossier on Senator Willingham, and showed him
a small, unused office where he could read through the file.

"Willingham's fiancée, a dancer, has a part in a Broadway musical, and he has publicly announced he will be
present on opening night," Boris told him, speaking in
Russian. "We have also targeted several speeches and a
dinner for the Canadian prime minister at the Waldorf-
Astoria, which Willingham will attend in late October, all of
them excellent opportunities for assassination. The man is
very visible and sometimes erratic, taking few real precau-
tions."

"Yes, yes, yes," Mikhail said impatiently.

"At Comrade General Vladmir Petrov's request we also
have prepared a list of assassins the Medellín cartel uses. It
includes information we have been given from CIA files."

"Yes," Mikhail said, taking the papers. He waited for the
man to leave him alone.

He read quickly through the file. Within minutes he came
to the conclusion that a hit in the Lederer theater would be
the most visible.

But wait. It was the production Valentina was in. He
began to sweat.

He picked up the folder that listed the various assassins,
and focused on a mysterious person known as Araña, whose
name meant "spider," and whose real identity was unknown.

The kill list attributed to Araña included some of the most
influential world leaders. Araña's trademark was a small
plastic spider left on the scene. There were often side murders
of family members, employees, or anyone else unlucky
enough to be in the immediate presence of the victim at the
time of the hit.

Multiple murders.

Mikhail began to smell the sharp, acrid scent of his own
fear. He remembered one Araña hit in Istanbul. Before the
"kill" was finished, the victim lay paralyzed from the neck
down, and three others were dead, including a thirteen-year-
old child.

After absorbing the materials, he rose to leave.

Exiting the embassy, he decided to take a long stroll
down by the Potomac. He'd come to the United States with
the idea of defecting . . . spending several weeks with his
sister before giving himself up. He would have to live the
life of a fugitive under another identity, for fear of KGB
retaliation, but he would be "free." Now, this! He was
morally committed to preventing this assassination.

No more killing, he told himself.

His first step, he decided, would be to warn Willingham
personally.

Arriving at the Capitol after lunch, Mikhail asked direc-
tions from the Senate page, and made his way to the elevator
of the Dirksen Senate Office Building.

An attractive, honey-blond receptionist looked up as he
entered Willingham's waiting room, which was hung with
poster-sized photographs of the scenic settings of Alabama.

"Can I help y'all?"

He smiled to put her at her ease, but spoke with the air of
authority that was second nature to KGB men of all ranks.
"I am here to speak with Senator Willingham."

"I'm sorry, he's in Bethesda today, I don't expect him
back until late afternoon, and he never sees anyone without
an appointment."

"I will wait."

"Can you state your business?"

"It's personal," he responded vaguely.

Just then a door swung open and Willingham himself
breezed into the office, his white hair disheveled from the
wind and his string tie flapping.

"Senator Willingham," began the receptionist nervously.
"This gentleman—"

"Senator," interrupted Mikhail. "I need to speak with
you, privately. At once, on a matter of greatest importance."

"Didn't Samantha tell you? You need to list with my
appointment book—"

"No appointments. I must warn you, Senator—"

"Warn me about what?" he replied, giving a slight nod to the receptionist.

"I am Mikhail Sandovsky, Valentina Lederer's twin brother," he began. "I have come here to this country from the Soviet—"

"A Soviet! From Russia! I heard all about you from Jinna! Well, young man, I don't know what you're up to and I don't want to know. Is this a threat?"

"No," began Mikhail urgently. "Senator Willingham, the threat is—"

But the door swung open again and two uniformed security men slammed in, striding up to Mikhail and gripping his arms. The Russian stood rigid and angry.

"There," Willingham said with satisfaction. "You see what a good security service we've got? Now, you listen to me, young Ivan, and you listen good. I get death threats nearly every week and I don't need any more warnings. My security service is top drawer and I also turn over my threats to the FBI. They cover me good. And if the threat is so doggone real, how come you know about it? Where is your Soviet Embassy in this matter? Why haven't I heard from y'all before now?"

"Senator Willingham, this assassination will be carried out by a professional assassin, one of the most—"

"It's all bullshit!" Willingham turned on his heel and irritably stomped into an inner office, slamming the door behind him.

Mikhail stared after him.

"Come on, buddy, get your Russian ass out of here . . . now, before we call your embassy and the FBI," said one of the men, pulling at Mikhail.

Mikhail shook himself free, then strode out of the office. He would have to warn the senator some other way. Also, he must report the incident to the Soviet Ambassador and military attaché so as to prevent any diplomatic ripples.

New York

A week after she returned to New York, Valentina drove out to LaGuardia to pick up Misha, who apparently had stopped in Washington first. At the gate she hugged him in an ecstasy of happiness.

She was so excited she could barely stop talking as they began walking toward the baggage claim area.

"Mikhail! This is just so wonderful! And I'm going to show you everything, even the real touristy places. I'll buy you a *Phantom of the Opera* T-shirt. And a Big Apple ashtray. And . . ."

"I just want a few months of peace," he told her quietly.

"Well, of course. You'll have the apartment to yourself most of the day starting next week, except for the nanny and Krista, because I'll be in rehearsal."

Mikhail gave one of his rare, sweet smiles. "I will enjoy playing with the baby. We Russians love babies, you know."

"We—yes, of course." Valentina sobered a bit. Mikhail *was* Russian, wasn't he? And she was American now.

During the next week, she outfitted Mikhail at Bloomingdale's, and introduced her brother to pizza, Pepsi-Cola, MTV, an Arnold Schwarzenegger movie, and the subway. She also brought him to the Lederer Theater and showed him where *Dr. Zhivago* would open.

"Our mother would be so happy," he told her, and she felt a tiny shock as she realized he was referring to Nadia, not Peaches.

But mostly they talked for hours, rehashing every memory they held in common. Mikhail, however, refused to talk about his KGB training, or any part of his job, becoming grimly silent whenever Valentina probed.

She told him at length about Orchid, and showed him photographs taken when Blue Orchids was at its peak.

"She is lovely," Mikhail said, gazing at the photograph for a long moment. "She looks very, how you say it, fragile?"

Valentina laughed. "She's as strong as iron! You'll meet her when rehearsals start. She is . . . gorgeous and selfish and funny and talented and cute and jealous." Valentina sighed. "She hates me since the breakup of Blue Orchids. She has never forgiven me."

"Perhaps she is still searching," Mikhail remarked.

Valentina frowned. "At the expense of everyone around her, and herself? Orchid detests herself as much as she hates me."

"But for some the search causes initially deep pain, because it involves finding and then understanding one's place in the world. Without a place, one is less than nothing. One is a zero, and angry. Have I said that correctly? My English—I have not learned your colloquial expressions well."

"I'd say your expressions are doing just fine," Valentina said.

"Do you wish me to introduce you to some nice women?" Valentina asked her twin as they were returning to her apartment after a late dinner.

"No."

"But I know some lovely ones."

"I am sure you do," he said, frowning. He was staring out of the dirt-smeared taxi window, his profile stern. "Perhaps while you are busy rehearsing, I will make a few short trips. Maybe to Washington again."

"Washington?"

"I want to see where your country is governed," he told her stiffly.

"Of course," she responded warmly. "I'll call ahead to the Washington Fitzgerald Hotel—they have wonderful suites with a fantastic view of the Potomac."

"I need no 'view,'" Mikhail began, but then, turning, he saw Valentina's expression, and he closed his hand over hers. "But I would appreciate one," he finished.

When they reached Valentina's apartment, Mikhail excused himself, going to his room and closing the door. He wanted to be by himself for awhile . . . and just think about the events of the last few weeks, especially Orchid. Since Yulia he'd had a few *prostitutkas,* but no woman who had interested him even slightly. He was unwilling to risk

his inner feelings, he knew. Or maybe he did not have any.
Perhaps his soul was as arid as the Kara Kum Desert.

The photograph he had seen of Orchid Lederer, however,
had struck him like a blow across the face. The woman
reminded him of a little Siberian kitten, all beauty and claws
and fierce eyes. But in her eyes he'd seen such pain . . .

Valentina had looked forward to the first rehearsal with
eager anticipation. Orchid would be there, of course, but she
was adult enough to handle it. They would have a polite
business relationship—nothing more. She'd insisted Keith
Leonard be the one to showcase her. She'd lived for the
moment when she'd be seeing Keith on a daily basis again.
Even to talk to him casually would be a joy.

But when she showed up at the rehearsal hall on the first
day, he was not present.

Bettina Orlovsky, who was again doing the choreography
for a Keith Leonard production, told her that Keith's wife
had suffered another heart attack and was in intensive care
in a hospital in Norwalk.

"Oh, no," Valentina whispered.

"Yes, isn't it a shame?"

"But—but the last I heard, Cynthia was f-fine," she
stammered.

"Not anymore she isn't."

That night she took a chance and phoned Keith at his
Connecticut estate, but the housekeeper told her he was still
at the hospital. Valentina hung up, astonished to discover
the depths of her jealousy for the dying woman who could
command Keith's emotions and loyalty.

Shaking, she washed her face and came out to the
kitchen, where she brewed a pot of Earl Grey tea for Misha
and herself.

"You are in love with someone, aren't you?" asked her
brother.

She jumped, startled, nearly spilling her tea. "How did
you know?"

"We are twins," he said simply.

"It's Keith Leonard. I've cared about him for years, I've

never loved any other man, and it's—'' She shakily rose to her feet, continuing, ''It's foolish and useless! It's never going to come to anything, and it's spoiling me—it ruined my marriage and it'll spoil any other relationship I try to have too. Oh, Misha,'' she wept, giving way to the emotions that tore at her. ''I want him! I just want him so much! I hate her sometimes! I hate her for coming between us! And I know she can't h-help it . . .''

Mikhail held her, and murmured endearments in Russian. Valentina slowly began to feel soothed and refreshed, as if, for a brief moment, she was once again wrapped in the warmth of her childhood.

The cast members filed into the rehearsal hall, yawning, taking seats scattered in the first few rows as they waited for rehearsals to begin. Orchid hesitated, noticing that Val's brother, that Russian, was already seated near the front.

He was the most magnificent man she'd ever seen. They'd been briefly introduced but it hadn't gone very well. He merely gazed at her with those green, piercing eyes, and she'd suffered a totally unexpected attack of shyness.

Go ahead, sit beside him . . . there's an empty seat, she told herself, but knew she wouldn't. She, Orchid Lederer, who'd made handsome hunks her favorite hobby, was getting *shy* at the sight of a man? Now that was weird!

She found a seat in the fifth row.

''Hi, yah,'' yawned Jinna Jones, throwing herself into the seat beside Orchid.

''In five minutes sharp I want all the members of the chorus in meeting room two,'' barked Bettina, coming to the apron of the stage. ''And I mean sharp. That means Miss Jinna Jones too.''

''Ouch,'' Jinna muttered. ''She's got a bee in her bonnet about me.''

''I'm sure that's not true,'' Orchid said.

Jinna sighed. ''It is true. I just found out that Charlie pulled some strings to get me in, and he went over Bettina's head. That's why she hates me. I think I'd have made this one on my own, but it was so dear of him, I can't fuss too much.''

In front of them, Mikhail had risen and was exiting to the aisle, his brow furrowed. Only a person who'd observed him as closely as Orchid did would notice the faint limp.

She told Jinna absently, ''Well, who cares why she hates you? You're in, aren't you? She can't get rid of you now.''

''Not without pissing Charlie off,'' Jinna giggled.

Two weeks into rehearsals, Keith Leonard had made only cursory appearances, and when he did show up, looking exhausted, he treated Valentina exactly as he treated Bettina, Orchid, Jinna, and everyone else—as if they were not quite there.

''Keith,'' called Valentina one afternoon, breaking into a run to catch up with him as he left the rehearsal room, glancing at his watch.

''Val, I'm afraid I'm in a hurry, I'm on the way to the hospital.''

''I know, oh, Keith, how is she?''

''Not good.''

''But is she . . . ? Keith . . . ?''

''Let's drop the subject,'' he snapped.

Fighting her hurt feelings, she hurried after him through the maze of dingy backstage corridors. ''Keith, I know she's ill, but aren't *we* still friends? You've been avoiding me purposely, I think. Have I done something wrong? I don't know how to act around you anymore.''

''Val. Please don't.''

''Don't what?''

''Val . . . Cynthia is dying,'' he whispered.

Valentina stopped short, fighting the ugly feelings that surged up uncontrollably from the center of her. ''I'm sorry!'' she cried. ''I'm very, very sorry for all of it! But I love you too! What about us, what about our love?''

Keith looked at her, his features contorted. ''Val, please, some other time,'' he began, but Valentina had already spun around. She ran down the corridor, back the way they had come, his rejection echoing in her ears.

Val, please, some other time.

Keith Leonard knew he was only giving the show a quarter of his attention. Still, *Dr. Zhivago* was shaping up well. By the fourth week of rehearsals, the dance numbers were completely choreographed, and the usual feuds, relationships, and friendly attitudes of any production were well under way.

Orchid and Valentina were on polite but distant terms. Two of the male dancers had begun a tempestuous, passionate affair. Jinna Jones, with her breezy, warm, southern good humor, had become one of the most popular members of the company. Senator Willingham, too, was a favorite after he'd had pizza sent in a number of times for the whole company.

"My Charlie's gonna be sitting front row center," she would tell everyone as they crowded into the greenroom at break time to raid the table laden with bagels, cream cheese, and coffee. "So I've gotta be the best for him. He doesn't know I'm just fighting to stay alive here."

She was referring to the conflict between her and Bettina. The choreographer berated Jinna sarcastically whenever she made a mistake—which was more frequently than the other dancers.

"Don't you think you're being a little harsh on her?" Keith asked Bettina one morning after he'd watched Jinna, tears streaming down her face, valiantly trying to dance one of the difficult combinations, to Bettina's exacting instructions.

Bettina snapped, "Harsh? I'm not being harsh enough!"

"But Jinna was crying."

"So? They all cry at some time or another. This isn't Miss Sophie's Jazz and Tap Class, this is Broadway, honey lamb. And furthermore—"

But she wasn't to finish. Keith's secretary had appeared in the doorway with a pink message slip in her hand. Her eyes were red. She motioned to Keith, who immediately jumped up and rushed out of the rehearsal room.

"Is this from the hospital?" he said, snatching the pink slip from her.

The secretary was crying. "Yes—Mr. Leonard—I'm sorry. She's . . ."

Keith stared down at the message slip, his eyes burning.

Two days after Cynthia's funeral, Keith returned to the rehearsal hall, looking as if he had aged ten years. His complexion was sallow and there were dark circles under his eyes. His suit jacket hung loosely on his body.

He looked so pathetic that Valentina let out a cry of anguish, and ran to him.

"Darling—oh, I'm *so* sorry! I know how you must feel—"

"Don't," he choked. "Please, Val—just don't."

She pulled back.

His voice was hoarse. "I know you're sorry. I'm sorry too. But that doesn't solve anything." He turned abruptly and walked away from her.

Three days passed, then four, and five. Keith adroitly managed to avoid speaking to Valentina. If she entered the greenroom, he left it. If she approached him in the corridor, he would nod curtly, and pass her by. He stood at the back of the theater while she was rehearsing her scenes, but when she came offstage, he disappeared into the stage manager's office.

"Keith!" she called one day, hurrying after him into the tiny, cluttered office. "Could I talk to you about—"

"I can't talk," he responded curtly.

"But—"

"Valentina, I have to use the phone. If you'll excuse me."

She'd backed away, humiliated and furious.

Peaches, in town to do some shopping, took her daughter to lunch at the Palm Court. In the palm and pastel setting of the Plaza Hotel lobby, Valentina poured out her distress to her mother.

"He's treating me like a damn Jezebel! He's acting as if I helped to kill her."

"Now, dear, you have to remember that he's got a lot of guilt feelings and he's had them for years. I'm sure Cynthia was well aware that Keith was in love with you. Who knows what she might have said to him when she was dying," Peaches soothed.

"Oh, God."

"Darling, all you can do is just let him work this through. He'll come around in time."

"If he doesn't feel so guilty that he starts to resent me," Valentina said bitterly.

After one particularly long day, during which Keith had ignored her and complimented everyone else on their wonderful performances, Valentina felt she'd had enough.

She waited until she saw him about to leave the theater, and followed him, calling his name.

If he had heard her, he didn't indicate it, and hurried on, his strides lengthening.

"Damn you!" she yelled. "Damn you to hell, Keith Leonard!" She raced up beside him and grabbed his arm.

"Let go." He shouldered his way ahead of her in the crowds and turned a corner, disappearing from sight. Suddenly she realized his destination—the apartment he kept in town.

"If that's the way he wants to play it!" she muttered to herself, racing into the street to hail a cab.

She was standing in front of the lobby doors to his building when Keith arrived on foot, looking hot and angry.

"We have to talk, and I'm not leaving until we've settled this," she said firmly, going up to him.

"No, dammit."

Her voice rose. "I told you, I'm not leaving until we talk."

"Sir? Is everything all right?" inquired the doorman.

"Yes, perfectly all right!" Valentina snapped, as Keith reluctantly nodded.

Neither of them spoke as they rode up in the elevator, and by the time the doors slid open, Valentina was near tears.

Grimly, Keith unlocked his apartment door and ushered her inside. "I'll fix you a drink and then you can leave," he said curtly, starting toward the kitchen.

"I don't want a fucking drink!" Valentina shouted. "I want to talk to *you*. What's wrong, Keith?"

"I—" Then Keith gave up, and sagged onto the sofa, putting his face in his hands.

"Keith?" She sat down beside him.

"It's terrible, Val—terrible. I wronged her, I wronged *you*, I sat on the fence, I didn't do one thing or the other, and then she died giving me total freedom from her."

"What?"

"She said—her self-respect—" His body shook with silent sobs.

She reached out a hand to touch him, to take him in her arms, and then pulled back, afraid he would reject her again.

"I was a shit!" Keith wept. "I loved you, Val . . . I always loved you . . . she knew it. How that must have hurt her. What did she have out of life? A husband who cared about someone else! I'm such a bastard! I despise myself for what I did to her. Goddammit to hell!"

Valentina bit her lip, searching for words that would not destroy, but heal.

"Keith, we all are given the same days to fill. Cynthia had many things of beauty in her life. She knew the marriage wasn't perfect but she chose to stay with you. She could have left but she didn't."

"Yes," he groaned.

"I don't have all the answers," Valentina admitted. "But if she found any realizations at the end, then . . . well, I know God is with her wherever she is."

Keith was crying again.

"Keith, you did your best," she whispered. "You stayed loyal, you gave her all the love you could . . . and it *was* love. I'm sure she knew it too. I—I'm glad you didn't leave her. I'm glad you were with her until the end.''

Their hands had found each other, fingers grasping, clutching, and then Keith pulled her against him. ''Val,'' he choked. ''I know I've wronged you. I've been so torn.''

''I know.''

''I love you so much.''

''And I you, my darling.''

''I need you so, Val . . . I've always needed you, and I always will, and God help both of us,'' Keith said as they walked toward the bedroom.

Chapter
Twenty-four

WILLINGHAM WAS SCHEDULED to be honored at an American Cancer Foundation award dinner in the Grand Ballroom of the Waldorf-Astoria in two weeks. One more opportunity for the Colombian hit man!

But that opportunity came and went.

It lent even more credence to Mikhail's belief that the hit would take place at the *Dr. Zhivago* opening night. The senator had discounted his warnings. Should he notify the FBI now? But the pervading view of the KGB was that the FBI and CIA were incompetent blunderers. Besides, both organizations were surely already guarding Willingham around the clock.

"I'm so happy," sighed Valentina one night as she and Mikhail were eating take-out Chinese food in her apartment. She told him about her new relationship with Keith Leonard.

"Happy," repeated Mikhail, looking at her. To him, she seemed beautiful and exotic, and sometimes it was hard for him to believe she was really his sister. In the past days she had seemed to glow with an intense brightness.

Valentina caught her breath. "Anyway, the other happy thing is *Dr. Zhivago*. Shirley Eder gave us a wonderful writeup in her syndicated column. She says we have a real chance at a major, major hit—we could be another *Phantom of the Opera*. Misha! Just think. Personal appearances, talk shows, and all the rest of the glamorous fanfare. If a Broadway show really hits big—it can be incredible."

He hesitated before changing the subject. "Have you ever

314

thought that perhaps your friend Jinna Jones should be dropped from the production?''

"What did you say?'' Valentina asked in a shocked voice.

"I said maybe you do not need her in your play. Surely such a dancer could be easily replaced.''

Valentina jumped up, her chopsticks clattering. "Misha, I can't believe you said that! What the hell does that have to do with anything we were discussing? Jinna is a fine dancer, even if Bettina doesn't like her. Why would you suggest such a thing anyway?''

"I cannot tell you.''

"You just don't understand,'' Valentina said, controlling her anger. "Jinna has lived for this show!''

Mikhail rose, and went to stand at the window, where he gazed out at the view of towers, sparkling with lights. How could he tell his beloved sister that he was a KGB agent? A killer sent to prevent an assassination attempt and then terminate the perpetrator.

Worse, how could he tell her that his instincts told him that the play was the venue—the target place.

"And you don't understand, dear sister,'' he said at last. "There is a matter—''

"Please,'' Valentina begged. "I just don't want to hear any more. Misha, will you please come back and finish your food?''

"Very well,'' he sighed.

The buzz of the intercom interrupted his troubled thoughts.

Valentina jumped up to press the button. She listened for a few seconds, then said, "It's Orchid. She's in the lobby.''

"I will leave then, and allow you some privacy,'' Mikhail said, pushing away his untasted food.

"But Misha, you're welcome to stay—''

He pretended he hadn't heard her. A headache was splitting his temples. He wanted only to be by himself in complete solitude.

Orchid paced impatiently, jabbing the up button several times as she waited for the elevator. When it finally arrived, she rushed forward, nearly colliding with a tall man in a corduroy jacket and jeans.

It was Val's brother, his brows pulled together in a glowering frown.

"Mikhail!" she gasped.

"Good evening, Miss Lederer," he murmured, brushing past her.

She opened her mouth to say something, to attract his attention and call him back, but nothing emerged. What was wrong with her? Every time she saw him she became tongue-tied. She stepped into the elevator and pushed the button for Valentina's floor.

"Mikhail seems so *brooding*," remarked Orchid, picking at the leftover Chinese food. The atmosphere between the sisters was strained. She could tell that Valentina was wondering why she was here. "He's sort of the Russian version of Heathcliff in *Wuthering Heights,* huh?"

"He's had a difficult life, Orchid."

"KGB, huh?"

"Whatever it was, it's scarred him badly, and he hasn't told me everything yet." She added, "What can I do for you this time, Orchid?"

"I want you to talk to Keith about increasing my lines. You know the part of Sonya is only fifty lines. That's hardly anything."

"But it could knock the script way out of balance," Valentina pointed out. "You know that even better than I do. The play's already running a little too long and they've been trying to figure out where to make some cuts now."

Orchid felt a rush of hot emotion. "Jesus, Val . . . you really don't give a shit about what's right for me, do you?"

"Of course I do."

"Then talk to Keith. It wouldn't hurt you a bit. Talk to your lover boy and tell him—"

Valentina recoiled. "Don't you dare use that term when talking about Keith and me."

"Oh, what is it, then, you and Keith have this major,

world-shaking romance? Well, if you ask me, you two have acted just like a couple of ghouls, fucking around before poor Cynthia's even cold in her grave!''

Valentina spoke through her teeth. ''*At least* I haven't screwed half of the male population on the North American continent and two-thirds of the sleazy playboy princes in Europe! *At least* I'm not a total, unmitigated, selfish asshole who doesn't care about anyone except herself!''

''Is that so?'' cried Orchid, breathing fast. ''Well, let me tell you something, cookie. If you think I'm that bad, I'll let you in on a big secret. *I fucked Paul.*''

''W-what?''

''Screwed him! Fucked him! And I did it two days before your wedding, sweetheart, I did it because you were just as shitty to me then as you're being right now. I'm soooo tired of you and your prima-donna bullshit!''

Valentina just stared at her for a minute or so. ''Get out of here, Orchid. Just get out. I'll deal with you at the theater because I have to, but as far as I'm concerned—we're through. You've got the morals of an alley cat.''

''You don't mean that.''

''The door is that way, Orchid. Use it and don't ever come to me with one of your bullshit requests for 'favors' again.''

Completely bewildered, Orchid got to her feet and stumbled through the living room.

''Please,'' she began as she reached the door. ''I'm really sorry.''

''Go away,'' Valentina said emotionally, almost hissing the words. ''It's too late for 'sorry.' ''

Orchid reached her apartment in a foul mood. She opened the set of four locks, and entered the cluttered apartment. The maid had cleaned it only three days ago, but the discarded lingerie, playscripts, and stacks of papers had mounted up again.

She ran into her bedroom and threw herself on her unmade bed. Her red satin sheets seemed to mock her with their slippery, sensuous feel. Then Orchid rolled onto her back, her shoulders shuddering with sobs.

The next morning, Peaches hung up from her phone call with Valentina, frowning as she turned to her husband.

"They've had another fight," she said to Edgar, who was stretched out in bed drinking his first cup of coffee and reading the Sunday paper.

"Mmm," he mumbled.

"I used to think they fought because of Orchid's obsession with being a star. Now I don't know. Orchid provokes Valentina, but sometimes I think Val purposely aggravates her too. Perhaps they were too dependent on each other," mused Peaches. "Maybe these fights are about growing up and becoming individuals."

"And it's just possible I'm Peter Pan," said Edgar, rattling newspaper pages. "I suppose now you're going to try to be the peacemaker again. Just let them be, will you? They can patch up their own quarrels."

"Yes, by the time they're fifty," she flared. "I don't want them to drag it on for another twenty years. That would be such a tragedy." She reached for the telephone and dialed Orchid's number.

"I *won't* make up with her," snapped Orchid, as she lunched with her mother that afternoon.

"I'm not asking you to make up with her. Just to—well, to realize that you have some wonderful qualities of your own, too, Orchid."

Peaches embarked on a twenty-minute pep talk, enumerating all of Orchid's achievements, but saw by her daughter's glazed-over eyes that she was being tuned out.

"You think I'm just jealous, don't you?" Orchid finally said, her face reddening. "You think I have *low self-esteem*," she sneered. "That's your opinion, isn't it, Peaches?"

"I just want you girls to end this ridiculous, childish conflict."

"And how do you suggest I accomplish that? By groveling after the star? Or even kissing her ass? I'm not going to—''

"Well, then," Peaches snapped, losing patience. "Van Cleef and Arpels is only a cab ride away. Why don't you go buy her something pretty—have it engraved with your apology. Valentina loves jewelry."

"An apology? Oh, sure! Oh, yes, I'll just do that. I'll run right out and buy her a pin with Blue Orchids on it—to symbolize the raw deal she gave me!"

But then Orchid looked quizzical for a moment or two, ducked her head and began eating rapidly. Peaches breathed a quick breath of relief. At least Orchid was beginning to listen. "Oh, and one more thing," she added. "Jule Styne is giving a little dinner party next week to show off his new duplex and he wants you to come with Daddy Edgar and me. We're in town for a few weeks."

"Oh, a party?" Orchid mumbled, forking up another mouthful of pasta. "Jule Styne? I haven't seen him in years. I really don't think—"

"He's invited some very exciting guests," Peaches said firmly. "And while you're there, I want you to look around his place very closely. I want you to count all the Tonys and Grammys and other awards that he has received over the years. You might be up for one of those awards, too, Orchid, if *Dr. Zhivago* becomes a—"

"I don't want to talk about that right now," Orchid grumped. "And anyway, I don't have a date."

"Well, perhaps Mikhail will escort you," Peaches suggested.

"But I barely know him. He hardly speaks to me."

"I'll call him," offered Peaches.

Orchid agonized for several days, wondering how to package herself for the date with Mikhail. Should she be supersexy and glamorous? But he seemed so conservative and might think her too flamboyant.

Finally, she decided on a simple ecru silk dress. It clung to her figure, revealing every pert curve. She threw on a wonderful gold and diamond lotus blossom pin she'd purchased from an estate sale, and added rows and rows of gold bangles on her wrists.

An hour later, when her buzzer sounded, she started toward the door, then stopped, and whirled to the mirror, where she inspected herself in frantic, last-minute alarm.

The buzzer sounded again.

"I'm coming! I'm coming!" she cried, frantically lunging toward the buzzer button.

"I do not know any of these people," Mikhail told her, as they jumped out of the cab in front of the Dakota. It was a glorious August evening, yellow light falling lazily between the buildings.

"Your American celebrities. To you they are famous, but in Russia for me they did not even exist."

Orchid felt a little shock. "Let's—let's go in," she quavered, again feeling that attack of shyness. She'd fantasized about this man for days, yet as soon as she was in his presence she couldn't even make conversation.

In the duplex on the tenth floor, they were greeted by Jule Styne at the front door. Peaches and Edgar had already arrived, but Valentina hadn't been able to make it—the baby had a cold.

A tall actress who resembled Anjelica Huston pulled Mikhail away. Orchid was left on her own, drawn into the usual round of predinner conversation. She did her best to chat about *Dr. Zhivago,* and her plans for another script, but her eyes kept following Mikhail.

Orchid wandered into a darkened music room, where a huge Steinway gleamed in the shadows, the walls crowded with photos and mementos.

She gazed with clenched teeth at the assembled awards of a show business career. She might as well face it. She'd rampaged through life using men like so many Kleenex tissues, and now she'd found one who was worth something, and she was so terrified she couldn't bring herself to pursue him, *because she might fail*! Maybe she should wait until Sadie Hawkins Day.

"You have eyes of sadness," Mikhail's voice said beside her.

"Do you usually startle people like that?"

"I am sorry. I wanted to be alone too. That is why I came in here. But if you want to be by yourself—"

"No!" she cried as he seemed about to leave. "I was just thinking that I've built a whole life on mistakes, and now when I want it so badly to be right, I don't seem to know how. Look out there." She pointed to the jeweled lights of the Big Apple below. "All those people, caught in their own, tiny lives—and I'm caught in mine too. I wish . . ."

She stopped, horrified. Why had she said such a thing to a man she she barely knew?

"Yes?" he said softly.

To her complete embarrassment, she started to cry. "I've *always* wanted something. Only I've never really known for sure what it was. Sometimes I thought it was being a rock singer, sometimes, a movie star, sometimes—" The tears threatened to become sobs. "Shit! Shit! Oh, shit!"

Mikhail slid his arm gently around her waist. "You can talk to me, Orchid. If you wish. There isn't any pain that I haven't felt too. I have made decisions . . . terrible mistakes far worse than you could ever dream of."

"It's just . . . it's just that I've been so . . . j-jealous," Orchid wept. "I'm jealous of my own sister and I can't help it. Valentina is one of the world's rare, beautiful, talented people. I wanted to be like her so much. From the first day I saw her I wanted to be j-just like her. And I can't be! And it kills me! *It just kills me!*"

She was about to say more, when their host poked his head around the corner. "People? So there you are. We're serving dinner now in the dining room—if you'd like to join us?"

Orchid and Mikhail looked at each other. Then Mikhail reached up with his forefinger and gently smoothed away her tear tracks. The act, so soft, startled her. "We will talk later," he quietly promised.

* * *

There were three tables of ten each, blue linen overlaid with lace, the centerpieces low vases filled with old English garden flowers and tea roses.

Orchid floated through dinner. She teased, she flirted, and she made witty conversation, she sparkled.

But all the while she was thinking of Mikhail, seated at another table. No one had ever spoken to her so gently, or offered such tenderness. She hadn't even known it existed! Jesus, *what had she missed*?

After espresso and cappuccino had been served in the living room, Jule gave Peaches a look, then took Orchid by the hand, announcing that he'd been asked to give Orchid and a few others a tour of the duplex.

Orchid flushed, remembering Peaches's lecture at lunch several days ago about all the awards Jule had won.

In the music room, Jule flipped on the lights and led the small group inside. Orchid glared at the armoire by the far wall that held the rows of Tonys, Oscars, Grammys, and other awards she had seen before. It was a gleaming Broadway treasure trove.

Everyone except Orchid exclaimed at the sight.

"I don't usually show them off this way," admitted Jule, "but tonight I made an exception for a friend." Again he glanced toward Peaches.

"Did you maneuver this?" Orchid took her mother aside as they left the music room. "To give me an object lesson or something?"

"Darling," began Peaches nervously. "You've always focused so hard on the performance aspect of stardom, but honey, look at Jule Styne or even Betty Comden. They don't need to be performing on a screen or a stage in order to feel good about themselves—or have a sense of accomplishment."

"So what? I don't *want* to be behind the scenes. It doesn't satisfy me! And I hate being dragged to a party and set up with a date, just to prove some stupid point!"

"Hush, darling, lower your voice. I only meant—"

"I don't care what you meant! I suppose you told Mikhail

all about my problems and asked *him* to talk to me too! How dare you!'' Orchid hurried toward the living room where she had left her purse.

"Orchid," Peaches called, but Orchid was too heartsick to pause. She snatched up her small, jeweled evening purse, flung the strap over her shoulders, and rushed toward the elevator. Let Mikhail wonder what happened to her—she just didn't care!

What a fool she was. All that tenderness and understanding from Mikhail had only been a stupid-ass favor he was doing for Peaches!

She reached the street, where a line of cabs waited. But instead of hailing one, she turned right. It was more than fifteen long blocks back to her apartment, but she didn't give a damn. She had to work out some of her frustration somehow.

She hated men right now! She hated everyone! All she wanted right now was to go home and rummage in her liquor cabinet until she found the biggest bottle of vodka she had.

"Orchid, you are walking very fast," said Mikhail, falling into step beside her.

"Go away!" she screamed. "You were a great date—now leave. You've done your duty, your favor for Peaches, you've given me my lecture. Now get out of my face!"

"I did not do a favor for her or for anyone."

"Oh, is that so! Everyone is trying to tell me how to run my life—how to let go of my damn jealousy—but I can't! I can't let go of it! She has what I want! She's always had what I want! I hate it! I hate her! I hate—"

She subsided into muffled sobs, the rest of her words lost. Mikhail grabbed her arm and steered her into a small, all-night coffee shop.

He pulled her toward a booth. "We will talk and have some of your American coffee."

"No," she snapped, resisting him, but then she changed her mind and slid into the booth. What did it matter? She was a leftover, a has-been, a *failure*. What did anything matter now?

Mikhail ordered coffee for her, tea for himself, and then both of them let their cups get cold as they talked.

"Orchid, I will tell you something I have not told even Valentina. I am a torturer and murderer—a KGB killer who has ended the lives of more than fifteen people in cold blood, some in screaming pain . . . terminated them . . . for a country I didn't even believe in!" Mikhail confessed bitterly. "Before that, in Afghanistan I killed hundreds more. I strafed innocent villages and watched the people run, flaming from the napalm I dropped."

Orchid felt faint, nearly gasping for air.

"If there is a God, He will look on me with shame," Mikhail grated. "I can never wipe it out, although for the rest of my life I will try. So that is why I can talk to you. That is why I can listen to you and why I do not care what you have done, or to whom."

"Or who I've slept with?" She sat shivering. "I've been looking all my life, but for what? Mikhail, I don't know for what! I'm lost! And I hate myself for it."

"Do not hate any longer, little one. Hatred is useless. I have had similar thoughts, many, many times. Sometimes, I think that some people are born to a particular thing. But they are like you, they cannot find it. But their instincts tell them it exists . . . somewhere."

"Yes, yes," she breathed.

"I have played all of the wonderful Blue Orchids music," Mikhail said after a pause. "All six albums."

"You listened to our albums?"

"Valentina has the tapes. Your voice is so pure and sweet. It made me think of a night I visited a nightclub in Moscow. They served Georgian food and there was a chanteuse."

"I didn't know they had nightclub singers in Russia."

"In certain clubs, yes. She sang with a voice like smoke, in Russian, French, and English." Mikhail's eyes clouded with memory. "She had her own following, you see . . . Without her, they would not have come to the club.''

"I see.''

"I cannot remember the woman's name now, but she was not like your American rock singers. Her audience was very few. She occupied a small space, in only one city. But in that space she was supreme.''

"You mean . . . she was a big fish in a little pond?''

"Is that your curious American idiom? Yes. But I prefer to think of it as a princess in a tiny kingdom. You could be that princess, Orchid. If you chose.''

She felt her heart give a strange twist inside her chest. Then a feeling slid over her like a homecoming. "A nightclub singer? My own following? Sort of like Michael Feinstein, even Bobby Short. Everyone adores them! But I don't know how to . . . ?''

"You will learn,'' he told her.

Orchid began to cry again. But this time gently.

They left the coffee shop, walking the remaining blocks to Orchid's apartment, Mikhail's hand clasping hers.

"Russians are very affectionate,'' he told her. "We are big bears. I hope you do not mind my taking your hand.''

"It's . . . it's wonderful,'' she told him, feeling secure.

When they reached her apartment, she said, "Will you come up?''

They both looked at each other. Then Orchid said, "No. No, Mikhail. I want you to be different from the others. I know I'm being silly, but just kiss me good-night for now, and let's promise ourselves to each other for tomorrow night. I . . .'' Shyness consumed her, and she stopped.

"I want to make love with only you,'' he whispered gently. His gentle kiss touched her soft, promising lips.

Orchid spent the entire next day in a fever of anticipation.

By the time Mikhail arrived, fifties love songs crooned into the room. Orchid was wearing a white silk jumpsuit that clung luxuriously to her curves. She'd brushed out her fiery hair and added just a touch of peachy lipstick. Her spicy perfume floated around her.

"Hello," he said huskily.

"Hello."

His eyes gripped her. "You are so beautiful."

"You too." She shivered as she inspected him. With his trendy pleated trousers and suspenders, his too-big striped shirt, he could have gone straight into a Saks catalog. But somehow the clothes didn't suit him.

"Your American shopping is a problem for me," he said, as if reading her thoughts. "I am not accustomed to so many choices."

Just looking at him made Orchid tremble with desire.

"I want you," Mikhail whispered, sensing her need and vulnerability.

"Mikhail . . . I'm—"

His green eyes searched hers, deep and tender. "It does not matter. Nothing matters between us, Orchid. We are just us, with all our flaws and mistakes, and all the love we have kept shut inside us for so long."

Mikhail lifted her up and carried her into the bedroom, lowering her gently onto the fresh sheets.

Orchid felt as if she were a virgin again—shy and tumultuous, anxious and love-swept. Mikhail kissed her neck, her arms and shoulders, and gently unzipped the jumpsuit, peeling it down over her hips. Beneath she wore only silver panty hose, and she heard his sharp intake of breath as he gazed at her body.

"I am not accustomed to being with such a beautiful woman," he admitted.

He touched the panty hose, his skin so hot she shuddered with pleasure. "I have never met anyone like you."

"Love me, just love me," she murmured, slithering out of the hosiery and reaching up to unbutton his shirt.

They lay together full-length, exploring each other's bodies.

Wonderingly, she ran her fingers down the jagged,

reddened scars that traversed his chest, shoulders, and upper right arm, twisted and ugly.

"I lay there on a mountainside in Afghanistan for hours, watching the stars blink on, one by one. I waited helplessly for the Afghanis to come and find me and torture me to death. They would have stopped at nothing, since I had strafed their villages. But while I waited, something happened. I became as lonely as a single star in the blackness of night. And I wondered . . ."

"Yes, Mikey?" she whispered, calling him by a nickname for the first time as she kissed the scars, one by one.

"I wondered if I would search the rest of my life. If the purpose of my life was only to search."

"And was it?"

"No," he murmured, pulling her on top of him. "No, my wonderful Orchid, the purpose of my life was to find you."

Their limbs intertwined, their skin moist, the boundaries of their bodies blended. His breath on hers, her gasp his. It was as if God had finally reached down a hand and touched them in benediction. Even as they made love, Orchid wept with unspoken prayers of thanks.

Mikhail's thrusts grew deeper, almost violent, and Orchid matched them. She looked down into the green pools of his eyes and clutched his shoulders, rocked by his storm.

Suddenly she exploded, then he followed.

"Orchid!" he shouted out in ecstasy. "Orchid! *Moya lubimaya! Dusha!*"

Araña walked through the stage entrance of the Lederer Theater, showing her forged pass to the security men seated at the door. It was the third day she had entered this way, and the other guard only nodded curtly.

She made her way down the backstage passage, lined with dressing rooms. No one even glanced at her in her uniform stolen from the apartment of one of the company's regular security guards. She was made up to look like a Chicana with a blotchy complexion—hardly worth looking at.

Reaching the backstage area, she positioned herself in the

wings. Her stolid presence would be as overlooked as the cables and hanging mikes.

She folded her arms across her chest and affected a bored expression, watching from narrowed eyes as ten dancers practiced intricate Russian folk steps. Among them was Jinna Jones, Senator Willingham's fiancée.

"Pianist!" Bettina yelled. "Stop the fucking music!"

The piano instantly died. "Jinna Jones!" snapped the choreographer. "This is *not* a junior high recital. Dearie, we are opening in Boston in three days and you can't even remember your combinations!"

"I—I think I've got the rhythm now," panted Jinna.

"You haven't got the rhythm of a Seventh Avenue hooker. Take five, everybody . . . no, make that twenty," Bettina told the assembled dancers. "And Jinna, I want to see you."

Araña watched as the group dispersed, except for Jinna, who approached the choreographer with reluctance. Anxiety was written on her face.

"I'm sure I can get it right in just a couple more tries," the dancer pleaded.

"I'm dropping you, Jinna. Sorry. I'll use one of the understudies—all of them have already got the combinations down perfectly."

"But—please—" Even from fifteen feet away, Araña could hear the desperation in Jinna's voice.

"If you want to be on the stage that badly, then get your husband to buy you a dinner theater," Bettina added. "*I* don't take people who are foisted on me from above—not unless they're Mary Martin, and honey, Mary Martin you ain't."

Devastated, Jinna rushed offstage, and Araña hid her shock behind an impassive face. Son of a bitch! She wanted to scream with disappointment and rage. If Jinna wasn't in the production, then Willingham certainly wouldn't attend opening night.

There were still fifteen minutes left on the break, and dressing room conversation shifted to gossip. Orchid, who wasn't interested in stage scuttlebutt, turned to leave, but was caught by a remark made by one of the dancers.

"My ridiculous ex has finally agreed to sell Rampage," the dancer said. "The stubborn asshole finally listed it with a realtor last week. Now our divorce can go through. Thank God! It's been three long, fucking years."

Orchid stopped short. Rampage was a small nightclub on Central Park South—she'd been there once with Roman Solenski. It had enjoyed a few years of trendy success. Then it had switched to a disc jockey format, rather than live music, and had fallen on hard times.

Thoughtfully she left the ladies' room. Her heart pounded fitfully as she remembered the sexy chanteuse Mikhail had told her about in Moscow. A small nightclub for sale! As she remembered, the place even had a tiny marquee, and a pretty little stage, just right for—

Now, don't get all excited, she told herself. *It's a crazy idea . . . there's probably a hundred reasons why it wouldn't work.*

"Orchid," called Pete Mazzini, the director. "I want to go over your Scene Four lines—five minutes, onstage. Your timing is still a shade off."

She nodded. There was a telephone in the greenroom. It wouldn't hurt to call a realtor, would it? Just to find out the asking price. And maybe—maybe she could call on a few friends to see if she could do a guest appearance somewhere, just to make sure she could be as hot as she thought she could.

"The beauty of this place is that it comes with a liquor license and a fairly new kitchen. Practically turnkey ready," said the real estate woman, as she ushered Orchid into the small, dark establishment. "A lot of great groups have played here. Patti LaBelle, the Pointer Sisters, even the Bee Gees."

Orchid went to a bank of switches and began flipping them one by one.

"Turnkey ready?" scoffed Orchid. "I'd say this place needs a major overhaul."

"But it has such possibilities, don't you think?"

Orchid caught her breath. It did.

Suddenly she knew how she'd decorate it—all in shades of violet and mauve and blue. She'd have recessed lighting—a sensuous, velvety violet. There would be urns filled with huge arrangements of tropical orchids. An orchid in a vase on each table. She'd call the place Orchids.

The real estate woman was going on about square footage, but Orchid had stopped listening. She felt her pulse pound recklessly.

She'd bring in a little of Pia Zadora's smoldering, husky fire.

She'd take a cue from Cher, and wear costumes so wildly sexy and original that people would flock here just to see them.

She'd sing *pure sex*.

Oh, God, it would work . . . she knew it would!

It had to! She didn't need a trial run to know this was going to be magic. She'd call Daddy Edgar tonight and see if he would swing her a loan for part of the down payment.

Flickering firewood danced shadows across the naked bodies of the two who lay wrapped together on a sheepskin rug in front of the fireplace.

"I never knew I could love anyone this much," Keith said wonderingly. "I never knew this kind of love could even exist."

They were both sated from hours of lovemaking.

"I'm thirty years old," Valentina mused. "You'd think I'd know all about love by now, but I don't. I feel like a baby. I feel so brand-new."

"A virgin?" he teased.

"Almost. In a way. You know I've had several other lovers. And one horrible husband."

"Hush," Keith said, pulling her close.

A knot in the firewood suddenly snapped. Valentina jumped violently.

"Darling!"

"I guess I'm just a little jumpy tonight," she excused

herself. "I've been having dreams lately—dreams about the play. I keep dreaming about guns . . . it's all very strange."

"Guns?" Keith's laugh was rich. "Guns in a dream is a phallic symbol, dear, and I think it has to do with something also besides guns." He pressed himself against her flank.

"Oh, ho," she said, giggling.

"Oh, ho, indeed," Keith responded. "You're insatiable, my love, and I adore it." Then he leaned over, stretching, and reached for a small package set inconspicuously on a tabletop. "I have something for you, Val. I've been waiting for this for weeks and I was going to give it to you on opening night. But, well, I can't wait any longer."

He was like an eager boy.

She sat up, reaching for the light quilt he'd brought from the bedroom, and wrapped it around both of them. Then she took the package. Inside was a small jeweler's box.

"Keith?" she gasped.

"Open it," he urged.

With trembling fingers, she lifted the lid. The ring inside was stunningly magnificent, a one-of-a-kind design. Its central square diamond was at least six carats, surrounded by rectangular baguettes that refracted the firelight in shimmering rainbow fire.

"Keith," she whispered. "God. It's so . . . it's the most beautiful ring . . . I . . ."

"I hope it fits," he said nervously. "I took your ring size while you were asleep."

"It's just so beautiful." Her laugh of pleasure turned to a half-sob as she slid the ring onto her third finger. She held it up like a section of star, caught on her hand. Then she turned to Keith, melting into his arms. *"Oh, Keith.* It's so overwhelming."

"I think we should set a wedding date," he said. "How about a week after *Dr. Zhivago* opens in New York?"

"A week!" Valentina's incredulous laugh trilled through the room. "Good grief, Peaches would have a fit if she thought she had to produce a wedding that fast. How about—"

"Two weeks after opening, then? That's the longest I can wait." And before she could respond he enfolded her in his arms and kissed her with all the passion and promise of a lifetime.

At two-thirty A.M., Pietro "Pete" Mazzini, the director of *Dr. Zhivago,* let himself into his Village apartment after having spent a satisfying four hours with his new girlfriend.

But he had not even thrown his jacket across a chair when his buzzer rang. Annoyed, he pressed the button. Probably some enterprising thief, ringing all the buzzers trying to find an empty apartment.

"Go away," he snapped, "or I'll call the police."

"It's Bettina," squawked a familiar voice, warped by the poor transmission. "I have to see you right away. It's important!"

Bettina Orlovsky was the last person on earth he wanted to see right now. But there must be some major problem on the set, or she wouldn't be here at this hour, so he punched the buzzer to allow her to come up.

He opened the door, then stepped backward in surprise. It wasn't Bettina at all, but a messenger with long, greasy blond hair, wearing a New York Mets cap pulled down low over his eyes. The messenger had dark brown eyes.

"But I thought—" he began stupidly.

But before he could close the door, the messenger lunged forward and flicked a thin wire over Mazzini's neck, tightening it from behind with a pair of steel handles.

"Aaah!" Mazzini, strangling, clutched at the wire, but it was embedded too deeply in his skin and he couldn't get his fingers underneath. Desperately he tried to suck air, his chest caving in.

"If the dancer Jinna Jones isn't back in the chorus tomorrow, you are dead," hissed a voice in his ear.

Horrible sounds came from Mazzini's mouth. He started to black out.

"Did you hear me?" whispered the messenger.

Mazzini nodded his head up and down.

The pressure applied around his neck relaxed. "Tomorrow. Bring her back tomorrow. Or I return here and cut your head off with this wire."

* * *

"But honey lamb, they can't do this to you," Charlie kept repeating, as Jinna threw herself into her fiancé's arms and sobbed like a child. She had taken the commuter flight to Washington, then waited in his apartment for him to get out of a late committee meeting.

"They can do it! They did do it! I'm not good enough, Charlie!"

"You're plenty damn good. You're the best. Just let me make a phone call—"

"No!" she cried. "That's why she dumped me, because you made a phone call and went over her head, Charlie. She hates me for that. Oh, shit, I wanted it so much . . . I can't believe I got that close and then was dumped. I w-wish I could just go to bed and sleep for hours . . ."

"Not without me," he told her.

But when they went to bed, Jinna was sobbing too hard for them to make love, so Willingham held her, and stroked her hair and crooned to her, like the father he sometimes was to her. "Baby, you're so beautiful, I love you so much, I don't care if you don't dance . . ."

"But you were so p-proud," she exclaimed, bursting into fresh tears. "You were gonna come and see me . . . Charlie, I'm finished! That was my only chance! I've had it! No one will want me now!"

"Hush," he soothed her.

Finally, exhausted from her emotions, Jinna fell asleep.

Early the following morning, the telephone rang. Jinna was still asleep, curled like a cat against his side, so groggily Willingham reached for it.

"Jinna Jones, please," said a hoarse male voice with an Italian accent. "I'm calling from New York."

"Honey lamb, it's for you." Willingham shook Jinna awake. "Hon, it's New York."

Jinna blinked, and then sprang awake, grabbing feverishly for the telephone. "Yes . . . yes . . . oh, my God . . . yes! I'll fly back right now. Oh, God . . . are you sure?" A pause, then sunlight spread across Jinna's face. "Good-bye!"

She slammed down the phone, and jumped out of bed, racing toward her suitcase, which she had not yet unpacked.

"I gather they want y'all back," he drawled.

"You gather right! Oh, Charlie! I don't know what happened, and I don't care! Pete said he had a long talk with Bettina first thing this morning and argued her down, and now she's taking me back, and I have to have extra rehearsals but I'm in, Charlie, and this time for good! Isn't that wonderful! Isn't that sensational! Oh, lordy lord!"

She danced around the room, a ridiculous, sweet, sexy figure wearing only a lacy pink teddy. "Pete has a doozy of a cold, though," she added. "It's kinda funny, because he was perfectly well yesterday. I hope he doesn't give it to everyone else."

The rehearsal seemed to drag on for an eternity. Araña wondered how actors could stomach the boredom of repeating the same lines over and over again, night after night, sometimes for four or five years. Her own profession was so much more exciting. Every "job" was different! And this one promised to be the best in a long time.

She was observing the furious expression on Bettina's face as she accepted Jinna Jones back, when she heard a sound to her left. Araña turned. A tall, dark man with chiseled features walked into the wings, giving Araña a sharp look as he passed her.

Then, as he stood talking to Valentina, he eyed her again. Just one flick of the eyes, but it was hard, cold, knowing. He was Valentina's brother, she knew—the Russian.

Araña felt a knife turn in the center of her stomach. She survived by her sharpened instincts, and every instinct told her that this man posed danger. He was KGB of course— she'd stake her children on it.

He suspected.

Something had to be done about him, or he'd fuck everything up. She sighed with anger. Now that she'd contracted for the hit and had been making elaborate plans with every detail in place, she would allow nothing to stop her, not even the KGB!

Chapter

Twenty-five

MIKHAIL EXITED VALENTINA'S apartment building, and began walking the four blocks to the garage where he parked his newly leased car.

At the parking ramp, a valet came trotting up. Usually Mikhail got his car himself, but today he gave his key to the attendant.

"Black Oldsmobile, second level, space one twenty," he instructed in his careful English.

"Yes, sir."

Pacing in the small cement waiting area, Mikhail thought about the production of *Dr. Zhivago,* now in Boston and due to open tomorrow evening. He had tried four more times to contact Willingham's staff, but each time had been given a curt brush-off. Willingham had announced publicly that he would attend the opening night in *New York,* but, Mikhail happened to know, the senator also planned to go to the opening in Boston.

Was it possible the assassin would strike in Boston, not wait for New York? If so, there was little time. Why was the feisty old senator so stubborn?

A loud explosion suddenly shook the waiting area, rocking out a blast of sound that momentarily deafened Mikhail. It came from the level immediately above—the exact spot where Mikhail's car was parked. Already the stench of cordite drifted from the ramp, a smell familiar to Mikhail from his days in Afghanistan.

A car bomb.

Mikhail turned, quickly striding onto the street, where he hailed the first available cab. There was no sense in giving the bomber a second opportunity. Someone had assumed he would pick up his car himself. He'd been a fool—a careless but lucky fool.

Boston

"Are you sure? Are you *sure* she's all right?" Valentina hung on to the pay phone wedged in a corner of the backstage hallway. Krista had a fever, and here she was in Boston's Wilber Theater over two hundred miles away!

"She's just fine," reassured the nanny. "Her fever's gone down two points and I'm sure it'll keep on going down now. She's past the crisis."

"You'll sponge-bathe her if it goes up again, won't you? And you'll call me right away? No matter what the hour?"

"Absolutely, Miss Lederer. Please don't worry."

Slowly, Valentina hung up and hurried into the room crowded with the twenty-two cast members, and a number of mob-scene extras, all of them exhausted from both a lighting and full dress rehearsal.

"Well, the queen finally arrives," Orchid called, her tone sarcastic.

"Excuse me . . . excuse me," Valentina murmured as she climbed over outstretched legs. Keith gave her one of his warm smiles, patting a place near him. She settled into it, stifling the hurt she felt at Orchid's sarcasm. She might as well face it—they were flagrant enemies now. Orchid really hated her and she wished she could feel the same. Maybe things would be easier if she did.

"Is Krista okay?" Keith whispered.

"She's cooling down, thank goodness. And she drank some orange juice."

He squeezed her hand.

Valentina looked around at the others. The cast had worked overtime assimilating a host of last-minute line and lyric changes, and were now tired, edgy with opening-night nerves. Patrick Swayze, seated next to the dainty Winona Ryder, was yawning. Jinna looked pale with anxiety. And near her, Bettina looked murderous.

"You are an excellent cast, the best," Pete Mazzini praised the assembled actors, beginning the task of pumping them up for the performance. "You are stars, every one of you, and tomorrow night we will prove it."

He was wearing a black cashmere jacket with a white silk ascot loosely tied at his throat. "We are here in Boston to 'shake out the glitches,' as you Americans say. Keith and I will be in the audience listening for the reactions, good and bad."

Mazzini went on, critiquing the errors that had been made, and going over areas where he felt the production still needed work. Valentina listened carefully at first, then found her mind beginning to drift. Mazzini looked tired, as if he were under a lot of stress. As the director spoke, his right hand kept going to his neck, where he plucked uneasily at the ascot.

He'd worn either an ascot or a turtleneck every day for the past week, even though the temperatures had been in the eighties.

The other production chiefs gave brief talks, and finally the meeting broke up.

Valentina decided to go back to her hotel and call the nanny again to see if the baby's fever had broken.

"Val—stay a minute," called Mazzini as she was leaving.

In the now empty greenroom, Mazzini poured them some strong coffee. As he handed her a cup, the ascot fell away, giving a brief glimpse of an angry red bruise.

"What happened to your neck?"

A flush spread across the director's face. "It is, ah, my new 'friend.' She is very, very passionate."

"Well, if that's the case, I hope she never gets really angry with you," she said, not really believing him. "Now, what is it you wanted to talk to me about?"

Half an hour later, after he'd gone over a last-minute reinterpretation of her part, Valentina hailed a cab and went back to her hotel, her mood thoughtful. When, exactly, had Mazzini started wearing the ascots and turtlenecks? Wasn't it just about the time that Bettina dropped Jinna from the production and then took her back—at Mazzini's insistence?

Valentina stripped off her clothes, dropping them in a trail that led to the bedside telephone. Once again, she dialed New York. The nanny picked up, and she spent ten minutes reassuring Val that Krista was fine.

Finally she hung up and headed for the shower, her uneasy speculations returning. The bruises on Mazzini's neck, Jinna's being dropped and replaced . . . Bettina's furious resentment.

Even Mikhail, she thought suddenly. Her brother had shown a deep interest in the production, asking her to get permission for him to attend rehearsals six or seven times. *Mikhail was KGB*—the thought suddenly hit her like triphammer blows to the stomach.

Then she shook her head, trying to rid her mind of such crazy thoughts. God, her opening-night jitters were a doozy this time, weren't they? Now she was imagining international intrigue.

She stepped into the luxurious shower and gave herself up to the pulsating massage of the needle sprays.

A noise outside the shower door startled her. Valentina jumped, letting out a sharp exclamation of fright. Her hip hit the lowest shower head, and she uttered another yelp of pain.

"Val? Jesus, you're really wired, aren't you? I'm sorry, I didn't mean to scare you like that."

Keith stood in the middle of the steamy bathroom, wearing nothing except a pair of white Jockey briefs.

"Keith, you scared me half to death!"

"Baby, baby," he said, holding her wet body. "I'm sorry."

"God . . ."

The water was still pouring out of the shower. She clamped her arms around him, clutching at his calm solidity. "Am I crazy? I have this feeling . . . Those dreams I've been having about falling, and guns . . . And now Mazzini's got a strange black and blue mark on his neck, and there's this weird security woman back at the theater in New York who keeps giving me these odd looks . . .''

Keith laughed. "Why, honey, she's probably just awed by you, that's all, maybe working up enough courage to ask for an autograph. I haven't really noticed her all that much. As for Mazzini, perhaps he fell. Who knows?''

"No," she began. "The marks weren't from falling. They went all the way around his neck, exactly like—''

But Keith had buried his face in her damp neck and was tonguing up the warm droplets from her skin. Valentina caught her breath. Moaning, she arched her hips forward, pressing her pelvis into his and reaching for the waistband of his underwear.

When the last shudder of pleasure was finished, Keith turned off the warm water, lifted her out of the shower, and wrapped her in a thick white towel. As if she were a goddess, he carried her into the bedroom to the bed, and laid her down, her wet hair trailing on the pillow.

"My water nymph," he murmured. "My sweet love. How I adore you, Val. You'll never know how much.''

They lay together locked in wet kisses that promised to turn to more lovemaking. Valentina snuggled into his chest, her uneasy thoughts totally forgotten.

An hour later, however, as they got up for a snack, her unease returned. Reaching for the bottle of mineral water, Valentina saw a headline in the *New York Times* financial section, which was lying across her table.

BROADWAY INVESTORS BECOME CAUTIOUS.

"Keith?" she said, leaning over to read its text. "What does this mean, 'cautious'?''

"Oh, just one of those meaningless squibs they print when they haven't got any better news," he replied off-handedly. "It doesn't mean diddly squat, it's just filling up space.''

Keith's name was mentioned as an investor who had already lost two and a half million dollars in his last productions, and now stood to lose another one and a half million if *Dr. Zhivago* bombed at the box office.

She read the story twice, her heart sinking. She knew
Keith's major investments were in shopping centers and
real estate. To him, Broadway had always been a fun,
creative way for him to put money to work earning even
more money. Now the financial climate was shaky, and if
the production folded he could actually be in serious
trouble.

"Now, put that away, darling," he said, planting a kiss
on her forehead. "Newspapers always exaggerate, you
know that."

"But Keith—"

"Honest, I'm fine."

She changed the subject, but still her mind continued to
swirl with the unexpected surprise. Keith needed the hit as
much as she did, but for different reasons. *Please,* she
prayed. *Let Boston love us, so we can both go on to New
York and be a smash success!"*

In Washington, D.C., Mikhail took a cab to the FBI
building on Pennsylvania Avenue.

Twenty minutes later he was being ushered into the office
of Assistant Deputy Director Herb Cannell. Mikhail suspected that Cannell's position was a front. The man's real
job was probably much more clandestine, just like in the
KGB.

"All right, I'll need some identification," Cannell said
after Mikhail had told him who he was and what he wanted.

Mikhail produced his Soviet passport and visa, waiting
while Cannell examined these minutely, searching for
forgeries.

"You say you're KGB?"

"Yes."

Cannell asked some identifying questions about the KGB
setup and current hierarchy that only an insider would
know. After discussing the purpose of Mikhail's coopera-
tion with the Bureau, he probed further. "They've had word
of a definite hit on Willingham?"

"Through Cuba, yes. Word is that the hit will be public,
and soon. The Colombians are behind the contract."

''You'll have to wait while I check all this out,'' Cannell said. ''There's a waiting room beyond the receptionist's desk—you may wait there, Mr. Sandovsky. Then we'll talk in detail.''

He was kept waiting more than an hour. Leafing through old copies of the *Congressional Record,* Mikhail suppressed his impatience. But he knew the huge bureaucracy moved as slowly as the KGB. Cannell would be calling the CIA, tracing him on computer and in other secret files.

Finally he was called back into Cannell's office.

The FBI man was sitting with a cup of coffee. ''Your credentials check out fine . . . but defection, well, that's another story. If you want to defect, we'll assist you but in return we want some help of our own. We want one helluva lot more than information from you. We need you to tell us everything you know about this possible hit and also be part of our team effort. *You'll help us in every way, up to and including the risk of your own life.* Later, if this works out, you'll be debriefed at length and then we will help you establish a new identity here in the U.S.''

Mikhail nodded coldly. ''I will do it. I have access to KGB files of international assassins, perhaps information you do not possess.''

A flare of interest lit Cannell's faded eyes. His hand tightened on the coffee cup. ''We want everything.''

Araña had flown into Boston a few days earlier than the cast and become part of the maintenance crew at the Wilber Theater. The day before the opening, she left the theater, changed out of the coverall uniform at a McDonald's, and ditched it in a waste bin. As she returned to her hotel room, she laughed to herself, thinking of her husband. He'd be with his mistress right now. He never asked her too many questions, because he had a lover of his own. Men were *estupidos*! Her thrills were far better than any lover.

She took out the suitcase she'd picked up at the bus station in D.C., and began rechecking the items inside, going over them one by one. The black tuxedo, a topcoat with a specially made inside flap pocket for a small, lightweight assault rifle. The man's white wig, the facial prosthesis, theatrical makeup, and plastic gum she would use to age her face. And the weapon itself, the Belgian-made semiautomatic. *A miracle of perfection!*

Her hands caressed the beautiful, silky barrel, stroking it like a phallus.

The plans for tomorrow were deadly simple. She would attend the opening dressed as a nondescript, older male theater patron. She would take a seat in the row behind the senator, and wait until intermission, when people would be getting up from their seats. In the confusion, she would shoot Willingham and several of the security people near him. The silencer on the gun would render the shots no louder than a finger's snapping.

It would take a second or two for anyone to react. By then she'd be in the aisle. She would drop a plastic spider onto the floor—her vain little idiosyncrasy. Then she would blend with the exiting crowds. As many of the audience thronged on the sidewalk for a quick smoke, she would slip away. Later, in another fast-food restaurant, the switch back to a female disguise would take only seconds. She had already booked a reservation for the next day on American's flight to Miami . . . then on to Rio via Pan Am, and home.

Jinna gripped the edge of the desk in her hotel room as she did barre exercises while talking on the telephone to Charlie.

Charlie had just told her he was afraid that he might have to chair an emergency meeting of the Investigations Subcommittee of the National Security Committee.

"*Please, please, please,* Charlie," she begged. "Don't let a subcommittee meeting interfere with your coming to Boston. I want you here so bad, baby. Bettina hates me and she's looking for any excuse to dump me again. Maybe if you were here, she wouldn't dare."

"I'll try. Our national security seems to have gone straight to hell, but I'll work all day to put out fires," the senator promised.

"And come afterward to the cast party, it's at Locke-

Ober's. Oh, Charlie! I'm *so* nervous. I wish you were here,"
she added plaintively. "I never sleep as well without you."

"Tomorrow night, I promise, I'll hold you all night
long."

Jinna giggled. "And we won't sleep at all?"

"Not if you don't want to. Baby . . . I wish I could hold
you right now, an' tell you just how much I really love you.
I'm one lucky son of a bitch to have you."

Mikhail took a red-eye flight back to Washington the next
day. He had been shuttling between Boston, New York, and
Washington for the past ten days.

He checked into a room at the Fitzgerald and fell into bed,
his sleep filled with dreams of the avalanche. Bundled in
black fur, Vladimir Petrov lifted him out of the snow and
carried him in his arms. But when Mikhail looked at his
father's face, he saw the hideous features of a desiccated
corpse.

I want a son, I want a son, whispered the leathery lips,
and Mikhail woke violently, jerking upright in bed. Sweat
poured off his skin, soaking the sheets.

"You bastard." Mikhail muttered the words in Russian,
as he clicked on the bedside lamp. He got up, pacing to the
window and opening the drapes. While looking out at the
night view of the Capitol, he allowed himself to think of
the two women in his life. Orchid and Valentina. Two
women who together held almost all the love he had ever
known.

He had to do this, for them.

A security guard stationed on the first level of the Senate
building accepted without question the identification
Mikhail handed him—that of a lobbyist for the National
Rifle Association, which he had had Boris obtain for him.
He might as well use the full services of the KGB desk at
the embassy while he had the chance.

He took the elevator to the third floor, and stationed
himself in the hallway near the meeting rooms where
Willingham's subcommittee was scheduled to meet.

He only had to wait twenty minutes before he saw
Willingham striding down the corridor accompanied by a
beefy young aide. ''Senator Willingham.'' Mikhail hurried
forward, quickly introducing himself.

The senator's bodyguard put his hand inside his jacket,
toward his shoulder holster, and Willingham stopped short.

''Sandovsky, is it?'' the senator growled, restraining the
guard. ''What is it, man, are you cracked or somethin'?
You've placed ten dozen phone calls to my staff. I got your
message loud and clear. I've taken appropriate action. Will
y'all now have the courtesy to let me alone? I have
important work to do.''

''Senator, give me two minutes of your time. I have been
asked by the Russian Embassy to apprise you of the exact
situation,'' Mikhail added. He took out his real identity
papers, stamped officially, and offered them to the senator.

Willingham narrowed his eyes at the visa stamps. Finally
he nodded. ''All right then. But make it fast. This committee
meetin' can't start without me.''

''Senator,'' said the guard.

''It's okay, Tommy Lee. No more than two minutes,'' the
senator said to Mikhail. ''You drink coffee?''

''I will drink coffee.''

The paneled lounge was furnished like a men's club,
filled with leather couches and overstuffed chairs.

''Senator,'' Mikhail said. ''I have come here to explain to
you the sizable risk you are facing. It's certain there will be
an assassination attempt, probably within the next few days
to three weeks.''

''The next few *days*? Aren't y'all bein' just a tad
dramatic?'' But he saw the senator pale slightly.

''Senator! This is terrorism. International terrorism!''

''I've got a sonofabitchin' guard with me everywhere I
go now except in bed with my lady, and I suppose that's
where he's gonna wanna be next,'' Willingham said bitterly. ''I think I've got it covered.''

''Senator Willingham, you have made a public announcement that you plan to attend Jinna Jones's Broadway opening. That would be the real opportunity for—''

"If they want to gun me down, they can damn well do it right here! Right now!"

As Mikhail stared at him incredulously, Willingham added, "I won't tolerate bein' scared off. Go back to your embassy and tell them that you did what you could. I'm the fool here, not you—but I like it that way."

Willingham turned on his heel and plowed toward the meeting room.

International assassins? Hell. Who did the fucking Colombians think he was, some soft southern belle? They forgot he'd been an ace fighter pilot at Ponyang, Pork Chop Hill, along the 38th Parallel and "MiG Alley," the air corridor over central Korea. He'd been a lot younger and thinner, true, but he flew more than sixty-five missions, and had been shot down twice. That didn't make him a Ninja, but he'd weathered one assassination attempt already and planned to survive another.

He might be sixty and over the hill, but he did not live his life based on fear—not then and not now. Not ever.

Lorren Jewel, his executive secretary, came hurrying up, breathless, to tell him that the President had just called. He wanted him to come to the White House tonight for a briefing on the current volatile situation between the Medellín cartel and a rival group of Columbians that was threatening to take it over.

"Shit," sighed Willingham. Jinna would be crushed, but even he couldn't ignore a direct request from the White House.

"Send her flowers," suggested the sympathetic Lorren, reading his thoughts. "If she's like most of us, she'll understand, Senator."

"I've been doin' that too much lately . . . All right, six dozen roses, you know the kind she likes, and let me dictate a note. 'I love you so much, darlin', and I'll be with you in spirit.' How does that sound?"

"Excellent," agreed Lorren, who wrote most of his letters.

They had reached the meeting room, where a buzz of voices could be heard from inside the doors. ''And I don't want you to tell anyone about that Sandovsky KGB man comin' here to see me, do you understand? That's our little secret, right?'' He drilled Lorren with his piercing blue eyes until she reluctantly nodded.

Boston

The Wilber Theater was filling up rapidly with a sell-out crowd, drawn by intensive advance publicity. The buzz of laughter and chatter filled the auditorium, as ushers handed out programs and tried to keep up with the crush.

Disguised as a 55-year-old man, Araña took a program and started down the aisle, careful not to make direct eye contact with anyone. The assassin knew her male walk was perfect, even with the necessary compensation for the weight and bulk of the automatic weapon concealed in her coat flap.

She looked around at the well-dressed crowd, thinking that most of the women here had probably seen her picture in *Vogue* or *Mirabella*. Now, none of them even glanced at her.

Araña sank into her third row seat, staring at the front row, where a block of four seats still remained empty. As the orchestra began to play the overture, and the houselights began to blink, Araña glanced uneasily at her watch.

Where was he?

The ''Theme from Dr. Zhivago'' drifted backstage from the orchestra.

Valentina thought momentarily about Nadia. She could almost feel her presence, see the smile. She seemed to radiate waves of encouragement.

Feeling serene, Valentina began to breathe deeply. She was barely aware of the people around her.

''Darling,'' said Keith, sliding his arms around Valentina. ''You look so beautiful. If you really lived back in the

days of Zhivago, he'd never be able to resist you. Oh, Val,''
he added, pulling her close. ''All the important things I want
to say to you. I feel so certain we're on our way now. I just
feel it.''

''I love you,'' she said simply.

The first song was nearing an end.

''Your cue,'' whispered Keith.

Valentina drew herself up, becoming Lara. She moved
toward the stage-left entrance, and walked onstage, speaking her first line.

The swell of applause that greeted her became a roar.
Valentina was back!

At intermission, Araña quietly exited the theater.
Willingham hadn't shown up.''

Did he suspect? Had he been warned? Or had something
else come up? Reaching the street, Araña strode toward an
idling taxi, and yanked open its door, jumping inside. Anger
seethed through her. She'd have to phone her husband in
Buenos Aires, and tell him she'd received another assignment. She needed more time to finish this job.

The private room at Locke-Ober's was jammed with
revelers. Theater people partied as hard as they worked, and
this celebration was well on its way to blast-off.

''They loved Valentina, they loved Patrick and Winona,''
gloated Keith, who had mingled with the crowd at intermission. ''We hit them in all the right places with the
emotions. Tremendous!''

''Broadway bound!'' screamed one of the male dancers.
The others, drunk more on success than champagne, took up
the shout. Four hard months of work had been vindicated.

The first reviews came in, all favorable. A few negatives
were mentioned, but nothing important that couldn't be
fixed. Orchid's performance as Zhivago's wife was called
''disappointingly not up to the level of the rest of the stellar
cast.''

Valentina felt a stab of compassion for her sister. She
decided to speak to Pete Mazzini. Maybe she could get the

director to work with Orchid some more to hone her performance.

"Pete," she said, spotting the director as he returned from the men's room."

"There she is—the *bellissima,* without whom we could not exist," he greeted her, his Italian accent much thicker under the influence of the free-flowing champagne.

She steered him away from the private party room toward the bar area of the restaurant, where a pianist played to a well-dressed crowd of regulars.

He slumped into an empty booth. "I am far, far too drunk," he told her. "I have had enough of this production. I am Pietro Mazzini, not some . . . some hoodlum who must be strangled into submission."

"Strangled? Pete, what are you talking about?"

"Things happen," he said mysteriously, looking frightened.

"What things? Did someone try to strangle you?"

"I . . . I must get back to the party."

"No! Not yet. Pete . . . who did that to your neck? And why? Please, tell me. I think it's important. It could be very, very important."

"He made me talk to the old bitch," Peter would only say, as he stood up and went weaving back to the party.

Valentina sat where she was, stunned and alarmed. The old bitch had to be Bettina. She remembered only one time when Pete had argued with Bettina—when he'd forced her to agree to take Jinna back in the show.

She caught her breath.

Back in Valentina's hotel room, Keith and Valentina undressed quietly.

"We really are Broadway bound," Valentina said in deep satisfaction. "All the reviews said so . . . thank God. Nothing can stop us now, can it?"

"What would stop us? And our success is due in no small part to you. Honey, remember years ago, when you auditioned for *Balalaika*? I knew that day you'd be a big star."

"Yes— But, Keith, it's about Pete Mazzini. I told you before, he had a—"

"Do we have to talk shop right now, honey? I've been wanting to make love to you all night long."

Without further hesitation, Valentina came to him, and kissed him lovingly. Within minutes they were lying on her bed, locked deep in the passion that consumed them like a hot flame.

Later, however, after Keith had drifted to sleep, Valentina's troubled thoughts kept her awake. She sat beside him in bed, the lamp turned on low, as she leafed through a copy of *Mirabella* she'd bought at the hotel newsstand. On the cover, a beautiful South American model called María Cristina Ramírez gazed sulkily at the camera, her dark sloe eyes smoldering with sex.

Valentina studied the cover model's stunning face. The dark, melting eyes . . . somehow they seemed very, very familiar.

She tossed the magazine aside, sighing. Everything was striking her wrong these days. Could someone have wanted Jinna to stay in the production badly enough to threaten the director?

That was exactly what it looked like to her. But why? she wondered. What would their motive be? Jinna was just an ordinary dancer. The only extraordinary thing about her was that she was the fiancée of Senator Charles Willingham, one of the most powerful men in Washington.

Willingham.

And then the realization hit her. Willingham had hoped to attend tonight, but backed out at the last minute. But he had *sworn* to attend the opening night on Broadway—"front row center."

She knew he had survived an assassination attempt several years ago. Could it be . . . Oh, God . . . *If Jinna wasn't in the show, then Willingham wouldn't sit in front row center.*

"Keith," she began, trying to shake him awake.

But Keith only muttered, turning over on his side as he uttered a tiny snore.

''Maybe it isn't true,'' whispered Valentina, sliding down on the pillow again.

Room service arrived with breakfast. The delicious aroma of fresh-ground coffee made Valentina's speculations of last night seem too fantastic to mention.

''You were restless last night,'' Keith remarked, spreading a croissant with the Meridien Hotel's special peach preserves. ''I felt you tossing and turning.''

''I guess I was.''

''Something bothering you? Or was it just opening night nerves?''

''Well, some of that,'' she admitted. ''But there's more, Keith.'' She told him about her conversation with Mazzini, and her idea that someone had wanted to keep Jinna in the production so that Willingham would attend opening night. About her fear that the senator was in danger.

''*Assassination?*'' Keith stared at her incredulously, his croissant pausing midway to his mouth. ''You can't be serious, Valentina? Don't even say such a thing.''

''Well? What if it's true?''

''I'm sure it isn't true. In fact, I've heard a nasty rumor about Pete Mazzini—his sex life may be a little, well, on the kinky side. Maybe one of his girlfriends—or boyfriends—gave him those marks all in the name of fun. Anyway, if anyone put pressure on him, it's probably Willingham himself. The old boy is smitten with Jinna and would do anything for her.''

''Not attack a director,'' she insisted.

''Hon, I think, well, your imagination might have run away with you just a little bit.''

She frowned. ''I'd feel better if you'd call him, Keith—or I will. He just charges ahead and doesn't think.''

''Hush,'' Keith said in a low tone. ''I told you, I'll call him.''

A blue sky blazed over Washington, D.C.

Senator Willingham had carried his portable cellular phone onto the balcony of his Watergate condo to catch the breezes. The phone call from Keith Leonard had stunned him. All he heard these days was assassination warnings. First the Russian, scaring the shit out of him. Now Leonard. Maybe, just maybe, he should pull his head out of the sand and face the facts. The Colombians hated his guts and had marked him for execution.

Dammit! He hated being made to feel like a helpless victim, some doddering old man who could only sit back and wait to be murdered.

They were targeting him for the Broadway opening. Yeah, they'd have a sniper with a high-powered weapon, and wouldn't he be an easy mark, with his white hair, his usual white suit, and his black string tie? Shit, he was more noticeable than a gorilla at the North Pole.

Of course, he'd have to cancel. He had no other choice.

Despondent, he reached for the cordless phone and was about to dial the number of his security man, when an idea hit him.

Damn, it just might work!

Five performances had been scheduled for Boston. Two down, three to go.

Bettina stalked around backstage, discontented and furious that Jinna Jones kept kicking a second too late, and once had missed two beats, throwing all the other dancers off. The audience might not notice, but Bettina did, and it drove her crazy.

"What are *you* staring at?" she snapped savagely at a new stagehand who'd been eyeing all the women.

"Nothing."

The man shifted his dark brown eyes elsewhere. Bettina strode toward Pete, who had just appeared from the backstage corridor.

"Pete, we must talk again and this time I won't be bullied."

"Later, later," muttered the director.

"Don't 'later' me," she snapped. "Jinna Jones is going to ruin my choreography. She can't get her timing right and she's uneven, and she makes mistakes, Pete—*mistakes that reflect on me.* She can finish here in Boston but after that, she's history! We don't need her.''

Mazzini turned white. "Now, Bettina, calm yourself. Jinna isn't that bad and she adds glamour to the chorus. People like to look at her."

"I don't give a flying fuck if they like to look at her. Can she dance? That's the big, fucking question, and the answer is, no, she can't. She is amateur hour, Pete. Do you want me to spell that out? A-M-A . . ."

"Enough," muttered Mazzini, cutting her off and hurrying away.

"Pete," she shouted after him. "I'll go over your head with this!"

He was gone. Enraged, she swiveled her head around, only to see the stagehand's eyes flick away from her, as if he'd been eavesdropping. Yeah, she knew everyone thought her a bitch, and she could see why. But she wasn't going to give up this easily—she'd talk to Keith again tonight. Nobody foisted a dancer she didn't want on Bettina.

Chapter
Twenty-six

ORCHID FLUNG OPEN the elegant door of Van Cleef and Arpels and hurried inside. Display cases glistened with trays of rings, diamond necklaces, and tennis bracelets. Orchid paused, the blood rushing to her cheeks. She'd been awake half the night, tossing and turning. This *had* to be right.

"I don't suppose you have any pins or rings that are shaped like an orchid?" she asked the smiling clerk.

"Are you referring to costume jewelry, then?"

"No . . . I need something more expensive . . ." Orchid gulped, running her hand nervously over her close-fitting hat, then suddenly snatched it off because her head felt too hot. "It's an apology," she whispered. "It has to be very special. I've been to six jewelers already and they didn't have anything."

"You say it has to be an orchid?"

"Um, yes. Some shade of blue, preferably dark blue."

The woman smiled. "Well, then, you might want to take a look at a new display we've just set up this week."

Orchid followed the woman to the other side of the store.

"Oh," she said, staring at a brooch that resembled two small, flute-shaped tropical orchids twined together. Their enamel was cleverly painted in shimmering blue-violet to resemble the delicate gradation in shade of the real flower. Diamonds had been set along the petals like dewdrops.

It was the one. It was perfect.

"Would you like to see it?"

"Oh, yes. I would." It probably cost over five thousand dollars, maybe a lot more, but suddenly Orchid didn't care. She'd hock everything she owned if necessary.

She went on, "I don't suppose you can engrave the back of it, could you? While I wait, I mean."

"It should take about thirty minutes. What do you want the engraving to say?"

Orchid hesitated. "Put down, 'Sisters Always, Forgive Me, Orchid.' Tears were rolling down her cheeks. "Yes," she added, sniffling. "That's exactly what I want it to say."

As the woman took away the pin to be worked on, Orchid found a chair at the back of the store and sat down. She felt as if all the energy had been drained out of her.

Bettina stalked into the lobby of the Copley Plaza Hotel, where she was staying, her anger still not dissipated. She hadn't been able to buttonhole Keith Leonard as she'd hoped—he'd had to fly back to New York for a rush meeting with the set designer.

Entering her room, she took off the black jeans and T-shirt she'd worn today, and slipped into a velour bathrobe. She moved to the phone and dialed room service.

"Just a garden salad," she specified. "With arugula, and radicchio. And some steamed vegetables and maybe a small slice of cheesecake. And a carafe of Piesporter."

Flicking on CNN, she felt herself relax as she watched the news. She'd talk to Keith in the morning. Room service arrived, and she went to the door to let in the attendant with her cart.

"Over by the bed," she specified, as the woman rolled the white-covered cart inside the room, dishes rattling.

The waitress did as she was told, closing the door behind her. Suddenly she lifted a long, napkin-wrapped object and pointed it at Bettina.

Bettina stared back, startled. "You should put that—"

Araña smiled as she gazed down at the sprawled corpse; then she reached into her pocket for a small plastic spider and dropped it on the floor. Grasping the handles of the cart, she wheeled it out of the room, dishes rattling as she renegotiated the door.

Valentina stepped out of the elevator, looking to her right and left. A Puerto Rican maid was rolling a room service cart, pushing it with slow, ponderous movements, her dark eyes almost too pretty to belong with the stained uniform, Valentina noted.

"Miss? Could you tell me where room ten forty-four is?"
The woman gestured back the way she had come.
"Thanks," Valentina said, turning around.

When she reached Bettina's room, Valentina rapped repeatedly, but got no response. Bettina was probably in the shower, she told herself, or maybe she'd already gone to bed. It had been silly to come here without calling first, but she had to talk Bettina out of dumping Jinna.

She turned to leave, deciding to arrive at the Wilber Theater early the next morning, and catch Bettina first thing.

Washington, D.C.

A tape recorder softly whirred, recording the debriefing that had been going on for ten hours a day, for the last five days.

"The opening *has* to be delayed," insisted Mikhail Sandovsky. "You can't let an assassin loose in a theater!"

Herb Cannell leaned back in his swivel chair and studied the angry Russian.

"Okay, I want it again, from the top—all the information you've got on these hit men, every fucking detail."

As Mikhail elaborated on the questions he had already answered fully, Cannell busied himself with thinking about exactly how they would use this penitent defector who had fallen so conveniently into their hands.

After another two hours, a phone call interrupted them. Irritably, Cannell picked up his phone.

"Yes?" he snapped. It was Will Chapin, the special agent in charge in Boston.

"Mr. Cannell, Bettina Orlovsky, the choreographer for *Dr. Zhivago,* has been found murdered in her hotel room at the Copley Plaza. Shot with a semiautomatic weapon, probably equipped with a silencer. Very professional. I thought you'd want to know right away."

"I see. When did this happen?"

"Probably last night around eleven P.M."

"Has next of kin been notified?"

"No, the police can't find any relatives, she lived alone. It's funny, though, Mr. Cannell, BPD did find a small plastic spider not far from the body."

Shit, thought Cannell. This proved everything the Russian had been telling them for the past few days.

"Well, Will, I suggest you tell the Boston police to keep a lid on this," he said casually. "I mean a *tight* lid. And give the director of the play some excuse or other—tell him Orlovsky had to go out of town unexpectedly. I want the opening night in New York to go on as scheduled."

Mikhail had started up from his seat. "But there will be hundreds of people there! You can't do that! We can't—"

"We want to catch us an assassin," Cannell drawled. "And you're going to help—that is, if you want U.S. political asylum, you will."

Mikhail stared at the FBI agent in shock as the man outlined what was expected of him. He knew the type well from the KGB—ambitious and greedy for recognition, someone who regarded intelligence activities as a test, rather than a risk of human lives.

"You want me to act as a *decoy*?"

"As a matter of fact, yes, we do. For the sake of U.S. security we must thwart the assassin and, my orders are, if possible, take him alive, it's of vital importance. I don't see any other way to do it than to be there, at the point of impacting events, so to speak."

Mikhail took a deep breath. "My sister is in that show—and the woman I love."

"I've told you—we need this killer, and we're going to get him. Now, I'll outline what's going down. You'll dress in a wig and white suit like the senator. You'll be plenty protected, bulletproof gear, the works, and you'll have loads of backup."

"No!"

"Willingham will be safe, he won't even be in the theater, and your sister and the rest of the cast will be in no danger, I promise you."

"In no danger! What if he sprays bullets indiscriminately! What if he takes out more than just his target?"

"We'll take him down before he can do all that," Cannell said. "Now it all boils down to this: will you do it? If you do, the gold key is yours, Sandovsky. We'll not only accept you, we'll provide you with identity papers, a house, relocation, protection, anything and everything you need to start a new life."

"And if I don't?"

Cannell grinned, but there was no mirth in his eyes. "We'll get someone else to be the decoy and we'll still carry out the project. That takes place whether you're in it or not. And you get slapped in Federal prison, buddy boy—without a key."

Mikhail stared straight ahead. This, too, was like the KGB. Why should they use their own manpower for the dangerous job when they had him, a totally expendable body?

"Well?" Cannell said.

"I will do it," he agreed.

New York

Three weeks later, Senator Willingham and Jinna were in bed in her small apartment in the Village.

"Charlie? Rub my back, will you, baby? I have such kinks. The muscles in my calves are killing me. Dancing is total hell on the body."

Jinna threw back the sheets, presenting her naked, well-formed body. Charlie, detecting the tense trill in her voice, knew her nerves were stretched near breaking point.

"I'll do a lot more than just rub your back," Willingham murmured, enjoying the silky feel of her skin. "I've got just the prescription for stress."

Later, Jinna rolled over until she was facing him. In the

semidarkness, her eyes glistened. "Charlie . . . opening night is tomorrow—"

"I'll be there, but I just won't be in my usual seat, that's all. Security, you know," he told her casually.

"Security? Oh, Char—"

"Hush," he said, putting his hand over her lips. "Now, you might hear that I'm goin' to be sittin' in the front row, but I'm not—I'm gonna be sitting somewhere else."

"I don't understand."

"It's just security bullshit, honey lamb. They've got some guy dressed up like me, and they told me to stay away. Well, I ain't stayin' away. Just don't tell anyone that I'm out there in the audience, all right? It's all very hush-hush," he explained. "Even my staff doesn't know all about it, and I want to keep it that way. But I promise, darlin', that I'll have a very good view. The best. I wouldn't miss seein' my beautiful Jinna dance for anything."

"I worry about you sometimes, Charlie," she sighed. "You think you lead such a charmed life, but no one really does. I just wish—"

"Be still and kiss me."

Orchid unlocked the four locks on her apartment door, and rushed inside, tossing off the fake fur, and hurling the matching hat onto the back of her overstrewn couch.

She fished the small jeweler's box out of her purse and set it in a place of honor on the coffee table, then sat gazing at it, not opening it, but only staring with misted-over eyes.

She'd give the brooch to Val tomorrow night. Opening night!

The buzzer from the lobby sounded, and she hurried to the intercom.

"Miss Lederer, it's a Mr. Mikhail Sandovsky."

Mikhail. "Send him up," she trilled happily.

She rushed to the door and waited impatiently until he arrived, then threw herself into his arms like a child. "Mikhail—! Mikey—!"

"Orchid." He gripped her hard, enfolding her.

"I can't believe you're here . . . where've you *been*? I called and called but you never answered. Oh, Mikhail, so much has happened—I've done an incredible thing . . ."

He looked like a man recently returned from a war. Weary, somber lines bracketed his mouth, and scored his forehead. There were new shadows under his eyes, which burned at her in a long, searching look. For the first time she noticed he had a few gray hairs at his temples.

"Mikey?" she asked in alarm. "Are you all right? Is anything wrong?"

He shook his head. His smile was tired but sweet, exactly like Valentina's. "I was in Washington, being debriefed. Long hours every day full of the same questions over and over. And they have not finished with me yet," he added wearily.

"Oh . . ."

"I am glad to be here in your apartment, *dushenka*. You don't know how very glad I am to see you."

She smiled at his use of a Russian endearment, then dragged him by one arm into her living room, where she first cleared a space from the clothing disarray, and then pushed him down on the couch, settling herself in his lap.

"And I'm *sooo* glad to see you! Mikey, I'm going to make it up with Valentina! I really, really am. We're going to be real sisters again. I'm so scared, it really scares me, but I'm going to do it. If she'll let me."

"Tell me about it," he murmured, "while I show you how much I love you."

Afterward, they ordered in Thai food and opened a bottle of Chablis. Then, while they sat on the floor with their plates, she told him about the nightclub. "It's a beautiful place! Well, it needs some work, but I can make it fabulous. If I handle it right, they'll line up on the sidewalk to get in. And the best thing of all, Daddy Edgar will put up the necessary money for a percentage of the profit. He thinks it's a terrific location for a small, intimate club. We've already made the offer—I can't wait to hear if it's accepted! Oh, did I tell you, I'm calling it Orchids."

"Orchids," he repeated, smiling.

"Yes, do you love the name?"

"I love you," he said gently.

They made love again, but this time, as Mikhail held her, his kisses seemed less lusty, and filled more with a sense of sorrow and loss.

"Orchid, *moya lubimaya*," he whispered as his hands worshiped every inch of her, committing her very skin to memory. "You have given me so much, more than you can ever guess. Your . . . unconditional acceptance. Your . . . forgiveness. I need your forgiveness." His voice broke.

"Don't *talk* like that! You make me scared. Mikhail, is something wrong? Did something bad happen when you were in Washington?"

"There are parts of me that you would not like, parts of me that *I* do not like. I must . . . deal with them, I must somehow pass beyond them."

She didn't understand.

"I will tell you, I promise, but not tonight, *moya dushechka*. Tonight is for us." Mikhail's voice caught and he grabbed her, burying his face in her shoulder.

"I love you," she gasped, suddenly terror struck. *He was acting as if she'd never see him again!* She clung to him, shaking, horrified by the thought of losing what she'd barely found. "You could have done anything and it wouldn't matter to me. Anything! Do you hear me? *I don't care what you've done! I don't care!*"

"I believe you," he whispered.

Chapter

Twenty-seven

Opening Night

IT HAD COME.

Crossing her dressing room to the small refrigerator, Valentina poured herself a glass of sweetened lemon iced tea.

There was an insistent knock on her door. It was Cassie Lee, the assistant to the company manager, delivering a batch of telegrams, and two more floral arrangements.

"More flowers are on the way, Miss Lederer—a whole van full of them."

"Oh . . ." Valentina felt suddenly overwhelmed by all the expectations. "Please put them all in the greenroom, Cassie. Then, well, tomorrow I'll give you a list of nursing homes and hospitals we can send them to."

After the girl left, Valentina slid a disc into her portable CD player. The rich, bluesy female voice that filled the room belonged to Abby McKay.

She threw herself on a chintz couch and closed her eyes, forcing away the nervous thoughts that skittered around inside her brain. Breathing deeply, in and out, visualizing a deserted beach, swirling traceries of foam on golden sands.

But the soothing images lasted for only thirty seconds. Valentina snapped her eyes open again. *Bettina,* she thought.

Bettina had been missing ever since Boston. The woman had just taken off, without a word of notice to anyone— something about her sister in San Francisco being sick, according to a typed note she'd sent to Keith. A *typed* note.

Valentina didn't believe it then, and she didn't believe it now. When you added Bettina's disappearance to Mazzini's bruises, and the on-again, off-again game that had been played with Jinna, it spelled trouble. Someone desperately wanted Senator Willingham to attend opening night.

A second knock on her door made Valentina jump. "Wardrobe, Miss Lederer."

The door opened and there was a banging sound as the dresser wheeled in a steel wardrobe hanger, on which Valentina's costume changes were arranged in order of appearance, plastic bags affixed to each hanger containing the jewelry, shoes, and accessories that went with each costume.

The costumes were sensational, a panoply of bright jewel colors and glorious trims.

The dresser took out the ballgown, made of pale jonquil watered silk. A boned waist cincher was pinned to the hanger, and would reduce Valentina's slim twenty-four-inch waist to a narrow twenty-two-inches.

Kristen wrapped the cincher around Valentina's waist, drawing it tight, while Valentina braced herself, holding on to a table edge, like Scarlett O'Hara did in *Gone With the Wind*. "I don't know how you can sing in this," the dresser remarked. "I'd be gasping for air."

"Well, it's only two scenes. Then I get to loosen it, thank God."

Another knock at the door interrupted them as Kristen was lowering a crinoline petticoat, trimmed with yards of French lace, over Valentina's shoulders.

"It's Grand Central Station in here," Valentina griped.

"It's me—can I come in?"

Orchid stepped into the dressing room. She had been through makeup, but was still in her street clothes.

"Hey, I found Jinna in the loo tossing her cookies. She says she always does it—you know, it's bad luck if she doesn't heave."

This was more than Orchid had said to Valentina in weeks. Valentina stared at her flamboyant sister. "Why aren't you getting in costume?"

"Oh, I will in plenty of time. I'm a fast dresser." Orchid eyed Valentina, who still wore only the petticoat and waist cincher, her bare breasts voluptuously full. "Too bad you can't go on like *that*. Can you imagine the reviews? Hey, Val," Orchid added nervously.

She fumbled in the pocket of her fringed leather jacket, bringing out a silver jeweler's box. She held it out, a pleading expression in her eyes. "For you, Val. I bought this just for you. I . . . I want you to love it. You *have* to love it."

"I'll be back in five minutes," the wardrobe woman said hastily. The door closed behind her.

Valentina stared at the Van Cleef and Arpels box.

"Please." Orchid's eyes beseeched her. "Val, I guess I'm kinda poor with words. I mean, these words. Oh, shit . . . I'll open it, then, if you won't."

Orchid fumbled open the lid of the case and held it out. Inside, nestled on midnight-blue velvet, gleamed a fabulously beautiful brooch, blue orchids, their symbol. The two orchids were twined together, stems interlocking. The shimmering enameled petals were rimmed with silver, and diamond dewdrops caught the light.

"T-the artist is Hawaiian," Orchid stammered. "It's an original. And . . . I had the back engraved. It says 'Sisters Always.'"

Valentina's heart leaped painfully within her, her eyes rising from the beautifully wrought pin, to search the pleading eyes of her wayward sister. *She wanted so much to believe.*

"I really . . ." she began.

"Please, just take it and read the engraving."

A third knock sounded on the dressing room door.

"Oh, fuck!" Orchid wailed. "Can't I even have one minute?"

"It's opening night," Valentina said, shrugging on a robe. "I was expecting Keith. I still have to finish dressing too. Wardrobe is waiting outside."

Orchid flinched, hurt spreading across her face, but

almost at once she recovered, smiling her brilliant, I-don't-care smile. "Okay, I'm gone," she drawled.

But she crashed into Keith as she tried to leave. Both of them stepped backward.

"In a rush?" Keith said to Orchid, as she flung herself past him. Then he turned to Valentina, warmth filling his voice. "Darling," he added, enfolding her in his arms. "I just had to give you a hug."

Valentina leaned gratefully into her fiancé's embrace. "Let's hold each other, just for a minute or two."

She embraced him, sensing the tension in him—a tension she felt too. "Things are just a little too crazy tonight," she murmured uneasily. "It's weird . . ."

"All that security," he said. "I've been trying to find out about it but no one will talk. No one seems to know where those people came from."

"It's Senator Willingham," Valentina said. "It's about him, I know it is. Keith, something is happening."

He nodded. "Yeah," he said. "I know."

So many florists had arrived with flowers for the cast members that the extra bouquets had been placed on a special, long table in the greenroom, their combined perfume overpowering. Western Union had made four more deliveries of telegrams. Three paparazzi had been thrown out of the backstage area.

In a corner of the dancers' dressing room, Jinna slid on the wig she would wear for the first scene, her hands quivering. She had the shakes, she'd already puked her guts out, and now she was beginning to wonder what kind of a fool she'd been to ask Charlie to attend the opening with all the wild rumors flying around.

Jinna stared glassy-eyed at her reflection. She almost felt disappointed that Bettina wasn't here. If she danced beautifully, she at least wanted Bettina to see her triumph!

But Charlie would be in the audience, she assured herself nervously. *He'd promised!*

Consumed with rage, Orchid rushed down the backstage corridor. Valentina had rejected her for the last time!

She ran into her dressing room, the box containing the orchid pin that was supposed to be her reconciliation with her sister burning a hole in her hand. She slammed the door shut on the opening-night hubbub, and angrily threw the box across the room. *Who the hell gives a fuck anyway?*

A sharp rapping at her door disturbed her. "Yeah?" she snapped.

"Anything broken in there? Miss Lederer," ventured Cassie Lee cautiously. "Twenty-five minutes."

"All right, all *right*."

She sat down and began brushing additional green eye shadow onto her eyelids, feathering it professionally. But she had only just finished when the beautiful eyes in the mirror began to leak hot tears.

She knew why she was so upset tonight. It was more than Valentina. It was Mikhail, too, and last night. Her horrible premonition that she might not ever see him again, that he'd been saying good-bye—permanently.

What if her feelings were—no, no, no—a portent of danger? *Or even worse!*

No, she thought, feeling an icy wash of terror. *Please . . . no, dear God. Don't take him from me too!*

The rain was thinning out, and the blare of taxi horns echoed wetly in the damp night air. Neon lights flashed on and off, revealing the gaudy beauty of Times Square through a misty haze.

Araña joined the crowds pressing toward the entrance of the Lederer Theater. She felt incredibly excited, yet calm, too, her nerves in icy control.

Car doors slammed as a succession of cabs and limousines dropped off first-nighters. Uniformed drivers handed out women in long designer gowns and furs. A crowd of gawkers had gathered to watch the arrivals, held back by a row of policemen.

In her protective disguise as an older man, Araña blended right into the opening night crowd.

She entered the theater, passing the ticket-taker, and began to reconnoiter the ornate lobby, lounges, stairs, and exits. She knew the theater intimately from her forays here as "security guard," but there was always the possibility that new security personnel might be posted on stairs or outside the rest rooms, or that closed-circuit TV, could have been installed earlier in the day. All of her senses were alerted. Police? Routine theater security?

Better to be cautious, than careless and dead.

Araña noted several additional men standing near the stairs to the mezzanine. One was speaking inconspicuously into a small walkie-talkie he held in his palm. She froze. She didn't like it. The bastards had added extra security!

She headed for the aisle door. The target would be arriving soon. Perhaps his limo was pulling up in front of the theater right now. Senator Willingham would be ushered to his prime seat at front row center.

Reporter Joe Donovan, accompanied by Rita Dougherty, his photographer, entered the glittering lobby.

His eyes darted around for signs that something was happening tonight—something blockbusting. He could sense it—he was a pro, and his abbreviated interview with Keith Leonard out by the stage door only sixty minutes earlier had whetted his sharpened instincts. Who were all the FBI-CIA type gonzos hanging around? In his career Donovan had covered more than two hundred opening nights, but he had never seen so much security before. They were everywhere, disguised as sellers at the refreshment concession, standing near the stairs and by the steps that led to levels A and B.

"Oh look, there's Arnold Schwarzenegger and Maria Shriver," crowed Rita. "Everyone's turning out for this, aren't they? And there's—"

"I hope you brought plenty of film," Donovan interrupted.

"Well, sure, but—"

"I want you to get lots of pictures tonight. I mean, let's saturate this crowd with film if we can, okay? Get as many of these people as possible. Start snapping, Rita."

"But—there's hundreds of people in here!"

"So? Stand by the ticket-takers and get each new group as they enter. I've got a feeling that we're going to get something we didn't bargain for. I want it all on film."

"What didn't we bargain for?"

"Who the hell knows what?" Donovan snapped irritably. "Just do it, Rita. Trust me. I'm the reporter, you're the eyes, all right?"

Rita obediently began clicking her shutter. "Okay, okay, you don't have to get pissed."

Standing on the sidewalk, Abby Mckay glanced around at the glitzy lineup of limousines, the TV minicams, and pushing crowd of gawkers. Overhead, the white marquee, bordered with flashing lights, spelled out Valentina's name, with Orchid's in smaller letters.

She arranged where her limo driver would pick her up, and walked into the theater.

Her girls.

Abby could hardly wait for the curtain to go up. She'd be intensely watching every turn and jump, rooting for every crystal-pure high note.

A trill of harp music over the PA system announced that there were only five minutes left to be seated. Abby glided through the lobby, finding the archway that led to level A.

Peaches and Edgar sank into their first-row seats. Edgar helped his wife slide her new Blackglama mink off her shoulders. Tonight Peaches wore a robin's egg blue Mary McFadden sheath with a beaded and embroidered bodice.

"Sell-out crowd," Edgar noted professionally, glancing around him. "And the advance box office is *wunderbar*—sold out until next January."

"Wonderful," breathed Peaches, gazing around her to spot friends, some of whom had flown in especially for this opening night from Detroit and Los Angeles.

She gave a finger-wave to Clive Barnes, drama critic for *The New York Post,* whose reputation was "tough, but fair."

She sighed. "I hope the critics are in a good mood, especially Clive."

"Don't *worry*. If a production is good, they'll recognize it."

Three latecomers entered their own row, settling into their seats only four away from the Lederers. One was a man Peaches recognized as Senator Charles Willingham. The senator's white sharkskin suit, flowing white hair, and trademark black string tie were eccentric apparel for an opening night—but he always wore them, she remembered.

Peaches smiled at him, but Willingham, staring straight ahead, did not seem to see her. In fact, he looked oddly grim and tense.

Peaches glanced away, feeling a ripple of unease that she could not explain.

Mikhail sank into his seat, feeling a wetness of nervous perspiration. The cumbersome white wig he wore and extra body weight provided by the abundance of Kevlar padding made him feel awkward and blatantly conspicuous. Peaches Lederer had stared straight at him! Maybe he should have greeted her, but his disguise would not pass close inspection.

His entire body was aching with nervousness. He felt his heart hammer at the walls of his chest.

On his right, in formal wear specially tailored to hide a shoulder holster, was Tom Manson from the CIA. Seated to his left was the FBI agent, Rosalie Greenfield.

Dotted among the patrons in the first ten rows were fifteen more federal agents, with others stationed on the aisles, in the back row, and working as ushers.

The danger sickened him. He listened as the overture began, its haunting Russian theme reminding him suddenly of Red Square on a winter night in February. White steam curling up from hundreds of chimneys, and his breath puffing frozen clouds. He had a brief, painful thought about his mother, Nadia . . . and then his father, buried in a frozen wasteland. His mind clouded over.

The sweat had begun to trickle down his back. He felt a

malevolent sensation of something *focused* on him. Waiting. Anywhere in the theater, even on one of the flywalks, the assassin could be poised with a high-powered rifle, red laser cross hairs fixed on his back or forehead.

Involuntarily, Mikhail glanced upward but saw nothing out of the ordinary.

Expiation, that was what tonight meant. Putting his life, so stained with blood, at risk for someone else. Making amends!

Mikhail knotted his jaw together, thinking about the past.

"Baby," drawled the senator, hunching over the phone booth in the lobby of the theater. "I'm here . . . I love you."

Over Jinna's delighted response, he heard excited female voices in the background. He'd dialed the public phone outside the dancers' dressing room.

He felt so proud of himself that he had to tell someone.

He went on, "But don't look for me in the first row, hon. And don't look for me in my white suit either. I'm dressed a lot different, and I'll be in the balcony. Just keep your mouth shut about it, okay, darlin'?"

"Sure, sure, baby . . . oh, God! They've just called the five minutes! Oh, Lord, Charlie, I'm terrified! Charlie, I've gotta go—"

"Love you," he said, but she'd already hung up.

The lobby lights were flicking in warning as Senator Willingham, accompanied by his bodyguard, hurried toward the stairs. He was wearing ordinary black evening wear, and a dark brown wig, as well as horn-rimmed glasses and a mustache, touches he had particularly liked. He knew no one would recognize him now. He looked so . . . ordinary.

He might be a lot of things, including a stubborn SOB, but Charles Willingham had never been ordinary. But for one night, he'd make the sacrifice.

Now, as he and Tommy Lee crossed the lobby and headed toward the stairs that led to the balcony, he began to feel fairly pleased with his plan. Actually, it was all so simple. He was supposed to stay home tonight. Instead, who would ever expect to find him in the balcony, "nose-bleed alley"?

They climbed carpeted stairs to the mezzanine, then a second flight to the balcony. Already they could hear the overture, some moody, romantic Russian composition.

"First row, sir," the young woman usher instructed them. "First row, center."

The senator nodded with satisfaction. He had fooled all the sons of bitches. He was here, and would still be in the first row—only it would be the balcony.

Keith Leonard was livid.

He had just been told about the FBI-CIA operation that was going down tonight—*on his parade!*—and he wanted to throttle someone with his bare hands.

"You bastards! You living fuck-ups! When has your agency ever done anything right? I can't believe you would put all these people at risk just to catch some asshole spy! Well, you are not doing it here tonight—not a chance in hell!"

"This is not just a 'spy,'" the man called Herb Cannell had told him coldly. "This is by order of the President himself. It's authorized in writing."

"You're lying. The President would never authorize such asininity! He's not a goddamn zealot like you and that boss of yours in Washington!"

"Isn't he?" Cannell produced a sheet of paper stamped with an official seal.

Keith scanned it, but he had no way of recognizing if any of the signatures on the paper were genuine, nor did he care.

"Mr. Leonard, let me put this to you in words you can understand," Cannell snapped. "This *has* been authorized by the White House. The assassin we are trying to trap has killed a number of known political figures, and it's just possible that Senator Willingham may be the target for tonight. We're not sure! Odds are the President himself is on the list, perhaps even next."

"So? Is that what this is all about, Willingham? Then

why doesn't he stay home instead of fucking up my show? How do you know that? I don't think you know shit," Keith spat out.

The FBI man moved slightly, and suddenly there was the glint of the barrel of an FBI-issue .38 Colt revolver. "You don't get to ask questions, bud. You just go about your business and put this show on. There isn't going to be any bloodshed—trust me."

Keith stared at him.

"Lives aren't going to be risked," Cannell urged. "Maybe you don't realize how many operatives I have placed out there. How about more than sixty! We intend to catch this sicko and I'm glad you finally understand."

Cannell's walkie-talkie suddenly blared out static. "Now, go do whatever it is you producers do. Please just stay outa my face. I have plenty of work to do or else we'll have bedlam tonight and you can kiss your show good-bye. Now, which one do you prefer? *It's your choice!*"

The orchestral music was at once lush and dark, a perfect backdrop for the sweeping saga of *Dr. Zhivago*. It drifted into the backstage area from the orchestra pit.

The final minutes were counting down to curtain time. Stagehands went to their posts, dressers added last-minute accessories to the dancers' ballgowns, a hairdresser sprayed down Valentina's hair, and cast members waited in their assigned spots for their cues. But there was the addition of the five extra men, dressed in dark business suits, that Keith now knew were FBI.

Keith swallowed down a burst of sour bile, blaming himself for the position they were in.

He strode through the backstage area, until he found Pete Mazzini, who was in earnest last-minute conference with the sound designer.

"Pete," he said urgently. "We have to postpone the opening. Like for about two weeks."

"Postpone?" Stunned, both men stared at him.

"You're not delaying anything," growled a voice behind

him. Keith felt something hard prod his side through the fabric of his evening jacket. A gun.

He turned. Herb Cannell was staring at him, his face grim.

Araña saw Senator Willingham, accompanied by two bodyguards, take his seat in the first row.

Her target! She studied the back of his head carefully, observing the flowing, slightly untidy, silver-white hair, and the white suit—all of it exactly as depicted in all the newspaper photos, and what she had seen for herself on her two personal observations of the senator as he conducted committee hearings.

She glanced around the theater, her senses taking in every detail, but inevitably her eyes kept being drawn back to Willingham. He wasn't talking much, she noticed. He barely spoke to his companions. Shouldn't he be talking more? Well, maybe he was nervous for his girlfriend.

Balalaikas added their plaintive twang to the horns, flutes, and clarinets.

Araña glanced again at her target, who was sitting far too stiffly and rigidly. And there was something about his hair. Alarmed, she swung her eyes toward the people seated ahead of her in the first and second rows.

Something was wrong.

There were too many men compared to the number of women, and the men all had a look . . . She shifted her eyes back to the senator, and now she realized that the white hair was a wig.

Maricones! Araña swore to herself. A wave of sickening anger crunched through her, shattering her icy calm. The man in the first row wasn't Senator Willingham at all, but someone dressed to resemble him, probably wearing complete bulletproof gear. The people on either side of him were either CIA or FBI agents, probably half the audience in the first fifteen rows was too.

She'd been had!

The volcanic anger in her broke to the surface.

They thought she was a fool! A cunt, a *puta! Que*

cabrones! Years of mistreatment and bloody battles in the *barrio* in Buenos Aires suddenly erupted in a gush of violence.

Enraged, her brain all red fire, wanting only to hurt, to destroy, Araña reached for the gun still in its sling inside her coat. She didn't take it out of her coat, just tilted the barrel upward. She stood up and squeezed out a shot, aiming low, for the body, below the level of the Kevlar vest. It barely coughed.

Latecomers were still being seated, a group milling in the aisle, and a saxophone soloist had merged with the balalaikas. *No one heard the shot.*

Mikhail had been thinking about his mother, Nadia, and of a moment in his childhood when he had been ill with a fever and she had sponged him off, soothing him with pale, restless fingers. Suddenly something slammed into his back, knocking him forward.

There was a swirling wave of numbness, then a shock wave of pain so intense that he started immediately to black out.

"I've been shot," Mikhail managed to gasp before he collapsed forward, his head pillowed on his knees.

Araña, under the confusion of people still looking for their seats, casually walked up the aisle, hurrying across the lobby to the men's room on the balcony level, where she'd left different clothing and disguise paraphernalia for just such an eventuality.

There were four persons in the men's room when she entered but none of them even glanced at her. Araña went into the end booth, where a locked maintenance cupboard in the wall held her extra supplies. She jimmied the lock and pulled out the garments she had stuffed here the previous day: a woman's blue cloth coat, an inexpensive black knit dress, high heels, pearl necklace, and pierced earrings—the evening garb of an office worker. There was a reddish-blond wig, tinted glasses, facial prosthesis, makeup, and a second ticket stub for row JJ, toward the back of the main floor.

She peeled off her white wig, the trench coat, and the tuxedo, stuffing the clothing back into the cupboard. None had labels, and all would be impossible to trace. Swiftly she removed her dental prosthesis and peeled off the plastic aging makeup.

Her last act was to transfer the gun from the hidden sling of the trench coat, to a similar sling she'd fashioned in the woman's coat.

Four minutes later she flushed the toilet and emerged from the stall, an attractive young woman, who looked as though she'd saved every penny to attend the opening.

Now several of the men did turn to look at her.

"Long line in the ladies'," she explained as she exited.

A man in a business suit wearing a bad brown wig and horn-rimmed glasses was just heading into the men's room. He paused to gaze at her in surprise.

"Y'all got the wrong toilet?"

"There was a long line in the ladies'," Araña swiftly explained, noticing his bristling white eyebrows at odds with the brown hair. And a thick southern drawl! The same drawl she'd heard dominate a committee room in Washington.

Willingham!

She laughed to herself as she scouted out a position near the phone kiosk where she would have a view of the exit door of the men's room. *El viejo* must have been warned, and sent a double in his place. A decoy to take his place in the first row. But he was still in the theater, only seated somewhere else. Her heart hammered with joy. The chicken had flown straight into the fox's den!

Herb Cannell couldn't believe his ears when Anson's voice blared into his ear, static rendering it only partially understandable.

"Team one to Red Fox Leader . . . Team one to Red Fox Leader. White Owl has fallen . . . the hit's already come down—they got White Owl—he took a shot."

"Code A, Code A," he snapped into the transmitter.

"Tell the little foxes to start scanning the crowd. Now! On the double! Blockade the doors—no one gets out."

Mikhail was half aware of being supported by the two Federal agents, held by the arms and helped out of the theater as if the senator had become suddenly ill. He was dead weight. His legs did not want to move. Lights flashed in front of him, telescoping and turning suddenly black. He was aware of faces . . . music.

The pain throughout his back and spine was splitting him apart. Had the bullet severed his spine? He couldn't move his legs!

"Radio ahead. All! We gotta get this one in fast," someone said. He was in the ambulance.

"Stat! Stat! Control that bleeding!" someone yelled.

Mikhail began to float off. Orchid . . . Valentina . . . The pain was going farther away now, he was drifting on top of it, it no longer concerned him. Softness . . . peace . . .

Valentina waited to go on, the backstage turmoil now seeming far away, part of another world. The real world for her now was full of swirling skirts, violins, and handsome dukes, and generals in medal-glittering uniforms.

Jinna appeared beside her, wearing the rose satin ballgown. Her state of nerves had progressed to a chattering euphoria.

"Oh, Val, I'm just so happy . . . Charlie's out there! He didn't let me down."

"What?"

"Oh, he's got some guy dressed like him sitting in the front row, it's all very hush-hush . . . I think Charlie's wearing a brown wig and glasses. Can you believe it? He's *such* a character."

Valentina froze!

"Jinna." She touched the dancer's arm. "What are you talking about?"

Jinna explained triumphantly. "He called me just before curtain, from a phone booth. He's here in the theater only he's not sitting in the first row where he's supposed to be. There's another guy there—a double. I think Charlie's in the balcony or something. Isn't it great?''

Assassination! That was what this was all about! And now the senator himself had apparently scrapped his own security measures and was actually *in* the theater. Jesus, he'd be a sitting duck for any professional killer.

And if Jinna had told her about his presence here, who else had she told? Somebody had to find the man and warn him.

Pete Mazzini stood a few yards away, talking to Orchid, and Valentina ran up to him. ''Pete,'' she gasped. ''Pete, there's an emergency, a possible assassination—oh, God, I haven't got time to explain. You've got to delay the curtain. *Please. Ten minutes, Pete!* No one out there will even notice.''

She saw Orchid's shock, the blood draining from her sister's face.

Mazzini seemed discomfited. ''But that FBI man already said—''

''To hell with the FBI. I know Willingham, I can find him, I'll warn him,'' Valentina blurted out. She turned, hurrying toward the backstage corridor, where a private staircase for the use of the production staff led to the balcony area.

Chapter

Twenty-eight

"*WHAT IS IT?*" demanded Orchid, grabbing Valentina's arms with both hands. "*What's happening?*"

"I haven't got time," Valentina said, attempting to pull away.

"Is it Mikhail? *It's Mikhail, isn't it? I know it is.*"

What was her sister talking about?

"No, no, it isn't Mikhail. Please, Orchid—not now. I've only got a few minutes." Valentina managed to pull herself loose and half ran toward the corridor. Orchid hurried after her, catching up.

"*A few minutes to do what?*"

"I think Senator Willingham is going to be assassinated."

"Oh, God," Orchid gasped.

"Just get out of here, Orchid, and let me handle this. I know the senator, I think I can recognize him, and I've got to tell him to leave, now, before something terrible happens."

The horror written on Orchid's face was growing. "No. Please. I can help," she insisted.

"I . . ." Then Valentina gave up. There wasn't time to argue. "All right, then come along," she agreed hastily.

"Let's hurry," said Orchid, pulling at her.

They lifted up their long skirts and ran.

They pelted down the old corridor, built to allow access to the mezzanine and balcony area, and a costume storage vault located off the same level.

"I don't understand," Orchid said as they ran.

"I think the Colombians want to kill Senator Willingham—he said he'd be first row center—he was supposed to stay away, only he didn't, he's in the balcony somewhere," Valentina panted. "He's c-crazy!"

"Mikhail has something to do with this," Orchid said as they reached the door that opened onto the mezzanine.

"Mikhail?" Valentina slowed her steps. Mikhail's trips back and forth to Washington, his insistence on coming to rehearsals, Mazzini's bruises, the uncharacteristic disappearance of Bettina. Bits and pieces that had not made much sense suddenly came together.

They pushed open the door, and stepped into the crowded mezzanine, and noticed immediately a conspicuous trio of men in dark business suits who were standing at the far end, speaking into walkie-talkies.

"Who are *they?*" Orchid asked in wonderment.

"Hurry," Valentina said, grabbing her sister's arm and pulling her toward the flight of stairs that led to the balcony.

They emerged into the lower level of the balcony. About fifty rows of seats stretched above them, and another twenty below, every seat filled.

"Can I help you?" asked an astonished usher, seeing the two actresses in their costumes.

"We're—looking for someone," Valentina blurted out. They walked a few rows down, then stopped, overwhelmed by the task of inspecting several hundred people, a third of whom were facing the stage, the backs of their heads to them.

"What is he dressed like?" whispered Orchid.

"He's in disguise," hissed Valentina, nudging her sister.

"What disguise?"

"I don't know. Brown hair. Glasses." Valentina stifled despair. "Oh, God, I can't believe this . . ." She added desperately, "But he was going to sit in the front row center—that's what he told Jinna before. Maybe he's in the first row of the balcony. It's worth a try."

Mikhail dimly heard the wailing scream of the ambulance as it wove through heavy evening traffic toward New York

Hospital. He drifted in and out of consciousness. He felt sure he had taken a fatal shot, and perhaps only had a few more minutes before he passed out for the final time.

"Come on, guy, come on, you're gonna make it," an EMS attendant urged in his ear, but the words seemed to come from very far away and have little relationship to him.

He wished he could have spent more time with both Valentina and Orchid, Mikhail thought, fighting for the remaining shreds of consciousness.

Valentina could get along without him—she'd done it for nearly thirty years. But Orchid . . . she was needy and wounded, in a way like him. His damaged flower. He wanted so much to be there for her.

Mikhail did not know that tears rolled down his cheeks as he thought of Orchid . . . his woman. He again passed into a black, peaceful unconsciousness.

Valentina was the one to spot Senator Willingham. He sat ensconced in a first row balcony seat next to the aisle seat, holding a pair of binoculars in his hand, ready to view the opening scene.

His bodyguard sat on one side of him, and the aisle seat on his right was vacant.

"I'll go and talk to him," Valentina whispered. "You stand here and wait."

"Hurry," Orchid urged.

"Senator," Valentina burst out, flinging herself into the seat beside the man. "You're in terrible danger."

Senator Willingham turned to gaze at her in obvious surprise.

"Why, Valentina, hon, why aren't you backstage?" Beside him the chunky bodyguard had shifted alertly, bringing one hand close to his coat jacket.

"Please," she begged. "Senator, I feel sure that you've been targeted for assassination, and they're going to do it in this theater, tonight. You've got to leave now. Please—before the performance starts."

"Leave? Not this here United States senator, darling. It was all right until you appeared on the scene but now you're drawin' all kinds of attention to me.'' Willingham gestured behind him, and when Valentina turned her head to look, she groaned. Hundreds were staring, astounded at the sight of the star herself in the audience.

"Oh, *shit*," she muttered.

"Look, dear heart, I've got Tommy Lee here and some of his agent friends, and we've got a look-alike downstairs takin' my place, so why don't you just go on backstage and get ready to give us the fantastic performance we all came here to see?"

Valentina clenched her hands in frustration.

"Please! Senator, I don't have all the facts, but I know someone wanted you at this opening night awfully bad, and Jinna—"

"Now, now." The distinguished politician shook his head. "I know that, but y'all can see my position here. I made a promise and I—"

"Don't you see why they wanted her to go on tonight?" Valentina interrupted desperately. "Because you said you'd sit in the first row center! It's a perfect setup for killing you. In public, where loads of people can see. Oh, Senator, for Jinna's sake if not for mine, will you please get up right now and—"

She heard a faint cry from Orchid, and turned. A woman had gotten out of her seat and was coming down the aisle. She wore a blue cloth coat, and her eyes were filled with a malevolent fury.

Araña, infuriated by the distinct possibility of being cheated of her prey, no longer cared. The woman gave a swift, catlike movement, reaching into her coat, and suddenly the senator's security guard stood up, too, gripping a revolver in both hands, and fired.

Araña screamed.

She reached again for the Belgian-made automatic, but the agony in her left shoulder made her movements awkward, throwing her off balance. The prick was readying himself for another shot.

Valentina, stunned by the sudden violence, had fallen back into the aisle seat. Desperately Araña reached down and grabbed the actress by the arm, jerking her to her feet.

The scheduled curtain time passed, then stretched on to five, then six, then seven minutes late. People had begun to glance at their watches.

At the orchestra level, Keith started up the center aisle, and gazed sharply toward section A, where, only minutes before, two CIA agents had hustled away the decoy in the front row who'd been dressed up to resemble Willingham. The guy looked as though he had collapsed.

He started up the aisle toward the lobby doors, scanning the audience, and that was when he heard the altercation in the balcony. Screams.

The late opening bothered Joe Donovan. He twisted impatiently in his seat, wondering what kind of backstage fuckup it meant.

Then Rita nudged him excitedly. "Look, Joe, isn't that Keith Leonard? The man's running."

Joe looked.

"Come on," he told his photographer, hauling her out of her seat. "Let's go!"

Valentina felt herself being jerked backward, off her feet, as a muscular forearm tightened around her neck, squeezing off her air. She struggled frantically, trying to kick, but the tight waist cincher, heavy crinoline, and voluminous fabric of the ball gown hampered her. Her air supply was being cut off!

"*Puta!*" grated Araña, tightening her strangle squeeze. "You're going to get me out of this."

Orchid screamed Val's name over and over as Araña attempted to drag her sister up the aisle toward the balcony exit. Federal agents were running from all over the theater. She watched in horror as Val clawed at the arm clamped around her neck. An icy horror froze her throat, and she was paralyzed.

"*Val!*" she screamed, hurling herself forward toward Araña.

Araña heard the choking, gagging sounds made by the woman she had captured, as she struggled to breathe. *It was all fucked up and it was her own fault.*

Orchid stormed forward and threw herself on Araña. *Nobody hurt her Val . . . nobody!*

Beleaguered and wounded, Araña dropped Valentina, who tried to roll out of the way. Orchid went crazy, all of her street-fighting ability returning as she knocked Araña down.

Keith came running up, his gun out.

"Down, Leonard, get out of the fucking way," Herb Cannell yelled behind him but Keith didn't hear. He raised his Colt .38 and aimed. Somehow Valentina managed to roll away, pulling Orchid with her.

Shots exploded.

Araña lay sprawled in the aisle, her body covered with blood. At least six shots had hit her, from the FBI and CIA men scattered in the area, from Herb Cannell, and Keith. Red soaked her chest and shoulder, shining dark red in the half-lights of the semidarkened theater. Her brilliant, melting eyes were wide open. She still breathed, but barely.

Valentina looked away, shuddering, as she pulled herself to a sitting position.

"Val, Val, Val," Orchid sobbed, getting to her knees. Her face was bruised and bloody. "Oh, Val, I thought she was gonna kill you . . ."

Tears ran down Orchid's face, smearing her makeup, and she convulsively gasped, reaching for Valentina. She threw her arms around her. "Jeez, Val," she choked.

"Orchie," Valentina gasped. Then there were no more words to say, and they just clutched each other, both of them shaking.

"I'm sorry, I'm sorry," Orchid wept, burying her head in Valentina's shoulder. "Can you ever forgive me?"

Keith didn't hear Val's response—but he didn't have to—as the two sisters desperately hugged each other; the tears that wet their cheeks were more than answer enough. Keith felt his own eyes fill.

Reviews and Press

Two weeks later, the delayed opening of *Dr. Zhivago* at last filled all fifteen hundred seats of the Lederer Theater, with more than one hundred standing room tickets sold.

Joe Donovan sat in the fourth row, listening to the *Zhivago* overture, nearly drowned out by the excited buzz of a pumped-up opening-night audience. *What a night.* Everyone had to pass through metal detectors. Every magazine, wire service, TV network, and tabloid was represented, and some two hundred security guards and police officers stood in rows at the back of the main level and balcony, and near the stage, just in case of any further disturbance.

"Hot damn," gloated Rita Dougherty beside him. "Can you believe the rarefied air in here? I heard that people paid two thousand dollars apiece for scalper's tickets. Even Mayor Dinkins couldn't get extra tickets."

"Yeah." Donovan craned his neck to see Peaches and Edgar Lederer file into their front row seats.

It was like a circus—almost. No drama like the one two weeks ago had occurred in an American theater since Lincoln's death. The debacle had left fourteen people injured, six enough to be hospitalized. One of these was Mikhail Sandovsky, Valentina's brother, who had pulled through after an eight-hour operation that nearly cost him his life.

And the assassin herself . . . a woman! Jesus, that was a whole new, incredible story. After being in intensive care for three days, she died. Fingerprints had brought up zero information. No one knew who she was, and it didn't look as if they were ever going to.

The houselights were dimming. The curtain ballooned majestically upward.

"Migawd," said Rita, catching her breath.

The audience gasped, and began applauding spontaneously. The set was a gorgeous gold and white ballroom. Its walls were hung with brocades, and tall pillars had been fashioned to look like white veined Carrara marble. Chandeliers sparkled like cut diamonds, spraying light. Women in satin ballgowns, and men in Russian uniforms or cutaways, dipped and twirled in an elegant Strauss waltz.

Caught in time, a glittering moment from the days of the czars.

"Beautiful, beautiful," murmured Rita, already captivated by the fantasy.

Two and a half hours later, the cast took their curtain call to tumultuous applause. First the chorus, who received storms of wolf whistles. Then Winona Ryder, Orchid, and the other supporting cast members, to wild cheers.

Finally Valentina linked arms with Patrick Swayze and came forward, curtsying as he bowed.

The audience went wild. The clapping intensified to shouts and whistles. Valentina and Swayze faced the applause, their smiles incandescent, and then Patrick bowed to Valentina, deferring to her as he stepped back.

A stagehand came onstage carrying an enormous basket heaped with blue cymbidium orchids. He handed it to Valentina, who ran back and pulled Orchid out of the row of cast members.

"The author of this musical production, Orchid Lederer," she said with her throaty voice into the mike, "just happens to be my *favorite* sister."

Applause roared, and then there was the deep rustle of fifteen hundred people getting to their feet as they gave Orchid and Valentina a standing ovation.

An ovation that went on and on.

Valentina's brilliant smile wavered and it was obvious that she was trying to hold her emotions in check. Orchid was openly crying. The audience screamed louder, projecting their love, in one of the rare, unforgettable Broadway moments of which legend is made.

Suddenly Orchid reached into the flower basket and grabbed up a handful of blue orchids. She glanced at Valentina and then tossed the handful across the footlights. A girl shrieked and jumped up to catch one.

Grinning, Valentina reached for a second handful and tossed them toward Peaches and Edgar, in the first row.

Blue Orchids was back together again.

The next morning, Jinna and Senator Willingham were having breakfast in Jinna's small Manhattan apartment. The table was littered with the remains of their southern-style breakfast, and on the floor were spread all the papers, opened to the theater sections.

Rave reviews, every one of them. Even Clive Barnes.

Valentina had been hailed as a major star. Orchid as the newest and brightest of Broadway playwrights.

"Read it again, Charlie," Jinna begged, picking up the *New York Post* and handing it to her fiancé.

The senator winked, and read the pertinent sentence aloud for the third time. "'A red-haired chorus dancer, Jinna Jones, caught the eye of the audience with her sinuous movements and bright verve.' You like that, honey? I love it."

"That's such music to me," Jinna sighed. "I tried so hard for so long. I wanted to see if I could really do it, *and I did*! I want to dance a full year in this show, Charlie—just to prove I really made it to Broadway. But after that . . ." Jinna snuggled onto his lap and wrapped both arms around his neck. "I want to take some time off to have a baby."

"Just one baby?" Willingham said gruffly, to cover the deep emotion in his voice.

Jinna giggled. "One? Just how many do you want, Charlie? Let's start off easy now. I'm not as young as I used to be," she teased. "But I *will* want to dance again. Me and my dancing are a package deal."

"Anything, darlin'," agreed Willingham happily. "Let's just get married tomorrow."

* * *

Mikhail Sandovsky floated somewhere between sleep and wakefulness, aware only of the small, strong hand that clasped his own.

He had nearly died. The bullet missed his spine by millimeters, and it had ruptured part of his colon. He was weak . . . terribly weak. And he'd have some new scars on his body. And yet that did not matter at all.

He heard the bedside telephone ringing.

"Mikey?" whispered Orchid, who had been by his side constantly, except for her performances, ever since it happened. "I'll get the phone."

He heard her pick up the phone, and respond, "Is this some kind of a practical joke?"

Mikhail took the telephone and listened, dazed, to the familiar voice as President Gorbachev praised him for his service to Russia. He had helped save the life of a man extremely important to the USSR's diplomatic relationship with the United States.

"I will offer you a well-deserved and long furlough for your complete recuperation," the President continued. "Also permanent posting with the embassy in Washington if you so desire."

Mikhail hung up, bemused. Things had changed so much! He didn't even have to defect.

"Mikhail," Orchid whispered, her voice trembling. He heard her gulp. "Do you have to . . . I mean . . . you don't have to go back to Russia, do you . . . ?"

"I'm staying," he said hoarsely. "I want to get into the nightclub business . . . *a place called Orchids.*"

Several days later, Edgar and Peaches were in their suite at the Pierre Hotel reading the newspaper accounts of the newest "hot ticket" show on Broadway, *Dr. Zhivago,* and the stunning cover story by Joe Donovan for *People.*

Edgar was on the phone to his lawyer, gesturing emphatically, while Peaches browsed through a fat issue of the *New York Times.*

It held a clipping telling about the recent Senate confirmation of Ambassador Robert Lovell to Russia.

"The club deal went through," Edgar said, hanging up with a grin. "And we got it for thirty thousand dollars less than what I was willing to pay. Next week we meet to sign the papers and get things rolling."

"Oh, Edgar," Peaches exclaimed, dropping the paper. "That's fabulous. You're so wonderful to her. Orchid really needed something like that—"

"Darling, this isn't exactly charity. Our redheaded daughter is a natural entrepreneur, and the ideas she has for that club—it's going to be the 'in' place, mark my words. A big money-maker. We'll have to step back and watch her become an overnight success," Edgar added with pride.

"To me, she always was," Peaches said lovingly.

Valentina and Keith were still asleep in her apartment, the floor by the bed covered with their mingled clothing.

On the floor lay a copy of the *New York Post,* as yet unread.

"Val," murmured Keith, his eyes still lazily shut as he stirred, running his hand along the silken curve of Valentina's flank.

"Hold me," she murmured, rising from the depths of sweet sleep.

"More than hold you, I'll love you . . . forever. As long as forever is."

"A very long time, I hope," she mumbled, wrapping her arms around him.

BLUE ORCHIDS
NO LONGER BLUE

UPI–Detroit. Blue Orchids, the Grammy-winning female singing duo which split up in 1985, sang together last night for the first time in eight years, raising more than $150,000 in a surprise appearance at a benefit for the St. Vincent and Sarah Fisher Children's home, in Farmington Hills.

In attendance were Michigan Governor John Engler and Madonna, Robin Williams, and George Peppard, all former Detroiters.

"It's great—it's fantastic to be together," enthused Valentina Lederer. "We feel such a strong surge of energy."

"I love my sister," added Orchid Lederer. "And I love Blue Orchids, I always have. We're already got a new album in the works called *Let's Dream Together*."

SNEAK PREVIEW

. . . of a spellbinding new novel by Nora Roberts!

No one combines suspense and romance as brilliantly as
Nora Roberts, the *New York Times* bestselling author of
Carnal Innocence and *Genuine Lies*. Her newest novel
unveils the dreams and schemes of an unforgettable
family—who turn fantasy into fame and risk everything for
love. . . .

HONEST ILLUSIONS

Here is an exclusive excerpt from this tantalizing new novel,
available July 1992 from G.P. Putnam's Sons. . . .

THE LADY VANISHES. It was an old illusion, given a modern twist, and never failed to leave the audience gasping. The glittery crowd at Radio City was as eager to be duped as a group of slack-jawed rubes at a dog and pony show.

Even as Roxanne stepped onto the glass pedestal she could feel their anticipation—the silvery edge of it that was a merging of hope and doubt glued together with wonder. The inching forward in the seat ranged from president to peon.

Magic made equals of them all.

Max had said that, she recalled. Many, many times.

Amid the swirl of mist and the flash of light, the pedestal slowly ascended, circling magestically to the tune of Gershwin's *Rhapsody in Blue*. The gentle three-hundred-and-sixty-degree revolution showed the crowd all sides of the ice-clear pedestal and the slender woman atop it—and distracted them from the trickery at hand.

Presentation, she'd been taught, was often the slim difference between a charlatan and an artist.

In keeping with the theme of the music, Roxanne wore a sparkling gown of midnight blue that clung to her long, willowy form—clung so closely that no one studying her would believe there was anything under the spangled silk but her own flesh. Her hair, a waterfall of flame curling to her waist, twinkled with thousands of tiny iridescent stars.

Fire and ice. More than one man had wondered how one woman could be both at the same time.

As in sleep or a trance, her eyes were closed—or seemed to be—and her elegant face was lifted toward the star-pricked ceiling of the stage.

As she rose, she let her arms sway to the music, then held

them high above her head, for showmanship and for the practical necessity that underscores all magic.

It was a beautiful illusion, she knew. The mist, the lights, the music, the woman. She enjoyed the sheer drama of it, and was not above being amused by the irony of using the age-old symbol of the lone, lovely woman placed on a pedestal, above the common worry and toils of man.

It was also a miserably complex bit of business, requiring a great deal of physical control and split-second timing. But not even those fortunate enough to be seated in the first row could detect the intense concentration in her serene face. None of them could know how many tedious hours she had put in, perfecting every aspect of the act on paper, then in practice. Unrelenting practice.

Slowly, again to Gershwin's rhythm, her body began to turn, dip, sway. A partnerless dance ten feet above stage, all color and fluid movement. There were murmurs from the audience, scattered applause.

They could see her—yes, they could see her through the blue-tinted mist and spinning lights. The glitter of the dark gown, the flow of flame-colored hair, the gleam of that alabaster skin.

Then, in a breath, in a gasp, they could not. In less time than it takes to blink an eye, she was gone. In her place was a sleek Bengal tiger who reared on his hind legs to paw the air and roar.

There was a pause, that most satisfying of pauses to an entertainer where an audience held its stunned collective breath before the applause thundered, echoing as the pedestal descended once more. The big cat leapt down to stalk stage right. He stopped by an ebony box, sent up another roar that had a woman in the front row giggling nervously. As one, the four sides of the box collapsed.

And there was Roxanne, dressed not in shimmery blue but in a silver cat suit. She took her bows as she'd been taught almost from birth. With a flourish.

As the sound of success continued to pound in her ears, she mounted the tiger and rode the beast offstage.

"Nice work, Oscar." With a little sigh, she bent forward to scratch the cat between the ears.

"You looked real pretty, Roxy." Her big, burly assistant clipped a leash to Oscar's spangled collar.

"Thanks, Mouse." Dismounting, she tossed her hair back. The backstage area was already hopping. Those trusted to do so would secure her equipment and guard it from prying eyes. Since she'd scheduled a press conference for the following day, she would see no reporters now. Roxanne had high hopes for a bottle of iced champagne and a stingingly hot whirlpool bath.

Alone.

Absently she rubbed her hands together—an old habit Mouse could have told her she'd picked up from her father.

"I've got the fidgets," she said with a half laugh. "Had them all damn night. It feels like someone's breathing down my neck."

"Well, ah . . ." Mouse stood where he was, letting Oscar rub against his knees. Never articulate under the best of circumstances, Mouse fumbled for the best way to phrase the news. "You got company, Roxy. In the dressing room."

"Oh?" Her brows drew together, forming the faint line of impatience between them. "Who?"

"Take another bow, honey." Lily, Roxanne's onstage assistant and surrogate mother, swept over to grab her arm. "You brought down the house." Lily dabbed a handkerchief around the false eyelashes she wore onstage and off. "Max would be so proud."

The quick twist in Roxanne's gut had her willing away her own tears. They didn't show. They were never permitted to show in public. She started forward, moving into the swell of applause. "Who's waiting for me?" she called over her shoulder, but Mouse was already leading the big cat away.

He'd been taught by the master that discretion was the better part of survival.

Ten minutes later, flushed with success, Roxanne opened the door of her dressing room. The scent hit her first—roses and greasepaint. That mix of fragrances had become so familiar she breathed it in like fresh air. But there was another scent here—the sting of rich tobacco. Elegant, exotic, French. Her hand trembled once on the knob as she pushed the door fully open.

There was one man she would forever associate with that aroma. One man she knew who habitually smoked slim French cigars.

She said nothing when she saw him. Could say nothing as he rose from a chair where he'd been enjoying his cigar and her champagne. Oh, God, it was thrilling and horrible to watch that wonderful mouth quirk in that very familiar grin, to meet those impossibly blue eyes with her own.

His hair was still long, a mane of ebony waving back from his face. Even as a child he'd been gorgeous, an elegant gypsy with eyes that could freeze or burn. Age had only enhanced his looks, fining down that compelling face, the long bones and shadowy hollows, the faint cleft in the chin. Beyond the physical, there was a drama that shivered around him like an aura.

He was a man women shuddered over and wanted.

She had. Oh, she had.

Five years had passed since she'd seen that smile, since she'd run her hands through that thick hair or felt the searing pressure of that clever mouth. Five years to mourn, to weep and to hate.

Why wasn't he dead? she wondered as she forced herself to close the door at her back. Why hadn't he had the decency to succumb to any of the varied and gruesome tragedies she'd imagined for him?

And what in God's name was she going to do with this terrible yearning she felt just looking at him again?

"Roxanne." Training kept Luke's voice steady as he said her name. He'd watched her over the years. Tonight he'd studied her every move from the shadows of the wings. Judging, weighing. Wanting. But here, now, face to face, she was almost too beautiful to bear. "It was a good show. The finale was spectacular."

"Thank you."

His hand was steady as he poured her a flute of

champagne, as hers was when she accepted it. They were, after all, showmen, cast in an odd way from the same mold. Max's mold.

"I'm sorry about Max."

Her eyes went flat. "Are you?"

Because Luke felt he deserved more than the slash of sarcasm, he merely nodded, then glanced down at his bubbling wine, remembering. His mouth curved when he looked back at her. "The Calais job, the rubies. Was that yours?"

She sipped, the silver sparkled on her shoulders as she moved them in a careless shrug. "Of course."

"Ah." He nodded again, pleased. He had to be sure she hadn't lost her touch—for magic or for larceny. "I heard rumors that a first edition of Poe's *House of Usher* was lifted from a vault in London."

"Your hearing was always good, Callahan."

He continued to smile, wondering when she'd learned to exude sex like breath. He remembered the clever child, the coltish adolescent, the irresistible bloom of the young woman. The bloom had blossomed seductively. And he could feel the pull that had always been between them. He would use it now, with regret, but he would use it to gain his own ends.

The end justifies everything. Another of Maximillian Nouvelle's maxims.

"I have a proposition for you, Rox."

"Really?" She took a last sip before setting her glass aside. The bubbles were bitter on her tongue.

"Business," he said lightly, tapping out the stub of his cigar. Taking her hand, he brought her fingers to his lips. "And personal. I've missed you, Roxanne." It was the truest statement he could make. One flash of sterling honesty in years of tricks, illusions and pretense. Caught up in his own feelings, he missed the warning flash in her eyes.

"Have you, Luke? Have you really?"

"More than I can tell you." Swamped by memories and needs, he drew her closer, felt his blood begin to pump as her body brushed his. She'd always been the one. No matter how many escapes he'd accomplished, he'd never freed himself from the trap in which Roxanne Nouvelle had caught him. "Come back to my hotel." His breath whispered over her face as she went fluidly into his arms. "We'll have a late supper. Talk."

"Talk?" Her arms wound sinuously around him. Her rings flashed as she dipped her fingers into his hair. Beside them the makeup mirror over her dressing table reflected them in triplicate. As if showing them past, present, future. When she spoke, her voice was like the mist she'd vanished into. Dark and rich and mysterious. "Is that what you want to do with me, Luke?"

He forgot the importance of control, forgot everything but the fact that her mouth was an inch from his. The taste he'd once gorged on was a wish away. "No."

He dropped his head toward hers. Then his breath exploded as her knee shot up between his legs. Even as he was doubling over, she slammed her fist into his chin.

His grunt of surprise, and the splintering of wood from the table he smashed on his way down gave Roxanne enormous satisfaction. Roses flew, water splashed. A few slender buds drifted over him as he lay on the dampening carpet.

"You . . ." Scowling, he dragged a rose from his hair. The brat had always been sneaky, he remembered. "You're quicker than you used to be, Rox."

Hands on her hips, she stood over him, a slim, silver warrior who'd never learned to sample her revenge cold. "I'm a lot of things I didn't used to be." Her knuckles hurt like fire, but she used that pain to block another, deeper ache. "Now, you lying Irish bastard, crawl back into whatever hole you dug for yourself five years ago. Come near me again, and I swear, I'll make you disappear for good."

Delighted with her exit line, she turned on her heel, then let out a shriek when Luke snagged her ankle. She went down hard on her rump and before she could put nails and teeth to use, he had her pinned. She'd forgotten how strong and how quick he was.

A miscalculation, Max would have said. And miscalculations were the root of all failures.

"Okay, Rox, we can talk here." Though he was breathless and still in pain, he grinned. "Your choice."

"I'll see you in hell—"

"Very likely." His grin faded. "Damn it, Roxy, I never could resist you." When he crushed his mouth to hers, he tossed them both back into the past.